NEW YORK REVIEW BOOKS
CLASSICS

BERLIN ALEXANDERPLATZ

ALFRED DÖBLIN (1878–1957) was born in German Stettin (now
the Polish city of Szczecin) to Jewish parents. When he was ten his
father, a master tailor, eloped with a seamstress, abandoning the
family. Subsequently his mother relocated the rest of the family
to Berlin. Döblin studied medicine at Friedrich Wilhelm University, specializing in neurology and psychiatry. While working at a
psychiatric clinic in Berlin, he became romantically entangled with
two women: Friede Kunke, with whom he had a son, Bodo, in 1911,
and Erna Reiss, to whom he had become engaged before learning
of Kunke's pregnancy. He married Erna the next year, and they
remained together for the rest of his life. His novel *The Three Leaps
of Wang Lun* was published in 1915 while Döblin was serving as a
military doctor; it went on to win the Fontane Prize. In 1920 he
published *Wallenstein*, a novel set during the Thirty Years' War,
which was an oblique comment on the First World War. He became
president of the Association of German Writers in 1924, and
published his best-known novel, *Berlin Alexanderplatz*, in 1929,
achieving modest mainstream fame while solidifying his position
at the center of an intellectual group that included Bertolt Brecht,
Robert Musil, and Joseph Roth, among others. He fled Germany
with his family soon after Hitler's rise, moving first to Zurich, then
to Paris, and, after the Nazi invasion of France, to Los Angeles,
where he converted to Catholicism and briefly worked as a screen-
writer for Metro-Goldwyn-Mayer. After the war he returned to
Germany and worked as an editor with the aim of rehabilitating
literature that had been banned under Hitler, but he found himself
at odds with conservative postwar cultural trends. He suffered from

Parkinson's disease in later years and died in Emmendingen in 1957. Erna committed suicide two months after his death and was interred along with him.

MICHAEL HOFMANN is a German-born, British-educated poet and translator. Among his translations are works by Franz Kafka; Peter Stamm; his father, Gert Hofmann; Herta Müller; and fourteen books by Joseph Roth. A recipient of both the PEN Translation Prize and the Helen and Kurt Wolff Translator's Prize, Hofmann's *Selected Poems* were published in 2009 and *Where Have You Been?: Selected Essays* in 2014. In addition to *Berlin Alexanderplatz*, New York Review Books publishes his selection from the work of Malcolm Lowry, *The Voyage That Never Ends*, and his translations of Jakob Wassermann's *My Marriage* and Gert Ledig's *Stalin Front*. He teaches in the English department at the University of Florida.

BERLIN ALEXANDERPLATZ

ALFRED DÖBLIN

Translated from the German and with an afterword by
MICHAEL HOFMANN

NEW YORK REVIEW BOOKS

New York

THIS IS A NEW YORK REVIEW BOOK
PUBLISHED BY THE NEW YORK REVIEW OF BOOKS
435 Hudson Street, New York, NY 10014
www.nyrb.com

First published as *Berlin Alexanderplatz* by S. Fischer Verlag in 1929.
The English-language translation is published here by arrangement with
Penguin Books, Ltd, London.

The translation of this work was supported by a grant from the Goethe-Institut.

Library of Congress Cataloging-in-Publication Data
Names: Döblin, Alfred, 1878–1957, author. | Hofmann, Michael, 1957 August 25–
    translator.
Title: Berlin Alexanderplatz / Alfred Doblin ; translated by Michael Hofmann ;
    afterword by Michael Hofmann.
Description: New York : New York Review Books, [2018] | Series: NYRB Classics
Identifiers: LCCN 2017046077 (print) | LCCN 2017047715 (ebook) | ISBN
    9781681372006 (epub) | ISBN 9781681371993 (paperback)
Subjects: | BISAC: FICTION / Psychological. | FICTION / Crime. | FICTION /
    Political.
Classification: LCC PT2607.O35 (ebook) | LCC PT2607.O35 B5113 2018 (print) |
    DDC 833/.912—dc23
LC record available at https://lccn.loc.gov/2017046077

ISBN 978-1-68137-199-3
Available as an electronic book; ISBN 978-1-68137-200-6

Printed in the United States of America on acid-free paper.
10 9 8 7 6 5 4 3

Contents

rainy – *Franz breaking and entering, Franz not under the wheels, he's in the box seat now, he's made it – Love's weal and woe – Dazzling harvest in prospect, but miscalculations have been known to happen – Wednesday, 29 August – Saturday, 1 September*

The subject of this book is the life of the former cement worker and haulier Franz Biberkopf in Berlin. As our story begins, he has just been released from prison, where he did time for some stupid stuff; now he is back in Berlin, determined to go straight.

To begin with, he succeeds. But then, though doing all right for himself financially, he gets involved in a set-to with an unpredictable external agency that looks an awful lot like fate.

Three times the force attacks him and disrupts his scheme. The first time it comes at him with dishonesty and deception. Our man is able to get to his feet, he is still good to stand.

Then it strikes him a low blow. He has trouble getting up from that, he is almost counted out.

And finally it hits him with monstrous and extreme violence.

With that, our man who had been doing so well is finished. He throws in the towel, he has no idea what day of the week it is, it seems all up with him.

Before he can make an end, however, his blindness is taken from him in a way I do not describe here. His fault is revealed to him in the clearest terms. It is indeed his, the fault of his plan, which may once have looked sensible enough to him, but now looks quite different, not unexceptionable and straightforward, but full of arrogance and ignorance, and further vitiated with impertinence, cowardice and weakness.

The terrible thing that was his life acquires a purpose. A radical cure has been performed on Franz Biberkopf. And in the end we see our man back on Alexanderplatz, greatly changed, considerably the worse for wear, but straightened out.

To see and hear this will be worthwhile for many readers who, like Franz Biberkopf, fill out a human skin, but, again like Franz Biberkopf, happen to want more from life than a piece of bread.

I

Chapter One

As our story begins, Franz Biberkopf leaves Tegel Penitentiary, where a previous foolish life has taken him. He has difficulty initially readjusting to Berlin, but finally, to his relief, he succeeds, and vows to stick to the straight and narrow from now on.

The 41 tram into the city

He stood outside the gates of Tegel Penitentiary, a free man. Only yesterday, he had been on the allotments with the others, hoeing potatoes in his convict stripes, and now he was wearing his yellow summer duster, they were hoeing and he was free. He leant against the red wall and allowed one tram after another to pass, and he didn't take any of them. The guard on the gate strolled past him a few times, pointed to the tram, he didn't take it. The awful moment was at hand (awful, why so awful, Franz?), his four years were up. The black iron gates he'd been eyeing with increasing revulsion (revulsion, why revulsion) for the past year swung shut behind him. He was being put out. The others were inside, carpentering, varnishing, sorting, gluing, with two years ahead of them, with five years. He was standing at the tram stop.

His real punishment was just beginning.

He shook himself, gulped. He stood with one foot on the other. Suddenly he took a run up and he was sitting in the tram, with passengers all around him. At first it felt like being at the dentist's, when the dentist has the offending tooth gripped in his pliers and is pulling, and it feels like your head will explode with the pain. He craned his neck to look back at the red wall, but the tram rushed him away down the tracks, and he was left merely facing the general direction. The tram turned a corner, trees and buildings interposed themselves. The streets were full of bustle, Seestrasse, people got on and off. Something in him screamed: Watch out, watch out. The tip of his nose felt cold, something brushed his cheek. *Zwölf Uhr Mittagszeitung, B.Z, Die neuste Illustrierte, Die Funk-stunde.* 'Any more fares? ' The police have blue uniforms now. He made his way off the tram unnoticed, mingled with the crowd. What was wrong? Nothing. Hey, watch where you're going or I'll whop you. The crowds, the crowds. My skull needs grease, it must have dried out. All that stuff. Shoe shops, hat shops, electric lights, bars. People will need shoes to run around in, we had a shoe shop too, once, let's not forget that. Hundreds of shiny windows, let them flash away at you, they're nothing to be afraid of, it's just that they've been cleaned, you can always smash them if you want. They were taking up the road at Rosenthaler Platz, he was walking on duckboards along with everyone else. Just mingle with the crowd, man, that'll make everything better, then you won't suffer. There were mannequins in the windows in suits and coats, in skirts, with shoes and stockings on their feet. It was all seething and swarming, but it had nothing going on! It wasn't alive. It had complacent facial expressions, it was grinning, it was standing in groups of two or three on the traffic island in front of Aschinger's waiting to cross, smoking cigarettes, browsing in newspapers. Stood there like lamp-posts, and getting stiffer all the time. It was just like the buildings, all painted, all wood.

He got a shock when he turned down Rosenthaler Strasse, and saw a man and a woman sitting together in the window, pouring beer down their necks from big steins, so, they were just having a drink, they had forks in their hands and they were jabbing at pieces of meat, and lifting them to their mouths, and pulling the forks out, and not bleeding. Oh, his body cramped, I can't get over it, what am I going to do with myself? The answer came: punishment.

He couldn't go back, he had come so far on the tram, he had been released, and he had to go on.

I know, he groaned, I know I need to dig deeper and that I've been released. They had to let me go, my punishment was up, that's the way it works, the administration is doing what it has to do. And I will go on digging, but I don't want to, oh God, I can't.

He drifted down Rosenthaler Strasse, past the Wertheim

department store, then swung right into narrow Sophienstrasse. He thought: less light, and the darker the better. Prisoners may be held in isolation, solitary confinement or general confinement. In isolation, a man is kept apart from his fellows day and night. In solitary, the prisoner is kept in a cell, but is permitted to exercise, take classes and attend worship with others. Traffic hooted and honked. The façades were never-ending. There were roofs on the buildings, floating on the buildings, his eyes bounced around. Heaven forbid the roofs should slip off, but no, the buildings were steadfast. Where am I poor devil going to go, he trudged along the wall, wall without end. I am a fool, surely I'll be able to make my way, five minutes, ten minutes, then sit down somewhere and have a drink. At the sound of the bell, work is to begin. It may only be suspended for purposes of meals, exercise and lessons. During exercise, inmates are enjoined to keep their arms straight, and to swing them back and forth.

There was one particular building, and here he lifted his eyes from the pavement, shouldered open a door, and a sorry 'oh' broke from his chest. He slapped his shoulders, best way to keep the cold off, mate. The door opened onto a courtyard, someone shuffled past him, stopped behind him. He groaned, it did him good to groan. In his first days in solitary he had groaned continually and taken pleasure in the sound of his voice, it gave him something, meant it wasn't all up with him. Plenty of people did that in the cells, some from the very start, others only took to it later, once the loneliness got to them. There was something human about it, something consoling. He stood in the entryway, no longer aware of the terrible din, the lurching buildings were no longer there. He pouted, grunted, balled his fists in his pockets to give himself some encouragement. His shoulders in the yellow duster hunched defensively.

A stranger stopped and watched him. 'Sir, is there something the matter with you, are you in pain?' He heard him and stopped his groaning. 'Are you unwell, do you live here?' It was a Jew with a red beard, a short man in a coat, a black velvet hat, a cane. 'No, I don't live here.' He had to leave the entryway, though he had enjoyed his time there. Now the street resumed, the façades, the shop windows, the hurrying figures in trousers or flesh-coloured stockings, all of them in a tearing rush, purposeful, one after another. He made his mind up and veered into another entry, but they were just opening the gates to allow a car out. Next door, then, where there was just a narrow passage beside the staircase. No car was going to bother him here. He gripped the newel post. And while gripping it, he knew he wanted to avoid his punishment (how are you going to do that, Franz, you'll never manage that), definitely, he knew the way out. Quietly he started his personal music again, the groaning and humming, I'll not go out on the street again. The red-haired Jew reappeared, failed to spot him right away, standing by the banister. Heard him chuntering. 'What are you doing here? Are you unwell?' He let go of the newel post, lurched back into the courtyard. As he reached the gate, he saw it was the same Jew as before. 'Leave me alone! What are you bothering me for?' 'Nothing. Nothing really. But the way you're moaning and kvetching, surely I can ask if you're all right.' Through the chink in the gate, the buildings, the swarms of people, the badly secured roofs. He pulled open the gate, the Jew behind him: 'What are you afraid of, mister, it won't be so bad. You won't die. Berlin's a big place. Where thousands live, there's room for one more.'

It was the well of a deep, dark courtyard. He was standing beside the garbage bins. And suddenly began ear-splittingly to sing. He pulled the hat off his head like a hurdy-gurdy man. The sound bounced off the walls. It was a good sound. His voice filled his ears. He sang more lustily than he had ever dared in prison. What was it he was singing, that came bouncing off the walls? 'Es braust ein Ruf wie Donnerhall'.[1] A martial earnestness and rigour. And then, in the middle of a song, 'Juvivallerallera'. No one paid him any heed. The Jew was waiting for him at the gate: 'You've got a good voice. You sing beautifully. With a voice like that you can make money.' The Jew followed him out onto the street, took his arm, towed him along, jabbering at him all the time, till they turned into Gormann Strasse, the Jew and the big, raw-boned fellow in the summer duster, who kept his lips pursed as though he tasted gall.

Still not there

He took him to a room heated by an iron stove, sat him down on the settee: 'There, now you've arrived. Sit soft. Keep your hat on, or take it off, just as you please. I'm going to bring someone who you'll like. I don't live here myself, see. That's the way of it, if the room's cosy and warm, one guest brings the next.'

The convict sat there all alone. 'Es braust ein Ruf wie Donnerhall, wie Schwertgeklirr und Wogenprall'. He took the tram, he looked out the side, the red walls were plainly visible between the trees, brightly coloured leaves were raining down. The walls were in front of his eyes, he was looking at them from the settee, looking at them incessantly. It's great good luck to live within these walls, you know how the day begins and how it continues. (Franz, you're not about to hide, are you, you've been hiding for four years, buck up, take a look around, it's time you stopped hiding.) All forms of singing, whistling and noise-making are forbidden. Inmates are required to get up the moment the signal is given to get up, then make their beds, wash, comb, clean their clothes and dress themselves. Soap is to be supplied in sufficient quantities. Boom, the sound of a bell. Get up, boom five-thirty, boom six-thirty, cells unlocked, boom boom, out you get, sunshine, breakfast time, work time, free association, boom boom boom, dinner time, come on son, don't make a face, you won't put on any weight here, singers are to present themselves, singers come forward at five-forty, I report hoarse, six o'clock lock up, g'night, that's been taken care of. A great joy to live within these walls, they ran me into the ground, I thought I'd committed murder but it was only manslaughter, GBH resulting in death, not so bad, I'd gotten to be a right s.o.b., a ruffian, little better than a vagrant.

A big old long-haired Jew, the little black skullcap on the back of his head, had been sitting facing him for a while. Now there was a

Jew in Susa the capital whose name was Mordecai, who brought up Esther, the daughter of his uncle, the maiden was beautiful to behold. The old man looked away, turned back to the red-haired Jew. 'Where'd you dig him up then?' 'He was going from door to door. He stopped in a yard, and started to sing.' 'Sing what?' 'Wartime songs.' 'He'll freeze.' 'Maybe.' The old man studied him. Jews may not handle corpses on the first holy day, nor on the second; and this applies to both New Year's Days. And who is the author of the following Rabbinical lesson: if a man eats of the carcass of a clean bird, he is not impure; but if he doth eat of the bowels or the craw, then he is impure? With his bony yellow hand the old man reached for the hand of the convict, which was lying on his coat: 'Will you not take off your coat, mister? It's warm in here. We are old people, we feel the cold all year, it'll be too warm for you.'

He sat on the settee, squinting down at his hand, he had gone from house to house, who knew where you would find something in this world. Now he wanted to get up and leave, his eyes were scanning the dark room for the door. The old man, though, pushed him back on the settee: 'Stay, where d'you think you're going.' He thought: out. But the old man held him by the wrist and squeezed. 'We'll soon see who's the stronger. Will you sit here when I tell you to,' the old man yelled. 'Sit, and listen to what I have to say. Get a grip on yourself.' And to the red-haired man who was holding him down by the shoulders he said: 'You can go. I never sent for you. I can manage him.'

What did these people want with him? He wanted out, he thrust up, but the old man pushed him down. 'What do you want with me?' he yelled. 'Scold all you like, you'll be scolding a lot more.' 'Let me go. I want to get out.' 'What've you got waiting for you, the street, the courtyards?'

Then the old man got up out of his chair, and went rustling up and down the room: 'Let him yell all he wants. Let him do as he pleases. But not here. Show him out.' 'But why, it's always noisy in here?' 'Don't bring me people who make more noise. My daughter's children are sick, they're in bed at the back, that's enough noise.' 'Oy, oy veh, I didn't know that, please forgive me.' The red-haired man clasped his hands together: 'We'd better go. The rabbi's house is full. The grandchildren are sick. We'll go somewhere else.' But now Franz didn't want to get up. 'Come.' He had to get up. Then he whispered: 'Don't pull me. Leave me be.' 'But the house is full, you heard.' 'Leave me be.'

With glittering eyes, the old man looked at the stranger imploringly. Jeremiah said we would heal Babylon, but Babylon would not be healed. Let us leave, let each one of us go home. The sword will fall upon the throats of the Chaldeans, and upon the inhabitants of Babylon. 'If he's quiet, he can stay with you. If not, he'd better go.' 'All right, we won't make a sound. I'll sit with him, you can depend on me.' The old man rustled out through the door.

The example of Zannovich

Then the discharged prisoner in the yellow duster was once more seated on the settee. Sighing and shaking his head, the red-haired man paced through the room. 'Don't be angry with the old man. He has a temper. Are you new in town?' 'Yes, I was in—' The red walls, the beautiful walls, the cells, he looked at them yearningly, his back was stuck to the red wall, a clever man had built them, he wasn't going anywhere. And the man slid down off the settee onto the floor, like a doll; as he went down, he pushed the table away. 'What's the matter with you?' cried the red-headed man. The prisoner writhed on the carpet, his hat rolled away between his hands, he drilled down with his head, he groaned: 'Into the ground, into the earth, where it's nice and dark.' The red-headed Jew tugged at him: 'For the love of God, you're among strangers. If the old man should come back. Get up.' But he wouldn't permit himself to be pulled back up, he clawed at the carpet, he groaned. 'For God's sake be quiet, what if the old man should hear you. You and I will get along.' 'No one's gonna get me out of here.' Tunnelling like a mole.

And as the Jew wasn't able to haul him upright, he scratched his sidelocks, shut the door and settled himself on the floor beside him.

He clasped his knees, and looked at the table legs in front of him: 'All right. Stay there. I'll stay with you. It's not so comfortable, but why not. You're not going to tell me what's the matter with you, so let me tell you a story.' The prisoner wheezed, head to the carpet. (Why is he groaning and wheezing? It's make up your mind time, you've got to choose a route, and you don't know any, Franz. You don't want the old stuff, and in the cells you only hid and groaned, and you didn't think, Franz, you didn't think.) The red-haired man said angrily: 'It's not right to make a show of yourself. Listen to other people. Who's telling you you're so special. God won't let anyone fall from his hand, there are other people besides you. Haven't you ever read about Noah, putting two of each kind in his Ark, in his boat, when the Flood came? Two after each kind. Did the Lord forget any of them? He didn't forget so much as the lice on their heads. They were all dear to him.' The man below whimpered. (Whimpering doesn't cost anything – a sick mouse whimpers.)

The red-haired man ignored the whimpering, scratched his cheeks: 'There's lots of things on this earth, no end of stories you can tell when you're young, and when you're old too. I'm going to tell you, yes, I'm going to tell you the story of Zannovich, of Stefan Zannovich. You won't have heard it before. Once you feel better, you can sit up, it's not good for you to have too much blood go to your head. My late father told us a lot of stories, he travelled as our people do, he got to be seventy years old, he outlived my mother, he knew a lot, a clever man. We were seven hungry mouths, and when there was no food in the house he would tell us stories. They may not fill you up, but you forget your hunger.' The dull moans continued. (A sick camel can moan too.) 'Well now, we know there are more things in this world than gold and beauty and joy. So who was Zannovich, who was his father, who were his forefathers? Beggars, like most of us, grocers, traders, commersants. Old Zannovich came from Albania and made his way to Venice. He will have known why. Some go from the city to the country, others from the country to the city. The country is calmer and quieter, people consider everything, you can talk for hours, and if your luck's in you'll earn a few coppers. It's no easier in the city, but the people are more densely packed, and they have less time. If it's not this man, it's that one. They don't have ox-carts, they have fast horse-drawn carriages. You win some, you lose some. Old Zannovich knew that. First, he sold what he had with him, and then he took out cards, and played. He was dishonest. He turned it to his advantage, the fact that people in the city are always in a hurry and want to be kept amused. He kept them amused. It cost them a lot of money. Old Zannovich was a card-sharp and a cheat, but he had a good head on him. The peasants used to make things difficult for him, life was easier in the city. He prospered. Till one day someone felt he'd been tricked. Well, old Zannovich wasn't prepared for that. Blows were exchanged, the police were called, and in the end old Zannovich had to leg it with his children. The law was after him, and the old man preferred not to argue with the law, the law of Venice wouldn't understand, and in fact it never caught up with him. He had horses and money, and he went back to Albania, and bought himself an estate, an entire village, and he sent his children to good schools. Then, when he was very old, he died quietly and respectably. That was the life of old Zannovich. The peasants mourned his passing, but he didn't care for them, because he never forgot the times he stood before them with his wares, his rings and his bracelets and his coral necklaces, and they handled everything and turned it this way and that, and finally they went off, and left him with it, and didn't buy.

'You know, if a father's a shrub, he'll want his son to grow up to be a tree. And if a father's a rock, he'll want his son to be a mountain. Old Zannovich told his sons: I was nothing in Albania for the twenty years I was a peddler, you know why? Because I didn't carry my head to where it belonged. But I'm going to send you to the great school at Padua, take horses and carriages, and then when you come to go out into the world, remember me, who had trouble with your mother and with you, and who used to sleep in the woods with you at night like a boar: it was all my fault. The peasants dried me out like a lean year, and I would have withered away, then I went to be among people, and I didn't die.'

The red-haired man chortled to himself, tipped his head to the side, waggled his behind. They were sitting on the carpet together: 'If someone comes in now, he'll think we're both meshugge, they supply us with a settee and here we are sitting on the floor in front of it. Well, if it's what you want, why not. Young Stefan Zannovich was a great talker, even when he was just a young man of twenty. He could twist and turn, ingratiate himself, he could flirt with the women and flatter the men. In Padua the nobility learns from the professors, and Stefan learnt from the nobility. Everyone liked him. And then when he went back to Albania, his father was still alive, and liked him and was happy to see him again, and said: "Take a look at him, he's a man of the world, he won't spend twenty years dickering with peasants, he's twenty years ahead of his old man." And the young man stroked his silk sleeves, brushed the pretty curls out of his face and kissed his proud father: "But you, Father, you've saved me the worst twenty years." "I want them to be the best twenty years of your life," the old man said, and he stroked and petted his son.

'And then young Zannovich seemed to experience a miracle, even though it wasn't a miracle. People came to him from everywhere. He was given the keys to every heart. He travelled to Montenegro with coaches and horses and servants, his father was delighted to see his son such a great man – the father a shrub, his son a tree – and in Montenegro they spoke to him as to a count and a nobleman. They would never have believed him if he'd said: my father's name is Zannovich, we come from the village of Pastrovich, that my father is proud of! They would never have believed him, such was his allure of a nobleman from Padua, and he looked like one and he knew them all. Stefan spoke and he laughed: "All right, have it your way." And he said he was a wealthy Pole, which is what they took him for, a Baron Varta, and they were glad, and he was glad.'

The convict had sat up with a sudden jerk. He squatted on his knees, listening to the other man below him. With an icy glare he said: 'Monkey.' The red-haired man replied indifferently, 'So I'm a monkey. A monkey that knows more than a lot of people.' The other was forced back down on the ground. (You have to learn contrition; understand what you've done; understand what you need to know!)

'So can we carry on then? There's always a lot you can learn from other people. Young Zannovich was on that path, and he carried on. I never saw him, and my father never saw him, but it's easy enough to imagine him. Let me ask you, you called me a monkey – one shall not despise any creature on God's earth, they give us their flesh, and they do us many kindnesses besides, think of the horse, the dog, the canary, monkeys I only know from the fair, they have to do tricks in chains, a hard lot, no man has a harder one – well, I want to ask you, and I can't ask you by name, because you haven't done me the courtesy of telling it to me: what was it that helped the two Zannoviches on their way, both the younger and the elder? You'll say they had brains, they were both clever men. But plenty of people have had brains, and at the age of eighty they're not so far along as Stefan was at twenty. The main thing about a man is his eyes and his feet. You have to be able to see the world and direct your feet to it.

'So hear what Stefan Zannovich did, who knew a bit about people, and who knew how little there was to fear from them. See how they smooth your path, almost as they show a blind man the way. They wanted him to be Baron Varta. All right, he said, I'm Baron Varta. Later on, that was no longer enough for him, or for them. Why just a baron, why not more? There's a celebrity in Albania who's already long dead, but they continue to celebrate him, the way the people like to celebrate their heroes, Skanderbeg was his name. If Zannovich had been able to, he could have claimed: I am Skanderbeg. As Skanderbeg was dead, he said, I'm descended from Skanderbeg, and strutted about and said he was Prince Castriota of Albania, destined to recover the lost greatness of Albania, his retinue was waiting for him. They paid for him to live as a descendant of Skanderbeg's ought to live. He was just what those people wanted. They go to the theatre and listen to things made up to suit them. They pay money for the privilege. So why not let them pay to hear nice things in the morning and afternoon as well, and that they can even play a part in themselves.'

Once again the man in the yellow summer duster pulled himself upright, he had a grim, creased face, he looked down on the red-haired man from above, cleared his throat, his voice was changed: 'Now hold on a minute, mister, you seem to be not all there. You're a bit short.' 'Not all there, maybe that's right. Now I'm a monkey, now I'm meshugge.' 'What do you think you're doing, gabbing this stuff to me?' 'Whose idea was it to sit on the floor, and not get up? It wasn't mine, was it? With a whole settee behind me? Well, if it bothers you, I'll be happy to shut up.'

At that the other, having shot a glance round the room, thrust out his legs and sat down with his back against the settee, propping his hands on the carpet. 'There, that's more comfortable, isn't it?' 'You can stop your nonsense now.' 'Whatever you say. I've told the story often enough, I don't care either way.' But after a pause, the other man turned to face him: 'You can carry on if you like.' 'Well, listen to that. People talk and tell each other stories, and the time passes more agreeably. All I wanted was for you to open your eyes. The Stefan Zannovich you were learning about, he got so much money he was able to travel to Germany. They didn't succeed in unmasking him in Montenegro. What you can learn about Stefan Zannovich is that he knew himself and he knew people. Even if he was as innocent as a chaffinch. You see, he had so little fear that the greatest historical figures were his friends, the most imposing: the Kurfürst of Saxony, the Crown Prince of Prussia, who was later a great war hero. The Austrian Empress Theresa quaked on her throne when he stood before her. Zannovich never quaked. So when Stefan got to Vienna and there were people sniffing around him, the Empress lifted up her hand and said: "Let the young man go free!" '

The story is concluded in an unexpected way; helping the freed man to acquire new strength

The other man laughed, whinnied against the settee: 'You're a card, aren't you. You could work for a circus. As a clown.' The red-haired man giggled with him: 'There, you see. Hush now, I can hear the old man's grandchildren. Maybe we should sit up after all. What do you say.' The other laughed, crept up, settled himself in one corner of the settee, the red-haired man in the other. 'You sit softer this way, and you won't get creases in your coat.' The man in the summer duster eyed the red-haired man in his corner. 'I've not met a bird like you in a long time.' With equanimity the red beard replied: 'Maybe you just didn't look, there's more than enough of us. Now you've gone and soiled your coat, they don't wipe their feet in this household.' The freed man, a man in his early thirties, had alert eyes, his expression looked fresher: 'Tell me, you, what do you deal in? I expect you live on the moon?' – 'Very well, let's talk about the moon then.'

A man with a curly brown beard had been standing in the doorway for the past five minutes or so. He now walked up to the table, and sat down on a chair. He was about the same age, and had on a black velvet hat like the other man. He waved his hand about, and his voice shrilled: 'Who's this then? What're you doing with him?' 'And what are you doing, Eliser? I don't know the fellow, he won't tell me his name.' 'You been telling him stories.' 'That's none of your business.' The brown beard to the convict: 'Has he been telling you stories?' 'He doesn't speak. He just walks around and sings in people's yards.' 'Then let him go.' 'What do you care what I do.' 'I listened at the door to what was passing between you. You were telling him all about Zannovich. That's all you ever do.' The stranger eyed the brown beard, growled: 'Who are you, and what are you doing here? Why do you care what he does?' 'Did he tell you about Zannovich, or didn't he? Of course he did. Nahum my brother-in-law goes around and talks and talks and never does anything.' 'I never asked for help from you. Wicked man, can't you see

the man's in trouble.' 'So what if he is. God didn't make you responsible for him, no, God waited for you to come along. On his own
God couldn't do anything for him.' 'Bad man.' 'You stay away from
him. He'll just fill your head with nonsense about Zannovich and
who else succeeded in this world.' 'Won't you leave us alone now.'
'Listen to the cheat, the doer of good deeds. He wants to tell me
what to do. Is this your flat? What did you tell him about Zannovich this time, your shining example? You should have been our
rabbi, and we'd have had the pleasure of feeding you.' – 'I don't
need your charity.' The brown beard raised his voice: 'And we
don't need scroungers hanging on our apron strings. Did he tell
you what happened to his Zannovich at the end?' 'Bastard, bad
man.' 'Did he tell you?' The convict blinked sleepily at the red-
haired man, who shook his fist and stalked over to the door, then
he growled after him: 'Don't run off, man, don't get het up, let
him speak.'

Then the brown beard started in on him, with jerky hand movements, slipping back and forth, with tongue clicks and head wags,
a new expression every other second, now addressing the stranger,
and now the redhead: 'He makes people stupid. Let him tell what
became of his Stefan Zannovich. He doesn't like to say, why doesn't
he like to say, I wonder.' 'Because you're a bad man, Eliser.' 'Better
man than you. They chased his Zannovich (both hands raised in
revulsion, terrible round eyes) from Florence like a thief. Why?
Because they saw him for what he was.' The redhead loomed dan-
gerously in front of him, the other motioned him away: 'I'm talking
now. He wrote letters to the nobility, a nobleman gets lots of
letters, you can't always tell from a letter what manner of man
is writing it. Then he puffed himself up, and he went to Brussels
as Prince of Albania or some such, and he got involved in politics. Well, it must have been his bad angel who led him on. He
presents himself to the government, the boy Stefan Zannovich,
and promises them a hundred thousand men for the war, or two
hundred thousand, don't ask me which, the government writes
him a letter, thanks but no thanks, it didn't want to get involved in

his uncertain business. Then the bad angel told Stefan: take this letter, and borrow money on it. Here's a letter from the minister addressed to His Highness, the Prince of Albania. They lent him money, and then the swindler was finished. How old did he get to be? Thirty – that was the reward for his crimes. He couldn't repay the loan, they tried him in Brussels, and it all got out. Your hero, Nahum! Did you tell the visitor about his grim death in prison, when he opened his own veins? And how once he was dead – nice life, pretty death, why not tell it all – once he was dead, the hangman came, the knacker with his cart full of dead dogs and dead horses and dead cats, and picked up his body, and wheeled him out of town to their gallows hill and covered the body with all sorts of rubbish from the city.'

The man in the summer duster sat there open-mouthed: 'Is that right?' (A sick mouse can groan.) The redhead had counted every word yelled by his brother-in-law. He waited with raised index finger in front of the brown beard's face, as if for a cue, and then jabbed him in the chest and spat at his feet, ptui, ptui: 'That's for you. That's what I think of you. My brother-in-law.' The brown beard waggled over to the window: 'There, and now you talk, and tell me it's not true.'

The walls melted away. There was a small space with a light bulb, two Jews running around, one with brown hair, one with red, both in black velvet hats, bickering. He applied to his friend, the redhead: 'You, listen to me, you, is it true what he said about the man, and how he lost his way and they put him to death?' The brown beard yelled: 'Put him to death, when did I say put him to death? He killed himself.' The redhead: 'He did very likely kill himself.' The freed man: 'And what did they do, the others in with him?' The redhead: 'Who, who?' 'Well, there'll have been others there besides him, besides Stefan. They won't all have been ministers and bankers and crooks.' The redhead and the brown beard exchanged glances. The redhead: 'Well, what do you think they did? They'll have sat and watched.'

The freed man in the yellow summer duster, the big fellow, picked up his hat, brushed it down, laid it on the table, all in silence, and unbuttoned his waistcoat: 'Here, look at my trousers. I used to be so fat, and now I can stuff both fists inside the waistband, that's what hunger did to me. It's all gone. My whole belly gone to pot. That's how you get ruined, for not always having been the way you were supposed to be. I don't think the others are that much better either. No I don't. They want to drive you crazy.' The brown beard whispered to the redhead: 'There you are.' 'Where am I?' 'Well, a jailbird.' 'So what if.' The freed man: 'Then it's: you're being released, and it's straight back in it, the same shit you were in before. Snow joke.' He buttoned up his waistcoat again. 'You can tell that by what they've done. They get the dead man out of his cell, the man with the cart comes along, and throws a dead human being on it, who's gone and killed hisself, poor bastard, I wonder why he wasn't brained right away, for transgressing against a human being, never mind what he did.' The redhead, sorrowfully: 'What can I say?' 'Is it that we're nothing, once we've done something? Anyone can get another go who's been to prison, never mind what it is they're in for.' (Regrets? You want to breathe! Cut loose! Then everything's in the past, fear and all.) 'I just wanted to show you: you shouldn't believe everything my brother-in-law says. Sometimes you can't do everything you'd like to, sometimes things get fouled up.' 'That's not justice, getting tossed in the garbage like you were a dead dog, and rubbish dumped on top of you, that's not what I call justice towards a dead man. No sir. But now I want to say goodbye to you. Gimme your paw. You mean well and so do you (he shook hands with the redhead). Biberkopf is the name, Franz Biberkopf. It was nice of the pair of you to take me in. My bird was singing back then, in the courtyard. Well, cheers to you both, it'll pass.' The two Jews shook him by the hand, smiled. The redhead clasped his hand a long time, beamed: 'Now, are you sure you're all right? I'll be happy to see you, whenever you have a moment.' 'Thank you kindly, I'll do that, I'm sure I'll have time, it's the money that worries me. And give my best to the old gentleman, too. He's got strength in his hand, he must have been a butcher or what? Oh, let me just straighten the rug, it's all skew. No, no, I'll take care of it, and the table too. There.' He worked on the floor, laughed at the redhead over his shoulder: 'So we sat on the floor and told each other stories. That's a nice place to sit, if you forgive my saying so.'

They walked him to the door, the redhead still concerned: 'Will you be able to walk on your own?' The brown beard jabbed him in the ribs: 'Don't be such a mother hen.' The freed man, walking upright, shook his head, displaced air with both his arms (You need to clear space for yourself, space is what you need, and nothing more): 'Don't you worry about me. You can let me go. You were telling me all about how important it was to have feet and eyes. Well, I still got them. No one's cut those off of me yet. Morning, gents.'

And he crossed the narrow, cluttered yard, the two of them peeking down after him from the stairway. He had his hat pulled down over his face, and was muttering as he jumped over a puddle of petrol: 'Filth. What about a cognac. Whoever comes near me gets one in the face. Let's see where I can get me a cognac.'

Markets opening directionless, gradually drifting lower, Hamburg out of bed the wrong side, London continuing weak

It was raining. On the left, down Münzstrasse, were blinking lights that indicated cinemas. On the corner he got held up, people were stood in front of a fence, there was a big hole there, the tramlines on their sleepers were crossing empty space, just then a tram slowly passed. Look at that, they're building an Underground, there must be work to be had in Berlin after all. Another cinema, no admission to anyone under seventeen. On the enormous poster was a red gentleman on a staircase, and a sweet girl was clutching at his legs, she was sprawled over the stairs and there was smuggins at the top. Below he read: Orphaned, the story of a child in six acts. Yes, think I'll treat myself to that. The orchestrion was grinding away. Admission: 60 pfennigs.

A man said to the cashier: 'Miss, is there a discount for an old reservist in good shape?' 'No, only for infants under six months with dummy.' 'That's me, then. Newborn on the never-never.' 'All right, then, fifty, come on in.' Behind him a skinny fellow with a kerchief round his neck cut in: 'Please, miss, will you let me in for free.' 'As if. Ask your mama to put you on the potty.' 'Well, can I?' 'Can you what?' 'Go in the flicker.' 'This ain't no flicker.' 'Oh, ain't it.' She called through the ticket window to the lookout by the door: 'Maxie, come here a minute. Here's someone who wants to know if this is a cinema. Hasn't got ny money. Show him what's here.' 'You wanna know what's here, young fella? Ain't it clicked? This is the poorhouse, Münzstrasse section.' He shoved the skinny fellow away from the box office, waved a fist in his face: 'And if you like, you can have that in writing.'

Franz pushed on in. There was a break in the programme. The long space was chock-a-block, 90 per cent of them men in caps which they keep on throughout. Three overhead lamps with red shades. At the front a yellow piano with parcels on it. The orchestrion grinding on without a break. The lights go down and the film begins. A goose girl is to be educated, why isn't immediately clear. She wiped her nose with her hand, scratched her bottom on the steps, the whole cinema laughed out loud. Franz was exhilarated by the sniggering all round. Here were lots of people, at liberty and enjoying themselves, no one's telling them what to do, how lovely, and yours truly in the midst of it! The show went on. The stuck-up baron had a lover who sprawled in a hammock and stuck her legs straight up in the air. She kept her knickers on though. There's a thing. What did people see in that dirty goosegirl, now she was licking her plate. Once again the one with the long legs came up. The baron had dumped her, she flew out of her hammock and lay sprawled on the grass for a long time. Franz stared at the wall, there was the next scene already, but he could still see her spilling out of the hammock and lying there motionless. He chewed on his tongue, my word. Then, when someone who was the goosegirl's beau embraced the lady, he got a rush of feeling across his chest, as if he was hugging himself. It affected him so much, he came over all weak.

A woman. (So there's more in the world than bother and dread.

What's it all for? Christ, man, air, a woman!) How had he failed to think of that. You stand at the window of your cell, staring out at the prison yard through the bars. Sometimes women go by, visiting, or children, or cleaners for the governor. The way they stand pressed to the windows, the convicts, eyeing, all the windows full, gobbling up any passing woman. A sergeant had a conjugal visit lasting a fortnight from his wife in Eberswalde, it used to be he only went to see her once a fortnight, he saved em up and cashed em in, and at work he can hardly keep his head up he's so shagged out.

Franz was already out on the street in the rain. What to do? I'm free – gotta have a woman. Where's a woman. Delightful, life on the outside. Be able to stand still and walk wherever. His legs were shaking, he felt no ground under them. Then on the corner of Kaiser-Wilhelm-Strasse there was one behind the market cart, and he stopped in front of her, didn't care what she was like. Crikey, where do these jelly legs come from all of a sudden. He sloped off with her, biting his underlip to stop it shaking, if you live any distance off, I'm not going. It was only diagonally across Bülowplatz, past the fences, through an entryway, across a yard and down half a dozen steps. She turned, laughed: 'Hold on a minute, just let me park my umbrella.' He squeezed, thrust, pinched at her, ran his hands over her coat, he was still in his hat, crossly she let the umbrella clatter to the floor: 'Let go of me, man,' he panted, faked a smile, 'What's the matter with you?' 'You're ripping my clothes. I don't spose you'll pay for the damage either. Well, then. No one gives us anything.' When he refused to let go of her: 'I can't breathe. What's wrong with you. Idiot.' She was sluggish, fat, short, he had to hand over the 3 marks first, she put them away carefully in her dresser and stuck the key in her pocket. He, not taking his eyes off her: 'I been inside for a couple of years, gal. Tegel, you can imagine.' 'Where's that?' 'Tegel, you can imagine.'

The fat woman laughed full-throatedly. She was undoing her blouse at the top. There were two king's children, who loved each other oh-so much. When the dog jumps over the kerb with the sausage in its teeth. She clutched him, pulled him to her. Chook, chook, chook, my little chicken, my little chickadee. Before long he had sweat on his face, he was groaning. 'What are you groaning for?' 'Who's the fellow running around next door?' 'That's no fellow, that's my landlady.' 'Well, what's she doing then?' 'How do I know. It's her kitchen.' 'I want her to stop it. Why does she have to do that now. I can't stand it.' 'Oh yes, I'll just tell her to stop then, would you like that.' What a sweaty man, won't you be happy to be rid of him, layabout, I'll put him out just as soon as I can. She knocked on the door: 'Frau Priese. Would you mind being quiet for a few minutes, I've got a gentleman I'm trying to talk to, it's important.' There, that's done, dear Lord, now you can be at peace, come to my bosom, but you'll be flying out in a jiffy.

She thought, her head on the pillows, the yellow shoes could do with re-soling, Kitty's new man will do it for a couple of marks if she doesn't mind, I'll not steal him away from her, or mebbe he could dye them brown to go with my blouse, which is an old rag already, it'll about do for a tea-cosy, the lace trim needs ironing, I'll tell Frau Priese as soon as I can, she'll have her hearth on still, wonder what's cooking today. She sniffed. Fried herrings.

Through his head rhymes rolled, incomprehensible stuff, a procession: cooking soup, Miss Stein, I'll have a spoonful, cooking noodles, Miss Stein, give me noodles, Miss Stein, I fall down, I get up. He groaned loudly: 'Don't you like me then?' 'Why wouldn't I sweetie, come here, love for a *Sechser*.' He tumbled into bed, grunted, groaned. She scratched her throat: 'You do make me laugh. You can lie still a moment. I'm not bothered.' She laughed, extended her plump arms, pushed her stockinged feet out of the bed. 'It's not my fault.'

Out on the street! Air! It's still raining. What can the matter be? I better find myself another one. Have a good sleep. Franz, my boy, what's wrong with you?

Sexual potency in the male is produced by the following, working in concert: 1. the glandular system, 2. the nervous system and 3.

the sexual organs. The glands involved are: the pituitary, the thyroid, the suprarenal, the prostate, the seminal vesicle and the epididymis. The lead role is taken by the sperm gland, the entire sexual apparatus from cerebral cortex to genitals is activated by its secretions. The erotic trigger releases the erotic tension of the cerebral cortex, the charge moves in the form of sexual excitement from the cerebral cortex to the switch centre in the interbrain. This charge then funnels down the spine. Not unimpeded, because before it quits the brain, it needs to pass the inhibitors, mainly intellectual inhibitors, moral scruples, lack of self-confidence, fear of humiliation, fear of infection and pregnancy, etc. etc. play a great part.

Then dawdled down Elsasser Strasse at night. Don't hang about, mate, don't pretend to be tired. 'How much you asking!' The dark-haired one is good, the hips on her like a pretzel. If a girl's got a guy she likes. 'You're in a good mood, darling. You must have come into some money.' 'Sure I have. I'm good for a thaler.' 'Why not.' But he's still nervous.

And then up in her room, flowers behind the curtains, tidy little room, sweet little room, she's even got a gramophone, she sings for him, in Bemberg's artificial silk stockings, blouse off, eyes blacker than kohl: 'You know, I'm a shantoose. Guess where? Anywhere that takes my fancy. I'm just between engagements now. I go to bars I like, and then I enquire. And then: my song. I've got a song. Hey, stop tickling me.' 'Come on, cut it out.' 'No, hands off, that's bad for business. My song, be nice, sweetie, I conduct a proper auction in the bar, no passing round a hat. Anyone who can afford it gets to kiss me. Wild, eh. In the public bar. None under fifty pfennigs. I get it every time. Here on my shoulder. You can, too.' She puts on a gentleman's top hat, cackles in his face, waggles her hips, arms akimbo: 'Theodor whatever did you have in mind when you eyed me up last night? Theodor what have you gone and done, you rotter when you trett me to champagne and trotters.'

The way she perches on his lap, sticks a cigarette in her bill that she's sneaked out of his weskit, looks meltingly in his eye, rubs her earlobes softly against his, tootles: 'Do you know what homesickness is? Homesickness that breaks your heart? Everything around feels so cold and empty.' She trills, stretches out on the chaise. She smokes, strokes his hair, trills, laughs. The sweat on his forehead! The fear again! And suddenly his brain gives another lurch. Boom, bells, get up, five-thirty, six o'clock unlocked, boom boom, a quick brush of the jacket in case the old man holds inspection, but not today. I'm being released soon. Psst, you, last night someone did a runner, Klose, the rope's still dangling over the wall, they're after him with dogs. He groans, his head lifts, he sees the girl, her chin, her throat. How will I ever get out of here. They won't let me out. I'm still not out. She blows blue smoke rings in his face, titters: 'Ooh, you, I'll pour you a Mampe for thirty pfennigs.' He lies there, full-length: 'What do I want with a Mampe? I'm all gone. I did time in Tegel, for what. First I was with the Prussians in the trenches and then in the big house in Tegel. I'm not a human being any more.' 'Oh come. You're not about to start crying on me, are you. Come on, big fella, open wide, a big fella needs a drink. Here is where we have fun, we enjoy ourselves, we laugh, from morning till night.' 'And that's what they give me shit for. They might as well have cut my throat, the sons of bitches. They might as well have thrown my body out on the dump as well.' 'Come on, big fella, another Mampe. If it's your eyes, go to Mampe, let Mampe light the way for you.'

'The girls chased after you like sheep, and you didn't so much as spit at them, and then suddenly you're flat on your face.' She picks up another one of his cigarettes which are tumbling out on the floor: 'Yes, you'd better go to the nice policeman and tell him.' 'I'm going.' He looks for his braces. And doesn't say another word, and doesn't look at the girl, slobberlips, who's smoking and smiles and looks at him, quickly scuffs a few more of his cigarettes under the chaise with her foot. And he grabs his hat, and down the stairs, takes the 68 to Alexanderplatz and sits and broods over a beer in a bar.

Testifortan, patent no. 365695, potency remedy endorsed by Drs Magnus Hirschfeld and Bernhard Schapiro of the Institute for Sexual Science, Berlin. The principal causes for impotence are A.

insufficient charge through malfunctioning of the glands; B. excessive resistance by exaggerated mental blocks, fatiguing of the erective centre. If the impotent man tries again, each case has to be handled individually. A rest can often be helpful.

And he eats his bellyful and gets a good night's sleep, and the next day on the street he thinks: I fancy this one and I fancy that one, but he doesn't proposition either. And the dummy in the shop window, the curves on that, she'd suit me, but I'm not propositioning her either. And he sits in the bar and looks no one in the face and eats his fill and drinks. From now on I'll do nuffink all day but eat and drink and sleep, and life will be over for me. Over, over.

Victory all along the line! Franz Biberkopf buys a veal escalope

And now it's Wednesday, the third day, and he gets into his coat. Who's to blame for everything? Ida, always Ida. Who else. I broke her fucking ribs, that's why they put me in clink. Now she's got what she wanted, she's dead, and I'm standing there. And wailing and running down the freezing streets. Where to? Where they used to live, at her sister's. Down Invalidenstrasse, into Ackerstrasse, whish into the house, back courtyard. No prison, no conversation with any Jews on Dragonerstrasse. The bitch is to blame, where is she. Saw nothing, noticed nothing on the way, just went there. The odd facial twitch, the odd twitch finger, that's where we'll go, rumbly bumbly kieker di nell, rumbly bumbly kieker di nell, rumbly bumbly.

Ding-dong. 'Who is it?' 'Me.' 'Who?' 'Open up, woman.' 'My God, Franz, it's you.' 'Open the door.' Rumbly bumbly kieker di nell. Rumbly. Bit of thread on my tongue, spit it out. He's standing in the corridor, she locks the door after him. 'What are you doing here. What if someone had seen you on the steps.' 'Doesn't matter. Let them. G'morning.' Hangs a left into the parlour. Rumbly bumbly. That thread on his tongue, can't seem to catch it. He picks at it with his finger. But it's nothing, just a stupid feeling on the tip of his tongue. So there's the parlour again, the horsehair sofa, the Kaiser on the wall, a Frenchie in scarlet troos is just handing his sword to him. Surrender bender. 'What are you doing here, Franz? You must be mad.' 'I'll sit down then, shall I.' I surrender, the Kaiser takes his sword, then the Kaiser has to give him back his sword, that's the way of the world. 'If you don't go, I'll scream the place down.' 'Why would you do that?' Rumbly bumbly, I've come such a long way, here I am, here I stay. 'Did they let you out already then?' 'Yes, I'm done.'

He stares at her and then he gets up: 'They let me go, so I'm here. They let me out all right.' He wants to tell her how, but he chews on his bit of thread, the trumpet is broken, it's over, and he's shaking and he can't cry, he stares at her hand. 'What is it then, what's the matter?'

There are mountains that have stood for thousands of years, and armies with artillery have passed over them, there are islands with people on them, jam-packed, all of them strong, solid businesses, banks, enterprises, dance, boom, import, export, social questions, and one day it starts to go: rrrrr, rrrrr, not from the battleship, but of its own – from below. The earth cracks, nightingale, nightingale, how beautifully you sang, the ships fly up to the sky, the birds fall down to the ground. 'Franz, I'll scream, let go of me. Karl will be back soon, he will be back any moment. You began like that with Ida too.'

What's the price of a woman between friends? The London divorce courts granted Captain Bacon's petition for divorce on the grounds of his wife's adultery with his colleague, Captain Furber, and awarded him damages of 750 pounds. The captain doesn't seem to have rated his faithless wife, who will go on to marry her lover, very highly.

Oh, there are mountains that have lain there quietly for thousands of years, and armies with artillery and elephants have passed over them, what can you do when they suddenly start to go: rrrrr rrrumm. Let's not give an opinion on it, let's leave it be. Minna can't get her hand back, and his eyes are staring into hers. A man's face is governed by rails, now there's a train crossing it, look at the smoke, see it go, it's the Berlin to Hamburg/Altona express, leaving 18.05 arriving 21.35, three and a half hours, there's nothing to be done about it, a man's arms are made of iron, iron. I'll cry for help. She cried. She was already lying on the carpet. His stubbled cheeks against hers, his mouth sucks at hers, she turns away. 'Franz, oh my god, have pity, Franz.' And – she saw rightly.

Now she knows, she is Ida's sister, he sometimes used to look at Ida like that. He is holding Ida in his arms, that's why his eyes are shut and he's looking happy. And there isn't any terrible fight between them and the hanging around, there isn't the prison! It's Treptow, Eden Gardens with jewelled fireworks, where he met her and took her home, the little seamstress, she had won a vase by throwing dice for it, the first time he kissed her was in the passage with the keys in her hand, she was up on tiptoe, she was wearing canvas shoes, she dropped the keys, and then he couldn't leave off her after that. That's good old Franz Biberkopf.

And now he can smell her again, it's the same skin, the whiff makes him dizzy, what's happening. And she, the sister, how strange she feels. The feeling is communicated from his face, from his quietly lying there, to her, she has to follow it, she fights it, but it passes into her, her face slackens, her arms are unable to push him away any more, her mouth is helpless. The man doesn't say anything, she leaves him him him her mouth, she's softening as in a warm bath, do with me what you please, she dissolves like water, it's all right, come to me, I know everything, I want you too.

Magical quiver. The goldfish flit in the pond. The room flashes, there is no Ackerstrasse, no building, no gravity or centrifugal force. It's all disappeared, sunk, wiped out: the refraction of the red rays in the sun's force field, kinctic gas theory, the conversion of heat into energy, electrical waves, induction phenomena, the relative densities of metals, liquids, non-metallic fixed bodies.

She lay on the floor, throwing herself back and forth. He laughed and stretched: 'You can kill me if you like, I'll keep still if you've got the strength.' 'You deserve it.' He scrambled up, laughing and spinning with delight, happiness, bliss. How the trumpets were blowing and tooting, huzzah hussars. Franz is back! Franz has been freed! Biberkopf is at large! He had pulled up his trousers, was hopping from one foot to the other. She sat down on a chair, wanted to cry: 'I'm telling my husband, I'm telling Karl, they should have given you another four years on top of what you had.' 'Tell him, Minna, be sure to tell him.' 'I will too, I'm going to call the police.' 'Minna, Minna, sweetheart, do, I'm so happy, I'm a human being again.' 'Christ, mad is what you are, they really messed with your head in Tegel.' 'You wouldn't have anything to drink, would you, like a pot of coffee or something.' 'And who's going to pay for my apron, look at it, it's nothing better than a rag now.' 'Franz will take care of it, leave it to Franz! Franz is back among the living!' 'You'd better take your hat and get out in case he sees you. You've giv me a black eye. And don't come back.' 'Goodbye, Minna.'

But he was back the next morning, with a small parcel. She didn't want to let him in, but he had his foot jammed in the door. She hissed at him through the crack: 'Go your ways, man, I told you!' 'Minna, it's just the aprons.' 'What aprons.' 'You're to choose the ones you like.' 'You can keep your stolen goods.' 'Nothing's stolen. Open up.' 'God, the neighbours will see you, go away.' 'Then open the door, Minna.'

She opened up, he dropped the parcel in the parlour, and as she didn't want to go in the parlour herself, with the broom-handle in her hand, pranced about in there all alone. 'I'm so happy, Minna. I've been happy all day long. I dreamt about you.'

He untied the parcel on the table, she came closer, felt the material, chose three aprons, but she remained firm when he took her hand. He packed up, she standing there broom in hand, pushing: 'All right then, away with you.' He waved to her in the doorway: 'Goodbye, Minnie.' She rammed the door shut with the broom-handle.

A week later he was back on her doorstep: 'I just wanted to check up on your eye.' 'It's fine, thank you, there's nothing for you here.' He had bulked up, was wearing a blue winter coat, a brown stiff derby: 'I just wanted you to see me, what I look like now.' 'I'm not interested.' 'Well, won't you at least give me a cup of coffee.' Then there was a sound of footfall on the steps, a child's ball bounced down, the woman, alarmed, opened the door and pulled him in. 'You standing there, that was the Lumkes, there, now go.' 'I just want a cup of coffee. You'll have one for me, won't you.' 'You don't need me for that. You've probably got someone anyway, from the look of you.' 'Cup of coffee.' 'You really know how to make someone unhappy.'

And as she stood by the coat stand in the corridor and he looked at her beseechingly from the kitchen door, she pulled up her pretty new apron, shook her head and began to cry: 'You make me unhappy, so you do.' 'What's got into you.' 'Karl didn't believe my story about the black eye. How could I bump into the cupboard like that. He wanted me to show him. Even if you can get a black eye from the cupboard if you leave the door open. He can try if he likes. But he won't believe me, and I don't know why.' 'I don't either, Minna.' 'It's because I've got some marks here, on my neck. I didn't even know I had em. What can I say when he shows em to me, there they are in the mirror, and I've no idea where they came from.' 'Oh, I don't know, you might have scratched yourself, you might have had an itch. Don't let the fellow bully you around. I'd have knocked some sense into him.' 'And you keep coming round. And the Lumkes will have seen you, I bet.' 'Well, they're not to give themselves airs.' 'Why don't you go away, Franz, and not come back, you just make me unhappy.' 'Did he ask about the aprons too?' 'I was always going to buy myself some new aprons.' 'Well, then I'll go, Minna.'

He reached round her throat, she let him. After a while, when he didn't let go, and wasn't pressing, she realized he was stroking her, and looked up in astonishment: 'Now get along with you, Franz.' He pulled her gently in the direction of the parlour, she resisted, but went with him step by step: 'Franz, is this going to start again?' 'Whatever is the matter, I just want to sit in your parlour.'

They sat peaceably on the sofa for a while, side by side, talking. Then he left, alone. She saw him to the door. 'Don't come back, Franz,' she cried and pressed her head against his shoulder. 'Goddamnit, Minna, the things you do to a man. Why shouldn't I come back? Well, then I won't.' She was holding his hand in hers: 'No, Franz, don't.' Then she opened the door, still holding his hand, and she gave it a hard squeeze. She was still holding it when he was standing outside. Then she let go, and quickly and quietly pushed the door shut. He ordered a couple of large veal escalopes to be sent up.

In which Franz swears to all the world and himself, to remain decent in Berlin, money or not

Now, he was nicely set up – he had flogged off his old bits and pieces, and he had a few pennies left over from Tegel, his landlady and his friend Mack loaned him some more – when he got a proper shock, though later it turned out to be a false alarm. One otherwise half-decent morning found a piece of yellow bumf on his table, official, printed and in type.

To reply to this communication, write to the President of Police, Department 5, ref. so and so, using the ref. no. On the basis of documents in my possession you have been punished for threatening behaviour, physical injury and grievous bodily harm resulting in death, and are therefore to be viewed as a risk to public order and decency. Consequently, I have decreed, on the basis of the powers vested in me by the laws of 31 December 1842, Paragraph 2, and the law governing freedom of movement of 1 November 1867, Paragraph 3, in addition to the laws of 12 June 1889 and 13 June 1900, to have you excluded for reasons of public order from Berlin, Charlottenburg, Neukölln, Berlin-Schöneberg, Wilmersdorf, Lichtenberg, Stralau and the administrative districts of Berlin-Friedenau, Schmargendorf, Tempelhof, Britz, Treptow, Reinickendorf, Weissensee, Pankow and Berlin-Tegel. You are hereby ordered to quit the exclusion zone within a fortnight. If you remain within the zone, or have subsequently returned to it you will be charged under Paragraph 132 section 2 of the general administrative law of 30 July Q II E 1883 under pain of a 100-mark fine for a first offence, or in the event of inability to pay, a custodial sentence of 10 days.

At the same time I am informing you that if you take up residence in any of the following outlying districts, Potsdam, Spandau, Friedrichsfelde, Karlshorst, Friedrichshagen, Oberschöneweide and Wuhlheide, Fichtenau, Rahnsdorf, Carow, Buch, Frohnau, Cöpenick, Lankwitz, Steglitz, Zehlendorf, Teltow, Dahlem, Wannsee, Klein-Glienicke, Nowawes, Neuendorf, Eiche, Bornim or Bornstedt, you may expect your exclusion from the aforementioned places. I. Ve Form No. 968 a.

Made a mighty impression on him. But there was a good place by the S-Bahn, Grunerstrasse, near the Alex, prisoners' welfare organisation. They take a look at Franz, ask him a couple questions, sign this: Herr Franz Biberkopf has placed himself under our supervision, we will check whether you are working, and you are required to present yourself every month. Done, taken care of, everything in clover.

Forgotten the panic, forgotten Tegel and the red wall and the groaning and whatever else – away with the damage, we're beginning a new life, the old one is done and dusted, Franz Biberkopf is back, and the Prussians are merry and shout hurray.

Then for four weeks he filled his belly with meat and potatoes and beer, and went back once to thank the Jews on Dragonerstrasse. Nahum and Eliser were quarrelling as per usual. They didn't recognize him as he walked in in his glad rags, plump and reeking of cognac, and respectfully, hat in front of his face, asked in a shy whisper whether the old gentleman's grandchildren were still unwell. They asked him in the corner bar, where he treated them, what business he was in. 'Business. I'm not in any business. With our sort, things go by themselves.' 'Then where have you got money from?' 'Left over from before, savings, money I put by.' He jabbed Nahum in the ribs, flared his nostrils, made sly, knowing eyes: 'You remember the story of old Zannovich. Great guy. He was a fine gentleman, then they put him to death. All that stuff you know about. I'd like to be a prince like that, and study. No, our sort don't study. Maybe I'll get hitched.' 'Good luck to you.' 'Then you'll be invited, there'll be plenty to eat, and, you know, drink.'

Nahum, the redhead, scratching his chin, surveyed him: 'Perhaps you'd like another story. A man once owned a ball, you know, a children's ball, not rubber, but celluloid, transparent, with little lead balls inside it. For children to rattle around and throw. Then the man aimed the ball and threw it, and he thought: there are lead balls in it, that way I can throw it, and the ball won't run on, it'll stop where it lands. But when he threw the ball, it didn't go where he wanted it to go, it took a bounce, and then it rolled on a bit, a couple of handbreadths further.' 'Leave him alone with your stories, Nahum. The man's not interested.' The plump fellow: 'What happened with the ball, and why are you arguing again? Take a look at the pair of them, landlord, they've been quarrelling ever since I've known them.' 'You have to take people as they are. Quarrelling is good for the liver.' The redhead: 'I'll tell you, I saw you on the street and in the courtyard, and I heard you sing. You sing very beautifully. You are a good man. But don't be so wild. Be gentle and patient on this earth. I know what you're like inside, and what God intends for you. The ball, you see, it won't go the way you throw it and the way you want it to go, it flies a little further, maybe quite a bit further, you know, and a little bit to the side.'

The fat fellow threw back his head and laughed, spread his arms, bear-hugged the redhead: 'You know how to tell a story, by gum you do. Franz has had some experiences. Franz knows life. Franz knows who he is.' 'Let me tell you, you once sang very sadly.' 'Yes, then, then. Past is past. Now we've reinflated our waistcoat. My ball flies well, let me tell you. No one can prove different. So long, and when I get spliced, you're invited!'

That's what he's like, then, the cement worker, later furniture mover, Franz Biberkopf, a coarse, rough man of repulsive appearance, back on the streets of Berlin, a man on whose arm a pretty girl from an engineer's family once hung, whom he turned into a whore and finally beat up so badly that she died. He swore to all the world and to himself that he would remain decent. And as long as he had money, he remained decent. But then he ran out of money, which was a moment he had been waiting for, to show them all what he was made of.

Chapter Two

Our hero has been successfully brought to Berlin. He has sworn to mend his ways, and we wonder whether we shouldn't simply stop here. An ending here would be optimistic and straightforward, an ending seems to be at hand, and the whole thing would have the advantage of brevity.

But Franz Biberkopf is not just anyone. I have not summoned him for my own amusement, but for his heavy, true and illuminating fate to be experienced.

Franz Biberkopf has been burnt, now he stands there in Berlin, feet apart and merry, and when he says he wants to be respectable, we believe this to be the case.

You will see how for several weeks he succeeds. But that's just a period of respite.

Once upon a time, two people lived in Paradise, and their names were Adam and Eve. They had been put there by Almighty God, who had also created animals and plants and heaven and earth. And the Garden of Eden truly was a Paradise. Flowers and trees grew there, animals frolicked about, no one bothered anyone else. The sun rose and set, the moon ditto, the livelong day in Paradise was a joy to behold.

So we begin in happiness. Let us sing and dance: we will clap clap clap our hands, and stamp stamp stamp our feet, and in and out and once about, it's not difficult.

Franz Biberkopf enters Berlin

Trade and Industry

Sanitation and Street-Cleaning

Public Health

 Planning and Architecture

 Art and Culture

 Traffic

 Banking and Finance

 Gasworks

 Fire Department

 Tax and Excise

Publication of a plan for the property An der Spandauer Brücke, 10. The design for an ornamental rosette on the front wall of the property defined in perpetuity as An der Spandauer Brücke, 10, in the borough of Berlin-Mitte, is now open to public inspection. Concerned parties, with relevant supporting documents, are entitled to make objections. The borough planning officer is similarly entitled to raise objections. Any and all such objections to be made in person, or addressed to the council offices of Berlin-Mitte, Room 76, Klosterstrasse 68, Berlin C-2.

– With the agreement of the Chief of Police I gave the lessee, Herr Bottich, a provisional permit to shoot wild rabbits and other pests in the Fauler Seepark on the following days of 1928: said shooting to take place in summer, from 1 April to 30 September and to be concluded by 7 p.m., and in winter from 1 October to 31 March by 8 p.m. During these hours, the public are under advisement not to enter said terrain.

(*Signed*) The Oberbürgermeister, in my capacity of Controller of Hunting Licenses.

– Master furrier Albert Pangel, at the end of almost thirty years' service, has laid down his title, in consequence of advancing years and removal from the district. For an unbroken period of years he served as welfare official, resp. head of welfare. The council has expressed its thanks in writing to Herr Pangel.

Rosenthaler Platz is abuzz.

Weather changeable, bright, just below zero. An anticyclone over Germany continues to determine the outlook. An area of low pressure is moving slowly south over a broad front. Daytime temperatures will be a little colder than recently. Now the prospects for Berlin and surroundings.

Tram 68 via Rosenthaler Platz: Wittenau, Nordbahnhof, Heilanstalt, Weddingplatz, Stettiner Bahnhof, Rosenthaler Platz, Alexanderplatz, Strausberger Platz, Bahnhof Frankfurter Allee, Lichtenberg, Herzberge Asylum. The three Berlin mass-transport firms, tram, rail (under- and overground) and omnibuses, form a single fare grouping. Standard adult fare is 20 pfennigs, half fare 10, children receive a reduction until the end of their fourteenth year, as do full-time students, trainees, war invalids, handicapped men and women with a permit from the local benefit office. Get to know your network. During the winter months, no ingress or egress through the front doors, 39 seats, 5918, to stop the conveyance pull the cord in a timely fashion, no conversation with the driver, getting on and off the moving vehicle is hazardous.

In the middle of Rosenthaler Platz a man with a couple of yellow parcels jumps off the 41 and is almost run over by a taxicab, the traffic policeman watches him scamper away, a ticket inspector turns up, inspector and policeman shake hands: that fellow and his parcels had a bit of a lucky break.

Fruit liqueurs at wholesale prices, Dr Bergell, solicitor and notary, Lukutate, the Indian specific for the rejuvenation of elephants, Fromms Akt, the best rubber sponge, what do people need so many rubber sponges for.

The principal thoroughfare leading away from the square on the north side is Brunnenstrasse, the premises of AEG are on the left, just before Humboldthain. AEG is a colossal enterprise which, according to the 1928 telephone book, comprises: Electrical Light and Power Plants, Central Administration, NW 40, Friedrich Karl Ufer 2–4, Local Network North 4488, General Management, Janitors and Maintenance, Electrical Bank Ltd, Division of Lighting, Russian Division, Oberspree Metallurgy, Machine Works Treptow, Brunnenstrasse Plant, Hennigsdorf Plant, Insulation Factory, Rheinstrasse Factory, Cable Works Oberspree, Transformer Factory Wilhelminenhofstrasse, Rummelsburger Chaussee, Turbine Factory NW 87, Huttenstrasse 12–16. The Invalidenstrasse winds away to the left, in the direction of the Stettiner Bahnhof, where trains from the Baltic come in: you're all covered in soot – yes, it's dirty all right. – Hello, goodbye. – Does sir have something to wear, 50 pfennigs. – You look refreshed. – Oh, the tan will wear off in no time. – Wonder where people get money to go on holiday from. – In a little hotel in a poky little side street a couple was found shot, a married woman and a waiter from Dresden, they'd signed in under assumed names.

From the south, it's Rosenthaler Strasse that enters the square of the same name. There, Aschinger's Entertainment and Victualling Business provides people with food and beer. Fish is nutritious, some people like to eat fish, others get the heebie-jeebies, eat fish, stay slender, hearty and hale. Ladies' stockings, real artificial silk, here's a fountain pen with an excellent gold nib.

On Elsasser Strasse they've fenced off the entire thoroughfare, with the exception of one lane. Behind the building fence a locomobile is puffing away. Becker-Fiebig Ltd, Construction, Berlin W 35. There's a constant din, dump-trucks are backed up as far as the bank on the corner, a branch of the Commerz- und Privatbank, safe deposits, securities, savings accounts. Five men are kneeling in front of the bank, tapping little stones into the ground. Pavours.

At the stop on Lothringer Strasse four people have just boarded a No. 4, two elderly women, a worried-looking working man and a boy with a cap and ear-flaps. The two women are together, they are Frau Plück and Frau Hoppe. They are buying a girdle for Frau Hoppe, the elder of the two, because she has a tendency to umbilical rupture. They are on their way to the trussmaker on Brunnenstrasse, then they are meeting their husbands for lunch. The man is a coachman, Hasebruck, who is having trouble with a second-hand electric iron he picked up cheap for his boss. He was given a defective one, his boss tried it out for a couple of days, then it no longer got hot, he tried to exchange it, but the vendor refused, he's going back for the third time today, with a little extra money. The lad, Max Rüst, will one day become a plumber, the father of seven little Rüsts, will work for Hallis & Co., installers and roofers, Grünau, at the age of fifty-two he will win a quarter-share of the Prussian State Lottery jackpot and retire, and then, in the midst of a case he is bringing against Hallis & Co., he will die at the age of fifty-five. His obituary will read: On 25 September, suddenly, from heart disease, my dearly beloved husband, our dear father, son, brother, brother-in-law and uncle Max Rüst, in his fifty-sixth year. This announcement is placed by the grieving widow, Marie Rüst, on behalf of all with deep grief. The rendering of thanks will go as follows: Being unable to acknowledge individually the many tokens of sympathy we have received, we extend thanks to all our relatives, friends and

fellow-tenants in Kleiststrasse 4 and our wider acquaintances. Espe-
cial thanks to Pastor Deinen for his words of comfort. – At present
this Max Rüst is fourteen and on his way home from school, via
the advice centre for those hard of hearing, with impaired vision,
experiencing difficulties of speech, dyspraxia and problems with
concentration, where he has been a few times already, about his
stammer, which seems to be getting better.

Little bar on Rosenthaler Platz.

At the front there's a pool table, in a back corner two men are
drinking tea and smoking. One has sagging features and grey hair,
he's still got his coat on: 'OK, fire away. But sit still, and stop
fidgeting.'

'You won't catch me playing pool today. My hands are shaking.'
He's chewing at a dry roll, doesn't touch his tea.

'Why should you. We're fine where we are.'

'It's always the same. Well, this time I did it.'

'You did?'

The other man, young, fair hair, taut features, taut body: 'Yeah.
You think it's always the others? Now it's all out in the open.'

'In other words, you're out of a job.'

'I spoke to the boss in words of one syllable, and he shouted at
me. That night I got my notice effective on the first of the month.'

'There are situations where you should never speak in words of
one syllable. If you'd spoken to him in words of two syllables, you'd
still be there.'

'What are you talking about, I am still there. I've just clarified
my position. They think I'm going to make life easy for them. Now
every day, at two in the afternoon, I'm going to turn up and make
life hell for them: you see if I don't.'

'Oh, Lord, Lord. I thought you were married and all.'

He props his head on his hand: 'That's the bind, I haven't told her
yet, I can't tell her.'

'Maybe it'll sort itself out.'

'She's expecting.'

'Your second?'

'Yeah.'

The man in the coat pulls it closer to him, smiles sardonically, nods and says: 'Well, that's all right then. Children give you courage. You could use some.'

The other shifts: 'Oh, come on. It's the last thing I need. I've got debts up to here. All those instalment payments. I can't tell her. And then to get sacked just like that. I'm used to a bit of organization, and this is a wretched outfit from top to bottom. The boss has his furniture factory, what does he care if I bring in orders for shoes? I'm superfluous. That's all there is to it. Standing round the office, asking: have the specials gone out? What specials? I told them six times, why should I keep chasing the customers. I'm just making a fool of myself. Either he lets the business go bust, or he doesn't.'

'Drink your tea. It seems for the moment he's letting *you* go bust.'

A man in shirt-sleeves wanders over from the pool table, taps the young man on the shoulder: 'Fancy a game?'

The other answers on his behalf: 'He's just had some bad news.'

'Pool helps.' He slopes off. The one in the coat sips at his tea: it's good to drink hot tea with sugar and a shot of rum, and listen to someone else's troubles. It feels cosy in here. 'So I guess you won't be going home tonight, Georg?'

'I don't dare. What am I going to tell her. I can't look her in the eye.'

'Just turn up and look her in the eye.'

'Oh, what do you know about it.'

He slumps across the table, pulling his coat tails over him. 'Listen, Georg, have a drink, or eat something, and stop belly-aching. I know all about it. I wrote the book. When you were yea-high, I'd been all over.'

'I'd like someone to put themselves in my situation. It could have been a half-decent job, and they ballsed it up for me.'

'I used to be a schoolmaster. Before the War. When the War started, I was already the way I am now. This bar was like it is now. They didn't enrol me. They've got no use for people like me, addicts. Or rather: they did enrol me, and I thought, fuck, I've had it. They took my needle away, and the morphine as well. And I joined up. I stuck it out for two days, that's how long my reserves lasted, and then so long, Prussia, and it was the loony bin for me. Then they let me go. Well, what was I saying, then the school fired me, morphine, sometimes you get a bit fuddled first off, it doesn't happen any more. Unfortunately. And my wife? And kid? Well, bye-bye Fatherland. My God, Georg, I could tell you some stories.' The grizzled man drinks, hands cupped round his glass, drinks slowly, deeply, stares at his tea: 'A woman and a kid. It feels like the whole world. I wasn't sorry, I don't feel guilty; you have to find a level for things, and for yourself as well. Don't make a cult of destiny. I'm not a believer in fate. I live in Berlin, not ancient Greece. Why are you letting your tea go cold? Here, take some rum in it.' The young fellow puts his hand over his glass, but the other pushes it away, and pours him a slug from a little metal flask he takes out of his pocket. 'I've gotta go. Thanks all the same. Walk off my nerves.' 'Oh, stay here, Georg, have a drink, play some pool. No disorder, no panic. That's the beginning of the end. When I found my wife and kid not at home, just a note, gone to Mum in West Prussia and so on, botched life, failed husband, the humiliation and all, I cut myself, here in my arm, it looked like an attempted suicide. Take every opportunity to learn, Georg; I'd studied Provençal, but this was anatomy. – I mistook the sinew for the pulse. I still don't really know any better, but I wouldn't make the same mistake again. You know, all that pain and remorse, it was so much bullshit, I was alive, my wife was alive, the kid was alive, she even went on to have a couple more, in West Prussia, I like to think it was remote control. Anyway, we're all alive. This place here makes me happy, the cop on the corner makes me happy, pool makes me happy. I'd like to hear someone say his life was better, and that I didn't know anything about women.'

The fair-haired man looks at him with distaste: 'You're a wreck, Krause, you know that. You're no sort of example to anyone. You're bad luck. Didn't you tell me yourself about starving on what you made from tutoring. I don't want to be buried like that.' The iron-haired man has drained his glass, sits back in his coat on the iron chair, blinks aggressively at the younger man, then he barks, cackles: 'No, no sort of example, you're right about that. Never said I was. No sort of example. Take the fly. The fly sits under a microscope and thinks it's a horse. Who do you think you are, Master Georg? Introduce yourself to me, why don't you: rep. for Smith & Co.'s, shoes. Stop kidding around, telling me about your misery: M for martyr, I for Idiot, S for stupid. You're barking up the wrong tree, mate, barking up the wrong tree.'

A girl gets out of the 99, Mariendorf, Lichtenrader Chaussee, Tempelhof, Hallesches Tor, Hedwigskirche, Rosenthaler Platz, Badstrasse, Seestrasse/Togostrasse, weekend service between Uferstrasse and Tempelhof, Friedrich-Karl-Strasse at fifteen-minute intervals. It's eight in the evening, she is carrying a music case under her arm, her collar is pushed up in her face, she is walking up and down on the corner of Brunnenstrasse and Weinbergsweg. A man in a fur coat accosts her, she jumps, and crosses over to the other side of the street. She stands under a tall lamp-post, observing the corner where she stood before. A compact, elderly gentleman in horn-rims appears, she runs across to him, walks giggling at his side. They go up Brunnenstrasse together.

'I mustn't be so late back tonight, I really mustn't. I shouldn't have come at all. But I'm not allowed to ring you.' 'No, only in an emergency. They listen in the office. It's for your own protection, child.' 'Yes, I'm worried, but I don't think it will get out, you won't tell a soul.' 'That's right.' 'My God, if Papa should hear, or Mama.' The elderly gentleman takes her affectionately by the arm. 'Nothing will get out. I won't say a word to a soul. What did you do in your lesson?' 'Chopin. I'm playing the nocturnes. Are you musical?' 'Yes, at a pinch.' 'I wish I could play for you sometime. But I'm so nervous of you.' 'Oh, come.' 'It's true, I've always been nervous of you, not very, just a little. Not very. But I don't need to be nervous of you, do I.' 'Not a bit. Honestly. You've known me now for three months.' 'It's Papa I'm afraid of, I suppose. If word got out.' 'Oh, come, surely to goodness you can step out with a friend every now and again. You're not a baby any more.' 'That's what I kept saying to Mama too. And I go out.' 'We'll go wherever we please, ducks.' 'Don't call me that. I only told you, so – well, never mind. Where shall we go today. I need to be home by nine.' 'In here. We're already there. Flat of a friend of mine. We can go upstairs without worrying.' 'I feel scared. Are you sure no one's seen us? Will you go on ahead. I'll come up after.'

Upstairs they exchange smiles. She is standing in the corner. He has taken off his hat and coat, she allows him to relieve her of her music and hat. Then she runs across to the door and switches off the light: 'But be quick about it, I haven't got much time, I have to go home, I'll keep my clothes on. Don't hurt me.'

Franz Biberkopf is on the job market, you need to earn money, a man can't live without money. And all about the Frankfurt Topfmarkt

Franz Biberkopf and his friend Mack sat down at a table where several other noisy men were already seated, and waited for the meeting to begin. Mack reasoned: 'You shouldn't go on the dole, Franz, you shouldn't do factory work, and it's too cold to be digging. Trade is best. Either in Berlin or the sticks. Take your pick. But trade is what'll keep you fed.' The waiter called out: 'Mind your heads, gents.' They sipped their beer. At that moment they heard footsteps overhead, Herr Wünschel, the first-floor administrator, was running for an ambulance, his wife had fainted. Mack was declaring: 'For the love of Gottlieb, just look at the people here. Do they look hungry to you? Can't you tell they're all decent people.' 'Gottlieb, you know nothing matters more to me than decency. Now cross your heart and hope to die, is this a respectable calling you're pressing on me or not?' 'Just look at the faces, don't they speak for themselves. Tip-top, take a look at them.' 'A solid foundation, that's what I'm about, a solid foundation.' 'This is the solidest thing going. Braces, stockings, socks, aprons, maybe neckties. Retail's where the profits are.'

On the platform a man with a hunchback was talking about the Frankfurt Fair. It is not possible to exaggerate the drawbacks of supplying goods to the Frankfurt Fair. The fair is in a bad location. Especially the Topfmarkt. 'Ladies and gentlemen, esteemed colleagues, whoever attended the Frankfurt Topfmarkt last Sunday will be able to confirm that it is not fit for the public.' Gottlieb gave Franz a nudge: 'He's talking about the Frankfurt Topfmarkt. You're not to go there.' 'No worries, this is a good guy, he knows his mind.' 'Anyone who has ever been to the Magazinplatz in Frankfurt will never go there again. That's as sure as eggs is eggs. It was filthy, it was a ploughed field. Take as further evidence the fact that the mayor of Frankfurt gave us just three days' notice before he said: it's the Magazinplatz for us, not the Marktplatz what we usually go to. And the reason he gave, here, brothers, try this on for size: because the weekly market is held on the Marktplatz, and if we go there, there'll be a disruption to traffic. That's a scandalous decision from the mayor of Frankfurt, that's a real smack in the face. A reason like that. They have four half-days of market there as it is, and they want us to make way. Why not the greengrocer and the butter lady? Why doesn't Frankfurt build itself an indoor market? Sellers of fruit and vegetables and other comestibles are equally as badly off as we are, thanks to the Frankfurt authorities. We all suffer from their poor decision-making. But that's enough of that now. Income from the Magazinplatz was piss-poor, it was nothing, it wasn't worth the candle. No buyers braved the mire and the rain. Those of us who went mostly didn't cover their expenses. Train fare, licences, setting up, taking down. And one other thing, I want to make this very clear, the condition of the lavatories in Frankfurt defies description. You'll know what I'm talking about. Such poor hygiene is unworthy of a great city; the light of publicity must be shone on that. Such conditions will not attract visitors to Frankfurt, and it's noxious to we traders. And on top of that, the way they jam the booths on top of each other, like so many flounders.'

Following the discussion, in which the executive did not escape a share of criticism for their previous passivity, the following resolution was unanimously adopted:

'We traders view the relocation of the fair to Magazinplatz as a smack in the face. The takings are significantly below what was realized at previous fairs. The Magazinplatz is unfit as a venue because it can't accommodate enough visitors for a viable fair, not by a long shot, and in respect of hygiene it's positively a canker on the fair face of the city of Frankfurt on Oder, and furthermore, if a fire had have broken out, we traders and our wares would have all been goners. Therefore we the assembled tradespersons look to the city authorities to restore the fair to the Marktplatz, because that and that alone is sufficient to guarantee a future for the fair. At the same time, we urgently request a reduction in the rate for a stall, since as things stand we are not in a position to fulfil our responsibilities, and would only fall burden on the welfare resources of the city.'

Biberkopf was irresistibly drawn to the speaker. 'Mack, that is a speaker, that is a man who is cut out for this world.' 'Try stepping on his toes, then, and see what he says.' 'You can't know that, Gottlieb. Remember, the Jews helped me out. I was going round the courtyards and singing "Die Wacht am Rhein", that's how desperate things were with me. Then these two Jews fished me out and told me stories. Words can be good too, Gottlieb, the things that a man says.' 'Stefan, that Polack crook. Franz, you're not playing with a full deck.' Franz shrugged: 'Deck here, deck there, Gottlieb, put yourself in my position before you open your mouth. That man up there with the hunchback, he's good, I tell you, he's good.' 'Well, never mind. You need to think about business, Franz.' 'Will do, everything at the proper time. I got nothing against business.'

And he pushed his way through to the hunchback. Meekly asked him for some information. 'What do you want?' 'I've come to ask for some information.' 'No Q. and A. Finished, over. It sometimes happens that we up on the platform have had enough too.' The hunchback was sharp: 'What do you want anyway?' 'I— There's all this talk about the Frankfurt Fair, and I thought you gave a first-rate speech, sir, splendid. That's what I wanted to say, on my own behalf. I entirely agree with you.' 'Thank you, brother. What's your name?' 'Franz Biberkopf. It did me good to see you go about your business, and give it to the people of Frankfurt.' 'The authorities.' 'Quite. You sorted their hash. They won't know what hit them. They won't try that again.' The little man got his papers together, clambered down from the platform into the smoky hall: 'Very nice, brother, very nice.' Franz, beaming and scraping along in his wake. 'Didn't you say you wanted some information? Are you a member?' 'No, actually.' 'Well, you can join here and now. Come over to our table.' He sat Franz down at the foot of the table, among red faces, drank, greeted friends, produced a form. He promised his contribution for the first of the month. Shake hands.

From a distance he waved the paper to Mack: 'I'm a member now, I am. A member of the Berlin chapter. You can read it yourself, it says: Berlin chapter, Reich Union, and then what's this here: itinerant tradesmen of Germany. There's a thing, eh.' 'So what are you now, a trader in textiles? It says textiles here. Since when, Franz? Show me your textiles!' 'I never said textiles. I said stockings and aprons. He kept saying textiles. Well, can't do any harm. And I don't have anything to pay till the first.' 'Now come on, where's the sense in selling dinner plates or buckets or cattle, like the gentlemen here: gentlemen, isn't it absurd that this fellow takes out a membership in textiles, when he's perhaps going to be selling beef?' 'I wouldn't do beef. Beef is off. I'd advise poultry.' 'But the point is he's not selling anything right now. Fact. He's sitting around, thinking about it. You can say to him, all right, Franz, what about mousetraps or garden statuary.' 'If that's what I have to do, Gottlieb, and if it keeps me fed. Maybe not mousetraps, there'd be too much competition from the poison industry, but garden statuary'd be a fine thing: why not be the man to introduce garden statuary into small towns?' 'There, you see, he takes out a membership in ladies' aprons and ends up flogging statues.'

'Oh no, Gottlieb, oh no, gentlemen, I mean you're right, but don't twist things like that. You need to shine a clear light on a subject, like what the little hunchback did with Frankfurt, only you weren't listening.' 'What do I care about Frankfurt. Nor do these others here either.' 'Fine, Gottlieb, very good, sirs, it's not a complaint either, but personally, myself, I was listening, and it was ever so good, the way he illuminated things, calmly, but with force, spite of his weak voice, and the man has a lung condition, and how everything was laid out, and then the resolution was put to the assembly, every point nice and clear, a fine thing, a good head on him, up to and including the toilets that they didn't like. I mentioned my own business with the Jews, you know. Sirs, when I was on my uppers, these Jews helped me, just by telling me stories. They talked to me, they were decent people who didn't know me from Adam, and they told me about this Polack, and it was just a story, but it was very good just the same, and it was very instructive for me in my position. I thought: a glass of cognac might have set me to rights just as well. Who knows. But afterwards I felt right as rain.' One of the dealers was smoking and grinning. 'What was it then, you were run over by a bus?' 'No jokes, gentlemen, please. Though I suppose you're right. It might as well have been a bus. It can happen in your life, that misfortune rains down on you and your legs turn to jelly. A mess like that can happen to anyone. It's what you do afterwards matters. Your knees are shaking. You run around the streets, Brunnenstrasse, Rosenthaler Tor, the Alex. It can happen that you're running around and not able to read a street sign. Some smart people helped me, they talked to me and told me stories, people with good heads on their shoulders, and so you should know: you shouldn't swear by money or cognac or a few pennies in contributions. The main thing is keeping your head, and using it, and knowing what's going on around you, so you don't suddenly come a cropper. That's all it is. There, gentlemen. That's all I have to say.'

'In that case, brother, we'll raise our glasses to that. Here's to our chapter.' 'The chapter, cheers, gentlemen. Gottlieb.' Gottlieb laughed and laughed: 'Now, man, now all that's left is the little question of where you'll pay your contribution, on the first of the month.' 'And then, young colleague, you must see to it now that you have your membership and belong to our chapter, that the chapter helps you to a proper wage.' The dealers and Gottlieb laughed for all they were worth. One of the dealers said: 'Take your membership to Meiningen, there's a market there next week. I'll be on the right, you on the left, and I'll be able to see how you're getting on. Just imagine, Albert, he's got a membership, and he's part of the chapter, and he's standing in his stall. Over where I am they're yelling: Frankfurter sausages, genuine Meininger rolls, and there he is yelling: Hello, hello, it's my first time here, but I belong to the union, big sensation at the market at Meiningen. My God, people will be falling over themselves to buy from him. Cor, what a horse's ass you are.' They smote the table in their mirth, Biberkopf among them. Carefully he stashed his papers away in his inside pocket: 'If a man wants to walk, he gets hisself a pair of shoes. I never said I was going to be a hotshot at business. But I didn't fall on my face either.' They adjourned.

Once on the street, Mack got into a vigorous argument with the two livestock dealers. They were maintaining their point of view in a law case that one of them was involved in. He had traded livestock in Brandenburg, when he was only licensed to trade in Berlin. A competitor had run into him and reported him to the police. But then the two livestock dealers, who travelled together, had got out of it prettily: the accused man claimed in court that he was just accompanying his friend, and was dealing on his behalf.

The livestock dealers declared: 'We're not paying. We're swearing on oath. He'll give a deposition, and he'll swear he was accompanying me, and he's been doing that for a while, and that's where things will rest.'

At that Mack got beside himself, seized the two traders by the scruffs: 'Listen, you're soft in the head, wanting to perjure yourselves over something like that. The only winner there is the nasty fellow that tried to put one over on you. You'll wind up in the newspapers. That nonsense before the court, m'learned friends and all, that's never law. Justice is something else.'

The second trader insists: 'Sure I'll swear, why wouldn't I? Do you think I should agree to a fine, three rounds of appeals, and the villain getting the last laugh? Envious so and so. I believe in chimneys, and a good draught.'

Mack struck his fist against his head: 'Oh, you nincompoop, you belong in the dirt you're lying in.'

They took leave of the livestock traders, Franz linked arms with Mack, and they made their way along Brunnenstrasse. Mack was still chuntering about the traders: 'Those brothers. They've got us on their conscience. The whole country, they've got them on their conscience.' 'What's that, Gottlieb?' 'They're craven wretches, instead of standing up to the court, wretches, the whole people, the traders, the workers, every man jack of them.'

Suddenly Mack stopped and drew up in front of Franz. 'Franz, I need to have a word with you. Otherwise I can't walk another step.' 'Well, go on then.' 'Franz, I need to know who you are. Look me in the eye. Tell me honestly and truly you've been inside, and that you know what's right and what's just. Because what's right is right.' ''S true, Gottlieb.' 'Now then, Franz, cross your heart. What did they do to you there?' 'You can set your mind at rest. Believe me: if you've got horns, you can take em off. Inside we read books and learnt stenography, and we played chess, and I did and all.' 'You can play chess?' 'Well, you and I, Gottlieb, we can go on playing our skat, but you know, you sit around, not got much aptitude for reflection, we transport workers get too tired in our muscles and bones, then one day you say: damn you, leave us in peace, stay away. Mitts off, humans. What are the likes of us going to do with law and police and politics, Gottlieb? We had a Communist in the big house, he weighed more than I did, he was involved in the uprising of '19 in Berlin. They didn't catch him, but he came to his senses later, meets a widow and joins her business. A clever lad, as you see.' 'How did he come to be with you?' 'He will have tried a spot of fencing. We always used to stick together and watch him getting roughed up. But best give the others a wide berth. Let them go. Stay decent and keep yourself to yourself. That's what I say.'

'I see,' said Mack and looked at him coldly. 'Then we could all pack up, that's pretty shabby of you, that puts the kibosh on everything.' 'It's only those who want to can pack up, we're not worried.' 'Franz, I'll say it again, you're a wet rag. You'll get your comeuppance.'

*

Franz Biberkopf strolls down Invalidenstrasse, his new girlfriend, Polski Lina, is with him. On the corner of Chausseestrasse there's a newspaper kiosk in an entryway, and people standing around, gabbing. 'Move along now, no loitering.' 'Surely we'll be allowed to look at the pictures.' 'Then make a purchase. Don't block the entryway.' 'Idiot.'

Travel supplement. When the bitter season has broken into our chilly northland, between snow-sparkling winter days and the first green of May, we feel drawn – an ancestral urge – to the sunny south beyond the Alps, to Italy. Whoever is lucky enough to be able to follow such a call. 'Don't get excited about the fellow. Observe the coarsening of morals: a man assaults a girl in the S-Bahn, half-kills her, all for fifty marks.' 'I'd do the same.' 'What?' 'Do you have any idea what fifty marks are worth. You got no idea, fifty marks. That's a pile of money for the likes of us, a pile of money, you know. Come back when you know what fifty marks are worth.'

Fatalistic speech from Marx, the Chancellor Marx: What lies ahead of us is according to my beliefs in Divine Providence. God has made His separate compacts with every nation. What individuals can do is strictly limited. All we can do is work as hard as we can, in accordance with our convictions, and so I will honestly and uprightly carry out the task I have been chosen to perform. I conclude, gentlemen, by offering my best wishes for a successful conclusion to your strenuous and magnanimous labours on behalf of our beautiful Bavaria. I wish them every success. Live so that when the time comes for you to die, it's as though you've had a hearty dinner.

'Finished reading, then?' 'What do you mean?' 'Would you like me to take the paper off the hook for you? I had a gentleman once who accepted my offer of a chair, so that he could read in comfort.' 'But the reason you hang out your pictures is so that—' 'Never you mind why I hang out my pictures. You don't rent my kiosk. Spongers are no good to me, they just keep away honest customers.'

That's the end of him, his shoes need cleaning, probably a dosser in the Palme in Fröbelstrasse, boards a tram. Bound to have a lapsed ticket. If they nab him, he'll have picked up the wrong one. Always those spongers, now here's two more. I've half a mind to put up a wire screen. Was that my stomach growling. Franz Biberkopf marches up in his stiff hat, with blowsy Polish Lina on his arm. 'Lina, look right, into the entrance. The weather's no good if you're unemployed. Let's look at the pictures. Pretty pictures, but there's a draught. Hey there, mate, how's business. Doesn't the chill get to you.' 'Well, it's no community hall.' 'Would you want to stand in a thing like that, Lina?' 'Let's go, the man's giving us dirty looks.' 'I'm just thinking some people might like that, to have you standing in an entryway, selling newspapers. You know, the feminine touch.'

Puffs of wind, the publications flutter on their brackets. 'Mate, you need to put up a paravang.' 'Yeah, that way no one can see anything.' 'What about a glass screen then.' 'Come along, Franz.' 'No, stop a minute. The man's been stood here for hours, he's not about to blow away. There's no need to be nervous, Lina.' 'It's because he's staring so.' 'That's my natural expression, miss, those are the features I was born with. I can't be blamed for that.' 'You hear that, Lina, he's always staring that way. Poor fellow, I say.'

Franz pushed his hat back, looked the newspaper seller in the eye and exploded with laughter, Lina's hand in his. ''S not his fault, Lina. He was like that when he was on the breast. You know what you look like staring like that? No, not like that. The way you were doing before. You know? As if he was at his mother's breast, and the milk was sour.' 'Get away. I was a bottle baby.' 'Joke.' 'Brother, tell me, how's the business treating you?' '*Red Flag*, coming right up. Let the man through, brother. Gangway.' 'It's you who's in the way.'

Lina towed him away, they sailed down Chausseestrasse as far as Oranienburger Tor. 'I wouldn't mind his job. I don't feel the cold. Just all that hanging around in the passageway.'

A couple of days later it's warmed up, Franz has hocked his coat, put on some warm underclothing that Lina had from somewhere, stands in front of Fabisch & Co. on Rosenthaler Platz, gentleman's outfitters, quality work and low prices are our hallmarks. Franz is selling tie-holders.

'A question: why is it that in the West the gentleman wears a bow tie, and the working man doesn't. Step nearer, sirs, you too miss, with your sweetheart, young people welcome, and you don't have to pay extra, neither. So why does the working man not wear a bow tie? Because he don't know how to tie it, that's why. So he buys himself a tie-holder, and once he's bought it, it turns out to be no good, and he can't tie his tie with it. That's a swindle, it embitters people, it immiserates Germany further than it is already. Why did they not wear this great tie-holder here? Because you didn't want to tie bandages round your neck. A man didn't, his wife didn't, not even their little baby did, if it could only speak. Don't laugh, gentlemen, don't laugh, we have no idea what goes on in those tiny brains. Oh Lord, such a dear little head, a sweet little head, and the fluffy little hairs on it, adorable aren't they, but paying child support, that's no laugh is it, that pauperizes a man. Buy yourself a tie at Tietz or Wertheim, or, if you don't want to take your custom to a Jew, go elsewhere. I'm an Aryan myself.' He doffs his hat, fair hair, red sticking-out ears, round blue eyes. 'There's no reason for me to go touting for the big department stores, they manage perfectly well without me. Buy yourself a tie like the one I'm wearing, and then think about how you're going to tie it in the morning.

'Gentlemen, who's got the time to tie a tie first thing in the morning, who wouldn't rather have an extra minute of shut-eye. We all need our sleep because we work so hard and earn so little. A tie-holder like mine will help you sleep at night. It will compete with the chemist's because if you buy one of my tie-holders, like I have here, you will have no reason to take sleeping draughts and sedatives and nothing. You will sleep like a baby in the knowledge that tomorrow there's no fuss or bother, the thing you need is all ready and waiting for you on top of the chest of drawers and just has to be inserted in your collar. We spend our money on all kinds of shoddy, useless things. Last year you saw the crooks in the

Krokodil, there were sausages on sale outside, at the back Jolly lay in his glass case, letting the sauerkraut grow round his muzzle. Every one of you will have seen that – move nearer if you will, so I don't strain my tonsils, my voice isn't insured you know, I still owe on the down payment – anyway you all saw Jolly lying in the glass cabinet. But what you didn't see was them feeding him chocolate. Here you'll be buying an honest product, no celluloid, vulcanized rubber, twenty pfennigs apiece, three for fifty.

'Step off the roadway, young man, else you'll get yourself run over, and I don't want to be the one to pick up the pieces. Now pay attention, I'm going to explain to you how you tie a tie. It's very simple, I don't have to din it into you. On the one side, you take a piece ten to twelve inches, then you fold it over, but not like that. That looks like a squashed bedbug on a wall – an indoor flounder, know what I mean – and no gentleman would wear one of those. Then you take my little contraption here. You need to save time. Time is of the essence, remember. The romantic age is dead and gone, these days we need to be able to do our sums. You can't tie a gas-pipe round your neck first thing every day, you take this finished civilized article here. You see, it's your Christmas present, it's your taste, sirs, it's for your benefit. If you've got anything left over from the Dawes Plan, then it's the head under your hat, and that is surely telling you, this is for you, sunshine, this is the thing you buy and take home with you, where it will be a solace to you and a source of comfort.

'Gentlemen, we all of us need to be comfitted, and if we're stupid, we go looking for it in the pub. But if you're sensible, you don't, not least because of the expense, because what publicans sell as drink nowadays is outrageous, and the good stuff is dear. So you take my little contraption, you pull the narrow end through, or you can take a wide piece too, like what the queer lads tie their shoes with when they go on their travels. Then you pull it through here, and you take the end. A German man is looking for a real product, like what I'm offering you.'

Lina takes it to the queers

But that's not enough for Franz Biberkopf. He casts his eyes about. With lovely, well-built Lina he takes in the street life between the Alex and Rosenthaler Platz, and he decides to get into newspapers. Why? They told him about the job, Lina would come in handy, and it's the right thing for him. In, out, it's not so very hard.

'Lina, I can't address the public, I don't know how to talk. When I'm barking, they understand what I'm saying all right, but it's no good. Do you know what intellect is?' 'No,' Lina looks at him enquiringly. 'Look at the fellows on the Alex and here, they've none of them got any intellect. Or the ones with the booths and the carts, they don't either. They've got smarts, they know what's what, don't need to tell me. But imagine a speaker in the Reichstag, Bismarck or Bebel – the ones they've got nowadays are no good – and by gum, they had intellect. Intellect is brains, not just a turnip or hat stand. None of them would get any prizes from me. A speaker's a norator.' 'But you are that, Franz.' 'Don't give me that, me a norator. Do you know who was a norator? You won't hardly believe this, your landlady.' 'Ma Schwenk?' 'No, the last one, where I went to get your things from, in Karlstrasse.' 'The one at the circus. I don't think so.'

Franz leans down discreetly: 'She was a norator, Lina, a textbook example.' 'Nonsense. She walks into my room, when I'm in bed, and pulls down my suitcase, just because I'm a month late.' 'All right, Lina, that wasn't nice of her, I know, but listen. When I'm upstairs and asking about your suitcase, you shoulda heard her.' 'I know that sort of talk. You won't catch me listening to that. Franz, you shouldn't get caught up in that.' 'Lets fly, I say, with paragraphs and the law, and how she managed to eke out a widow's pension for her old man who had a stroke, and nothing to do with the war. Since when does it take a war to bring on a stroke. She says. But she got her way. Sheer obstinacy. She's got intellect, any amount. She gets her own way, and that's more than earning a few pennies. There you show your mettle. You can breathe. My, I'm still done in.' 'Are you still going up and seeing her, then?' Franz gestures dismissively with both hands: 'Lina, it's your turn. Go and collect your suitcase, show up on the dot of eleven, by twelve you'll be making your excuses, and quarter to one you'll still be standing there. She talks and talks, and you still won't have your suitcase, and chances are you'll leave without it. I tell you, that woman can talk.'

He studies the table top, draws something in a beer puddle with his finger: 'I'm going to report somewhere and flog papers. That's solid.'

She is left speechless and faintly offended. Franz does what he likes anyway. One lunchtime finds him on Rosenthaler Platz, she's bringing him sandwiches, then he's off, leaves her his soapbox and his carton of wares, and pushes off to learn about newspapers.

First, an old man on Hackescher Markt and Oranienburger Strasse urges him to get into sexual enlightenment. That's a booming industry right now. 'What's sexual enlightenment?' asks Franz, feeling a bit squeamish. The greybeard points to his display: 'See for yourself, then you won't have to ask.' 'I can see drawings of naked ladies.' 'That's about the size of it.' They smoke in silence for a while. Franz gets up, takes in the pictures top and bottom, blows out smoke, the old man takes no notice. Franz fixes him: 'Now, brother, do you get a kick out of that, those girls, I mean, and pictures? *The Gay Life.* So they go and sketch a naked lady and a little pussy cat. Can you tell me what she's doing with her pussy cat on the stairs? Doesn't seem right to me. Does it not bother you, brother?' The other man sighs loudly in his folding chair: there are donkeys the size of tenements, proper camels who go running round the Hackescher Markt in the middle of the day, and who even stop in front of you, if your luck's out, and gabble on and on. When nothing is forthcoming from the greybeard, Franz unpegs a couple of the publications: 'You don't mind do you, brother. What's this one called, *Figaro*. And this one: *Marriage*. And this one's *Ideal*

Marriage. Must be different to *Marriage*. And *Women in Love*. All for sale separately. There's a lot of information there, I'll be bound. If you've got the dough, but it costs. And there's a snag somewhere.' 'There's no snag. Everything's allowed, innit. Nothing's banned. What I have on sale here, I have a licence to sell, and I tell you there's no snag. I wouldn't touch the other stuff.' 'I'm just telling you, though, looking at pictures is no good. I know. It destroys a man, it really makes a mess of him. It begins with looking at pictures, and afterwards you're not capable of nothing natural no more.' 'What's your point. And don't drool over my publications, they're expensive, cost money, and stop soiling the covers and all. Here, look at this one: *Unmarried*. They've covered all the angles, everything's got its own mag.' '*Unmarried*, well, why wouldn't there be, I'm not married to my Polska neither.' 'Now look at this, and tell me if this ain't right, 's just one instance: to attempt to regulate the sexual life of the partners by contract, to define and insist on conjugal rights, as the law claims to do, is nothing but the vilest and most humiliating servitude imaginable. What do you say to that then?' 'How d'you mean?' 'Well, is it right, or ain't it.' 'I wouldn't know, doesn't apply to me, does it? A woman asking for it, well, I never heard of such a thing. Have they got that, then?' 'It's in black and white.' 'Well, I can't believe that. I'd like to meet her.'

In perplexity, Franz reads the sentence over again, then he jerks his head up and points to a passage: 'Look, what about this here: I should like to furnish an example from the work of d'Annunzio, *Lust*, watch out, d'Annunzio is the name of that pervert, he must be a Spic or an Eyetie or an American. Here the thoughts of the man are so consumed with the absent beloved that in the course of a night of passion spent with another woman who stands in for her, he lets slip her name. That's where the fun stops. No, no, brother, you'll not catch me doing something like that.' 'First, show me the place, here, let's see.' 'Here. Stand in for. Artificial rubber for the real stuff. Rutabagas instead of real food. Have you ever heard of that, a girl, a woman, as a substitute? He helps himself to another one, because his own bird happens not to be available, and she notices, and she's supposed to be fine with it? That's what that Spaniard has the neck to print. If I was his typesetter, I'd refuse.' 'Come on, be reasonable. Your tiny mind can't understand everything that a proper writer, and a Spaniard or Italian at that, is trying to say, and in the Hackescher Markt too.' Franz reads on: 'A great void and silence thereupon filled her soul. I'll bet. I'd like someone to explain that to me. Anyone. Void and silence, since when. I can say as much as he does, and the girls won't be that different to what they are wherever. So I had one once and she noticed something, name I wrote in me address book, you think: she's noticed something, and she's shut up? That's what you think, and you know women. You should of heard her. The whole house echoed with her screams. She didn't let me get a word in edgewise. On and on like a banshee. People came to see what the matter was. I tell you, I was pleased to get out.' 'Well, there's something you're missing, a couple of things, in fact.' 'All right' 'If a man takes a paper from me, he buys it and takes it home. The words don't matter anyway, he's only after the pictures.' Franz Biberkopf's left eye looked deprecating. 'And then we've got *Women in Love* and *Friendship*, and they don't natter, they fight. For human rights.' 'What do *they* want?' 'Paragraph 175, if you really want to know.' There's a public lecture in the Alexander Palais on Landsberger Strasse, where Franz would be able to hear about the injustice visited on a million people in Germany on a daily basis. It would make his hair stand on end. The man jammed a stack of old journals under his arm. Franz sighed, looked at the heap of old papers; yes, he expected he would attend. What am I going to be doing there, will I really go, is that a proper trade, those papers. The gay lads; he palms them off on me, I'm supposed to lug all that home with me and get across it. Sure, my heart bleeds for em, but do I really care.

He went off in a great confusion, the whole thing was so unkosher that he didn't say a word about it to Lina, and put her off that night. The old newspaper seller pushed him into the little hall, where there were almost nothing but fellers, most of them very young, and a handful of young women, but they were taken up with each other. For fully an hour Franz said not a word, though under his hat he was grimacing. Come ten o'clock he could no longer keep a straight face, he had to leave, the whole affair and those people were too weird, so many queers in one place, and him bang-smack in the middle of them, he had to rush out and laughed all the way to the Alex. The last thing he remembered hearing was one speaker talking about Chemnitz, where there was a police by-law dating from November of '27. Persons of the same sex may not go out on the street together and not visit public conveniences, and if they are caught, there is a 30-mark fine. Franz looked for Lina, but she was out with her landlady. He went to bed. In his dream he was laughing and scolding a lot, keeping company with an idiotic coachman who kept driving him round and round the Roland fountain on the Siegesallee. The traffic policeman was already giving pursuit. In the end, Franz jumped out, and then the car was driving round and round the fountain and around him like a mad thing, and it went on and on and wouldn't stop, and Franz was standing with the traffic policeman and they were pondering: what do we do with this one, he must be mad.

The following morning he goes to meet Lina in the bar, same as always, and he has his magazines on him. He wants to tell her what boys like that are put through, with Chemnitz and the 30-mark fine, even though it's none of his business, and let them sort out their paragraphs by themselves, also Mack might show, with some job for the livestock dealers. But no, he's not interested, he doesn't want anything to do with them.

Lina can see at a glance that he's slept badly. Then he shyly pushes the journals across to her, pictures on top. Lina puts her hand to her mouth in alarm. Then he gets going on intellect again. He reaches for yesterday's beer puddle on the table, but it isn't there any more. She backs away from him: is he by any chance interested in the kind of thing the journals go on about. She doesn't understand, there was no sign of it before. He fiddles about, draws lines on the wood with his dry finger, then she grabs the whole clutch of papers, drops them on the bench, stands there like a Maenad, they glower at each other, he like a small boy up from under, and she stomps off. And he's left sitting there with his papers, free to think about queers.

A baldie goes for a walk one evening, meets a pretty boy in the Tiergarten, who straight away links arms with him, they stroll about for an hour, then the baldie feels the wish, the desire, o the urge, irresistible, to be very sweet to the boy. He is married, he feels these stirrings occasionally, but now it must be, it is lovely. 'My sunshine, my gold.'

And the boy's so gentle. That there should be such a thing. 'Come with me, we'll go to a small hotel. You can give me five marks or ten, I'm all washed up.' 'Whatever you say, honeybunch.' He gives him his whole wallet. That there should be such a thing. That's almost the sweetest thing of all.

But the room has peepholes in the door. The hotelier sees something, and he calls his wife, who sees it too. And afterwards they tell each other they're not going to stand for it in their hotel, they saw it and he can't deny it. And they weren't going to allow it, and the man should be ashamed of seducing boys, they will take him to court. The handyman and a chambermaid also come and grin. The next day the bald man buys himself two bottles of Asbach Uralt, goes on a business trip to Heligoland to get dead-drunk and washed overboard. He gets drunk and he goes on the ship, but two days later he's home with his wife, and nothing has happened.

And nothing happens all month, all year. Only one thing: he inherits 3,000 dollars from an uncle in America, and can afford to take things easy. Then one day, he's away taking the waters in a spa, his wife receives a summons for him. She opens the envelope and reads all about peepholes and his wallet and the sweet boy. And when the bald man comes home from his holiday, everyone is in floods of tears all round him, his wife, his two grown-up daughters. He reads the summons, he can barely remember it all, it feels like a piece of gobbledygook from the year dot, but here it is, and it's all true. 'Your Honour, what have I done? I didn't cause any public offence. I went into a room and locked the door. Is it my fault if there were holes drilled in the door? Nothing illegal took place.'

The boy confirms it. 'So what did I do wrong?' The bald man in his fur coat begins to cry: 'Did I steal anything? Did I break and enter? All I broke into was the heart of a person dear to me. I said to him: you're my ray of sunshine. And so he was.'

He is acquitted. At home everyone goes on crying.

'Magic Flute', palais de danse with American-style dance hall on the ground floor. Oriental casino open for private parties. What shall I give my girl for Christmas? Transvestites: after years trying all sorts of things, I finally found a cure for hair-growth. Every part of the body can now be made smooth and hairless. At the same time, I found a way of growing a proper female breast in double-quick time. No drugs, absolutely harmless preparation. And as proof: myself. Freedom for love all along the line.

A clear, starry sky looked down on mankind'n dail wino places. Kr ik iuon Castle lay in profound nocturnal peace. But a curly-haired blonde tossed and turned and could find no rest. In the morning, her dearest was leaving. A whisper went (coursed) through the gloomy, impenetrable (dark) night: oh, Gisa, stay, stay (don't leave me, don't go away, don't fall down, please have a seat). Don't leave me. But the dismal silence had neither ear nor heart (nor foot nor nose either, for that matter). And there, separated from her by a few thicknesses of wall, a pale, slender woman was lying with eyes wide open. Her dark, luxurious hair lay tangled on the silk sheets (Kerkaucn Castle, renowned for its silk sheets). Shudders of cold convulsed her. Her teeth chattered as in an icy frost, full stop. She, comma, though, comma, did not draw the blankets around her, full stop. Her shapely ice-cold hands lay still (as in a deep frost, shuddering with cold, slender woman with eyes wide open, renowned silk sheets), full stop. Her shining eyes wandered flickeringly in the dark, and her quaking lips breathed, colon, open quotation marks, capital o-aitch Helena, em-dash, em-dash, Helena, cm-dash, close quotation marks, rotation marks, flotation marks.

'Nah, I'm not going out with you any more, Franz. I'm done with you. You get lost.' 'Oh, Lina, please, I'll take his stuff back to him.' And as Franz took off his hat and laid it on the chest of drawers – all this was in her room – and made a few convincing moves in her direction, she first of all clawed his hand, and then she went off with him. They each took half of the questionable publications and approached the front line that led along Rosenthaler Strasse, Neue Schönhauser Strasse, Hackescher Markt.

There, on the battlefield, Lina, short, buxom, unwashed, tear-stained, dirty Lina, charged forward on her own à la Prince of Homburg: Noble uncle Brandenburg! Natalie! Let be! Let be! O God, he is undone, but onward, onward! She made a beeline, an A-line, an I-line, straight for the stall of the greybeard. Franz Biberkopf, the noble tolerator, preferred to loiter in the rear. He stood in the lee of Schröder's Cigars (Import, Export) and surveyed the action, mildly impeded by mist, trams and passers-by. The principals were in a clinch. They felt for each other's weaknesses. The bundle of newspapers was thrown down, hurled to the ground, by Lina Przyballa, only legitimate surviving daughter of farmer Stanislaus – after two miscarriages, both of whom were also to have been called Lina. The rest of the action was lost in the sound of traffic. 'Attagirl, attagirl!' thus admiringly groaned Franz the tardy tolerator. In lieu of cavalry, he approached the mid-point of the conflagration. Then from outside Ernst Kümmerlich's licensed premises there beamed at him the heroine and victrix of the hour, sluttish Miss Lina Przyballa, ecstatic and asquawk: 'I shown him, Franz!'

Franz already knew. In the bar, she slumped against that part of him she took for his heart, but that underneath his woollen shirt corresponded to his sternum and the upper lobe of his left lung. As she swigged her first Gilka she crowed: 'And he can scrape his periodicals off of the pavement, where they belong!'

Now, o immortality, you are all mine, dearest, what lustre spreads, and hail, hail the Prince of Homburg, victor of the battle of Fehrbellin, hail! (Court ladies, officers and torches appear on the castle ramparts.) 'Gimme another Gilka!'

The Neue Welt, in Hasenheide, if it's not one thing it's another, no need to make life any harder than what it is already

And Franz is sitting in Fräulein Lina Przyballa's room, laughing: 'Do you know what a stock-girl is, Lina?' And he gives her a poke in the ribs. She sits there open-mouthed: 'Well, the Fölsch woman, she's a stock-girl, she looks out the records at Fritz's.' ''S not what I had in mind. If I give you a push, and you wind up lying on the sofa with me beside ya, then you're the stuck girl and I'm the stuck man.' 'Yes, and wouldn't you like that?' She squawked.

And so it's time again, so it's time, fol de rol rol lala, to make merry, make merry, trallala. And so it's time again to be merry la la, time again to make merry.

And they get up off the sofa – you're not ill, are you, sir, otherwise you'd best be off to see the quack – and they wander merrily off to Hasenheide, to the Neue Welt, where things are swing, where the fires of joy are lit, where prizes are awarded for the trimmest calves. The band sat onstage in Tyrolean dress. They softly sang: 'Drink, little brother, drink, leave your worries at home, feel no trouble, feel no pain, life is a jolly refrain, feel no trouble and feel no pain, life is a jolly refrain.'

And the rhythm got them going, and they smirked and hummed among the beer steins and they swayed their shoulders in time: 'Drink, little brother, drink, leave your worries at home, feel no trouble, feel no pain, life is a jolly refrain, feel no trouble and feel no pain, life is a jolly refrain.'

Charlie Chaplin was there in person, whispering a north-easterly variant of German, waddling around the balcony in baggy trousers and enormous shoes, pinched the leg of a lady not in the first flush of youth, and sped down the slide with her. Numerous families sat clustered round tables. You can buy a long stick with paper tassels for just 50 pfennigs, and establish any connection with it you want, the neck and throat are sensitive, and so are the backs of the knees, afterwards you pick up your leg and turn round to look. Who's here? Civilians of both sexes, plus a sprinkling of Reichswehr with their escorts. Drink, little brother, drink, leave your worries at home. Everyone's smoking, clouds of smoke from pipes and cigarettes and cigars fog the whole huge hall. When it gets too smoky for the smoke, it looks for a way out which, thanks to its lightness, it can, through chinks and holes and ventilator shafts, all of which are under instruction to see it out. Once outside, though, there's only black night and freezing cold. Then the smoke regrets its impulsiveness, and opposes its nature, but the ventilators turn only one way, and there's nothing to be done about it. Too late. It's subject to physical laws. The smoke's not sure what it thinks about that, it tries to touch its brow and there's nothing there, it wants to think and it can't. The wind, the cold, the night, have it in their grip, and it is never seen again.

At one table are two couples, watching the passers-by. A man in a pepper-and-salt check inclines his moustaches over the available bosom of a well-stacked brunette. Their sweet hearts are trembling, their noses snuffling, his over her bosom, hers over the pomaded back of his head.

Next door a lady in loud yellow checks is laughing. Her swain lays his arm around her chair. She has buck teeth, a monocle, a wall-eye (the left), she grimaces, smokes, shakes her head: 'How can you ask such a thing?' A young chick with blonde marcel waves sits at the next table, or if you prefer, eclipses the iron seat of a low garden chair with the planet of her powerfully made derrière. Under the effect of a steak and three lagers she is humming happily along to the music. She blabs and blabs, lays her head on his shoulder, the shoulder of a partner in a firm in Neukölln, whose fourth relationship this year is this particular chick, while he is her tenth, if not her eleventh if you count her cousin, to whom she is engaged to be married. Her eyes widen in panic, because it looks as though Chaplin is about to fall on top of them. The manager puts out both hands in the direction of the slide, where it seems something is about to happen. They order pretzels.

A gentleman of thirty-six, co-proprietor of a small grocery, invests in six large balloons at 50 pfennigs a pop and releases them one at a time in the aisle in front of the band, hoping thereby for want of other attributes to secure for himself the attention of girls, women, spinsters, widows, divorcees, adulteresses alone or in pairs, and effect an easy introduction. It's 20 pfennigs in the rear aisle to test your strength. For a look into the future: with a well-moistened finger touch the chemical preparation in the circle with the two heart shapes and rub it on the empty sheet of paper, and the visage of your future spouse will become clear. You have been on the right road since childhood. There is no shred of falsehood in your heart, and yet with a finely honed instinct you sense each trap your envi-ous friends will set for you. Trust to your instinct, because the star under whose light you came into this world will lead you to the consort who will perfect your happiness. The partner you can trust has the same reserved character as you His suit will not be stormy, but all the more durable will be your quiet happiness at his side.

From a balcony near the cloakroom in a side hall, a band was playing. They were all kitted out in red weskits and they kept yell-ing that they had nothing to drink. Below them stood a solid-looking man in a frock coat. He was wearing a striped paper hat, and while singing along, he was trying to insert a paper flower into his buttonhole, which he kept failing to do, in consequence of eight beers, two punches and four cognacs. In the crowd he sang up to the group, and he footed a waltz with an old and extraordinarily digressive looking person, with whom he was tracing wide circles around himself. As she danced, this person seemed to disintegrate further, but luckily she still had enough presence of mind, just before she exploded, to sit on three chairs.

Franz Biberkopf and the man in the frock coat found themselves under the balcony during an interval in which the band were clam-ouring for beer. One beaming blue eye stared at Franz, O moon of Alabama, his other was sightless, they raised their white beer steins together, the invalid wheezed: 'You're another one of them traitors, the others are all stuffing themselves in the food hall.' He gulped: 'Don't stare at my eye like that, look at me, where did you serve?'

They toasted one another, little fanfare from the band, we've got no drink, we've got no drink. Hey, you, stop that, relax, relax, here's a toast, a toast to geniality. 'Are you German, are you German to the core? What's your name?' 'Franz Biberkopf. You don't know me.' The invalid whispered, hand to mouth, he burped: 'Are you really a German man, cross your heart. You're not a Red, else you'd be a traitor. No traitor can be a friend of mine.' He hugged Franz: 'We give our blood for the Fatherland against the Poles and Frogs, and this is how the nation thanks us.' Then he pulled himself together, danced another round with the reassembled extensive person, always slow waltzes, irrespective of the tempo. He stood, lurching, and looked. 'Over here!' called Franz. Lina came for him, and he took a turn with Lina, arm in arm he appeared before Franz at the bar: 'Forgive me, with whom do I have the pleasure, the honour. Your name, sir, if you please.' Drink, little brother, drink, leave your worries at home, feel no trouble, feel no pain, life is a jolly refrain, feel no trouble and feel no pain, life is a jolly refrain.

Two pigs' knuckles and one corned beef, the lady ordered extra horseradish, the wardrobe, yes, where did you leave your coat, there are two cloakrooms here, are prisoners in remand allowed to keep their wedding rings? I say no. The festivities in the rowing club went on till four o'clock. The roads are unspeakable, you bounce against the roof of the car the whole time, it's like total immersion.

The invalid and Franz are sitting arm in arm at the bar: 'They cut my pension, I tell you, I've half a mind to join the Reds. The Archangel drove us out of Paradise with the sword of flame, and we're never going back. We're sitting up at Hartmannsweilerkopf, then I says to my captain, who's from Stargard, same as me.' 'Storkow?' 'Naa, Stargard. Now I've lost my carnation, oh no, there it is.' He who has kissed by the beautiful sea, while the billows listened and rippled with mirth, he knows what life's greatest charm can be, he has whispered to love upon this earth.

Franz is now dealing in Nationalist newspapers. Not that he's got anything against the Jews, but he is a supporter of order. Because there must be order in paradise, anyone can see that. And the Stahlhelm, he's seen those boys, and their leaders as well, well, they've got something. He stands at the exit to Potsdamer Platz underground station, in the passage in the Friedrichstrasse, under the Alexanderplatz station. He is of one mind with the invalid from the Neue Welt, the one-eyed geezer with the fat lady.

To the German people this First Sunday in Advent: destroy false idols and punish those who would lead you astray with their lies! The day will come when Truth will rise up on the field of battle with the sword of righteousness and unstained buckler, to put the foe to flight.

'As these lines are being written, the case against the knights of the Reichsbanner is being heard, whom a fifteen- to twenty-fold superiority in numbers permitted such expression as much of their renowned pacifism as of their indomitable courage in the line of duty that they ambushed and beat up a handful of National Socialists, killing in foulest wise our own party member Hirschmann. From statements of the accused who have legal licence and party duty to lie, it emerges with what deliberate, programmatic violence – clearly betraying the hand of a system – they here saw fit to proceed.

'True federalism is anti-Semitic. The fight for the independence of Bavaria is the fight against international Jewry. Long before the meeting commenced, the great Mathäser Festival Hall was full to bursting, and ever more joined the throng. Those present were kept entertained by the brisk marches and soulful ballads of our S.A. band. At half past eight, party member Oberlehrer opened the meeting with a heartfelt welcome, and gave the floor to party member Walter Ammer.'

In Elsasser Strasse, the brothers laugh themselves silly when he walks into the pub at lunchtime, with his Fascist armband tucked in his pocket as a precaution, but it doesn't take them long to pull it out. Franz cuts them dead.

To the young out-of-work engineer he says – and he sets down his pint pot in astonishment: 'What're you laughing at me for, Richard? Because you've got a wife? You're twenty-one and she's eighteen, what do you know about life? Zero minus three. I tell you, Richard, if we talk about our lasses, and you've got a little boy too, then you'll be in the right because of that brat. But what else? Hello.'

The lens-grinder and polisher Georg Dreske, thirty-nine, presently locked out, waves Franz's armband around. 'Look here, Orge, there's nothing on that banner that can't be defended. I ran away, man, same as what you did, but what happened after? If a fellow wears a red sash or a gold one or a black-white-and-red one, it doesn't make his cigar taste any different, does it. It's the tobacco that matters, the tobacco and the wrapping leaf and the drying and where it comes from. Say I. So what have we done, Orge, tell me.'

Orge quietly lays the sash on the bar in front of him, sups his beer, speaks hesitatingly, stammering occasionally, and moistening his lips frequently: 'I just looks at you, Franz, and I'm just saying I've known you a long time, from Arras and Kovno, and I say they've soft-soaped you.' 'You mean, all on account of the sash?' 'Yes, and everything else as well. Let it go. You don't need to go around in that.'

At that Franz gets up, and he pushes aside the young engineer Richard Werner with the green shirt, who wants to put a question to him: 'No, little Richard, you're a good sort, but what we're dealing with here is man stuff. Just cos you've joined the electoral roll don't mean you can talk with the grown-ups.' Then he stands pensively next to the lens-grinder at the bar, the publican in his big blue apron is the other side, looking alert in front of his selection of spirits, with his big hands in the sink. 'All right then, Orge, what was that about Arras?' 'What do you mean? You're the only one who knows. And why you made a break for it. And the sash. Christ, Franz, I'd sooner use it to hang myself wiv than wear it. They've really made a muggins of you.'

Franz has a confident expression and with it he fixes the lens-grinder, who stammers and throws his head around: 'I want to know what you means about Arras. Let's test it out. If you even were in Arras!' 'You're crazy, Franz, I'm not going to talk to you, you're drunk.' Franz waits, thinks: I'll pull one over on him, he's pretending not to understand, he's playing the smart guy. 'Of course we were, Orge, of course we were at Arras, along with Arthur Böse and Bluhm and the little sergeant major, what was his name again, he had a funny name.' 'I forget.' Let him talk, he's drunk, the others will notice too. 'It's on the tip of my tongue, Bista or Biskra or something. Little guy.' Let him talk, I'll shut up, he'll tie himself in knots, then he'll stop. 'Yeah, we all knew him. But that's not what I'm talking about. Where we went after Arras, when it was all over, after '18, when the next show started, here in Berlin and in Halle and Kiel and . . .'

Georg Dreske has had enough, this is too much, I'm not listening to this: 'Oh, give over, I'm going. Tell it to little Richard. Come on, Richard.' 'He acts so splendid to me, the Baron. He only talks to other barons now, you know. And him condescending to visit us in our bar.' Clear eyes in Dreske's flickering ones: 'That's really what I mean, Orge, when we were in Arras after 1918, field artillery or infantry or flak or radio brigade or engineering corps or whatever else. Where were we afterwards, in peacetime?' Ah, I see where this is going, just wait, sonny, you really shouldn't mess with that. 'Well, I'm going to finish my beer, and you, Franzeken, all those places you were at afterwards, and where you ran and didn't run, where you stood your ground, or sat it, I suggest you look them up in your papers if you happen to have them on you. A trader has to have his papers on him, isn't that right?' Now you've probably caught my drift, all right, now remember. Calm eyes in Dreske's cunning ones: 'For the four years after 1918 I was in Berlin. The whole war previously weren't no longer than that, innit, and I was running around, and you was running around, and Richard here was holding on to his mammy's apron strings. Well, and what had Arras done for us when we got back here? Did you notice anything? We had Inflation, paper money, millions with a b., and no butter and no meat, worse 'n before, and we noticed, you did too, Orge, and what became of Arras, you can work it out on the fingers of your hand. Weren't nothing, right? We was just a rabble, nicking potatoes from the farmers.'

Revolution? Unscrew the flagpole, fold the flag in an oil-cloth wrapper and shove it in the wardrobe. Get Mama to bring you your slippers and take off your fire-red tie. The only way you make a revolution is with your gob, your republic's nothing but a train wreck!

Dreske thinks: he's getting to be dangerous. Richard Werner, that young fool, opens his beak again: 'Then probably you'd rather we had another war, that's what you'd like, and us to fight it for you. Let's get up and whip France. But I tell you, you're making a big hole in your pants.' Franz thinks: an ape, a mulatto, paradise for Negroes, the only way he knows war is from the movies, pop him one and he'll shut up.

The landlord is drying his hands on his blue apron. A green flyer is in front of the rinsed glasses, the landlord puffs out his cheeks and reads: Nonpareil hand-picked come-again roasted coffee! Popular coffee (second grade and roast). Pure unground beans 2.29, Santos guaranteed, excellent Santos domestic blend strong and economical, Van Campina's strong clean-tasting blend, exquisite Mexico melange, an attractively priced plantation coffee for 3.75, prompt despatch by rail, 36 pounds minimum, make your own selection. A bee, a wasp, some buzzy thing is circling high up under the ceiling by the stovepipe, a miracle of nature at this time of winter. Its fellows, fellows of species and genus and outlook are dead, already dead or not yet born; it is the ice age that this solitary hummer is living through, not knowing how and why. The sunshine, however, that silently covers the front tables and section of floor, divided in two by the sign 'Löwenbräu Patzenhofer', that is ancient, and actually everything looks transient and meaningless when you look at it. It has covered x miles to be here, having zipped past star y, the sun has been shining for millions of years, since long before Nebuchadnezzar, Adam and Eve and the ichthyosaur, and just now it is shining through the window of a small beer joint, is divided in two by a tin sign, 'Löwenbräu Patzenhofer,' spreads across the floor and tables, sliding imperceptibly forward. It covers them, and they are aware of it. It is cheerful, light, more than light, light-light, it has come down from on high.

Two large mature mammals, two fully clothed human males, Franz Biberkopf and Georg Dreske, a newspaper seller and a locked-out lens-grinder and polisher, are standing at the bar in an upright position on their trousered hindlegs, propping themselves on the bar with their arms, which are in cylindrical coat sleeves. Each of them thinks, notices and feels something, though not what the other feels, notices and thinks.

'Then you might as well know and commit it to memory that there was no such thing as Arras, Orge. We just didn't do it, I might as well say so. Or you, or whoever happened to be there. There was no discipline, we had no one in charge, it was always each man for himself. I ran away from the trenches, and you and Böse with me. Well, and then back home, what happened then, who fled here? Everyone did, without exception. No one stayed behind, you saw it for yourself, maybe a handful, the odd thousand, OK.' So that's where he's coming from, the blithering idiot, well, he's trapped now. 'It's because we were betrayed, Franz, in 1918 and 1919, by the politicians, they killed Rosa and they killed Karl. We shoulda stuck together and made common cause. Look at Russia, and Lenin, they stuck together, that binds. But let's wait and see.' 'Blut muss fliessen, Blut muss fliessen, Blut muss fliessen knüppelhageldick'.[2] 'I don't care. But the world will go to pieces while we wait, and you with it. So sod that for a laugh. For me that's the proof: they didn't pull it off, and that's enough for me. Not the least little thing came about, no different than that Hartmannsweilerkopf that geezer was banging on about, the invalid who sat at the top, you don't know him, not even that. And now—'

Franz stretches, picks up his sash off the table, stuffs it inside his jacket, moves his left arm from side to side, as he slowly makes his way back to his table: 'And I'll say what I always say, listen, Krause, and put it behind your ear too, Richard: those causes of yours won't produce anything. That's not how it's done. Who knows if anything will come of this sash here either. I'm not claiming it will, but that's another story. Peace on earth, as they say, that's the thing, and whoever wants to work should be allowed to, and it'd be a shame to come to blows over that.'

And he sits down on the window seat, wipes his face, blinks into the sunny room, tweaks a hair out of his ear. The No. 9 tram grinds round the corner, Ostring, Hermannsplatz, Wildenbruchplatz,

Treptow Station, Warschauer Brücke, Baltenplatz, Kniprodestrasse, Schönhauser Allee, Stettiner Bahnhof, Hedwigkirche, Hallesches Tor, Hermannplatz. The landlord props himself against a brass beer tap, his tongue prods a new filling in his lower jaw, it has a metallic taste, little Emilie needs to go out in the countryside this summer, or to Zinnowitz to summer camp, the girl's ailing, his eyes encounter the green leaflet again, it's lying a little slant, he straightens it, a touch of obsessiveness there, he can't stand to see anything crooked. Bismarck herrings in gourmet spices, tender fillets no bones, rollmop herrings, tender with pickled gherkins, jellied eels, big chunks, delicate flesh, fried herrings.

The words, sound waves, sonorities filled with meaning, rock him gently about the room, from the mouth of Dreske the stammerer, who's smiling down at the floor: 'Well, good luck to you, Franz, on your new chosen path, as the priests like to say. When we go marching in January to Friedrichsfelde, where Karl and Rosa lie, I guess you won't be with us.' Let him stammer, I'll concentrate on flogging my papers.

The publican smiles at Franz when they're alone together. Franz stretches his legs under the table: 'Why do you think they hightailed it, Henschke? The sash? They've gone to get reinforcements!' He won't leave it alone. They'll come for him. 'Blut muss fliessen, Blut muss fliessen, Blut muss fliessen knüppelhageldick.'

The publican probes his filling, I should move the goldfinch nearer the window, the little perisher needs some sunshine. Franz gives him a hand, knocks in a nail behind the bar, the publican carries the birdcage with its fluttering occupant: 'It's dark today, innit. The buildings got too much elevation.' Franz clambers up on the chair, hangs up the birdcage, climbs down, whistles, raises his finger, whispers: 'Now just leave the little birdie alone for a bit. 'll get used to the new place. It's a goldfinch, you know, a she.' Then they're both perfectly still, exchange nods, look up, smile.

Franz is a man of some scale, and he knows what's what

That evening, Franz gets given the bum's rush at Henschke's. He comes trotting along at nine, looks for the bird, who's sitting in the corner on her pole, with her beak tucked under her wing, amazing that a critter like that doesn't just fall off; Franz whispers with the publican: 'What about that, able to sleep in so much din, what do you say to that, I think it's incredible, she must be so tired, and whether all that smoke is doing it any good for those little lungs?' 'She's not known nothing else here with me, it's always smoky in here. 'S not even all that thick today.'

Franz sits down: 'Well, I'm going to hold off smoking for today, else it'll get too thick, and we can throw open a window later, there won't be a draught.' Georg Dreske, young Richard and three other fellows are sat by themselves at another table, along with a couple more fellows, Franz doesn't know them. That's all that's in the pub. When Franz walked in, there was a great to-do and talking and scolding. Then as soon as he walks in the door, it gets quieter, the two new fellows keep looking across in his direction, bend across the table and lean back cheekily, toasting each other. When dark eyes wink, when full glasses clink, then there's one reason more, one reason more to drink. Henschke, the bald-pated publican, busies himself at beer tap and sink, he doesn't step out like he normally does, there's always something for him to do back there.

Then all of a sudden the conversation at the next-door table gets a little loud, one of the new fellows is speechifying. He wants a sing-song, there's not enough going on here, there's no piano neither; Henschke calls across: 'It's more than the business will provide.' What they have it in mind to sing Franz already knows, cither it's the 'Internationale' or 'Onward, brothers, to light and freedom',[3] unless they've got some new addition to the repertoire. They begin. The 'Internationale' duly rings out.

Franz chews, thinks: this is for my benefit. I wouldn't mind if it meant they smoked any less. Leastwise when they sing, they don't smoke, which is noxious to the poor dicky bird. But old Dreske hanging out with such green guys, and not even coming over to say hello, that was something he wouldn't have thought possible. The old geezer, he's married, he's an honest geezer, and he's sitting with those flash harries listening to their banter. One of the youths calls over: 'How'd you like our song, then, comrade?' 'Me, oh you don't need me. You've got good voices.' 'Join in then?' 'I'd rather eat. Maybe when I've finished my dinner I'll sing along or sing something on my own.' 'Deal.'

They go on chatting, Franz eats and drinks contentedly, thinks about Lina, and about how the little bird is managing not to fall off its perch in its sleep, and looks across to see who's smoking a pipe. He's had a good day today, though it was cold. From over there, there's always someone checking on his eating. Must be 'fraid I'll choke on something. There was a man once who ate a sausage sarnie, and when it was down in his tummy it had a think and it went back up his throat again and said: ere, no mustard! and only then did it go down properly. That's what a self-respecting sausage sarnie does. And when Franz is finished, and is pouring his beer down after, the fellow calls over: 'Now what about it, comrade, you gonna give us a song?' They seem to be a choral society or something, perhaps we should charge admission, still, when they sing they don't smoke. Well, I'm in no hurry. I keep my promises. And Franz is thinking, while wiping his nose, which started dripping the instant he walked in out of the cold, you can suck it back up but it doesn't help, he's thinking what's keeping Lina, and perhaps I should order a couple more frankfurters, but I'm putting on weight too fast, what am I going to sing them, they don't understand the first thing about life really, but a promise is a promise. And suddenly a sentence is going through his head, a line, something from a poem he learnt in prison, they used to recite it all the time, it went through all the cells. He's all caught up in the moment, his head is hanging down and warm and red from the warmth, he is serious and thoughtful. With his hand on his beer mug, he says: 'There's a poem I remember from prison, I think his name was, wait a minute, Dohms.'

It was. He's given it away, but it's a nice poem. And he's sitting all alone at his table, Henschke is working away at his sink, and the others are listening, no one coming in, the stove is crackling away. Franz, chin on his fists, recites Dohms's pohm, and there's the cell again, and the prison yard, he doesn't mind them now, wonder what lads are in there now: now it's himself going out in the yard, which is more than the fellows over there can do, what do they know about life.

He says: 'If you, o man, desire to become a human male on this earth, then consider carefully before suffering the midwife to bear you into the light! The earth is a pit of lamentation! Trust the writer of these lines, who often chews over this foolish but tough food. Quote pinched from Goethe's Faust: "The only time man is happy in this life is when he's in the womb!" . . , There's good further state, who torments you from early till late. He squeezes you and exploits you with his paragraphs and laws. His first law is: man, shape up! The second: shut yer trap! So you live in confusion, in a state of dimming. And if you try and drown your worries in beer, or in wine if that way inclined, then all you get for your trouble's a hangover. And by now the years are rolling round, your scalp's moth-eaten, the beams are creaking, the sinews are stiff and squeaking; the brains are eddled in your skull, and ever shorter is your human thread. In a word, it's autumn now, you've had your chips, and you turn to face the wall and die. Now I ask you, friend, with trepidation, what is man, what is life? The great Schiller was wont to say: "Not a whole hell of a lot." But I say, it's like a chicken ladder, from top to bottom, and so on.'

No one spoke. After a pause, Franz says: 'Well, that's what he reckoned, he was from Hanover, but the one what committed it to memory was me. Good, eh, a piece of wisdom to accompany you through life, but harsh too.'

From over there comes the judgment: 'Well, just you remember the bit about the state, good old father state, and the one who terrorizes you is the state. But rote learning isn't enough, comrade.' Franz's head is still propped in his hands, the poem is still with him: 'Yes, they haven't got caviar and oysters, and we haven't neither. A man needs to earn his daily bread, it's difficult for a poor devil. You should be grateful still to have your own legs, and be breathing the air.' They continue to plug away at him, surely the fellow will get riled up eventually: 'You know, there's various ways of earning your daily bread. In Russia there was spies back in the day, they earned a lot.' The other new fellow trumpets: 'And there's others over here who're sitting at the top table, because they've betrayed the workers to the capitalists, and are getting paid for it.' 'They're no better 'n whores.' 'Worse.'

Franz thinks about his poem, and wonders what the lads are doing out in Tegel, there'll be a lot of new fellers, after all there's transports every day, and then they're calling out to him: 'Here, what happened to our song? We've got no music, there's a promise that weren't kept.' Well, they can have one: I keep what I promise. Wet my whistle.

And Franz orders a fresh mug of beer, makes a big hole in it, what shall I sing; just then he sees himself standing in the court-yard yelling something at the walls, the kind of thing people sing these days, what was it again? And with majestic slowness he sings, it seems to come into his mouth: 'Ich hatt' einen Kameraden, einen bessern gibt es nicht. Die Trommel schlug zum Strei-heite, er ging an meiner Sei-heite in gleichem Schritt und Tritt, in gleichem Schritt und Tritt.' Pause. He sings the second verse: 'Eine Kugel kam ge-flogen, gilt sie mir, oder gilt sie dir; sie hat ihn weggeri-hissen, er liegt zu meinen Fü-hüssen, als wärs ein Stück von mir. Als wärs ein Stück von mir.' And then, loudly, the third verse: 'Will mir die Hand noch reichen, dieweil ich eben lad. Kann dir die Hand nicht ge-heben, bleib du im ew'gen Le-heben, mein guter Kame-herad, mein guter Kame-herad.'⁴

Loud and slow, leaning back he finishes singing, bravely and full-throatedly he sings. As he finishes, they've got over their consternation and are growling along and beating on the table, and squawking and carrying on: 'Mein gute-her Kame-kame-hera-had.' But while Franz is singing, he remembers what it was he actually wanted to sing. He was standing out in the courtyard, now he's happy he's remembered it, he doesn't care where he is now;

he's singing, and it must out, there are the Jews, they're bickering, what was the name of the Pole, and that decent old gent; tenderness, gratitude: he roars out into the pub: 'Es braust ein Ruf wie Donnerhall, wie Schwertgeklirr und Wogenprall: zum Rhein, zum Rhein, zum deutschen Rhein, wir alle wollen Hüter sein! Lieb Vaterland, magst ruhig sein, lieb Vaterland, magst ruhig sein. Fest steht und treu die Wacht, die Wacht am Rhein! Fest steht und treu die Wacht, die Wacht am Rhein!' All that's behind us, as we know, now we're sitting here, and life is beautiful, everything's beautiful.

Thereupon they go all quiet, one of the new fellers calms them down, they let it wash over them; Dreske's sitting there slumped, scratching his head, the landlord comes out from behind the bar, sniffs and sits down next to Franz. As he ends, Franz greets the whole of life, he swings his pint mug: 'Prost!', bangs on the table, beams, all is well, he is full up, only where is Lina, he can feel his full face, he's a hefty man, firm-fleshed with a little ruffle of fat. No one says anything. Silence.

One of the fellows over there swings his leg over his chair, does up his jacket, tugs the tails straight, a long lanky geezer, a new fellow, here comes trouble, and he stalks over to Franz, who thinks he's going to cop one, that is, if the guy swings at him. He jerks out a chair at Franz's table and sits down astride it. Franz follows all this, waits: 'Come on, surely to goodness there's more free chairs in this pub.' The guy points down to Franz's plate: 'Wassat you ad to eat?' 'I said, come on, there's more free chairs in the pub, if you've got eyes to see. I'm thinking the bathwater must have been too hot when you were a kid.' 'Thassnot what we're talking about. I wanna know what you 'ad to eat.' 'Cheese sammidges, you oaf. Here's a rind. Now get away from my table if you got any manners left.' 'I can tell they're cheese sammidges. I can smell. Just where from.'

But Franz, with red ears, is up on his feet, them at the other table are as well, and Franz picks up his table, turns it over, and sends the new fellow, with plate, mug and mustard pot, sprawling on the floor. The plate is broken. Henschke was waiting for it to happen, and stamps on the shards: 'No fisticuffs in here, I'm not having fights in my bar, if you can't keep the peace, get out.' The long tall fellow is up on his feet, barges Henschke aside: 'You get out of my road, this ain't fisticuffs. We're having a settling of accounts. If either of us breaks anything, he'll pay the damages.' I gave in, thinks Franz, he presses himself against the window by the blinds, if anyone lays a hand on me I'll explode. I hope to God they don't, I get along with everyone, but if anyone's stupid enough to lay a hand on me, there'll be trouble.

The lanky fellow pulls up his trousers, so, here it comes. Franz senses something, what's Dreske up to, he's just standing by and watching. 'Hey, Orge, what's this lad you've brought, where'd you get snot features from?' He keeps working at his trousers, they must be slipping off him, he needs a new button or two. The lanky fellow mocks the landlord: 'Always let everyone have their say. Fascists welcome. Whatever they want to say, they have the freedom to say it here.' And Dreske whoas with his left arm: 'No, Franz, I didn't get involved, you should see what kind of trouble you get into by yourself and your songs, I'm staying out of this, this isn't my doing.'

'Es braust ein Ruf wie Donnerhall', aw, it's what he sung in the courtyard they're getting at, that's what's bothered them.

'Fascist bloodhound!' the lanky boy yells in Franz's face. 'I want your sash! Give it me!'

Here goes, the four of them are going to set on me, I'll keep my back to the window, better see about a chair. 'The sash! I'll take it out your pocket. I want the sash.' The others are all by him. Franz has a chair in his hands. Grips it firmly. First grab hold of it, then biff bang.

The landlord is trying to hold the lanky boy back, begging him: 'Just leave! Biberkopf, please go.' He's worried on account of his premises, he probably hasn't insured his winders, well, it's no skin off my nose. 'Sure, Henschke. There's no shortage of pubs in Berlin, just I happened to be waiting for Lina in this one. But are you taking their side? Why throw me out when I comes here every day, and those two new fellows never bin here before.' The landlord has managed to pull back the beanpole, the other new one spits: 'Coz you're a Fascist, you've got yer sash in yer pocket, you're a Swazzy Nazi.'

'What if I am. I told Orge I was. And why. You don't understand, so you start shouting.' 'Na, it was you that were shouting with that Watch on the Rhine!' 'If you walk over to my table and cause a commotion like now, then there won't be any rest in the world. Not a hope. And it needs rest, so that people can live and work. Factory workers and traders and everyone, so that there's order, otherwise no one will be able to do their job. Then what will you live off, you loudmouths? You get drunk on your slogans! All you're good for is creating scenes and provoking other people, till they get mad enough to go and biff you. You try being walked over the way you walk over other people!'

Suddenly he's yelling too, something has happened in him, and is bubbling out of him, there's a red mist in front of his eyes: 'You bunch of crooks, you don't know what you're doing, a man has to knock the weevils out of your brains, you'll wreck the entire world, watch out something doesn't happen to you, you miserable wretches!'

It's bubbling up out of him, he has done time in Tegel, life is grim, what kind of life is it, the man singing knows it, what I went through, Ida, best not think about it.

And he goes on yelling in a fit of dread, an abyss is opening up, fight it off, stamp it down, yell it down. The pub is rocking. Henschke is standing in front of him by the bar, doesn't dare approach him because of the look on his face, and the roaring coming out of his throat, and now he's foaming at the mouth: 'You've got nothing to say to me, not one of youze can come up to me and say "we know better", that's not why we was in the big house, and laying in the trenches, to have you making trouble. Troublemakers, it needs quiet and calm, quiet I say, you can put that in your pipes and smoke it, just quiet (yes, that's it, that's where we've got to, that's the truth), and whoever turns up now to cause a commotion, they need to be strung up along an avenue (black poles, telegraph poles, a whole row of them along the Tegeler Chaussee, I know), and then you'll believe it, when you see them dangling there, then, yes. Then you can make a note of it and what you do, you criminals. (Yes, and then there will be quiet, they'll keep shtum, that's the only truth, we'll see.)'

Franz Biberkopf is rampant, rigid. He is squawking blindly out of his throat, his eyes are glazed over, his face is blue, swollen, he is spitting, his hands are on fire, the man is beside himself. All the time his fingers are gripping the chair, but only so that he has something to hold on to. Next he will pick it up and start swinging it.

Careful, danger, clear the road, fire, fire, fire.

All the time, the man who's standing there yelling can hear himself from a distance, see himself. The buildings, the buildings want to collapse, the roofs want to collapse on top of him, he won't allow it, they're not to come to me with that, I won't let them, we need quiet.

And the feeling goes through him: it will start any moment, I will do something, grab someone by the throat, no, no, I'll fall over, hit the ground, any second, any second now. And there I was, thinking the world was quiet and orderly. In his dimness he shudders: something is wrong in the world, the terrible way they're standing over there, he can see it plain as day.

But once upon a time there dwelt in Paradise two people, Adam and Eve. And that Paradise was the splendid Garden of Eden. Birds and animals played in it.

Well, the fellow's clearly bonkers. They pause, even the beanpole at the back is snorting and gesturing to Dreske; let's just sit back down, and change the subject. Dreske stammers into the silence: 'Well, best you be going, Franz, let go your chair, you've done enough talking.' And the pressure in him lets up, the cloud passes. Passes. Thanks be to God, passes. His face lightens, sags.

They stand by their table, the lanky fellow is sitting and drinking. The lumber manufacturers insist on their margins, Krupp starves his pensioners, one and a half million unemployed, up by 226,000 in a fortnight.

The chair drops from Franz's hand, his hand has gone soft, his voice sounds normal, he has lowered his head, they're no longer riling him: 'All right. I'm going. My pleasure. I'm not bothered with what's going on in your heads.'

They listen without replying. Let the renegade rascals abuse the democratic constitution to applause from the bourgeoisie and the social chauvinists. It all deepens and accelerates the breach between the revolutionary workers of Europe and the Scheidemanns and the rest of them. The mass of the oppressed classes is with us.

Franz takes his cap: 'I'm sorry something like this came between us.' He extends his hand, Dreske doesn't take it, sits down in his chair. 'Blut muss fliessen, Blut muss fliessen, knüppelhageldick.'

'Well, I'll be going then. What do I owe, Henschke, and for the glass and the plate as well.'

That's his order. For fourteen children a china cup. A welfare reform from the Centrist minister Hirtsiefer: confidential! In view of the slender budget at my disposal, qualification is determined not only by an exceptional number of offspring – twelve? – but also where raising of said offspring has been performed in an exemplary and self-denying way.

Someone behind Franz yells: 'Heil dir im Siegerkranz, taters with herring schwanz!' He needs his bottom smacking. Too bad I didn't get my mitts on him. Franz has pulled his cap on. He thinks of the Hackescher Markt, the gay boys, the greybeard's kiosk with the publications, he didn't feel like it, he hesitates, he goes anyway.

He is out in the cold. Outside he walks into Lina, who is just on her way to meet him. He walks slowly. Ideally he would go back inside and tell them all how crazy they are. Crazy, intoxicated, when he knows they're not really like that, not even the beanpole, the cheeky one who plonked himself down at his table. They just don't know what to do with all that blood, yes, they are hot-blooded, if they were out in Tegel or had done anything in their lives, they would see the light sure enough, hundred candle-power.

He has linked arms with Lina, is looking round the ill-lit street. They could use a few more street lights here. What's wrong with people, first the queers who he doesn't care about one way or another, and now the Reds. What do I care, so long as they mind their own business. Leave me out of it; a man can't even drink his beer in peace these days. I have half a mind to go back and trash Henschke's bar for him. There's more flickering and throbbing in Franz's eyes; his brow swells, and his nose. But after a while it goes away; he squeezes Lina, scratches her on the wrist, she smiles: 'That feels nice, Franz, a little scratch of yours.'

'Let's go dancing, Lina, I don't feel like going in some smelly dive, I've had my fill of smoke. You know there's a little goldfinch there. It can't be doing her any good, but do you think they even care?' And he explains to her how right he was a moment ago, and she sides with him. They get on the tram and ride down to Jannowitzbrücke, to Little Walter's Ballroom. Him just exactly as he is, and Lina's not to go back and change, she's lovely enough without all that. And the stout one pulls out a little newspaper from her pocket when they're in the tram, it's all crumpled. She brought it for him, it's the Sunday edition of the *Friedensbote*. Franz says it's not a paper he keeps, he presses her hand, he likes the name and the headline on the first page: 'From Misfortune to Good Fortune.'

Clap clap your hands, tap tap your feet, fishes, birds, all day, paradise.

The tram jolts along, but in the dim light they put their heads together and read the poem on the front page that Lina has ringed in pencil: 'Walking is best when we're two', by E. Fischer. 'When we walk alone, it's a walk of woe, The foot oft stumbling, the heart bowed low: Walking is best when we're two. And if you fall, who'll take your arm, If weary, who'll ward off all harm? Walking is best when we're two. You silent rover through world and time, Take Jesus as your mate sublime. Walking is best when we're two. He knows the road, he knows the lane, With word and deed he heals your pain, Walking is best when we're two.'[5]

I still feel thirsty, though, thinks Franz while reading, two pints wasn't enough. All that talking dried my throat. And then he recalls his singing, and he feels at home and squeezes Lina to him.

She feels optimistic. As they walk down Alexanderstrasse to Holzmarktstrasse, she presses herself softly against him: perhaps he'll ask to make an honest woman of her soon?

The scale of this Franz Biberkopf. A match for the heroes of old

This Franz Biberkopf, previously cement worker, then furniture removal man and so forth, currently newspaper seller, weighs nigh on two hundredweight. He has the strength of a cobra snake and has joined an athletics club again. Decked out in green puttees, hobnail boots and a bomber jacket. You won't find much money on him, it only comes to him in small amounts, but even so it's worth trying to get to know him.

Is he prey to conscience from back then, Ida and so on, nightmares, restless sleep, torments, the Furies from the time of our great-grandmothers? Uh *uh*. Consider the changed situation. A criminal, in his time a man accursed (how do you know, my child?) at the altar, Orestes, has bludgeoned to death one Clytemnestra – not an easy name to say – and she was his mother. (At what altar do you mean? You'll have a job finding a church that stays open at night.) I say, times have changed. HOI HO HATZ, terrible beasts, old raddled women with snakes, dogs without muzzles, an unsympathetic menagerie snapping at his heels, but they can't get near him because he's standing in front of the altar, that is an antique notion, and then the whole pack of them dance furiously round him, dogs and whatnot. Harpless, as it says in the song, the dance of the Furies, they whirl around their victim, insane delusions, bending of senses, preparation for the asylum.

They don't bother Franz Biberkopf. Let's make that perfectly clear, here's mud in your eye, he drinks one beer after another at Henschke's or wherever, interspersed with the odd tot to lucubrate his heart. That's how the furniture removal man and so forth, newspaper vendor Franz Biberkopf from Berlin north-east, end of

1927, may be distinguished from famous old Orestes. So who wouldn't rather be in his boots, then.

Franz killed his girl, Ida, never mind the last name now, in the flush of her youth. This happened in the course of a spat between Franz and said Ida in the flat of her sister Minna, in which the following organs of the woman received superficial injuries: the skin on the bridge of her nose, the bone beneath and cartilage, which wasn't noticed until hospital, and was to play a part in the subsequent court proceedings, also left and right shoulders, which suffered contusions and ecchymosis. But then the argument really took off. The words 'pimp' and 'skirt-chaser' had a huge effect on the honour-conscious if somewhat lapsed Franz Biberkopf, who had reasons of his own for being tense. His muscles were quaking. He didn't pick up any weapon beyond a little wooden-handled eggwhisk, because he was in training at the time and had hurt his hand. And this egg-whisk with its wire spiral he brought down with an enormous twofold impact on the thorax of Ida, with whom he had been engaged in debate. To that date Ida's sternum had been fully intact, the whole little person, which was very pleasant to behold, was not – by the way, the man, who was living off her, supposed not incorrectly that she had it in mind to get rid of him in favour of a recently appeared fellow from Breslau. At any rate, the attractive breastbone had not been built to withstand the impact of an egg-whisk. At the first blow she yelled Oh! and didn't say dirty pimp but Christ. The second impact happened with Franz in the same position, but followed a quarter-turn to the right on the part of his Ida. Thereupon Ida said nothing at all, but opened her mouth in an odd duck's-beak-like manner, and both her arms shot up in the air.

What had happened to the female's sternum involves mechanical laws of rigidity and elasticity, impact and resistance. Without knowledge of these laws, it is hardly comprehensible. The following formulae will be of assistance:

The First Newtonian (njuːˈtəʊnɪən) Law, which goes: a body exists in a state of rest, so long as no force causes it to change its state (with reference to Ida's ribs). Njuten's Second: the movement is in proportion to the force exerted, and will continue in the same direction (the force here being Franz, more specifically his arm and implement-bearing fist). The size of the force is expressed with the following formula:

$$f = c \lim \frac{\Delta v}{\Delta t} = cw.$$

The force acceleration, and therefore the degree of disruption, is expressed in another formula: —

$$\Delta v = \frac{1}{c} f \, \Delta t$$

The outcome was wholly predictable: the spiral of the egg-whisk is compressed, the wood itself struck. On the other side, inertia, yes, very good, resistance in the form of broken ribs, the seventh and eighth, in line with the left rear shoulder-blade.

The contemporary account leaves the Furies out of it. One can follow, blow by blow, what Franz did and what Ida suffered. There are no unknowns in the equation. It only remains to list the further consequences of the process thus initiated: loss of verticality on the part of Ida, reversion to the horizontal, in the form of colossal impact, at the same time as breathing difficulties, intense pain, shock and physiological loss of balance. Franz would have gone on to bludgeon the injured party, who was well known to him, like a roaring lion, had not her sister come running in from the other room. The shrill screams of that woman put him to flight, and later that evening a police patrol picked him up in his own flat not far away.

'Hoi ho hatz', cry the old Furies. O the dread sight of an accursed man at the altar, hands dripping with blood. Their snores: are you asleep? Put aside your slumber. Up, up. Agamemnon, his father, had set out for Troy many years before. Troy had fallen, there were beacons announcing the fact, from Mount Ida to Athos, always burning pine torches to Cithaeron.

How wonderful, by the way, these glowing reports from Troy to Greece. Isn't it splendid the progress of that fire across the sea – light, heart, soul, happiness, outcry!

The dark red fire, glowing red over Lake Gorgopis, and then seen by a sentry, who shouts out for joy, that's life, lit and passed on, the news and the excitement and joy, all together, and the hop across the bay, rushing up to the heights of Mt Arachnaeon, shouting and madness, visible, glowing red: Agamemnon is coming! We have nothing comparable to offer. We acknowledge the fact.

For transmission of news we avail ourselves of some of the results of the experiments of one Heinrich Hertz, who lived in Karlsruhe, died young, and, at least in a photograph in the graphic collection in Munich, wore a beard. We have the wireless telegraph. Through mechanical transmitters in great stations we produce high-frequency alternating currents. By oscillations of one oscillatory circuit, electrical waves are produced. These oscillations radiate out in a circular pattern. And then there is an electron tube of glass and a microphone whose glass vibrates now more, now less strongly, and which produces the same note that previously had entered the machine, and that is astonishing, subtle, treacherous. Difficult to wax enthusiastic about; it works, *suffit*.

How different the pine torch announcing Agamemnon's return! It burns, it flares, at every moment, in every place it speaks, it feels, and everything cheers: Agamemnon is coming home! A thousand men glow in every place: Agamemnon is coming, and now there are ten thousand, a hundred thousand along the coast.

And then, cut to the chase, he is home. Things there are different. Very different. The worm turns. As soon as his wife has him back, she sticks him in a bath. In an instant she shows him just what a fiendish harridan she is. She throws a fishing net over him, so that he cannot defend himself, and then she has a hatchet with her, as though to chop wood. He groans: 'Oh woe, I am struck!' Outside they are asking: 'Who is that crying out?' 'Oh woe again!' The antique witch does him in, she doesn't bat an eyelid, she even condescends to boast outside: 'I have done the deed, I cast a fisherman's net over him, and struck him twice, with two sighs he stretched out his limbs, then with a third blow I sent him to Hades.' This troubles the chorus of elders, but they manage to observe, aptly: 'We are astounded by your bold speech.' That, then, was the woman, that witch of old, who, in the course of marital duty with Agamemnon, had become mother to a boy who was given the name Orestes. Later she was killed by that fruit of her joys, and he was the one subsequently plagued by the Furies.

Our Franz was not like that. After five weeks Ida dies, in Friedrichshain hospital, complications from broken ribs, punctured lung, subsequent empyema, pleural infection, lung inflammation, God, the fever won't break, look at yourself, God, you look done in, you've had it, you can pack up. They conducted an autopsy, and put her in the ground in the Landsberger Allee, ten feet under. She died hating Franz, his fury with her didn't abate after her death. Her new friend, the boy from Breslau, visited her in hospital. There she's been lying now, for five years, horizontal, on her back, the boards are starting to rot, she is turned to sewage, she, who once in Treptow danced with Franz in white canvas shoes, who loved and played games, now she's keeping perfectly still and is no longer extant.

He's done his four years. The man who slew her walks around, lives, flourishes, eats and drinks, spills his seed, continues to spread new life. Even Ida's sister didn't escape his clutches. It'll all catch up with him one day. Various other odds and sods have gone on. But he's got a long life ahead of him. He knows. So he's still breakfasting in bars and in his way praising the sky over Alexanderplatz: since when has your gran played the trombone, and: my parrot don't eat hard-boiled eggs.

And where are the red prison walls of Tegel now, the ones that so intimidated him that he didn't like to look at them. The guard is standing in front of his black iron gate, which had once aroused such disfavour in Franz, the gate is still on its hinges, it doesn't bother anyone, it is well aired, at night, like any good gate, it is kept locked. Now in the morning the guard is standing in front of it, smoking his pipe. The sun is shining. It is always the same sun. Its position in the sky's arc is always calculable. Whether it is visible or not depends on the cloud cover. A few individuals are just getting off the No. 41 tram, carrying flowers and small parcels, they are probably going to the sanatorium straight ahead, left down the avenue, and they are all shivering with cold. The trees are in a black row. Inside, the prisoners are huddled in their cells, tinkering in the workrooms, or goose-stepping round the exercise yard. Strict orders not to appear in free association without boots, cap and neckerchief. The old man does his rounds of the cells: 'What was the soup like last night?' 'I wouldn't have minded a bit more of it, and better seasoned.' He doesn't listen, acts deaf: 'How often do you get a change of linen here?' As if he didn't know.

One man in solitary writes: 'Let the sun in! That's the call echoing round the world today. Only here, behind prison walls, does it not find an echo. Are we not worthy? Prison design means there are some north-east-facing blocks that don't see the sun all year. Not one sunbeam loses its way into these cells to greet their inmates. Year in year out, they need to wither and work without its cheering rays.' A commission is coming to inspect the building, the wardens run from cell to cell.

Another: 'To the prosecution service at the county court. During the proceedings against me in the criminal court the presiding judge, Dr X, told me that after my arrest belongings of mine had been taken from my flat at Elisabethstrasse 76 by an unknown party. Since this has been officially recorded in my file, a search must have been instigated by the police or public prosecution service. I had heard nothing about my property being taken at any point until then. I am writing to ask the prosecution service for the result of this inquiry or to lodge a copy of the report in my file, so that I may be able, if the need should arise, to bring charges against my landlady for negligence.'

As far as Ida's sister Minna is concerned, she's very well, thank you. It's now twenty past eleven, she's just coming from the market in Ackerstrasse, a yellow municipal building that has another exit on Invalidenstrasse. She chooses the Ackerstrasse exit, though, because it's more convenient for her. She's purchased a cauliflower and a pig's head, as well as a bunch of celery. From a stall outside she buys a fat flounder and some camomile tea; you never know when that might come in handy.

Chapter Three

Here decent, well-intentioned Franz Biberkopf suffers a first reverse. He falls victim to a cheat. The shock is profound.

Biberkopf has sworn to be decent, and as you've seen, he has been decent for several weeks, but that was really just temporary. In the long run, life finds that too prissy, and it cunningly trips him up. But to him, Biberkopf, that doesn't seem very nice on the part of life, and for a long time he is disgusted with such a mean, dastardly existence in the teeth of all his good intentions.

Why life proceeded as it did is something he doesn't understand. He has a long way to go before he does.

Yesterday on the backs of steeds . . .

Since Christmas is icumen in, Franz makes a switch into seasonal
products, for a few morning or afternoon hours it's shoelaces, first
on his own, then with one Otto Lüders. Lüders has been out of
work for two years, his wife takes in washing. Fat Lina brought
him along one day, he's her uncle. For a few weeks in summer he
was the Rüdersdorf Peppermint Man with swizzle stick and uniform. He and Franz wander through the streets together, go inside
the houses, ring doorbells and meet up afterwards.

One time, Franz Biberkopf checks into the pub. He has the fat
girl with him. He is in a particularly sunny mood. He gobbles down
the fat girl's sandwiches, then, still chewing, he orders a round of
pigs' ears with peas for everyone. He snogs his girl so much that
after she's finished her pigs' ears she trots off pink-faced. 'Not a bad
thing for her to push off, Otto.' 'She's got her place. She's always
traipsing after you.'

Franz lurches across the table, gives Lüders the look from below:
'Guess what's just happened, Otto?' 'How d'you mean?' 'Go on,
have a guess.' 'I don't know what you're talking about.'

Two beers, a lemonade. A new customer catches his breath,
wipes his nose on the back of his hand, splutters: 'A cup of coffee.'
'Sugar?' The landlady is washing glasses. 'No, but make it quick.'

A young fellow in a brown sports cap walks smartly through the
bar, warms himself at the stove, takes a peek at Franz's table, then
the one beside it. 'You seen anyone in a black coat wiv a brown
fur collar?' 'Is he a regular here?' 'Yeah.' The older man at the table

97

turns to the pale-looking one next to him: 'Brown fur collar?' Pale fellow: 'Loads of people come here in fur coats.' The man with grey hair: 'Where are you from? Who sent you?' 'Never you mind. If you ain't seen him.' 'There's loads in here in brown fur. Need to know who sent you.' 'I've no need to explain my business to you.' The pale fellow is getting excited: 'If you ask him if someone's been here, then surely he can ask who sent you.'

Already the guest is at the next table: 'I asked him the question. What's it matter who I am.' 'Come on, you ask him something, he asks you something back. You didn't have to ask him.' 'I don't need to tell him why.' 'In that case he don't need to tell you if the fellow was here or not.'

The visitor goes to the door, turns round: 'If you're such a clever dick, just stay that way.' Turns away, pulls open the door, and out.

The two at the table: 'D'you know him then? I don't.' 'He's never been here before. God knows what he wants.' 'He was a Bavarian, weren't he?' 'Nah, he was a Rhinelander. From the Rhineland, you know.'

Franz grins at bashful Lüders: 'So you won't, eh? Give you a clue: it involves money.' 'Well, you got any then?'

Franz has his fist on the table, opens it, grins proudly: 'All right, how much?' Lüders, the wretched manikin, is leaning forward, whistles through a loose tooth: 'Two tenners, no shit.' Franz lets them clink on the table. 'How about that. Earned it in fifteen minutes, twenty at the most. Absolute tops.' 'Christ.' 'No, it's not what you think, under the table, the back way. Honest, Otto, it's decently come by, legit, promise.'

They start to whisper together. Otto Lüders leans in. Franz rang a woman's bell, Makko laces, for yourself, for your husband, for the kids, she took a look at them, then she looked at me, she's a widder, still in good nick, we were in the corridor talking then I asks her if I couldn't get a cuppa coffee, winter's so cold this year. I drunk coffee, she with. And then one thing led to another. Franz blows into his hand, chortles, scratches his jawbone, rams his knee against Otto's: 'I left all my stuff with her. D'you suppose she noticed?' 'Who?' 'Well, who'd'you fink, the fat girl, coz I had no goods left on me.' 'What if she does, then you just sold everythink. So where was this?'

And Franz whistles: 'I'm gonna go back there, but not too soon, it was a back house on Elsasser, a widder. Christ, twenty marks.' They eat and drink until three. Otto gets a fiver as his share, but is just as glum as before.

So who's this creeping across Rosenthaler Tor with his shoelaces the next morning? Otto Lüders. Waits at Fabisch's on the corner, till he sees Franz trotting down Brunnenstrasse. Then he nips along Elsasser himself. There, that's the number. Maybe Franz has already been up. Look at the people calmly walking up and down the street. Think I'll just stand in the doorway a bit first. If he comes, I'll tell him, what do I tell him, I've got palpitations, they bother me all day and I can't work. The doctor can't find anythink wrong with me, but there is. A man perishes in his old rags, still got me old wartime gear on. Up the stairs.

He rings the bell. 'Makko laces, lil' lady? No, I just wanted to ask. Hey, listen up a minute, won't you.' She makes to shut the door, but he's shoved his foot in the way. 'See, I'm not alone, my mate, you remember him, he was here yesterday, and he left his clobber here.' 'Oh God.' She opens the door, in a trice Lüders is in, hurriedly pushes the door shut behind him. 'What's the matter, oh Lord!' 'Nothing at all, little lady. Why're you shaking?' He's shaking himself, he's surprised himself getting this far, what's next, whatever comes, he'll find some way. He needs to be seductive, but he can't find a voice, he's got a wire net clamped across his nose and mouth, all the way up to his forehead and both cheeks, if my cheeks freeze, then I've had it. 'I just come for his fings, that's all.' The little woman runs into her parlour to fetch the parcel, and he's already back on the threshold. She chews and looks: 'There's the parcel. Oh God.' 'Why, thank you, thank you very much. But what are you trembling for, ma'am? Say, it is nice and warm in here. And couldn't you maybe give me a cup of coffee?' Stall, talk, anything so as not to go out, strong as an oak.

The woman, who's skinny, delicate, stands in front of him, her hands are clasped in front of her: 'Did he tell you anything? What did he tell you?' 'Who d'you mean, my friend?' Talk, talk, the more you talk the nearer you get, now the net is just a tickle under his nose. 'Oh, nothing else, no, what would there be. What would he have said about a cup of coffee. And now I've got his things.' 'I'll just go in the kitchen.' She's scared what I'll say about her coffee, I make it better myself, it'd be cosier in the bar, she's trying to duck out of it, but, hey, I'm still here. Good the way I managed to hang on in, it was pretty easy really. But Lüders is still afraid, he listens for the door, the staircase, upstairs. He goes back in the parlour. Had a lousy night's sleep, kid kept him up coughing all night, let's get comfortable. And he sits down on the red plush sofa.

This is where she did it with Franz, for the moment she's still making me coffee, I'll take my hat off, my fingers are icy. 'There's a cup for you.' She's scared isn't she, quite presentable, though, wouldn't mind trying something on with her. 'Won't you have any yourself? To keep me company?' 'No, no, my tenant'll be along any moment, he has the parlour.' She's trying to scare me off, where's her tenant, why, there's not even a bed in here: 'Is that all? You can leave him out of it. A tenant – he won't show up in the morning, he's got work to go to. Yes, that's all my friend said. I was just to collect his things for him' – sips pleasurably at the coffee – 'ah, that's better. Ooh, it's parky out, so what do you think he might have told me. Maybe the fact that you're a widder, but that's no secret, is it.' 'I spose not.' 'What happened to your husband? Died in the war, I spect.' 'I'm busy, I have to cook.' 'Then you could make me another cup of coffee. What's the rush. We won't see each other like this again. You got any kids then?' 'Why don't you leave me alone, you got what you came for, I haven't any time.' 'Now, ma'am, let's not get frosty, you can always call the cops, but there's no need of that with me, I'll go, you won't mind if I finish my coffee first. All at once you're pushed for time. The other day you had all the time in the world. Know what I mean. Well, I'm not like that, I'm off.'

He rams his hat on his head, gets up, jams the little package under his arm, slowly pulls open the door, already he's past her, when he quickly spins round: 'All right then, where's your small change.' His left hand extended, beckoning with his index finger. She claps her hand to her mouth, little Lüders is very close to her: 'You know, if you shout. Only make a donation when you've been had. You see, we know everything really. Being friends, we don't keep secrets from each other.' Fucking outrage, bitch, bitch, black dress, my eye, I'd really like to give her a smack in the chops, how is she any better than my old lady. Her face is burning, but only the right side of it, her left is white as a ghost. She has her purse in her hand, her fingers are picking around in it, but all the while she's looking wide-eyed at Lüders. Her right passes him coins. Strange expression on her face. He gestures impatiently to keep it coming. She empties the purse into his hand, now he goes back to the parlour, to the table, picks up the red crocheted cloth, she wheezes, can't get a word out, can't open her mouth any wider than it is already, stands quietly beside the door. He picks up a couple of sofa cushions, then over to the kitchen, rips open the drawers, looks, looks. All trash, better run, else she'll start screaming. Now she's keeled over, I'm out of here.

Down the corridor, the door squeezed shut, down the stairs, into the next house.

Today, shot through the chest he bleeds

Paradise was wonderful. The waters were, oh, ateem with fish, trees sprouted from the earth, the animals played together, by land and water and air.

A tree rustled. A snaky snake snake thrust out its head, there was a snake living in Paradise, and it was more cunning than all the beasts of the field, and lo, it began to speak, and it spake snake to Adam and Eve.

Just as Franz Biberkopf is cheerily climbing the stairs a week later, with a bouquet of flowers wrapped in silk paper, thinking about his old lady getting on his case, but not altogether seriously, stops, she is a good girl, what is it with these old goats, leave it out Franz, bah, it's business, and business is business. Then he rings the bell, smiles in anticipation, smirks, nice cup of coffee, little dolly bird. He hears footfall, that'll be her. He puffs out his chest, extends the bouquet, the chain is put on, his heart is pounding, is my tie straight, her voice asks: 'Who is it?' He sniggers back: 'It's the postman.' Little crack in the door, her eyes, he bends down tenderly, waggles his bouquet from side to side. Crash. The door slams shut. Krrr. The bolt is thrown. Cunt. What do you do now. She must be crazy. Can't have recognized me. Brown door, door-frame, I'm standing on the step, my tie's straight. Unbe-fucking-lievable. He looks at his hands, bunch a flars, bought em at the corner for a mark, silk paper and everything. He rings again, a second time, keeps his finger down. She's got to be still standing by the door, and she's just keeping it shut, she's not moving, she's holding her breath, and not letting me in. Even though she's still got me laces, all me goods, must be 3 marks' worth, I'm entitled to pick em up, inni? Now there's movement, she's going away, she's in her frigging kitchen. Well, Jesus—.

Down the steps. Then back up again: I'm going to give her one more ring to make sure, she can't have seen me, she must have mistook me for someone else, some beggar, sure she gets all sorts. But once he's standing in front of the door, he doesn't ring the bell. He feels nothing. He's just waiting, standing there. There, she's not letting me in, I just wanted to see. I won't sell in this building any more, what do I do with the flars, cost me a mark they did, I'll chuck em in the gutter. Suddenly, as if under orders, he rings, calmly waits, right, she's not even answering the door, she knows it's me. I'll leave a note with the neighbours, I gotta have my goods back.

He rings next door, there's no one home. So. Let's write the note. Franz goes over to the window on the landing, tears off a corner of a newspaper, writes with the little pencil stub: 'You're not opening, but I need my goods back. Leave them in Klaussen's on the corner.'

Christ, bitch, if you knew who I am, and what I've had occasion to do to a woman before, then you would not behave like what you are. Got half a mind to take an axe and chop the door down. He pushes the note under the door.

Franz goes around glumly all day. The next morning, while he's waiting for Lüders, the publican gives him a piece of paper. It's her reply. 'Was that all?' 'What are you expecting?' 'A package with my goods.' 'No, this is what the boy brung last night.' 'So I'm supposed to go up and collect it, am I?'

A couple of minutes later, Franz goes over to the window next to the displays, slumps onto a stool, holding the note in his nerveless left hand, presses his lips together, stares across the table. Lüders, the wretch, walks in the door, sees Franz sitting there, guesses what's what, and he's out the door.

The landlord comes over: 'What's that Lüders in such a hurry for, he's not collected his goods yet.' Franz sits and sits. How can something like this be. I've been sawn off. It's not possible. Has anyone ever heard the like. I can't get up. Lüders can run, he's got legs, he'd better run, I ain't got words for im.

'Do you want a cognac, Biberkopf? Is it someone in the family?' 'Nah, nah.' What's he saying to me, I can't hear too good, feel like I got cotton wool stuffed in my ears. The publican persists: 'What come over Lüders to make him run off like that? No one's got it in for im. As if he ad someone chasin after im.' 'Lüders? Expect he's busy. Yeah, let's have a cognac.' He knocks it back, his thoughts seem to keep disintegrating. Jesus Christ, this business with the facking note. 'Here, you seem to've dropped the envelope. Do you want paper?' 'Thanks.' He goes on pondering: I wonder what thing she's talking about, in her letter. Lüders is a respectable man, he's got kids and all. Franz wonders what happened, and he can feel his head hanging, feels it getting heavy like when he's dropping off to sleep sometimes, the landlord thinks he's tired, but it's pallor, emptiness and distance, it's making his legs slither away from under him, and then he slumps completely, turns his head to the left, and he's gone.

Franz is lying slumped across the table, under his arm he's peering at the deal boards, blowing across the grain, keeping his head still: 'Is my old lady bin in yet, you know, Lina?' 'Nah, she'll not be by before noon.' See, it's just nine in the morning, ain't done nuffink yet, Lüders is off.

What to do? And then it pours through him, and he bites his lip: this is the punishment, they let me out, the others are digging potatoes in the big pile of manure at the back, and I have to catch the tram, goddamnit, I was all right there. He stands up, maybe go out on the pavement a minute, push it away, not get scared again, I'm on my feet, no one can touch me, no one: 'If my old lady comes in, tell her I suffered a bereavement, an uncle or something. I won't be in at lunchtime, so she needn't wait for me. What do I owe?' 'Just a beer, as usual.' 'There.' 'And you're leaving the package here?' 'What package?' 'You are in a bad way, Biberkopf. No sweat, keep your chin up, lad. I'll look after your package for you.' 'What package?' 'Go out and get some fresh air.'

Biberkopf is outside. The landlord watches him through the window: 'I wonder if they won't bring him in right away. He's in a mess. Strong man like that and all. His old lady will be in for a surprise.'

A pale little man is standing outside the building, his right arm is in a sling, his hand in a black leather glove. He's been standing in the sun for an hour or so already, without going inside. He has just come from the hospital. He has two grown-up daughters and a little boy, just four years old, and yesterday in hospital the boy died. First, he had a sore throat. The GP said he'd be over right away, but it was evening before he showed, and then he says right off: hospital, suspected diphtheria. The boy lay there for four weeks, he was on the mend, but then he caught scarlet fever. And yesterday, after two days, he passed, the hospital doctor said it was heart failure.

The man is standing in front of the house, up inside his wife will be shouting and carrying on like she was yesterday and all night, and blaming him for not taking the boy out of hospital three days ago when he was better. But the nurses said he's still infectious, and it's a risk to allow children home in that condition. His wife didn't agree right off the bat, but there was a chance that something might have happened to him, like with the other children. He stands there. They are yelling next door. Suddenly he remembers them asking him in hospital when he brought the boy in, if he had

had an injection with the serum. No, he hadn't. He waited around all day for the GP, then it was evening, and he said: hurry, no time to lose.

And straight away the man gets going with his war limp, crosses the main road, walks up to the corner, to the doctor, who apparently isn't in. But he starts yelling, it's morning, the doctor's got to be in. The surgery door opens. The bald, portly doctor looks at him, pulls him inside. The man stands there, tells him about the hospital, the boy is dead, the doctor clasps him by the hand.

'You kept us waiting the whole of Wednesday, from early till six at night. We sent for you twice. You didn't come.' 'Of course I came.' The man starts yelling again: 'I'm a war cripple, we gave our blood in the trenches, and now we're at the back of the queue, you think you can do what you like with us.' 'Sit down, sir, calm yourself. Your child didn't die of diphtheria. Cross-infections in hospital are a fact of life.' 'Fact of life, sure,' he goes on yelling. 'But we're left waiting, we're last in line. It's fine for our children to die, same as it was fine for us to die.'

After half an hour he walks slowly down the steps, takes a turn in the sun outside, and goes home. His wife is busy in the kitchen. 'Well, Paul?' 'Well, ma'am.' They clasp hands, and their heads sink. 'You've not had anything to eat yet, Paul. I'll get you something right away.' 'I was at the doctor's, told him he didn't come on Wednesday. I told him.' 'But our little Pauly didn't die from the diphtheria.' 'Never mind that. I told him and all. If he'd had the injection right away, then he wouldn't have had to have gone to hospital even. Not at all. But he never showed. I told him. He needs to think about other people in that position in the future. It can happen any day, who knows.' 'Well, better eat your dinner now. What did the doctor say?' 'Oh, he's all right. He's not as young as he was, and he's got a lot on his plate. I know. But if something goes wrong, it goes wrong. He give me a glass of cognac and told me to calm myself. And his wife came in and all.' 'Were you shouting, Paul?' 'No, not a bit of it, just to begin with, then it all passed off very quietly. He admitted it himself: he needs to be told. He's not a bad man, but he needs to be told.'

He's trembling violently while he eats. His wife is crying next door, then they both drink their coffee together by the stove. 'Proper coffee, Paul.' He sniffs at the cup: 'Yup, I can smell it.'

Tomorrow in the chill tomb, no, we'll keep our composure

Franz Biberkopf has disappeared. The afternoon of the day he gets the note, Lina goes up to see him in his room. She wants to leave him a brown sleeveless jumper she's knitted him. And then the man's home, when usually he's out selling, specially now with Christmas coming up, he's sitting on his bed, with the alarm clock in pieces on the table in front of him, fooling around with the pieces. It's a shock to find him home at all, and he might have spotted the jumper, but he hardly seems to notice her, just keeps staring at the table and his clock. She's not unhappy about that, because it means she can leave the jumper by the door. But he's hardly speaking, what's up with him, has he got a hangover, and what's that expression on his face, I'd hardly know it was him, fooling around with that ruddy clock, he must be stewed. 'What are you doing, Franz, it was a good clock.' 'Nah, it wasn't, it don't go off properly, it just makes this rattle stead of ringing, I'll sort it out, don't worry.' And he goes back to his fooling around, and then he leaves it alone, and just picks his teeth and doesn't even look at her. At that she leaves, she feels a bit scared, maybe he needs a proper rest or something. Then when she comes back in the evening, he's gone. He's paid the rent, packed his stuff and gone. All the landlady knows is that he's paid up, and she's to write on his registration form: gone, whereabouts unknown. Probably needed to do one, I suppose?

Then there were twenty-four grim hours before Lina finally caught up with Gottlieb Mack, who can help. He wasn't easy to find either, she spent all afternoon running from one pub to the next, finally she runs him to ground. He doesn't know about anything, what will have happened to Franz, he's a strong boy, and he's savvy, it's normal for him to disappear once in a while. Is he in some kind of pickle? No chance of that, not with Franz. Did they have a tiff, then, him and Lina. Not a bit of it, how could you think that, I was just taking him his new jumper. Mack agrees to go along to Franz's landlady the next day at noon, Lina keeps nagging at him. Yes, Biberkopf moved out in a hurry, there was something amiss, the man was always so chirpy, as recently as that morning, something must have got to him, she's quite adamant about that; he moved out, taking every last scrap of his, you can see for yourselves. Then Mack tells Lina to keep calm, he will look into this. He thinks about it, and straight away as an old trader he has a hunch, and he goes and he looks up Lüders. Lüders is at home with his kids: hey, where's Franz got to? Well, he says sullenly, he's gone and stood him up, he even owes him this and that, coz Franz forgot to settle with him. This Mack absolutely does not believe, but the conversation goes on for over an hour, and there's nothing more to be got out of the man. And then in the evening they catch up with him, Mack and Lina do, in the pub opposite. And that's when things come to a head.

Lina is crying and carrying on. Oh, doesn't he know where Franz has got to, surely he must know, they were together only that morning, Franz will have said something to him, just a word. 'No, that's just it, he didn't say nothink.' 'But then something must have happened to him?' 'To him? He will have slung his hook, that's what.' No, he's not in trouble, Lina won't be persuaded otherwise, he's not done anything, she'd swear blind, they should maybe go and ask at the police station. 'You're saying you think he might have got lost, and they're to do a missing person number on him.' Lüders laughs. The wretchedness of the fat little lady. 'What shall we do, what are we going to do?' Till Mack, who sits there keeping himself to himself, has had enough, and he winks at Lüders. He wants a tête-à-tête with him, all this is doing no good. Lüders steps out with him. In seemingly innocent conversation, they walk up Ramlerstrasse as far as Grenzstrasse.

And there, where it's pitch-black, Mack suddenly lays into little Lüders. He give him a terrible beating. As Lüders was lying on the ground howling, Mack pulled the handkerchief out of his pocket and stuffed it in his mouth. Then he stood him up again, and showed the little man his shiv. They were both of them out of breath. Then Mack, who wasn't back to normal yet, advised him to get on his bike and start looking for Franz. 'I don't know how you find him. But if you don't find him, there'll be three of us looking for you. And we'll find you, sunshine, never you worry. Even if you're with your old lady.'

The next evening, pale and quiet little Lüders followed a nod from Mack to step into the parlour next door. It took a while before the landlord got the gas lit for them. Then they stood there. Mack said: 'Well, you bin there?' Lüders nodded. 'See. Well?' 'There's no well.' 'What did he say, then, how can you prove you even saw him.' 'You're imagining he would have beaten me up, Mack, like what you did. No, I was ready and waiting.' 'So what happened?'

Lüders came even closer: 'Listen to me, Mack. I want to tell you that if Franz is your friend, it's not right the way you talked to me yesterday. That was aggravated assault. When there's no bad blood between us or nuffink. Not over that.'

Mack was staring at him expressionlessly, he was cruising for another one, and then there's no knowing what will happen. 'He's crazy! Haven't you ever noticed that, Mack? No lights on upstairs.' 'Now that's enough of that. He's my friend, all right, and I've got itchy fingers.' Then Lüders tells him, and Mack listens.

He had seen Franz between five and six; he was living very near his old digs, only two or three houses further on, the neighbours had seen him go up carrying a pair of boots and his box of gear, and he was in a room in the back building. When Lüders knocked on the door and walked in, there's Franz lying on the bed with his feet hanging off the end in their boots. He recognizes Lüders all right, there's a little flicker of something, that's Lüders, there's the rascal, but what's up with him, Lüders has a blade in his left pocket, where his hand is too. In his right he's got some money, a few marks, and he puts them on the table, starts talking, turns this way and that, his voice is hoarse, he shows Franz the lumps he got from Mack, his cauliflower ears, he's practically weeping with rage.

Biberkopf sits up in bed, sometimes his face looks all hard, sometimes there are little bunches of movement in it. He points to the door and softly says: 'Get out!' Lüders has put down a few marks, thought about Mack and how he would be waiting for him, and begs Franz for a note to confirm he'd been there, or else permission for Mack or Lina to come up. At that Biberkopf gets up out of bed, straight away Lüders has oiled over to the door, and is all ready, gripping the doorknob. But then Biberkopf walks to the washstand at the back of the room, takes the basin and – what about this then – slings the water across the room at Lüders's feet. For dust thou art, and unto dust shalt thou return. Lüders stares at him, moves aside, turns the doorknob. Biberkopf picks up the ewer, which has water in it as well, plenty more where that came from, we're going to clean up this mess, for dust thou art. He hurls it against the door, and Lüders can feel it splatter against his mouth and throat, icy water. Lüders slips out and is gone, the door is shut behind him.

In the bar room he hisses: 'He's insane, can't you see that, that's all there is to it.' Mack asked him: 'OK, what's the number? What name?'

Subsequently Biberkopf continued throwing water around his room. He flung it through the air: everything must be cleansed, everything must be purified; now open the window and blow; all this is nothing to do with us. (No collapsing buildings, no roofs sliding off, that's in the past, once and for all in the past.) When it started to get cold by the window, he stared at the floor. Should mop it up really, it'll drip on the people below, stain the ceiling. Shut the window, lay down flat on the bed. (Dead. For dust thou art, and unto dust shalt thou return.)

Clap clap clap with his hands, trap trap trap with his feet.

That evening found Biberkopf no longer up in his eyrie. Mack was not able to establish where he had moved to. He took little Lüders, who was sullen and obstinate, with him to his pub with the drovers. Let them ask Lüders what had happened and what the story was about the note the publican had kept for him. Lüders remained obstinate, he looked so twisted that finally they let him go. Mack himself said: 'He's had enough punishment.'

Mack speculated: either Lina had cheated on Franz, or he was angry with Lüders, or it was something else. The drovers said: 'That Lüders is a louse, there's not a word of truth in what he says. Maybe Biberkopf is short of a few. He did behave strangely, come to think of it, like his tradesman's licence when he didn't even have any goods for sale. When there's trouble, such traits might be apt to come to the fore.' Mack was unshaken: 'Well, I can see it might affect a man's gall bladder, but not his brain. Brain is out of the question. He's an athlete, a labourer, he was a first-rate furniture-removal man, pianers and what not, his brain wouldn't be affected.' 'He's exactly the type whose brain would be affected. It's sensitive. The brain gets too little to do, and if there's a call, it's overtaxed.' 'Well, and what about you and your court cases? You're all healthy, I suppose.' 'A drover has a hard shell. See. If they wanted to get het up about something, they could all get checked into Herzberge. We don't get excited. Order goods and then not come through or try and stiff you, we get that every day. We know people are short of money.' 'Or they don't have cash to hand.' 'Sure.'

One drover looked down at his soiled jumper: 'You know, when I'm home I like to drink my coffee out of a saucer, it tastes better that way, but it do make a mess.' 'You need to wear a napkin.' 'Yeah, and make my old lady laugh. No, it's my hands getting shaky, see this.'

Mack and Lina don't find Franz Biberkopf. They go looking for him through half the city, without success.

Chapter Four

Franz Biberkopf was not really struck by misfortune. The ordinary reader will be surprised, and ask: so what was it? But Franz Biberkopf is no ordinary reader. He thinks his orientation, in all its simplicity, must be mistaken in some way. He doesn't know how, but the mere fact of it digs him into a deep pit.

You will see the man turn to drink and almost lose himself. But that's not enough, Franz Biberkopf is reserved for a still harder fate.

A handful of people round the Alex

On Alexanderplatz they're tearing up the road for the underground railway. People are made to walk on duckboards. The trams cross the square and head up Alexander- and Münzstrasse to get to Rosenthaler Tor. There are streets on either side. In the streets, there's one house after another. They are full of people, from cellar to attic. On the ground floor are usually shops and businesses. Bars and restaurants, greengrocers and grocers, delicatessens and haulage businesses, painters and decorators, ladies' outfitters, flour and grain products, garages, insurance: the advantages of the fuel injection engine are simple design, ease of use, light weight, no clutter. – My fellow-Germans, never has a people been more shamefully deceived, more shamefully, wickedly cheated than the German people. Do you remember Scheidemann on the Reichstag balcony on 9 November 1918 promising us peace, freedom and bread? What happened to those promises! – Plumbing goods, window cleaners, sleep is medicine, Steiner's paradisal bed. – Bookshop, the contemporary library, our collected editions of the works of leading writers and thinkers together make up the contemporary library. Here are the great representatives of the European mind. – The tenancy protection law isn't worth the paper it's written on. Rents are going up all the time. The middle class are finding themselves out on the street, bailiffs and debt collectors are making hay. We demand state-guaranteed credits up to 15,000 marks, with immediate cessation to all closures of small businesses. – To approach the critical hour well prepared is the duty and desire of all women. All the thoughts and feelings of the mother-to-be are concentrated on her unborn. Hence her choice of beverage is of particular importance. Engelhardt's authentic caramel malt beer combines like no other the attributes of flavour, nutrition, wholesomeness and refreshment. – Provide for your future and family by taking out a life insurance policy with a leading Swiss insurance firm, the Zurich Rentenanstalt. – Your heart laughs! Your heart laughs for joy when you own a home furnished with celebrated Höffner furniture. Everything you dreamt of in terms of amenity will be outdone by the blissful reality. Years can go by, but the sight will continually cheer your eyes, and its durability and practical design will continue to delight you.

Private security companies look after everything, they do their rounds, punch clocks, keep time, alarm premises, Guardians and Security for Greater Berlin and beyond, Watch and Protection Services Gross-Berlin, Germania Round the Clock, and the one-time security section of the Economic Association of the Society of Berlin Property Owners and Landlords, now reincorporated as Western Security, Watch and Protection Company, the Sherlock Group, Sherlock Holmes collected works of Arthur Conan-Doyle, Watching Company for Berlin and Environs, Wachsmann the educator, Flachsmann the educator, washeteria, Apollo custom wash, Adler Laundry, handles all household and personal linens, specializing in ladies' and gentlemen's delicates.

Above and behind the commercial premises are apartments, and behind them are more courtyards, side buildings, cross-buildings, back-buildings, garden-buildings. Linienstrasse, that's where the building is where Franz Biberkopf took refuge after the schlimazel with Lüders.

At the front is a fine shoe shop, with four gleaming windows, and six girls to serve the customers when there are any customers to serve; they make 80 marks per month each, and if things go well and they grow old in the job, then they might make 100. The business belongs to an old lady who married her store manager, and since then she has been sleeping behind the shop, and regretting it. He's a good-looking fellow, he's made her business bloom, but he's not yet forty, and that's the bane of it, and when he gets in late, then the old lady is still awake, and too angry to sleep. – On the first floor is a solicitor. Is the wild hare to be included in the list of beasts for hunting in the Duchy of Saxony-Altenburg or not? The defence wrongly contests the District Court's assumption that the wild hare in the Duchy of Saxony-Altenburg is included among huntable animals. Which animals are huntable and which are subject to hunting without licence has evolved differently in the different states of Germany. In the absence of legislation, the matter is usually left to local custom and practice. There is no reference to the wild hare in the Game Control Bill of 24 February 1854. – At six in the evening a cleaning lady comes into the office, swabs the linoleum in the waiting room. The solicitor has not yet run to a vacuum cleaner, miserly git, when the man's not even married and Frau Zieske, who calls herself housekeeper, would know. The cleaning lady scrubs and scours away, she is incredibly thin but supple, she works to feed her two children. The role of fat in nutrition, fat covers jutting bones and protects the sensitive tissue below from pressure and impact, excessively thin persons may complain of pains in their footsoles when walking. That at least wasn't the case with the cleaning lady.

At seven in the evening the solicitor Löwenhund is sitting at his desk with two lamps, working. For once, the telephone is quiet. In the case of Gross A 8 780 27, I enclose the power of attorney given me by the accused Frau Gross. I would like authorization to enter into direct communication with the accused. – To Frau Eugenie Gross, Berlin. Dear Frau Gross, a further visit on my part is overdue. I'm afraid pressure of work and ill health have precluded me from doing so. I hope to find time for you next Wednesday, and would ask you to remain patient till then. Respectfully, Löwenhund. Letters, moneys and parcels are to be addressed to the prisoner by name and number (name alone is not sufficient). The street address is Berlin NW 52, Moabit 12 a.

To Herr Tollmann. In the case relating to your daughter, I must request payment of a further 200 marks. Instalments are acceptable. Secondly, resubmit. – Dear Solicitor, I want to visit my poor daughter in Moabit, but have no idea how to go about it, can you find out for me when such a visit would be possible. At the same time, I want to lodge a petition with the authorities: I'd like to send her a fortnightly food parcel. Hoping for a prompt reply, ideally end of this week or early next. Frau Tollmann (mother of Eugenie Gross). – Solicitor Löwenhund gets up, cigar in mouth, peers through the chink in the curtains at the brightly lit Linienstrasse and thinks, do I call her or do I not call her. Sexually transmitted diseases as consequence of personal negligence. Superior District Court, Frankfurt 1, C5. One may feel less strongly about the morality of sexual congress with unmarried men, while still admitting that in point of law there is blame involved, that extramarital congress, as Staub argues, is an extravagance associated with risks, and that the risks must be borne by the extravagant party. Also Planck, in the spirit of this decision, sees illness stemming from extramarital intercourse as a form of gross negligence. – He picks up the telephone, Neukölln exchange, please, ah, the number has been reassigned to Bärwald.

Second floor: the janitor and two fat couples, the brother and his wife, the sister and her husband, and there's an invalid girl as well.

Third floor a furniture polisher, sixty-four, widower, bald. His daughter, divorced, keeps house for him. Every morning he clatters down the steps, he has a dickey heart, and will soon go on invalidity benefit (arteriosclerosis, myodegeneratio cordis). Back in the day he used to row, what can he do now? Read his paper in the evening, light his pipe, while his daughter gossips on the landing. His wife passed away at forty-five, she was energetic and splenetic, could never get enough, you know, and then whoops-a-daisy, never breathed a word, the next year she might have had her menopause, went to get it taken care of by one of those women, and then hospital, where she pops her clogs.

Next door is an engineer, thirty-odd, has a little boy, sitting room and kitchen, his wife has gone on too, phthisis, he's coughing too, the boy is in a crèche by day, at night the man takes him home. Once he's put him to bed, the man brews up his infusions, tinkers with radio sets till late, he's a ham radio enthusiast, he can't sleep without fiddling with his circuits.

Then there's a waiter with a woman, parlour and kitchen, all piccobello, gas chandelier with glass pendants. He's home till two in the afternoon, either asleep or playing his zither, at the same time as Master Löwenhund is in District Courts 1, 2, 3, running around the corridors in his black gown, out of the lawyers' room, into the lawyers' room, into the courtroom, out of the courtroom, the case is adjourned, I apply for a judgment by default against the accused. The waiter's girlfriend is supervisor in a department store. Or so she says. When he was married, his wife cheated on him mercilessly. But she was always able to reassure him, until one day he finally walked out. He was nothing more than a bedfellow, kept running back to his wife, and when the thing came to court, because he had no evidence against her, he was found to be the one guilty of desertion. He met his present companion in Hoppegarten, where she was on the prowl. The same type as his first, naturally, only a little bit more cunning. He doesn't smell a rat when she leaves every other day for her so-called business, since when does a supervisor have to go on the road, well, it is an unusually responsible position. But now he's sitting on his sofa with a damp towel round his head, crying, and she has to look after him. He slipped on the pavement and couldn't get up. Or so he says. Someone tipped him off. There is no so-called business. Wonder if he suspected something, that would be a pity, he's such a good-natured idiot. It'll sort itself out.

Right at the top of the house there's a tripe butcher, which of course means stink and alcohol and lots of squalling children. Next door to that is a baker's apprentice with his wife, who works in a print shop. She has an ovarian cyst. What does life have to offer the two of them? Well, first they have each other, then last Sunday there was music hall and cinema, then various club meetings and visits to the in-laws. Is that it? Now, sir, don't be giving yourself airs. Throw in the weather, fair or foul, trips to the countryside, warming up by the stove, breakfast together, so on and so forth. What have you got that's so special, Captain, General, Jockey? Don't kid yourself.

Biberkopf anaesthetized, Franz curls up,
Franz doesn't want to see anything

Watch yourself, Franz Biberkopf, you boozehound! Lying around in your room, nothing but sleeping and drinking and more sleeping! Who cares what I get up to. If I feel like it, I can sleep in all day and not get up. – He chews his nails, groans, tosses his head from side to side on the sweaty pillow, blows his nose. – I can lie here till Doomsday if I like. If only the facking landlady would turn on the heat. Lazy cow, only thinks of herself. His head turns away from the wall, on the floor by the bed is gruel, a puddle. – Spew. Must of been me. Stuff a man carries around in his stomach. Yuck. Spiders' webs in the corners, you could catch mice in them. I want a drink of water. Who gives a shit. My back hurts. Come on in, Frau Schmidt. Between the spiders' webs at the top of the picture (black dress, long in the tooth). She's a witch (coming out of the ceiling like that). Yuck. Some idiot asked me why I'm hanging around in my room. In the first place, idiot, I say, who are you, secondly when I stay here from eight till noon. And then in this stinky room. He says he was joking. That wasn't a joke. Kaufmann said I might apply to him. Maybe I will and all, in February, February or March, March feels about right.

Did you lose your heart in nature? No, I didn't, not there. When I stood facing the Alpine massif or lay by the shore of the foaming ocean I had the feeling that the primal spirit wanted to tear me away. I felt swayed and buffeted in my bones. My heart was shaken, but I never lost it, neither where the eagle nests, nor where the miner tunnels for hidden veins of ore in the bowels of the earth.

Then where?

Did you lose your heart in sport? In the rushing stream of the youth movement? In the skirmishings of politics?

I didn't lose it there.

Have you not lost it anywhere?

Are you one of those who lose their hearts nowhere, but keep it for themselves, nicely conserved and mummified?

The road to the world beyond the senses, public lectures, All Saints' Day: Is Death Really the End? Monday, 21 November, 8 p.m.: Is Faith Still Possible? Tuesday, 22 November: Can Man Change? Wednesday, 23 November: Who Is Just Before God? We draw special attention to the sermon on 'St Paul'.

On Sunday, the slightly earlier time of 7.45.

Evening, Your Reverence. I'm the labourer Franz Biberkopf. Casual labourer, truth to tell. I used to work as a removal man, presently unemployed. I wanted to ask you something. What can be done about stomach pains. I'm a martyr to acid reflux, Ooh, there it is again. Yuck. Bitter gall. It's from the drink, I'm sure. Forgive me for accosting you on the public street. I know I'm keeping you from work. But what can I do about my gall bladder. Isn't a Christian duty-bound to help his fellow-man. You're a good man. I won't get to Heaven. Why? You ask Frau Schmidt who keeps popping out of the ceiling. She's in and out, and she's forever telling me to get up. But no one tells me what to do. If there are criminals, though, then I know all about them. Honour bright. We swore to Karl Liebknecht, we hold out our hands to Rosa Luxemburg. I'll go to paradise when I'm gone, and people will bow when I pass, and say, look, there goes faithful Franz Biberkopf, raise high the flag, the black and white and red, but he kept it to himself, he didn't turn to crime, not like some other fellows who claim to be good Germans and cheat their fellow-citizens. If I'd had a knife, I'd a stabbed him in the belly with it. Yes I would. (Franz tosses and turns, thrashes around.) Now it's your turn to run to the preacher man, son. Sonnymylad. If you'd like that, if you can still wheeze out a word, you. In honour true, I'll quit, Your Reverend, it's not worth it, crooks don't even go to prison; I was in prison though, know it like the back of my, first-class establishment, outstanding wares, there's no getting around it, no crooks go in there, least of all no one like him, not even ashamed in front of his wife, as he should be, and the whole world besides.

Two plus two makes four, no getting around that. You see before you a man, sorry to bother you on your way to work, sir, I have such bad stomach pains. I'll learn to control myself. A glass of water, Frau Schmidt. The bitch sticks her nose in everywhere.

Franz, on the retreat, plays a farewell march for the Jews

Franz Biberkopf, strong as a cobra but wobbly on his pins, has got up and gone to the Jews on Münzstrasse. He didn't go the straight way there, he made an almighty detour. The man wants to sort a few things out. The man has issues. So here we go again, Frankie BBK. Dry weather, cold but fresh, who would want to be a street vendor now, standing out in an entryway, and still freezing your tootsies off. In honour true. Good to be out of the room and not have to listen to women squawking. Here comes Frankie Biberkopf down the street somewhere near you. Pubs all empty. How come? The clientele still asleep. The landlords can drink their piss by themselves. Industrial piss. We're not in the mood. We're drinking spirits.

Franz Biberkopf steered his body in grey-green soldier's coat through the crowd, little women standing at stalls buying vegetables, cheese, herring. Someone was flogging onions.

People do their best. Kids at home, hungry mouths, little beaks, open, shut, open, shut, click clack, just like that.

Franz walked faster, stomped round the corner. There, fresh air. He slowed down as he passed the big shoe shops. How much for boots? Patent-leather shoes, dancing pumps, gotta look class; a little lass with dancing pumps on her feet. Dandy Lissarek, once of Bohemia, now of Tegel, the old fellow with the nostrils, he had his wife, or that's what she claimed to be anyway, bring him nice silk stockings every fortnight, one pair new and one pair worn. What a gas. Even if she had to lift them, he had to have em. One time they caught him with them on, queer bugger, ogling his nasty legs and getting his kicks, and the fellow blushed beetroot, what a gas, furniture on the instalment plan, kitchenalia, twelve affordable payments. Biberkopf wandered happily on. Only he had to inspect the pavement every so often. He checked his stride and the firm, well-laid paving stones. But then his regard slid up the front of the buildings, examined the façades, made sure they were standing still and not moving, a building like that must have a shedload of windows, which makes it easy for it to keel over. And that in turn affects the roofs, which can start to sway. They start to sway, and swing and shake. The roofs can slip off at an angle, like sand, like the hat off your head. I mean they're all set up skew on their rooftrees anyway, right the way along a terrace. But they're nailed down, strong beams under them, and then the roofing felt, and the tar. 'Fest steht und treu die Wacht, die Wacht am Rhein', good morning, Herr Biberkopf, we're walking nice and upright today, chest out, back straight, old son, along Brunnenstrasse. God has compassion on all men, we are, as the prison director reminded us, German subjects.

Fellow in a leather cap, white sagging face, picking at a spot on his chin with his pinkie; his mouth hanging open while he does it. A man with a broad back and baggy trouser-seat standing skew next to him, blocking the way. Franz walked around the pair of them. The one with the leather cap now digging in his right ear.

He noted to his satisfaction that people were proceeding calmly along the public thoroughfare, deliverymen were loading and unloading goods, the authorities were looking after the buildings, 'Es braust ein Ruf wie Donnerhall', so it's all right for us to walk here too. A poster pillar on the corner, on yellow paper in black italic script: 'Hast du geliebt am schönen Rhein',[6] 'The Doyen of Centre Forwards'. Five men stood around in a little gaggle, swinging hammers, cracking the asphalt, we know the fellow in the green woollen jacket, deffo, he's got a job, we can do that too, later, grip with your right hand, pull it back over your head, hold hard and down. That's what we are, we the workers, the pro-ho-le-ta-ri-at. Up with the right, join left, smack. Caution, building site, Stralau Asphalting Company.

He wandered around, along the creaking tramline, do not dismount while tram is moving! Wait till vehicle has come to a complete standstill! A policeman is supervising the traffic, a mail guard is in a hurry to get across. Me, I need no excuse, I'm just going to see the Jews. They'll be around later as well. The dirt you get on your boots, but then they're not polished anyway, who's going to clean them for me, not Frau Schmidt for sure (spiders' webs on the ceiling, a sour belch, he sucked at his gums, turned his head to look at the windows: Gargoyle Mobil Oil Vulcanizing, Bubi Unisex Hair Styling, Marcel Wave a speciality, on blue ground, Pixavon, refined tar product). Would Polish Lina agree to polish his boots maybe? He was stepping out a little now.

That cheat Lüders, the woman's note, I'll stick a knife in your guts, see if I don't, o God, don't for heaven's sake, we'll control ourselves, we don't attack people, we've done time in Tegel. Now then: Gentlemen's Suits, Made to Measure, that first, then next Automobile Parts, just as important for speedy driving, but not too speedy.

Right, left, right, left, easy does it, now there, don't barge, miss. Uh-oh, here's the filth. What did the queer policeman say? Cop-a-doodle-do, cop-a-doodle-do. Franz was chipper, the faces all looked friendlier.

He immersed himself happily in the street. A chill wind blew, mixed with the aromas of each respective building, cellar fug, domestic and imported fruit, petrol. Asphalt doesn't smell in winter.

At the Jews' Franz sat on the settee for fully an hour. They spoke, he spoke, he was surprised, they were surprised, for the length of a whole hour. What surprised him sitting on the sofa while they and he spoke? The fact that he was sitting there speaking and them speaking, and above all that he was surprised at himself. Why was he surprised at himself? He knew it and detected it himself, he sensed it as an accountant detects a faulty calculation. He detected something.

It was all resolved, and he was surprised at the degree of resolution he found in himself. The resolution said, all the while he looked them in the eye and smiled and asked questions: Franz Biberkopf, they can say what they like, they're wearing robes, but they're not priests, it's called kaftan, they're from Galicia, around Lemberg as they told me, they're clever, but they're not fooling me. I'm sitting on the sofa here, and I'm not doing any trades with them. I've done what I can.

The last time he was here, he had sat down on the rug with one of them. Wheesh, you slide down, I could try that. But not today, those times are gone. We're sitting in our trews, staring at the Jews.

A man can't do any more, he's not a machine after all. The Eleventh Commandment goes: and don't stand for any bullshit. The brothers have a nice pad, simple, tasteless, nothing fancy, The y don't impress Franz, Fi and to well in control of himself. All that's in the past. To bed, to bed, you've got a woman, you've got none, you go to bed anyway. No more working. That's all a man can do. If the pump's choked with sand, it doesn't matter what you do, it won't work any more. Franz is drawing retirement pay without a pension. How does that work, he thinks subtly, looking along the edge of the sofa, retirement pay without pension.

'And if you have strength as you, such a well-built man, then you should thank your Creator. What can happen to you? Do you need a drink? You do this, you do that. You go to the market, you stand in front of the shops, you go to the railway station: what do you think someone like that took off me just the other day when I was arriving from Landsberg the other week, how much do you think he took off me. You have a guess, Nahum, a man as big as a door, a Goliath, may God protect me. Fifty pfennigs. That's right, fifty pfennigs. Just for a little case, from here to the corner. It was the Sabbath, I didn't want to carry it. The man takes me for fifty pfennigs. I looked at him. Well, you can also – you know, I know what I mean. Feitel the grain merchant, you know Feitel.' 'Not Feitel, I know his brother.' 'Well, you know he's in grain. Who's his brother?' 'Feitel's brother. Nuff said.' 'Do I know everyone in the whole of Berlin?' 'Feitel's brother. A man with an income like . . .'

His head waggled from side to side in helpless admiration. The red-haired one raised his arm, lowered his head. 'Take your word for it. But from Czernowitz.' They'd forgotten all about Franz. They were both intent on Feitel's brother's fortune. The red-headed one went around in some agitation, making gurgling noises through his nose. The other purred, emanated satisfaction, smiled mischievously at the other's back, picked at his nails. 'Huh. The things you tell me. Wonderful.' 'Whatever the family does turns to gold. Not a manner of speaking. Gold.' The redhead wandered around, finally sat down shattered beside the window. What was going on outside filled him with contempt, two men in shirtsleeves washing a car, an old jalopy. One had his braces down, they were lugging buckets of water, the yard was half underwater. With his thoughtful expression, dreaming of gold, he looked at Franz: 'What do you say to that?' What can he say, he's a poor sap, half crazed, what does someone like that know about the wealth of Feitel from Czernowitz; he wouldn't let him wipe his shoes. Franz looked back at him. Good morning, Your Reverence, the trams always go jangling past, but we know what made the bell go, no man can do more than he can. There'll be no more work, even if all the snow catches fire, we won't lift a finger, we're obstinate.

The snake rustled from the tree. Thou art cursed above all cattle, and above every beast of the field; upon thy belly shalt thou go, and dust shalt thou eat all the days of thy life. And I will put enmity between thee and the woman. In sorrow thou shalt bring forth children, Eve. Adam, cursed is the ground for thy sake; in sorrow shalt thou eat of it all the days of thy life; thorns also and thistles shall it bring forth to thee; and thou shalt eat the herbs of the field.

We're not working any more, it's not worth a candle, and if all the snow should burn, we won't lift a finger.

That was the first iron crowbar Franz Biberkopf got to hold in his hands, with which he sat, and later passed through the door. His mouth said something or other. He had been brought here reluctantly, he had been released from Tegel prison some months before, he had ridden on the tram, whoosh along the streets, past the buildings, the roofs were sliding off, he had sat with the Jews. He stood up, let's go on, back then I went to see Minna, what am I doing here, let's go to Minna, let's take a good look at everything and how it all came about.

He pushed off. He wandered around in front of Minna's house. Mariechen sitting on a stone, all alone, no bone. What do I care. He snuffled round the house. What do I care. Let her be happy with her old man. Sauerkraut and beet, chased me away, if my mother had cooked meat, I'd have been happy to stay. The cats here stink the same way they do elsewhere. Little bunny, disappear, hide the sausage in your ear. I'll stand around here and boggle at the house. And the whole company goes kikeriki.

Kikeriki, kikeriki. Thus spake Menelaus. And without intending to, he made Telemachus' heart so mournful that the tears coursed down his cheeks and he gripped the purple robes in both hands and pressed them to his eyes.

Meanwhile Helen wandered out from her women's apartments, like unto a goddess in beauty.

Kikeriki. There are many types of chicken. If you ask me which my favourite is, cross my heart, etc., then I will say right out and unhesitatingly: the fried. Pheasants also belong in the chicken family, and in Brehm's *Life of Animals* it is written: the Little Crake is distinguished from Baillon's Crake by its very small size, but also by the fact that in spring, the sexes are almost indistinguishable. Asian experts are also familiar with the Himalayan or King's Monal, called Lophophorus by zoologists. Its colours are so magnificent as to elude description. Its call, a long plaintive wail, may be heard in the forests at any time, but most regularly before dawn and at dusk.

But as its habitat lies in the remote region between Sikkim and Bhutan, this is, as far as Berlin is concerned, a fairly abstruse piece of knowledge.

For as with animals, so it is with man; the one must die, the other likewise

The slaughterhouse in Berlin. The various structures, halls and pens are bounded in the north-east of the city, from Eldenaer Strasse, taking in Thaerstrasse and Landsberger Allee as far as Cothenius Strasse, along the ring road.

It covers an area of 47.88 hectares, or 187.5 acres. Not counting the buildings on the other side of Landsberger Allee it cost 27,093,492 marks to build, with the cattleyard accounting for 7,682,844 marks, and the slaughterhouse 19,410,648 marks.

Cattleyard, slaughterhouse and wholesale meat market make up one fully integrated economic entity. The administration is in the hands of the committee for stockyards and slaughterhouses, comprising two city officials, a member of the District Board, eleven councillors and three members of the public. It employs 258 officials, including vets, inspectors, stampers, assistant vets, assistant inspectors, clerical staff and maintenance workers. Traffic ordinance of 4 October 1900, general regulations governing the driving of cattle and the supply of feed. Tariff of fees: market fees, boxing fees, slaughtering fees, fees for the removal of feed troughs from the pork market hall.

Eldenaer Strasse is lined by dirty grey walls with barbed wire on top. The trees outside are bare, it is winter, they have secreted their sap in their roots and are waiting for spring. Butchers' carts draw up at a steady clip, yellow and red wheels, light horses. Behind one runs a skinny horse, from the pavement someone calls out, hey, Emil, what about the horse, 50 marks and a round for the eight of us, the horse goes a little crazy, trembles, nibbles one of the trees, the coachman tears it away, 50 marks and a round, Otto, else we go. The man smacks the horse on the cruppers: deal.

Yellow administration buildings, an obelisk for the war dead. And either side of that long halls with glass roofs, these are the pens, the waiting rooms. Outside notice boards: Property of the Association of Wholesale Butchers Berlin, Ltd. Post no bills: special permission only, the Board.

The long halls are fitted with numbered doors, 26, 27, 28, black openings for the animals to enter through. The cattle building, the pig building, the slaughter halls: courts of justice for the beasts, swinging axes, you won't leave here alive. Peaceful adjacent streets, Strassmann-, Liebig-, Proskauer Strasse, parks where people stroll. Close-knit communities, if someone here has a sore throat, the doctor will come running.

But on the other side, the rails of the circular railway extend for ten miles. The beasts are brought in from the provinces, ovine, bovine, porcine specimens from East Prussia, Pomerania, Brandenburg, West Prussia. They come mooing and bleating down the ramps. The pigs grunt and snuffle, they can't look where they're going, the drovers are after them, swinging sticks. They lie down in their pens, tight together, white, fat, snoring, sleeping. They have been made to walk a long way, then shaken up in rail cars, now the ground under their feet is steady, only the flagstones are cold, they wake up, seek each other's warmth. They are laid out in levels. Here's two fighting, the bay leaves them enough room for that, they butt heads, snap at each other's throats, turn in circles, gurgle, sometimes they are completely silent, gnashing in fear. In panic one scrambles over the bodies of the others, and the other gives chase, snaps, and those below start up, the two combatants fall, seek each other out.

A man in a canvas coat wanders through the passage, the bay is opened, he parts the combatants with a stick, the door is open, they push out, squealing, and a grunting and screaming begins. The funny white beasts are driven across courtyards, between halls, the droll little thighs, the funny curly tails, red and green scribbles on their backs. There is light, dear piggies, there is the floor, snuffle away at it, look for the few minutes that are left to you. No, you're right, we shouldn't work by the clock, snuffle and rootle to your heart's content. You will be slaughtered here, take a look at the slaughterhouse, it's for you. There are old abattoirs, but you are entering a new model. It's light, built of red brick, from the outside one might have guessed engineering works, shop or office premises, or a construction hall. I'll be going the other way, dear little piggies, because I'm a human, I'll be going through this door here, but we'll see each other soon enough.

Shoulder the door open, it's a swing door, on a spring. Whew, the steam in here. What are they steaming? It's like a Turkish bath, maybe that's what the pigs are here for. You're going somewhere, you can't see where, your glasses are misted over, perhaps you're naked, you're sweating out your rheumatism, cognac alone doesn't do the trick you know, you're shuffling along in your slippers. The steam is too thick, you can't see a sausage. Just squealing and gurgling and clattering, shouts, clatter of equipment, lids banging down. The pigs must be somewhere in here, they made a separate entrance. The dense white steam. There are the pigs, some are hanging up, they're already dead, they've been topped, they look almost ready to eat. There's a man with a hose, washing down the white split carcasses. They're hanging on iron stands, head down, some of the pigs are whole, their forelegs are in a wooden stock, a dead animal can't get up to any mischief, it can't even run away. Pigs' feet lie there in a pile, chopped off. Two men emerge from the fog carrying something, it's a cleaned opened animal on an iron spreader. They fasten the spreader to a hoist. Lots of their fellows come trundling along after, staring dully at the tiled floor.

You walk through the hall in fog. The stone flags are grooved, damp, and also bloodied. Between the stands the ranks of white, disembowelled animals. The killing bays must be at the back, it's from there you hear smacking sounds, crashing, squealing, screaming, gurgling, grunting sounds. There are big cauldrons there, which produce the steam. Men dunk the dead beasts in the boiling water, scald them, pull them out nice and white, a man scrapes off the outer skin with a knife, making the animal still whiter and very smooth. Very mild and white, deeply contented as after a strenuous bath, a successful operation or massage, the pigs lie out on wooden trestles in rows, they don't move in their sated calm, and in their new white tunics. They are all lying on their sides, on some you see the double row of tits, the number of breasts a sow has, they must be fertile animals. But they all of them have a straight red slash across the throat, right in the middle, which looks deeply suspicious.

More smacking sounds, a door is opened at the back, the steam clears, they drive in a new collection of pigs, running in, I've left through the sliding door at the front, funny pink animals, funny thighs, curly-wurly tails, the backs with coloured scribbles. And they're snuffling in this new bay. It's cold like the last one was, but there is something wet on the floor that they're unfamiliar with, something red and slippery. They rub their muzzles in it.

A pale young man with fair hair plastered to his head, a cigar in his mouth. Look at him, he will be the last human with whom you will have dealings! Don't think badly of him, he is only doing his job. He has official business with you. He is wearing rubber boots, trousers, shirt and braces. That's his official garb. He takes the cigar out of his mouth, lays it aside on a bracket in the wall, picks up a long-handled axe that was lying in the corner. This is the sign of his official rank, his power over you, like the detective's badge. He will produce his for you any moment now. There is a long wooden pole that the young man will raise to shoulder height over the little squealers who are contentedly snuffling and grunting and truffling. The man walks around, eyes lowered, looking, looking. There is a criminal investigation against a certain party, a certain party in the case of X versus Y – bamm! One ran in front of him, bamm, another one. The man is nimble, he has proved his authority, the axe has crashed down, dipped into the seething mob, with its blunt side against a skull, another skull. It's the work of a moment. Something continues to scrabble about on the floor. Treads water. Throws itself to the side. Knows no more. And lies there. The legs are busy, the head. But it's none of the pig's doing, it's the legs in their private capacity. Already a couple of men have looked across from the scalding room, it's time, they lift a slide to the killing bay, drag the animal out, whet the long blade on a stick, kneel down and shove it into its throat, then *skkrrk* a long cut, a very long cut across the throat, the animal is ripped open like a sack, deep, sawing cuts, it jerks, kicks, lashes out, it's unconscious, no more than unconscious, now more than unconscious, it squeals, and now the arteries in the throat are open. It is deeply unconscious, we are in the area of metaphysics now, of theology, my child, you no longer walk upon the earth, now we are wandering on clouds. Hurriedly bring up the shallow pan, the hot black blood streams into it, froths, makes bubbles, quickly, stir it. Within the body blood congeals, its purpose is to make obstructions, to dam up wounds. It's left the body, but it still wants to congeal. Just as a child on the operating table will go Mama, Mama, when Mama is nowhere around and it's going under in its ether mask, it keeps on going Mama till it is incapable of calling any more. Skkrrik, skkrrak, the arteries to left and right. Quickly stir. There, now the quivering stops. Now you're lying there pacified. We have come to the end of physiology and theology, this is where physics begins.

The man gets up off his knees. His knees hurt. The pig needs to be scalded, cleaned and dressed, that will happen blow by blow. The boss, feisty and well fed, walks around in the steam, with his pipe in his mouth, taking an occasional gander at an opened belly. On the wall by the swing doors hangs a poster: Gathering of Animal Shippers, Saalbau, Friedrichshain, Music: the Kermbach Boys. Outside are announcements for boxing matches. Germaniasäle, Chausseestrasse 110, tickets 1.50 to 10 marks. Four bouts on each bill.

Today's market numbers: 1,399 cattle, 2,700 calves, 4,654 sheep, 18,864 pigs. Market notes: prime cattle good, others steady. Calves smooth, sheep steady, pigs firm to begin with, then sluggish, fat pigs slow.

The wind blows through the driveway, and it's raining. Cattle low, men are driving along a large, roaring, horned herd. The animals are obstinate, keep heading off in wrong directions, the drovers run around with their sticks. In the middle of the gathering a bull tries to mount a cow, the cow runs off to left and right, the bull is in pursuit, and repeatedly tries to climb her withers.

A big white steer is driven into the slaughter hall. Here there is no steam, no bay as for the wee-weeing pigs. The big strong steer steps through the gate alone, between its drovers. The bloody hall lies before it, with dangling halves and quarters and chopped bones. The big steer has a wide forehead. It is driven forward to the slaughterer with kicks and blows. To straighten it out, the man gives it a tap on the hind leg with the flat of his axe. Then one of the drovers grabs it round the throat from below. The animal stands there, gives in astonishingly easily, as though it consented and, having seen everything, knows: this is its fate and there is no getting away from it. Possibly it takes the drover's movement for a caress, because it looks so friendly. It follows the pulling arms of the drover, bends its head aside, its muzzle up.

But then the knocker, with hammer upraised, is standing behind it. Don't look round. The hammer, picked up in both hands by the strongly built man, is behind it and above it, and then: wham, crashes down. The muscular strength of a powerful man like an iron wedge in its neck. And at that same moment – the hammer has not yet been taken back – the animal's four legs jerk apart, the whole heavy body seems to lift off. Then, as if it had no legs, the animal, the heavy body, lands with a thud on the floor, on its cramped stiffly protruding legs, lies there for a moment, and keels over onto its side. From right and left the knocker approaches him, gives him another tap on the head, to the temples, sleep, you'll not wake again. Then the fellow next to him takes the cigar out of his mouth, blows his nose, unsheathes his knife, it's as long as half a sword, and drops to his knees behind the animal, whose legs are already uncramping. It jerks in spasms, slings its rump this way and that. The slaughterer is looking for something on the floor, he doesn't apply the knife point, he calls for the bowl for blood. The blood is still circulating sluggishly, little moved by the beating of the mighty heart. The marrow is crushed, but the blood is still flowing through the veins, the lungs are breathing, the intestines moving. Now the knife will be applied, and the blood will jet out, I can picture it, a beam of it thick as my arm, black, lovely, jubilant blood. Then the whole merry crowd will leave the house, the guests will go dancing out, a tumult, and no more lovely meadows, warm shed, fragrant hay, gone, all gone, a void, an empty hole, darkness, here comes a new picture of the world. Wa-hey, a gentleman has come on the scene who has bought the house, a new road, improved economy, and he is having it torn down. They bring the big basin, press it against him, the mighty animal kicks its hind legs up in the air.

The knife is jolted into its throat next to the windpipe, feels for the artery, these arteries are thick and well protected. And then it's open, another one, the flow, hot, streaming blackberry-red, the blood burbles over the knife, over the slaughterman's arm, the ecstatic blood, the hot blood, transformation is at hand, from the sun is come your blood, the sun has been hiding in your body, now look at it come out to play. The animal draws a colossal breath, as though it had been throttled, a colossal irritation, it gurgles, rattles. Yes, the beams are cracking. As the flanks are so terribly aquiver, a man comes to help. When a stone wants to fall, give it a push. The man jumps on the animal, on its body, with both feet, stands on it, balances, steps on the guts, bounces up and down, the blood is to be expelled quicker, all of it. And the gurgling gets louder, it's a long-drawn-out wheezing, with light futile tapping of the hind legs. The legs are waving now. Life is draining away, the breathing is stopping. Heavily the hips turn and slump. That's earth, that's gravity. The man bounces up. The other on the ground is already peeling back the skin from the neck.

Happy meadows, warm fuggy stall.

The well-lit butcher's shop. Shop lighting and exterior lighting must be brought into harmony. Strong light is indicated. In general, direct illumination is appropriate, because the counter and chopping board must be well lit. Artificial daylight, produced by the use of blue filters, is inappropriate for butchers' shops, because meat requires light that will not harm its natural colours.

Filled pigs' feet. After the hooves have been well cleaned out, they are split lengthwise, leaving the rind intact, then folded together and secured with thread.

Franz, it's two weeks now you've been squatting in your wretched attic. Your landlady is about to evict you. You can't pay your rent, and she's not a landlady for the fun of it. Unless you get a grip on yourself, you'll land up in the homeless shelter. And what then. Yes, what then. You don't air your room, you don't go to the barber, you're growing a heavy brown beard, surely you can afford 15 pfennigs for a shave.

Conversation with Job, it's up to you, Job, you don't want to

After Job had lost everything, everything a man can possibly lose, not more and not less, he lay in the cabbage patch.

'Job, you're lying in the cabbage patch, just far enough away from the doghouse for the dog not to bite you. You hear him gnashing his teeth. The dog will bark if you take so much as a single step. If you turn round or make to get up, he will growl, rush at you, rattle his chain, jump out, drool and snap at you.

'Job, there is your palace, and there are the gardens and fields that once were yours. This watchdog was not even known to you, and this cabbage patch where you have been thrown was not even known to you, any more than the goats they drove past you in the mornings that would take a mouthful of grass as they passed, and grind it between their teeth and fill their cheeks with it. They were yours.

'Job, you have lost everything. You are allowed to shelter in the barn at night. Everyone is afraid of your contagion. You once rode in splendour over your estates, and people used to flock around you. Now you've got the wooden fence in front of you, and you can watch the snails creep up it. You can make a study of the earthworms. Those are the only creatures that aren't afraid of you.

'You hardly ever open your crusty eyes, you bundle of misery, you human swamp.

'What is the worst torment, Job? The fact that you lost your sons and daughters, that you own nothing, that you're cold at night, the boils on your throat, on your nose? Tell, Job.'

'Who's asking?'

'I'm just a voice.'

'A voice comes out of a throat.'

'You mean I must be a human being.'

'Yes, and therefore I don't want to see you. Go away.'

'I'm just a voice, Job, open your eyes as far as you can, and then you'll see me.'

'I'm raving. My head, my brains, now I'm being driven mad, now they're taking my thoughts away from me.'

'And if they were, would that matter?'

'I don't want them to.'

'Even though you're suffering so much, and suffering so much by your thoughts, you still don't want to lose them?'

'Don't ask. Go away.'

'But I'm not taking anything. I just want to know which torment is the worst.'

'That's nobody's business.'

'You mean, nobody but you?'

'Yes. Yes. Certainly not yours!'

The dog barks, growls, snaps at the air. The voice returns after a while:

'Is it your sons you are lamenting over?'

'No one need pray for me when I'm dead. I'm poison to the earth. When I am gone, just spit. Forget Job.'

'And your daughters?'

'My daughters. Ah. They're dead too. They're fine. They were pictures of women. They would have given me grandchildren, and they were dashed from me. One after the other was dashed to the ground, as though God had taken her by the hair, and lifted her up and thrown her to the ground, broken.'

'Job, you can't open your eyes, they are gummed shut. You are lamenting because you are in the cabbage patch, and the doghouse is the least thing that is yours, that and your disease.'

'The voice, you voice, whosesoever voice you are, and wherever you are hiding.'

'I don't know why you're lamenting.'

'Oh. Oh.'

'You groan, and you don't know either, Job.'

'No, I have—'

'You have?'

'I have no strength. That's it.'

'So you'd like strength.'

'No strength with which to hope or wish. I have no teeth. I am soft, I feel ashamed.'

'So you say.'

'It's the truth.'

'Yes, you must know. That's the worst.'

'So it's already written on my brow. That's what a rag I am.'

'That's what is causing you the most suffering, Job. You would like not to be weak, you would like to resist, or to be wholly riddled, your brains gone, your thoughts gone, just an animal. Make a wish.'

'You've asked me so many things, voice, I think you must be allowed to ask. Heal me. If you can. Whether your name is Satan or God or angel or man, heal me.'

'Will you accept healing from anyone?'

'Heal me.'

'Job, think carefully. You can't see me. If you open your eyes, perhaps you will be shocked to see me. Perhaps I will charge a great and terrible price.'

'All will be seen. You speak like someone who is serious.'

'What if I am Satan or the Evil One?'

'Heal me.'

'I am Satan.'

'Heal me.'

The voice withdrew, became weaker and ever weaker. The dog barked. Job listened fearfully: he is gone, I must be healed, or I must die. He squawked. A terrible night broke in. The voice came back once more:

'And if I am Satan, how will you deal with me?'

Job screamed: 'You will not heal me. No one will help me, not God, not Satan, and no angel, and no human.'

'And you yourself?'

'What about me?'

'You won't.'

'What.'

'Who can help you when you don't want to help yourself?'

'No, no,' burbled Job.

The voice in front of him: 'God and Satan, angels and humans, all want to help you, but you will not help yourself – God out of love, Satan so as to control you later, the angels and men because they are helpers of God and Satan, but you don't want to.'

'No, no,' burbled Job, and screamed, and flung himself to the ground. He screamed all night long. The voice called uninterruptedly: 'God and Satan, angels and men, all will help you, but you will not help yourself.' Job uninterruptedly: 'No, no.' He tried to stifle the voice, it grew louder and ever louder, it was always a degree ahead of him. All night long. Towards morning, Job fell on his face.

Job lay there silent.

That day the first of his boils healed.

And they all have one breath, and man has no more than the beasts

Today's market: pigs 11,543, cattle 2,016, calves 1,920, sheep 4,450.

Now what is this man doing with his cute little calf? He leads it in by itself on a rope, this is the enormous hall with the bellowing steers, now he leads the little beast to a bench. There are many benches stood together, beside each one is a wooden mallet. He picks up the delicate little vealer in both arms and lays it down on the bench, it calmly allows itself to be laid down. He pushes his left hand underneath the animal, and holds on to one hind leg, to prevent it from kicking. Then he takes the rope on which he led it, and fastens it to the wall. The animal is patient and still, it is lying here now, it doesn't know what will happen to it, it's a little uncomfortable on its slab, it butts its head against a rod, it doesn't know it, but it's the handle of the mallet with which it is about to be hit. That will be its last negotiation with the world. And then the man, the old simple man who stands there all alone, a gentle man with a soft voice – he is talking to it now – the man takes the mallet, picks it up a little way, it doesn't need much power for such a docile creature, and taps it on the back of the neck. Very gently, as he led the animal here, and told it to lie still, he lays the blow on its neck, without anger, without excitement, without grief either, no, this is how it is, you're a good animal, you know it must end like this.

And the little calf: *brr, brr*, very stiff, rigid, puts out its little legs. The black velvety irises are suddenly very big and still, and ringed with white, then they roll to the side. The man is familiar with this, yes, that's the way animals look, but we have a lot to do still today, and he feels underneath the little calf for the knife, there it is, with his foot he moves the basin for the blood into position. Then *skkrkk*, right across the throat he pulls the knife, through the windpipe, all the cartilage, the air escapes, through the neck muscles, the head has no more support, it lolls against the bench. The blood spurts, a thick blackish-red effervescing liquid. But he goes on cutting, with the same tranquil expression, with the blade he feels between two bones, the tissue is very young and soft. Then he is finished with the animal, the knife clatters onto the bench. He washes his hands in a bucket and walks away.

And now the animal is all alone, pitifully on its side, the way he made it fast. The hall is full of noise and commotion, people are working, lugging carcasses, exchanging shouts. Terribly the head hangs down, only on a piece of hide now, between the two table legs, full of blood and drool. The purplish tongue is jammed between the teeth. And horribly, horribly the animal on the bench continues to gurgle. The head trembles on the end of its flap of hide. The body twitches. The legs quiver and push, thin, knobbly legs. But the eyes are stiff and sightless. They are dead eyes. The animal is no more.

The peaceable old man stands by a pillar with his little black notebook, looks across at the bench, and does sums. Times are hard, the sums are difficult, it's difficult to keep up with the competition.

Franz's window is open, sometimes amusing things happen in the world

The sun rises and sets, brighter days are coming, prams are out in force, let's see, we are February 1928.

In his distaste and repugnance, Franz Biberkopf has carried on drinking into February. He drinks away whatever he has, he doesn't care what becomes of him. He wanted once to be respectable, but the world is full of bastards and parasitical villains, and so Franz Biberkopf wants nothing more to do with the world, even if he becomes a vagabond, even if he drinks up every penny he has.

When Franz Biberkopf has rampaged on into February, he is awoken one night by a noise down in the yard. There are some wholesaler's commercial premises at the back. He looks down in his stupor, throws open the window, shouts down: 'Shut it, you brutes, you layabouts.' Then he lies down and doesn't think about them any more, as far as he's concerned they're gone.

A week later, the same thing again. Franz is on the point of pulling the window open and hurling the wooden wedge at them when he thinks: it's one o'clock, he might as well have a look at the lads who are making the noise. What are they up to in the wee small ones. What business do they have here, do they even live here, this is maybe worth looking into.

And he's right, there is something dodgy going on, they're sliding along the walls, up at the top Franz cranes his neck as far as it will go, one fellow is standing by the gate, he's keeping watch, they're doing a job, they're busy with the big cellar door. Two more of them are fooling around with it. Bold as brass. Then there's a groan, they've did it, one of them stays out in the yard, in a patch of shadow, the other two are off down the cellar. It's dark enough, that's what they're banking on.

Quietly Franz shuts the window. The air has cooled his head. So this is the kind of thing people get up to, day and night, jiggery-pokery like that, he wishes he had a row of flowerpots, then he could let them have it. What are they doing in my building, the cheek of it.

It's quiet, he sits down on his bed in the dark, he has half a mind to go over to the window and take another look: what are those guys up to, in my building. And he lights a wax candle, looks for a bottle, and, once he's found one, he doesn't pour himself a drink. A bullet came flying, is she mine or is she thine.

Then it's midday, and Franz is down in the yard. A bunch of

people are standing around, including Gerner the handyman, Franz knows him, and they get talking: 'They've done another job, ain't they.' Franz gives him a nudge: 'Guess what, I saw them, I'm not about to shop them, but if they come in my yard where I live once more and where I sleep and where they've got no business, then I'll go downstairs, and sure as my name is Biberkopf, I swear they can pick their bones up off the ground when I'm through with them, I don't care how many of them there are.' The carpenter grabs hold of Franz: 'Listen, mate, if you know something, go talk to the boys in blue, you can earn yourself some dough.' 'Ah, leave it aht. I never squealed on anyone yet. Let them do their own work, after all, it's what they're paid for, innit?'

Franz pushes off. Gerner's still standing around when a couple of detectives come up to him, asking to speak to a party by the name of Gerner. Well, blow me down. The man turns pale down to the corns on his toes. Then he says: 'Let me see, Gerner, he's the chippie, inne, I'll take you there.' And he doesn't say anything, rings his own doorbell, his wife opens the door, the whole company troops in. Last of all, Gerner himself, he winks at his wife, mum's the word, she has no idea what's going on, he's milling around with the others, hands in his pockets, the cops and two more fellows besides, they're from the insurance company, all taking a good look at his flat. They want to know how thick the walls are and what the floor's like, and they tap the walls and take measurements and write things down. It's a bit much with these break-ins at the wholesaler's, the fellows are so downright cheeky, they had a go at tunnelling in through the walls, because the door's alarmed and the steps, and they seemed to know that. Yes, the walls are incredibly thin, the whole building wobbles, it's not much better than an eggbox really.

They step back out into the yard, Gerner still playing the innocent. Now they're taking a look at the new iron doors to the cellar, Gerner hard by. And then, as luck would have it, he takes a step back out of the way, and, as luck would have it, he knocks against something, the thing falls over, and as he looks down to see what is, it's a bottle, and it's fallen on some paper, which is why no one else heard nothink. So there's a bottle in the yard, and they missed it, well, I'll have that. And he bends over as if to tie his laces, and he snaffles the bottle and the paper. And that was how Eve gave Adam the apple, and if the apple hadn't have fallen off the tree, then most probably Eve wouldn't have picked it up, and Adam wouldn't ever have come across it. Later on, Gerner has stashed the bottle in his jacket, and taken it across the yard to his old lady.

'What d'you say now, sugar?' And she beams: 'Where'd'ye get that from, August?' 'I bought it when there was no one home.' 'Ya never!' 'Danziger Goldwasser, what do you know?'

She beams, she beams away like a lighthouse. She draws the curtains: 'Is there any more where that came from, did you get it over there?' 'It was standing by the wall, they'd have picked it up if they'd seen it.' 'Man, you have to hand that in.' 'Since when is Goldwasser treasure trove then? When was the last time we had a classy bottle like that, with times as bad as they are. You're having a laff.'

Eventually she comes round to his way of seeing, she's not really that pernickety anyway, the woman, what's one stray bottle to a great big company like that, and anyway, if you think about it, it doesn't even belong to the company any more, it belongs to the robbers, and we're surely not supposed to give it back to them. That'd be compounding a felony. And they have a little drink, and a little more, sure, keep your eyes peeled, it doesn't have to be gold either, silver's nothing to sneeze at.

The following Saturday the thieves are back, and a funny thing happens. They notice a stranger in the yard, or at least the one who's standing in the lee of the wall, he notices, and the other two with their torches are off out of the hole like leprechauns, and racing out the gate. That's where Gerner is though, and them going like the clappers across the wall next door. Gerner is after them, but they can't wait: 'Don't be stupid, I'm not going to hurt you, God you bloody idiots.' He watches as they scramble over the wall, his heart is breaking, two of them have scarpered already, guys, don't be stupid. Then the third of them, straddling the wall, shines a torch in his face: 'What's your game?' Perhaps he's just a colleague who's queering their pitch. 'I'm on your side,' says Gerner. What's up with him. 'I'm on your side, what are you running away for.' Finally the man crawls down, takes a look at the chippie, who seems a little the worse for wear. The smell of drink emboldens him. Gerner holds out his hand. 'Shake, mate, are you in?' 'Is this a trap?' 'I don't understand.' 'You putting one over on me?' Gerner acts offended, the man isn't taking him seriously, hope he doesn't run off as well, the Goldwasser was lovely, his wife would be on his case too, if, God forbid, he came back empty-handed. Gerner begs him: 'No, no. You can come down, I live here.' 'Who are you?' 'I'm the caretaker, for Christ's sake, but I wouldn't mind a piece of the action.' The thief has a little think, it would be great if this guy came in; so long as it's not a trap; well, and if it is, we're armed.

And he leaves his ladder propped against the wall, crosses the yard with Gerner, and the other two are long gone, sure they're thinking I got stuck. Then Gerner rings the bell: 'Why are you ringing, who do you think lives here?' Gerner proudly: 'None other. Watch this.' And he lifts the latch and enters noisily: 'Well, do I or don't I?'

And he switches on the light, and there's his wife standing in the kitchen doorway, shaking like a leaf. Gerner does the honours: 'Now, this is my wife, Gusti, and this is my new colleague.' She's still shaking, refuses to come out, then suddenly she gives a solemn nod, he's a nice young man, a very presentable young man. She comes out, and suddenly she's all: 'Paul, how can you leave the gentleman to stand in the corridor, step this way sir, take your cap off.'

He wants to be gone, but they won't let him, can it really be, two such respectable people, they must be doing badly, you always hear about the middle classes suffering, what with the Inflation and all. The little woman is gazing at him adoringly, he takes a glass of punch to warm up, then he pushes off, he's not entirely sure what that was all about either.

Anyway, the young man, now obviously sent by his gang, turns up again the following morning after tiffin, enquires whether he left anything behind. Gerner's not there, just the wife, who receives him warmly, yes, submissively, dutifully, and offers him a drink, which he condescends to take.

To the consternation of the caretaker couple the thieves then
stay away all week. Paul and Gusti talk the thing through a thousand times, did they perhaps scare them away, but they don't feel
they've done anything wrong. 'Perhaps you were a bit rough with
them, Paul, you know, sometimes you get like that.' 'No, Gusti, it
wasn't nothing I done, I'm thinking maybe it was you, you had an
expression on yer face like you was in holy orders or something,
and that put him off, they can't seem to shake down with us, it's too
bad, but what are we to do about it.'

Gusti is already in tears; even if just the one boy came again;
she's forever hearing her husband's reproaches, and it really wasn't
nothing she done.

And Friday rolls around, and the moment has come. There's a
knock on the door. Did you hear a knock? And even as she opens
the door and doesn't see anything, because in her haste she has forgotten to switch on the light, she knows who it is. It's the tall fellow
who always acts so proper, and he wants to have a word with her
husband and he's terribly brisk with her. She's alarmed: has anything happened. He calms her down: 'No, purely a business
conversation', says something about premises, and you don't get
something for nothing in this life, and so on. They are sitting in the
parlour, she's so happy he's here with her, and now Paul can't go on
claiming she scared them off, and she says that's what she always
says too, that you don't get something for nothing. A long discussion ensues, and it turns out that they both know sayings from
their parents and grandparents and in-laws that come to the same
thing: there's no such thing as a free lunch, and they are both insist-
ent on the point, so certain are they, and they were of one mind.
They came up with example after example, from their own past,
from the neighbourhood, and they were in the midst of this when
there was a ring, and in walk two gentlemen who identified themselves as detectives, and with them three insurance company
representatives. The one detective addressed the visitor without
any preamble: 'Herr Gerner, we need your help, it's to do with the
many break-ins at the back. I would like you to take part in a special
watch. My colleagues from the insurance company will of course

cover your costs.' They talk for ten minutes, the woman listens to everything, at twelve they leave. And the two parties left behind felt so relaxed after this conversation, that at around one something quite unmentionable transpired, to the shame of both parties. Because the woman was thirty-five, and the young man was maybe twenty or twenty-one. It wasn't just the age difference – or the fact that he was six foot two, and she five foot even – as the fact that it happened at all, but it seemed so natural, what with the conversation and the excitement and the making monkeys of the policemen, and in a way it wasn't a bad thing either, only a little shaming *après*, at least where she was concerned, but then she got over it all right. At any rate by two o'clock Herr Gerner came home to such a cosy scene that he couldn't have wished for anything more cordial. He himself slotted right in.

They were still sitting together at six o'clock, and he and his wife were listening in raptures to the stories the tall geezer was telling. Even if they were only part-true, they were a first-rate bunch of lads, and he was amazed at the sensible views a young person like that took of the world. He had certainly knocked around, and the scales fell from his, Gerner's, eyes. Yes, when the lad was gone and they went to bed at around nine, Gerner said he had no idea what such smart lads were doing with a fellow like him – there had to be something, Gusti would surely admit, something he had to offer them as well. Gusti quite agreed with him, and the old fellow stretched out.

In the morning, early, before he got up, he said to her: 'Now Gusti, call me Paul Piependeckel if I ever approach a foreman on a building site for work again. I had my own business and that went tits up, and this is no occupation for a man who used to be his own boss, and ideally they'd throw me on the scrapheap because I'm too old. And why shouldn't I earn my cut, from this gang. You could see for yourself what a bright bunch of lads they were. You've got to be bright these days, otherwise you've had it. That's what I say. What about you?' 'I've been saying that for a long time.' 'You see. I wanna go at the fleshpots myself, and not freeze my extremities off.' Out of gratitude and enthusiasm for everything he offered and would offer she gave him a hug. 'Do you know what we should do then, you and me, old lady?' He pinched her in the leg and she screeched. 'You join in.' 'Nah.' 'And I'm saying yes. You're thinking we can manage without you. We need you in with us.' 'Five of you, and all strong fellows.' Strong, and how! 'I can't stand guard neither,' she goes on, 'standing is murder on me varicose veins.'

'As far as helping goes, how'm I sposed to help?' 'Are you scared, Gustelchen?' 'What do you mean, scared. You should try running with me veins. A dachshund's faster. And then when they nab me, you're in the soup, because I'm your missus.' 'Is it my fault you're my missus, then?' He pinched her in the leg again, with feeling. 'Stop that Paul, you don't know what that does to a person.' 'You see, take you away from pickled cabbage, and you turn into someone else.' 'Well, I'm game, that life makes me mouth water.' 'You know that little bit, that weren't nothing, you need to take the cotton wool out of your ears. I've half a mind to go into business by meself.' 'What? And the rest of the boys?' The shock of it.

'That's just it, Guste. We'll do it without them. You know, these joint ventures, they never work, it's well known. So, are you in or not. I'm going solo. We're at ground zero here, it being my building and all. What d'you reckon?' 'How'm I going to help, Paul, with my varicose veins and all.' Not to mention various other regrets. And with a bittersweet expression the missus agrees, but inside, where the feelings are, she is saying: no, and again: no.

And that night, once the whole gang have left the cellar at six o'clock, and Gerner is all alone in there with his wife, and it's nine, and nothing's stirring in the house, and he is about to start working, and the watchman will be out patrolling in front of the house, what happens? There's a knock on the cellar door. A knock. I'm thinking, that's a knock. When who on earth could be knocking. The business is shut. A knock. And another. The pair of them quiet as mice, not a stir, and not a word either. Again a knock. Gerner gives her a nudge: 'That's a knock.' 'Yes.' 'Who can it be?' She, oddly enough, not at all afraid, just says: 'Oh, it won't be anything, and they won't kill us.' No, but he'll do something else, my phantom visitor, I know who it is anyway, and he's not come to murder me, he's got two long legs, and a wee little moustache, and when he comes won't I be happy to see him. And then there's another knock, sharp but quiet. For God's sake, it's a signal. 'It's someone who knows us. It's one of our boys.' 'That's what I concluded too, missus.' 'Then why don't you say so.'

And suddenly Gerner is on the staircase, how do they even know we're in here, they've caught us out, the man outside is whispering: 'Sst, Gerner, open up.'

Then, whether he wants to or not, he has to open up. It's a nasty dirty business, in fact it's a blooming disgrace, he'd like to smash the world in pieces. He has to open, it's the lanky one, by himself, her fancy man, Gerner doesn't notice anything, she has shopped him, she is that beholden to her fancy man. She beams to see him down there, she can't help herself, her husband stands there like a bulldog, swearing: 'What have you got to grin about then? Oh, I was so worried it might be someone from the building, or else a watchman.' They have to share and share alike, and swearing won't make it any better, goddamnit.

When Gerner tries his luck another time, and this time parks his old lady upstairs, because he swears she only brings him bad luck – then there's more knocking, but this time it's three of them, and they're pretending he invited them up, there's nothing to be done about it, he's not even the master in his own house, there's nothing he can do about those fellers. Then, furious and checkmated, Gerner vows: I'm going to pitch in tonight, birds of a feather and all that, but tomorrow I'm through: and if those bastards come knocking again in my building, where I'm the janitor, and they stick their noses in my business, then I'll make them acquainted with the police. Those fellows are profiteers, extortionists is what they are.

And then they work away for all of two hours in the cellar, carrying most of the loot over to Gerner's flat, sackloads of coffee, currants, sugar, they clean up, then crateloads of booze, schnapps and wine, they empty out half the storeroom. Gerner is hopping mad because of having to share it all with them. His wife tries to comfort him: 'I wouldn't have been able to carry it all with my varicose veins.' He's sarky back, they're still carrying stuff: 'You and your varicose veins, you should have worn support stockings long ago, that's all down to your economies, you're always trying to economize at the wrong time.' But Guste only has eyes for her lanky fancy man, who's throwing his weight around in front of the other lads, because he fixed it all, and this is his show now.

The minute they're gone, having worked like dogs, Gerner shuts his front door, locks up and starts hitting the booze with Guste, at least let him have some of that. He wants to try out all the kinds and flog the best of the stuff, he's got a couple of guys in mind for that, and they're both looking forward to it, Guste too, he is a good man and she's married to him, and she will help him out. And from two till five in the morning they sit up and diligently and methodically sample all the drink. Thoroughly pleased with themselves and their night's work, they stagger into bed, they've both had a skinful, they dropped like sacks.

At noon they're called upon to open. There's a ringing and a jingling and a tinkling. But who doesn't open is the Gerners. How could they with what they've drunk. But the noise doesn't stop, there's loud banging on the door now, and that gets through to Guste, who sits up with a jolt and hits Paul to wake him: 'Paul, there's knocking, you've gorra open.' First he replies: 'What? Where?', then she pushes him out because they'll have the door down, it'll be the postie. Paul gets up, pulls on a pair of trousers, opens the door. And they breeze in past him, three of them, a whole band, what are they doing, is it the gang come to collect the goods already, no, these aren't the same guys. These are cops, detectives, and their case is out on a plate. Their jaws drop. Their jaws drop, the janitor, the flat is jam-packed, the corridor, the parlour, with sacks and crates and bottles and straw, all of a heap. The detective says: 'I've not seen such a disgraceful case in all my years of service.'

And Gerner, what does Gerner say? What can he say? Not a dicky bird! He just gawps at the coppers, and on top of that he's feeling a trifle nauseous, the bloodhounds, if I had a revolver they wouldn't take me alive. A man is sentenced to life on a building site, and it's all exploitation. If they'd only let me have one more glassful. But there's nothing for it, he has to get dressed. 'Surely you can give me a minute to do up my braces and all.'

His wife is drooling and trembling: 'I had no idea, Inspector, we're respectable people here, someone must have pulled the wool over our eyes, those boxes, we were fast asleep. They must have seen that, and someone in the building played a trick on us. Oh, Inspector, you surely won't. Paul, what are we going to do?' 'You can tell us all about it at the station.' Gerner chips in: 'Now they've gone and broken into our place, it must be the same band as did the jobs at the back, and they want to talk to *us*.' 'You can tell us about it back at the station.' 'I'm not going to the bloody police.' 'We're going.' 'My God, Guste, I didn't hear a thing, they broke in here, and I was sleeping like a rat.' 'But so was I, Paul, so was I.'

Guste would like to take a couple of letters from her chest of drawers, billets doux she had from the lanky boy, but one of the detectives spots her. 'Let's see that. Or just put them back. We'll have the place searched later anyway.'

She says mutinously: 'You will, will you. Well, you should be ashamed of yourselves, breaking into a respectable flat like this.' 'Get a move on, will you.'

She cries, avoids looking at her husband, throws herself on the ground, they have to frogmarch her out. The man is swearing and has to be restrained: 'Take your hands off her.' The hoodlums, the vile band of blackmailers are gone, and they left me in it up to my neck.

Hopp, hopp, hopp, horsey does gallop

Hands in pockets, collar up past his ears, head and hat thrust between his shoulders, Franz Biberkopf takes no part in any of the various conversations in hallway and staircase. Just listened to one group, picked up something from another. Afterwards watched as they formed a guard of honour as the carpenter and his fat little missus are taken down the passage onto the street. Now they're gone. Well, I was on the lam once meself. That were night-time, though. Look at them all staring. Should be ashamed of themselves. Yeah, yeah, I see the tongues hanging out. You know what a person's feeling inside. Those curtain-twitchers are the real miscreants, but of course nothing ever happens to them. Unbelievable, those crooks. Now they're opening up the Black Maria. In you go now, my little ones, in you go, the little woman as well, my, isn't she's tiddly, and why not, why not indeed. Let them laugh. They should see what it's like. I'm outta here.

People were still putting their heads together when Franz Biberkopf stood outside the door, it was vilely cold. He saw the door from outside, from the other side of the road, what's a man to do now, eh. He shifted his weight from foot to foot. Damned cold. Bitching cold. I'm not going upstairs. What will I do.

There he stood, turned – and hadn't realized he was back. He had nothing to do with the pack that was standing there ogling. I'll see what's happening somewhere else. Screw this. And he sets off at a good lick, along Elsasser Strasse, along the security fence where they're building the new underground, to Rosenthaler Platz, oh, anywhere.

And so it came to pass that Franz Biberkopf left his burrow. The man they expelled through the guard of honour, the plump, tiddly woman and the Black Maria all went with him. But when he saw a pub on the corner, that's when it started again. His hands felt for his pockets, and no bottle there for refilling. Nothing. No bottle. Left it upstairs. All because of that bloody kerfuffle. When the noise started, he slipped his coat on, ran out and didn't give the bottle a thought. Damn! Do I go back? Then it set up in him: yes no, no yes. So much shrugging, back and forth, scolding, agreeing, fussing, well what is it, leave it out, I want to go in, that hadn't been seen in Franz for an eternity. Do I, don't I, I'm thirsty, well, there's always seltzer water, if you go in, you'll only drink, Christ, yes, I've got a powerful thirst on me, massive, unholy thirst, God I need a drink, so stay here, don't go back to your place, otherwise you'll be prostrated like before, you, and then you'll be back at the old lady's again, like before. And then there was the Black Maria, and the carpenter couple, and scoot, right about, no, not here, maybe somewhere else, walk on, on, walking, always walking.

And so Franz, with 1.55 marks in his pocket, trotted along as far as the Alexanderplatz, snuffing the air and sometimes breaking into a run. Then, even though he didn't want to, he forced himself to go into a restaurant and eat a proper meal, his first proper meal in weeks, beef cheeks with potatoes. After that his thirst felt less, he still had 75 pfennigs in his pocket, which he jingled between his fingers. Do I go to Lina, bah, Lina, I don't even like her. His tongue felt rough and sour, he was spitting feathers. I'd better have that seltzer water after all.

And then – as he drank it down he knew it, in the pleasantly cool tickle of the carbonated bubbles in his throat – he knew where he wanted to go. To Minna, he had sent her the veal, she refused the aprons. Yes, that's right.

Up we get. Franz Biberkopf straightened himself out in front of the mirror. Who wasn't pleased at all to see his pale, flabby, pimpled cheeks was Frankie BBK. My God, what a face, red lines across his brow, where on earth d'he get these red lines from, his cap, he supposed, and his schnozz, Christ, man, a thick red schnozz like that, doesn't have to be from schnapps, I suppose, it's cold out; but the glooping peepers, like a cow's, where do I get those calves' eyes from, and staring as if they were nailed fast. As if someone'd dunked me in syrup. But Minna won't mind. Plaster my hair down. There. Now let's see about seeing her. She'll give me a few pennies to see me through till Thursday, and then we'll see.

Out of the establishment, onto the cold street. Loads of people. Loads of people all round the Alex, all with stuff to do. Lucky them. Franz Biberkopf was making the running for them, turning his head left and right. Like when a horse has slipped on the wet asphalt and gets a kick in the guts, and scrambles up, and starts going like the clappers. Franz had muscles, he had been a member of the athletics club; now he ambled down Alexanderstrasse and relished his stride, click tick, like a blooming guardsman. We march just exactly like the others.

Weather report from noon today: bryter layter. Temperatures are still unusually low, but the barometer is rising. We may even catch a little sun. Expect further improvement in the days ahead.

And the person at the wheel of the NSU 6-cylinder is enraptured. Let me steer, o let me steer, my dear.

And when Franz is in her building and standing in front of her door, there's a bell. And he doffs his hat, pulls the bell, and who will open, who will it be, we perform a bow, if a girl has a gentleman, who will it be, dilly dilly. Shock. A man – her husband! That's Karl. Her engineer. But that don't matter. You can scowl all you like, mush. 'You? What you doing here?' 'Let me in, Karle, I won't bite you.' And he's inside. There's that taken care of. What a louse, did you ever see anything like it.

'Dear Karl, even if you're a qualified engineer, and I'm a casual labourer, you shouldn't give yourself airs. You can say hello to me, when I greet you.' 'What are you on about? Didn't I let you in? What are you doing barging into my house anyway?' 'Is your wife home? Maybe I can say hello to her.' 'No, she's not home. She's not home to you ever. No one's home to you.' 'Oh, really.' 'Yes. No one.' 'Well – but I see you, Karl.' 'No, I'm not here either. I've just been in to get my pullover and I'm going back out to the store.' 'So, business going well, I take it.' 'Yes.' 'You really are throwing me out.' 'I never let you in. What are you doing round here, man. Aren't you ashamed to come up here and embarrass me, when everyone in the building knows who you are.' 'Let them talk if they want to. That's not our concern. I wouldn't want to see inside their parlours neither. You know, Karl, there's no call to worry about them and what they might say. Today in my place, they arrested a guy, the police did, who was a qualified carpenter, and the janitor of the building. Imagine. And his wife as well. They were thieving like magpies, the pair of them. Am I a thief? Well?' 'Christ, I've had enough standing around with you. Push off. If you see Minna, you'd better be ready, she'll get her broom out and hit you in little pieces.' That's all he knows. A cuck like that, trying to lay the law down to me. I could laugh my boots crooked. If a girl has a man, what she likes and understands. Karl steps up to Franz: 'What are you doing still standing there? We're not related, Franz, there's nothing between us at all. And now you're out of jug, you'd best see how you get on.' 'I never asked you for favours.' 'No, and Minna still hasn't forgot Ida. A sister's a sister. You're the guy who did it. You're finished.' 'I never killed her. It could happen to anyone, they lose their temper, their hand slips.' 'Ida's dead, now push off. We're decent people here.'

The dog, with his horns, the poisonous louse, I feel like telling him, I'd take his wife off him like that. 'I served every last minute of my four years, and if I'm squared away with the law, that should be enough for you.' 'What do I care about the courts. Now get lost. Once and for all. This house here is no longer for you. Once and for all.' My, what's got into Mr Engineer here, he seems like he's about to lamp me.

'But I'm telling you, Karl, I've done my time, I want to make peace with you. I'm extending to you the hand of friendship.' 'Well, I'm not taking it.' 'That's all I needed to know. (Grab hold of the fellow, take him by the legs, and slam his head against the wall.) Now it's on if I had it in writing.' Slaps the hat down on his head with the same élan as before: 'Well, then, good morning to you, Master Engineer. Give Minna my best, let her know I came calling, just to see how she's doing. And you are the worst shit in the world. This is my fist, if you ever want anything. I feel sorry for Minna with a piece of shit like you.'

And exit. Exit calmly. Calmly and slowly down the stairs. Let him come after me if he likes. And over the road, knocked back a single short, to revive his heart. Maybe he'll come over. I'll wait. And very contentedly Franz moved on. I'll get hold of some money from somewhere. And he felt his thick muscles, and I'll get back to my fighting weight and all.

'You want to block my path and throw me down. But I have a hand that can strangle you, and you can't do anything against me. You attack me with scorn, you want to cover me with your contempt – not me, not me – for I am very strong. I can hear past your scorn. Your teeth are helpless against my armour, I am proof against vipers. I don't know where you get the power to oppose me. But I am able to resist you. The Lord set my enemies against me with their necks towards me.'

'You talk all you want. How prettily birds sing once they've escaped the polecat. But there are lots of polecats and a bird can only sing! You still have no eyes for me. You still don't need to look at me. You hear the babble of humans, the noise on the street, the rattling of the tram. Breathe, listen. In amongst it all you will hear me too.'

'Hear whom? Who's speaking?'

'I won't say. You will see. You will feel. Gird up your heart. Then I will speak to you. Then you will see me. Your eyes will see nothing but tears.'

'I don't care if you talk another hundred years like that. You make me laugh.'

'Don't laugh. Don't laugh.'

'Because you don't know me. You have no idea who I am. Who Franz Biberkopf is. He is afraid of nothing. I got fists. See my muscles?'

Chapter Five

A speedy recovery, the man is back where he was, he has learnt nothing and understood nothing. Now the first heavy blow strikes him. He is caught up in a crime, he doesn't want to be, he tries to resist, but he gotta gotta.

He resists bravely and furiously with fists and feet, but there's no help, it's bigger than he is, he gotta gotta.

Reunion on the Alex, bitching cold. Though next year, 1929, will be even colder

Boom boom goes the steam pile-driver outside Aschinger's on the Alex. It's as big as a house, and it drives the piles into the ground like nobody's business. Glacial air. February. People in coats. Whoever owns a mink wears it, whoever doesn't, doesn't. The women wear thin stockings and are freezing, but it looks nice. The tramps have melted away. When it warms up, they'll stick their noses out. In the meantime they're on double rations of canned heat, but you wouldn't want to be the corpse pickling in that stuff.

Boom boom goes the steam pile-driver on the Alexanderplatz.

Lots of people take the time to watch the pile-driver at work. A man at the top keeps pulling on a chain, and bam! the pile gets one on the lid. Men and women stand there and boys especially and take pleasure in the easy motion: bam! the pile gets one on the lid. By the end it's no bigger than the tip of your finger, but it still gets another bam!, there's no getting around it. Finally, it's gone altogether. Crumbs, they got rid of that all right, and people move off satisfied.

Everything is boarded up. Berolina used to stand outside Tietz's, one hand out, a colossal wench, they've dragged her away. Maybe they'll melt her down to make medals out of.

They're everywhere, like a swarm of bees. Building and fiddling around the livelong day and night.

Boggler boggler go the trams, yellow ones with extra carriages, over the boarded-up Alexanderplatz. Do not dismount while vehicle is moving. The station is cut off, one-way street to König-strasse, past Wertheim. If you're looking to go east, you need to follow Klosterstrasse round the back of the police headquarters. The trains boggle from the station to Jannowitz Bridge, the loco-motives let off steam, it's slap bang on top of the Prälaten, Schlossbräu, entrance next block.

Across the road, they are knocking everything down, whole buildings along the S-Bahn are being demolished, where do they get the money from, Berlin is a rich city, and we pay our taxes.

Loeser & Wolff with the mosaic sign outside has been torn down and rebuilt twenty yards away, and there's another branch outside the station. Loeser & Wolff, Berlin-Elbing, first-class prod-ucts in all types, Brazil, Havana, Mexico, Little Comfort, Liliput, No. 8s, 25 pfennigs apiece, Winter Ballad, packs of 25, 20 pfennigs, cigarillos No. 10, unsorted, Sumatra leaf, a special at the price, in boxes of a hundred, 10 pfennigs. I beat all comers, you beat all com-ers, he beats all comers with boxes of 50 and packs of 10, despatched to anywhere in the world, Boyero 25 pfennigs, this new product has made many converts, I beat all comers, you beat flat.

There is space next to the Prälaten, that's where the carts are with the bananas. Give your kids bananas. The banana is the most sani-tary of fruits, its peel protects it from insects, worms and germs. (Except such insects, worms and germs as penetrate the peel.) Dr Czerny advises that even the very youngest infants may. I smash everything, you smash everything, he/she/it smashes everything.

The Alex is always windy, on the corner in front of Tietz's there's a howling gale. The wind blows in between the buildings onto the digs. You feel like taking shelter in a bar, but who can afford to do that, the wind blows the cash out of your pockets instead, you notice there's something going on here, no faffing about, you need to be up for it in this weather. Early in the morning the workers roll in from Reinickendorf, Neukölln, Weissensee. Cold or not cold, wind or no wind, coffee can out, pack me lunch, we gotta work, the parasites sit up at the top, they sleep in their featherbeds and leech us dry.

Aschinger's has a large café and restaurant. Them as don't have a paunch can acquire one here, them as do can extend it ad libitum. Nature won't be swindled! Whoever thinks bread and baked goods made from depleted white flour can be improved by artificial additives is mistaken, and is leading their clients astray. Nature has laws, and it punishes infractions. The impaired health of almost every advanced nation may be traced to indulgence in devalued and refined foods. Fine sausages, home deliveries possible, cheap liver sausage, blood sausage.

The highly interesting *Magazine* retails for 20 pfennigs instead of 1 mark, *Marriage*, highly interesting and saucy, 20 pfennigs. The vendor is smoking cigarettes, is wearing a peaked cap, I challenge all comers.

From the east, from Weissensee, Lichtenberg, Friedrichshain, Frankfurter Allee, the yellow trams collect on the square via Landsberger Strasse. The 65 comes in from Central Abattoir, Grosser Ring, Weddingplatz, Luisenplatz, and the 76 from Hundekehle via Hubertusallee. On the corner of Landsberger, they bought out Friedrich Hahn, Kaufhaus as was, gutted it and will return it to its ancestors. That's where the trams and the 19 bus to Turmstrasse stop. They've pulled down the place where Jürgens the stationers used to be, and put up a wooden fence. Here's an old man with a set of doctor's scales: check your weight, 5 pfennigs. O brothers and sisters, swarming over the Alex, take a moment, look through the gap next to the set of scales, where Jürgens once flourished, and where Kaufhaus Hahn still stands, emptied out, gutted, with only a few scraps of the red legend *Closing Sale* still stuck in the shop windows. There is a rubbish tip in front of you. For dust thou art, and unto dust shalt thou return, we builded here a splendid house, now no man goes rein or raus. As busted as Rome, Babylon, Nineveh, Hannibal, Caesar, all busted now, oh, think of them. Firstly, I would observe that these cities are even now being exhumed, as depictions in last Sunday's papers show, and secondly they have served their purpose, leaving us free to build new ones. You don't go wailing about your old pants when they're ancient and full of holes, you get yourself a new pair, that's the way of the world.

The police assert their control of the square. They are multiply present. Each specimen looks knowingly left and right, and knows the traffic laws off pat. It wears puttees on its legs, a rubber truncheon dangles by its right hip, it swings its arms horizontally from west to east, then north and south must stand idle, while the east pours west, and west east. Then the model automatically reverses itself: the north pours south, the south north. The policeman is thick-waisted and highly specialized. At a peremptory twitch, about thirty individuals cross the square towards Königstrasse, some of them stopping on the traffic island, some of them getting all the way to the opposite side, there to continue on their way on duckboards. An equal number have gone east, swimming in the contrary direction, they fared similarly, but none of them came to grief.

They are men, women and children, the last-named mainly holding the hands of women. To list them all and describe their destinies would be daunting, only a few instances would be possible. The wind sprinkles all of them with bits of straw. The faces of the eastbound are in no way distinguishable from those of west-, south- or northbound persons, they exchange roles, and the ones now crossing the square towards Aschinger's can be found an hour later in front of the vacated premises of Hahn's. And similarly, those coming from the direction of Brunnenstrasse on their way to the Jannowitz Bridge mingle with those going the opposite way. Many turn aside, from south to east, from south to west, from north to west, from north to east. They are as indistinguishable as those others sitting in trams and buses. They all sit in different postures, adding to the declared weight of the carriage. What is going on in them, who could write it, a monstrous chapter. And if someone did, then what? New books? The old ones don't sell, and in the year 1927 the sale of books year on year from 1926 has gone down by so and so many per cent. Take those individuals who have paid their 20 pfennigs (excluding the others who own season tickets, and the schoolchildren who pay 10 pfennigs), so there they are adding their weight of on average one to two hundredweight, fully clothed, with bags, satchels, door keys, hats, dentures, trusses across the Alexanderplatz and keeping in their hands the inscrutable ribbons of paper on which is written: Line 12, Siemensstrasse DA, Gotzkowskistrasse C, B, Oranienburger Gate, C, C, Kottbus Gate A, enigmatic runes, who can guess, who can explain and who can tell, three markings I tell you pregnant with meaning, and the paper ribbons are punctured four times in particular places, and on them is written in the same German as the Bible and the civil code: valid for the destination given by the shortest route, no transfers.

They are reading newspapers of differing political stripe, keeping their balance by means of the labyrinthine passages in their ears, breathing oxygen, dozing off or looking at each other; they feel pain, feel no pain, make eye-contact, make no eye-contact, are happy, unhappy, are neither unhappy nor happy.

Bam bam goes the ram, I smash therefore I am, another rail. There's a whirring noise from in front of the police headquarters, that's where they're banging, a cement mixer empties its contents. Herr Adolf Kraun, janitor, looks on, he finds the toppling-over of the wagon gripping, you slam everything, he smashes everything. He always waits there tensely when the wagon containing sand lifts up to one side, then it's at the top, and whoosh, it drops again. Wouldn't it be awful to be thrown out of bed like that, legs up, head down, then you're lying there, scary, but that's the way they do it.

Franz Biberkopf has his pack on his back and is selling newspapers. He has changed his pitch. He has quit Rosenthaler Tor for Alexanderplatz. He is doing all right now, five foot eleven tall, his weight is down, but that makes it easier to lug around. He's got a cap with the paper's logo on it.

Crisis talks in the Reichstag, fresh elections possible by March or April, whither, Joseph Wirth? Middle-German stand-off continues, Arbitration committee to be appointed, Robbery on Tempelherrenstrasse. His pitch is at the U-Bahn exit on the Alexanderstrasse side, opposite the UFA cinema, that's where Fromm the optician has set up his new business. The first time he's standing in the bustle, Franz Biberkopf looks down Münzstrasse, and thinks: wonder how far it is to those two Jews, they're not far from here, that was after I had my first mischance, maybe I'll look in on them, see if they're good for a copy of the *Völkischer Beobachter*. Why shouldn't they be, they don't have to like it, just buy one off me. The thought makes him grin, the old Jew in his slippers was too funny. He looks around, his fingers are clammy, near him is a little stunted man with a hooked nose, probably broken. Crisis talks in the Reichstag, Premises on Hebbelstrasse 17 vacated thru' risk of collapse, Trawler crime: mutiny or insanity.

Franz Biberkopf and the stunted fellow blow into their hands. Mid-morning, trade is dragging. A scrawny old guy, shabby and run-down, goes up to Franz. Has on a green felt hat and asks Franz what business is like. Something Franz once asked hisself too. 'Who knows if you're cut out for it, mate.' 'Yeah, I'm fifty-two.' 'Well, quite, that's why, at fifty arthritis sets in. In our regiment we had an old reserve captain who was just forty, from Saarbrücken, lottery ticket seller – tobacconist to you, he says – he had arthritis at forty, in the lumbar region. He pretended it was his martial posture. He went around like a broomstick on wheels. He always had himself rubbed down with butter. And when there weren't no more butter, 1917 time, just Palmin, first-class vegetable oil, and rancid it were too, then he got himself shot.'

'What's the use, they won't take you in the factory any more either. And last year I had an operation in Lichtenberg, the Hubertus hospital. I lost a testicle, testicular tuberculosis they said it was, I tell you, it still hurts.' 'You watch yourself, they'll be coming for the other one too. Then you'll be ready for a sedentary occupation. Ever think of being a cabbie?' Middle-German stand-off continues, negotiations fail, Tenant protection law under attack, watch out, tenants, or they'll whip the roof off over your heads. 'Yes, mate, you can flog papers, but you need to be able to run around, and you need a strong voice, red-tops need a vox. See, that's what it's about in my sector, you gotta be able to run around and sing. We need loudmouths. Loudspeakers do most business. It's a cut-throat society, I tell you. Have a look, how many coins have I got in my hand?' 'Looks like four to me.' 'Correct. Four to you. That's what it's about. But if a fellow's in a hurry, and he reaches into his pocket, and he finds a five-pfennig piece, and a mark, or maybe ten marks, ask my mates, they're all dab at giving change. They're that shifty, they're the real bankers, they wrote the book on giving change, they take their cut, and you won't even notice, that's how quick they are about it.' The old fellow sighs. 'Yeah, fifty and arthritis. Mate, if you're married, then you're not on your own, then you take on a couple of lads, gotta pay them of course, maybe half what you make, but meanwhile you look after the business, and spare your voice and your shoe leather. You need connections and a good pitch. When it rains, it gets wet. Sporting events and government reshuffles are what you need. You wouldn't believe the way the newspapers were flying out of my hands when Ebert died. Don't look like that, it may never happen. Look at the ram over there, imagine that thing hitting you on the head, why waste your time thinking?' Tenant protection law under attack. Comeuppance for Zörgiebel. British censor Amanullah, Indians kept in the dark.

Opposite at Web's radio store – introductory special, we load your battery for free – stands a pale-looking girl with her cap pulled down over her face, apparently lost in thought. The taxi driver next to her wonders: is she thinking about getting a ride somewhere, and isn't sure if she can afford the fare, or is she waiting for her boyfriend. She is hunched over in her velvet coat, as if she was twisted inside, then she walks on, she's just poorly, and every time it feels like hot coals. She is studying for her teaching exams, tonight she will stay home and apply hot compresses, it's never so bad in the evening.

Nothing for a while, pause for rest and recuperation

On the evening of 9 February 1928, the day the Labour government fell in Oslo, the last night of the Stuttgart six-day bicycle races – Van Kempen and Frankenstein were the winners with 726 points, 2,440 kilometers – the situation in the Saarland deteriorated, on the evening of 9 February 1928, a Tuesday (excuse me a moment, you see the enigmatic countenance of an unknown woman, the question posed by this dusky beauty addresses itself to all mankind, yourself included: have you tried Garbaty Kalif cigarettes?), that evening found Franz Biberkopf standing in front of an advertising pillar on Alexanderplatz, contemplating an invitation from the allotment gardeners of Treptow-Neukölln and Britz to a protest meeting in Irmer's Festival Halls, subject: wanton dismissals. Below was a poster: the torment of asthma and costume rental, large selection for both sexes. Then all of a sudden little Mack was standing next to him. Mack, you remember Mack. See him coming right along, on his lips a merry song.

'Hey, Franz, Franz', was Mack ever glad to see him, no, glad is what he was, 'Franz, Christ, I don't believe it, it's you, I thought you'd disappeared for good. I could have sworn—' 'Sworn what? I can imagine, that I got in trouble again. No, not me.' They shake hands, shake arms up to their shoulders, shake shoulders down to their ribs, pat each other on the back, both men staggered and swayed.

'It just happens from time to time, Gottlieb, that people don't see each other. I'm in business around here.' 'Here on the Alex, Franz, well I never, I'm surprised I never run into you before now. Must of walked right past you.' 'Sure you did, Gottlieb.'

Arm in arm, drifting down Prenzlauer Strasse. 'Do you remember, Franz, you wanted to trade in plaster casts.' 'I don't have the nous for plaster casts. For plaster casts a man's got to have learning, and I've not got that. I'm back in newspapers, newspapers keep a man fed. How's about you, Gottlieb?' 'I'm over on Schönhauser in men's apparel, anoraks and trousers.' 'Where do you get the product from?' 'Same old Franz, always asking about where a thing's from. Like a girl when she's wondering who the father is.' Franz stomped along silently beside Mack, grim-expressioned: 'You do your crooked thing until one day you land up in the soup.' 'What are you talking about, crooked and soup, Franz, a man needs to be an entrepreneur these days, he needs to understand about buying and selling.'

Franz was no longer in the mood, he was stubborn. But Mack had his hooks in him, chattering away and not letting go: 'Come down the pub, Franz, maybe take a look at the drovers, you remember, the ones with the court case pending that were sitting at our table at that meeting, where you got your membership. They came quite a cropper with their case. They're at the deposition stage now, and they're scratching around for witnesses. I tell you, they're cruising for a fall, and head first.' 'Nah, Gottlieb, I'm not really in the mood.'

But Mack didn't give up, it was his good old friend, the best friend he had in the world, except for Herbert Wischow, but he was a ponce, and he was through with that, never again. Arm in arm, down Prenzlauer Strasse, drinks factory, textile works, jams and marmalades, silk, a contemporary fabric for the stylish woman of today!

By eight o'clock, Franz was sitting at a corner table with Mack and someone else who didn't speak, only gestured. Things were going with a swing. Mack and the other were astounded at the way Franz seemed to thaw out, and eat and drink with glee two servings of pigs' trotters, then some baked beans, and the halves of Engelhardt kept coming, and he treated them. The three of them stuck out their elbows to make sure no one joined them at their little table and put a crimp on things; only the scrawny landlady was permitted to clear the table every so often and refresh the drinks. At the next table sat three old fellows, who occasionally stroked each other's bald pates. Franz had his mouth full, beamed, his half-shut eyes slid across to them. 'What are they up to over there?' The landlady brought him mustard, a second pot already: 'Fond of each other is what they are.' 'Oh, I believes yer, I believes yer.' And the three of them whinnied, chomped and guzzled on. Franz kept announcing: 'A man needs to fill hisself up. A strong man has gotta eat. If you don't fill up yer belly you're no good for nothing.'

The beasts are brought in from the provinces, from East Prussia, Pomerania, West Prussia, Brandenburg. They come mooing and bleating down the ramps. The pigs grunt and snuffle. You're walking in fog. A pale young man picks up the axe, thwack, the blink of an eye, and lights out.

At nine they freed up their elbows, stuffed cigarettes in their fat mouths and started belching out fatty restaurant smoke.

Then something happened.

First a youth came in, hung up his coat and hat and began to play the piano.

The pub filled up. There were some standing at the bar debating. Some sat down next to Franz at the other table, elderly fellows in caps, and a young one with a stiff hat, Mack knew him, and the talk went back and forth between them all. The young guy, with flashing black eyes, a smart boy from Hoppegarten, said:

'D'you know what they first saw when they got to Straylier? Sand and scrub and desert and no trees and no grass and nothing. Just barren waste. And then millions upon millions of yellow sheep. They were living there in the wild. They were what the first settlers lived on. Then later they exported them. To America.' 'Where they need Australian sheep.' 'South America, it's a fact.' 'Where they have all the cattle, you mean. They got more cows there than they know what to do with.' 'But sheep, you know, for wool. The country's full of Negroes, and they feel the cold. As if the English din't know what to do with their sheep. You get to worrying about the English. But what happened to the sheep afterwards? You try going to Australia now, someone said to me, and you won't see a sheep anywhere, for love nor money. All gone. And why? What happened to them?' 'Wild animals gottem, I spose.' Mack gestured irritably: 'Wild animals! Plagues, I say. Them's always the biggest affliction for a country. They die off, and leave you not knowing what hittem.' The boy with the stiff hat was not inclined to think that plagues had been a material factor here. 'Sure, plagues, some. Wherever you got such a lot of animals, you'll get some on em dying, and then they rot away, and you get your scourges. But that's not what I'm thinking. No, they all stampeded into the water once the British got there. There was an outbreak of panic among the sheep all through the country when the British got there, and was rounding em up and putting them in wagons, so thousands of the animals ran off and into the sea.' Mack: 'Well, what if. Let them. It's for the best. It'll save the British on rail freight.' 'Oh, rail freight, yes, I would just think so. It took the British for ever to realize what was even happening. There they were, in the interior and catching em and rounding em up, and putting them on wagons, and such a normous country, and no infrastructure, you know, the way it always is at the beginning. And afterwards, well, it's too late, innit? The sheep are all out to sea, full of salt water.' 'Well, so?' 'Well so what? You try being thirsty and nothing to eat and drinking salt water.' 'Drownded, I shouldn't wonder.' 'You betcha. Thousands upon thousands of them were laying there stinking, and away with the lot of them.' Franz affirmed: 'Animals is sensitive. It's one of them things wi' animals. You need to have a way with them. If you don't know how to deal with them, best keep yer hands off.'

They all drank glumly, exchanging remarks about the waste of capital and the things that went on in America, where they let the wheat rot on the stalk, whole harvests, it had been known to happen. 'Nah,' put in the fellow from Hoppegarten with the dark eyes, 'there's much more of that in Straylier. Nothing's known about it, and there's nothing in the papers, and they don't write about it, don't know why, could be because of immigration, cos otherwise no one would even go there any more. There's sposed to be a kind of lizard that's ancient, prehistoric-like, yards and yards of it, and they don't even ave em in zoos, because the British won't allow it. There was one example that they took off a ship, and they put it on show in Hamburg. But then straight away they slapped a ban on it. Nothing to be done about it. They live in pools of mud and water, no one knows what they lives on. Once a whole column of cars just sank; they didn't even dare try and dig them up to see what happened to them. Nothing. No one would dare. Fact.' 'Blimey,' said Mack, 'did they try poison gas?' The boy considered this: 'Might be worth a try. Couldn't hurt.' Which made sense to the company.

An old man took a seat behind Mack, with his elbow across Mack's chairback, a short stout geezer, flushed red face and bulging eyes swivelling this way and that. The others made room for him. Before long he and Mack got to whispering. The geezer wore polished knee boots, had a calico coat over his arm, and seemed to be a drover. Franz was talking across the table to the entertaining youth from Hoppegarten, who he had taken a bit of a shine to.

Then Mack tapped him on the shoulder, inclined his head to the side, and they stood up, the sawn-off drover as well. They went off a little ways to be by the iron stove. Franz expected it would be about the drovers and their court case. He was about to signal his lack of interest in the matter. But then it was just more pointless standing around. The little guy wanted to shake hands with him, and hear what line of business he was in. Franz patted his newspaper bag. Well, if he ever fancied selling some fruit and veg on the side; his name was Pums, and he was a fruiterer, every so often he could use an extra stallholder. To which Franz responded with a shrug of the shoulder: 'That depends on the kind of margins.' Thereupon they sat back down. Franz thought about the little fellow's energetic spiel; exercise caution, shake well after use.

The conversation had moved on, and Hoppegarten had the bit between his teeth; they were talking about America now. The Hoppegarten youth had his hat on his knees: 'So he's getting married to an American bird, so what. Turns out she's a Negress. "What's this," he says, "is it true you're a Negress?" Bang, she's out on her ear. The woman had to strip in open court. To her bathing drawers. First, she tries to refuse, then she's told not to take on so. Skin was perfectly white. Coz she was mixed race. The fellow maintains she's a Negress. And on what basis? Because the roots of her nails is brown, not white. Makes her a mosquito.' 'Well, and so what's she want? Divorce?' 'Nah, damages. He married her after all, and maybe she quit her job for him. Who wants a divorcee. Gorgeous woman, petal-white, descended from Negroes, maybe dating back to the seventeenth century. Damages.'

There was some commotion at the bar. The landlady was squawking at an excited driver. He stood up for himself: 'I'm not having any malarkey with my food.' The fruit seller yelled: 'Quiet!' The driver turned round angrily, saw the fat fellow, who flashed a grin at him, and there was a tense silence in the bar.

Mack whispered to Franz: 'The drovers won't be coming today. They've got everything sorted. They've got the next hearing in the bag. Take a look at the yaller geezer, he's the ringleader.'

Franz had been staring at the yaller geezer, as Mack dubbed

him, all evening. He felt powerfully drawn to him. He was slender, wore a battered army coat – could he be a Commie? – had a long, bony, yellowish face and striking horizontal creases on his brow. He was in his early thirties, no more, but there were deep pleats from the nose down either side of the mouth. The nose, Franz was looking at him precisely and often, was short, blunt, matter-of-fact. He inclined his head towards his left hand, which was holding a lit pipe. His hair was black and spiky. When he went across to the bar later – he seemed to be dragging both feet, it was as though they were forever getting stuck in something – then Franz could see that he wore wretched yellow boots, with thick grey socks falling over the tops of them. Was it TB? They should stick him in a sanatorium, Beelitz or somewhere, stead of letting him wander around. Wonder what his thing is. The man came drifting up, pipe in his mouth, cup of coffee in one hand, lemonade in the other with a big tin spoon. Then he sat down in his old place, taking alternate sips of coffee and lemonade. Franz couldn't take his eyes off him. What a sad expression. He'll have been inside, I guess; he'll come over, see if he don't, thinking I'll have done time as well. That's right, sunshine, Tegel, four years, so now you know, what next?

There was nothing else that night. But Franz got in the habit of going to Prenzlauer Strasse regularly now, and hurled himself at the man in the old army coat. He was a hell of a fellow, only he had a big stammer, it took him forever to say what he had on his mind, that's why he had such big round imploring eyes. It turned out he hadn't been inside after all, but one time he'd been involved in politics, almost blown up a gasworks, they were snitched on, but he was never nabbed. 'Well, and what are you doing now?' 'Oh, fruit and veg mostly, helping out. If things are bad, down the dole office.' Franz Biberkopf was in shady company, most of the types here were dealing in 'fruit and veg', and doing pretty well by it too, the little fellow with the red face was the supplier, the wholesaler. Franz gave them a wide berth, but they him too. Somehow it didn't quite stack up. So he told himself: stick to newspapers.

Booming trade in girls

One night the fellow in the greatcoat, Reinhold's his name, got talking – or rather, got stammering – but he was surprisingly fluent, and the subject was women. Franz couldn't stop laughing because of the way the fellow was going off the deep end. He'd never have suspected it: so that was his craziness, everyone here seemed to have some defect or other, one here, another there, no one was actually sound all the way through. He had this drayman's missus, and she had already left her husband on his account, and that was the trouble, Reinhold had gone off her. Franz gurgled with glee, the fellow was hilarious: 'Then let her go.' He stammered and glowered terribly: 'That's too hard. Women don't get it, even if you put it in writing, they still don't get it.' 'Well, and did you give it to her in writing, Reinhold?' He stammered, spat and contorted himself: 'Told her a hundred times. She says she doesn't get it. Drives me mad. She doesn't understand. Which means I gotta keep her till the day I die.' 'Could be.' 'Well, that's what she says.' Franz laughed volcanically. Reinhold was angry: 'Christ, don't be such an arse.' No, it wasn't really any of Franz's business, a cheeky fellow, fearless, carries dynamite into a gasworks, and now he's sitting there all blue. 'Take her off me,' stammered Reinhold. Franz slammed the table with delight: 'And what do I do with her?' 'Well, you can send her packing.' Franz was beside himself with joy: 'I'll do you the favour, you can depend on me, Reinhold, but – but first they'll put you in nappies.' 'Take a look at her before you makes any promises.' Both of them were happy with that.

So next day, Fränze (her name) pops up at Franz Biberkopf's pad. Soon as he heard what she was called, he was happy, they made a good pair, because his was Franz. She was bringing Biberkopf a pair of stout shoes from Reinhold; my thirty pieces of silver, Franz chuckled to himself. That Reinhold is a piece of work, getting her to bring me my wage and all. Well, one good turn deserves another, he thought, and that evening he went out with her looking for

Reinhold, who, as arranged, could not be found, whereupon out-
burst of rage from Fränze, and consolation duet in his room. The
next morning the drayman's wife turns up at Reinhold's, who for
once wasn't stammering: he's not to put himself out, she don't need
him no more, she's got someone else. But she won't tell him who.
No sooner is she gone than Franz shows up at Reinhold's in his new
boots, which aren't too big for him any more, because he's wearing
two pairs of wool socks, and they throw their arms round each
other, and pat each other on the back: 'It's just a favour for a friend,'
said Franz, declining all honorifics.

This drayman's wife had fallen for Franz with some élan, she
had an elastic heart which she had been unaware of thus far. Being
philanthropically and analytically inclined, he was happy she felt
herself in possession of this new force. He observed with pleasure
how she settled down with him. it was a familiar sequence to him;
first off, women are always kept busy washing underpants and
darning. The fact that she also cleaned his boots every morning –
the boots he had from Reinhold – that had him in stitches regularly.
When she asked him what he was laughing about, he said: 'It's
because they're so big, they're too big for one single person. Don't
you think we'd both fit inside them?' They even tried getting into
the boots together, but it turned out to be an exaggeration, and not
possible.

Now the stammerer Reinhold, Franz's true friend, had himself
another girlfriend who was called Cilly, or at least so she claimed.
Franz Biberkopf didn't care either way, and he ran into Cilly sometimes on Prenzlauer Strasse. But a dark suspicion rose in him when
the stammerer asked after Fränze after about a month, and whether
Franz had moved her on yet. Franz replied that she was a nice
enough bird, and he didn't quite understand. Then Reinhold
claimed Franz had promised to get rid of her before long. Which
Franz denied, saying it wasn't time for that yet. He was happy to
keep her till spring. He had already seen that Fränze didn't have a
summer wardrobe, and he couldn't afford to buy her one, so she
would have to go in summer. Reinhold observed critically that
Fränze looked pretty down at heel already, and you couldn't call

those proper winter clothes, they were more in between, not really suitable for these temperatures. Thereupon there was a long discussion of temperatures and the barometer and the overall outlook, which they looked up in the newspaper. Franz insisted that you could never be sure which way the weather was going to turn, whereas Reinhold saw a sharp frost coming. Then it dawned on Franz that Reinhold was looking to get shot of Cilly too, who went around in fake rabbit. He couldn't stop talking about that pretty fake bunny fur. 'What am I going to do with that bunny rabbit,' thought Franz, 'that fellow is certainly set in his ways.' 'You're a bit slow today, I'm not going to be able to take on another, when I've got one already and business isn't exactly flourishing. Where to take without stealing.' 'Who said anything about two. Did I say two. Will I force a man to take two women. I'm not a Moslem.' 'That's what I was saying.' 'Well, that's not my point. When did I tell you you need to take on two women. Why not three. Nah, chuck her out – haven't you got someone lined up?' 'What someone?' What's he on about this time, the fellow's full of odd ideas. 'Someone who'll take that Fränze bird off your hands.' Was our Franz ever happy, he bangs him on the arm: 'Christ, you're ruthless, you wrote the book on this, my God, hats off. So we're doing chain-selling, right, like in the Inflation?' 'Well, why not, there's no shortage of women is there.' 'Too many, if you ask me. Christ, Reinhold. You're a card, I can't get my head around it.' 'So what now.' 'We'll do it, it's OK. I'll find someone. I feel stupid in front of you. I'm still a bit gobsmacked.'

Reinhold looked at him. He had bats in the belfry. How could a man be such a fool as Biberkopf. Did he really think he would keep two women at the same time.

Meanwhile Franz was so enthused by the idea that he set off right away, and looked up little stunted Ede in his building; did he want a girl, because he had one that was going.

That suited Ede down to the ground, he had felt like quitting work for a while, he had some invalidity benefit due, and could take some time off, and she can do errands for him and collect. But settling down with me is out of the question, mind.

The next day, before he went out selling papers, Franz made a scene with the drayman's wife about nothing. She exploded. He shouted happily away. An hour later everything was set: the hunchback helped her pack, Franz had run off in a rage, the drayman's wife got moved in with the hunchback because she had nowhere else to go. And the hunchback went to see his doctor, reported sick, and that night the two of them muddied Franz Biberkopf's name together.

Whereas Cilly now comes calling on Franz. What's it about, girl. Something bothering you, got an itch. 'I'm to deliver a fur collar to you.' Franz weighs the collar appraisingly in his hand. Sleek thing. Wonder where he gets this merchandise from. Last time it was just a pair of boots. Cilly, clueless, witters on: 'You must be a very good friend of Reinhold's?' 'Lord, yes,' laughed Franz, 'he likes to send me little delicacies and items of clothing, when he has something over. Lately he sent me some boots. Just boots. Wait a mo, you could have a look at them.' So long as Fränze hasn't taken them with her, where are they keeping, ah, there. 'See, Cilly, this is what he sent me the last time. What do you say to those gun barrels then? It'd take three men to fill those. Why'n't you try putting your little tootsies in there.' And already she's climbing in, giggling, sweet little creature, nicely dressed, what do you say, nice enough to what, looks ever so pretty in her black coat with the fur trim, what a woodentop Reinhold is, shifting her on, and wonder where he keeps on getting these sweet little things from. And there she is standing in the gun barrels. And Franz remembers the last time, women are like a monthly wardrobe to me, and he's slipped his shoe off and he's pushing one foot into the boot behind hers. Cilly squeals, but he gets his leg in, she tries to scamper off, but they're both hopping, and she is forced to take him with her. Then by the table he pushes his other foot in the gun barrel. They're tipping over. They tip over, there's more squealing, screeching this time, now, miss, control your imagination, just leave the pair of them to have a little giggle by themselves, they're seeing private patients only, panel patients later, from five till seven.

'Reinhold's expecting me, Franz, you won't say anything, will you?' 'As if.' And that evening he saw the whole of her, the little fountain of tears. In the evenings they always love a good scold, and she is a very attractive person, has a nice wardrobe, the coat's practically new, a pair of dancing pumps, she's bringing all that with her. Christ, all that's a present from Reinhold, he must get them on lend-lease.

It's always with admiration and contentment that Franz now goes to meet Reinhold. Franz's job isn't easy, he's already dreaming anxiously about the end of the month, when the taciturn Reinhold will begin to speak again. Then one night, Reinhold's standing next to him at the U-Bahn exit on Landsberger Strasse, asking him whether he's got any plans for the evening. What's this, it's not the end of the month yet, what's up, and Cilly's expecting Franz – but of course he can't top going somewhere with Reinhold. And they set off slowly on foot, where do you think, down Alexanderstrasse as far as Prinzenstrasse. Franz keeps pressing Reinhold to learn what the plans are. 'Are we off to Little Walter's then? Dancing?' No, he's going to the Salvation Army on Dresdener Strasse. E wants to listen to the music. Well, who'd of guessed. Typical Reinhold. The ideas in that fellow's head. And so for the first time in his life Franz Biberkopf experienced an evening at the Salvation Army. It was very funny, full of surprises.

At half-nine, when they began with the appeals to sinners, Reinhold started behaving strangely, then ran off as though someone was chasing him, Christ, what's the matter with you. On the steps he lectured Franz: 'You gotta look after the young ones. They'll work on you till you get all out of breath and just end up saying yes to everything.' 'Oh, well I'm not in that sort of shape yet, not by a long chalk, they'd have to get up a lot earlier to catch me out.' Reinhold was still cross in Hackepeter on Prinzenstrasse, and then he was away and what was it this time. 'Franz, I need to do something about these women, I can't do it any more.' 'Crikey, and there I was looking forward to the next one.' 'Do you think I enjoy it, going up to you in another week and asking you to take Trude, my blonde off of me? No, on that basis . . .' 'Well, it's none of my fault. You know you can depend on me. You can come to me with ten women if you want, Reinhold, and I'll manage to place all of them.' 'Leave me alone with women. I've had enough, Franz.' Well, pick the bones out of that, and is he ever wrought-up. 'Well, if you don't fancy them, that's perfectly simple, just leave your hands off of them. We'll manage. The one you've got right now, I'll take her off your hands, and then you can leave it for a while.' Two plus two is four, if you can count, understand, there's no call for those big eyes, Christ, does he ever stare. If you like, you can even hang onto the one you got now. Oh, what is it now, he's come over queer, now he's getting his usual coffee and lemonade, he don't do strong drink he says, wobbly on his pins, and then women on top of that. For a while Reinhold didn't speak, and only when he's had three cups of coffee in him does he spill the beans some more.

The fact that milk is a valuable food is not seriously contested, particularly for children, it is recommended for infants and small children, and to strengthen invalids, especially as part of a protein-rich diet. Another widely recognized invalid food, though unfortunately not often prescribed, is mutton. Nothing against milk. Only the propaganda shouldn't take on such simplistic form. Anyway, thinks Franz, I'm sticking to beer; if it's well kept and drawn, there's nothing the matter wi beer.

Reinhold levels his eyes at Franz – the fellow looks all in, as if he's about to cry: 'I bin there twice already, you know, the Sally Army. I talked to someone as well. I says "yes" to him, try and come up to snuff, then later I fall off.' 'What are you on about now?' 'You know I get fed up with a woman so quick. You can see it for yourself. By the end of four weeks, it's over. Search me why. Don't want her any more. When before I used to be crazy for her, you should see me, crazy, so crazy you'd want to put me in a padded cell. And then: nothing – she's gotta go, I can't stand the sight of her, I'd even be prepared to pay money not to have to see her any more.' Franz, astounded: 'Well, who knows, perhaps there really is something the matter with you. Let's see . . .' 'So I goes to the Salvation Army, and I told someone there about it, and we prayed together . . .' Franz's surprise knows no bounds: 'You prayed?'

'Christ, if you feel that bad, and you've got no other way out.' Wow. So that's how it is with the lad, who'd a guessed. 'It helped too, for six, eight weeks, takes your thoughts off it, you pull yourself together, it was better, it was better.' 'Well, Reinhold, maybe you should try the hospital. Or maybe you shouldn't have dashed out the way you did just now. You could of sat quietly on the bench at the front, you know you've no call to be ashamed in front of me.' 'No, I've had enough of it, and it doesn't help any more, and it's just a load of crap anyway. Why should I crawl over there and pray when I'm not a believer.' 'Oh, I understand. Well, it's no good if you're not a believer.' And Franz looked at his friend, who was staring bitterly into his empty coffee cup. 'If there's anything I can do for you, Reinhold, well – I don't know. I need to give it some thought. Perhaps you should allow yourself to get thoroughly disgusted with women or something like that.' 'The thought of Trude is just about enough to make me vomit right now. But you should see me tomorrow or the day after when there's some Nelly or Guste or what have you in play, see your Reinhold then. With his red ears. Nothing but gotta have her, gotta have her, even if she cleans me out.' 'What is it that gets you about women?' 'You mean, how they get hold of me? Yeah, what. Nothing. That's just it. One has – I don't know – say she's got a bob, or she likes cracking jokes. I don't know what I see in her, Franz, I never know. You should ask the women maybe, when I make sheep's eyes at them, and won't leave them alone. Ask Cilly. But I can't kick it, I can't kick it.'

Franz continues to watch Reinhold.

There is a reaper, Death yclept, by Almighty God employed. His blade he whets, it cuts much better, soon he will cut, and we must suffer.

Strange boy. Franz smiles. Reinhold doesn't.

There is a reaper, Death yclept, by Almighty God employed. Soon he will cut.

Franz thinks: we'll give you a bit of shaking up. Maybe push your hat down another four inches at the back. 'OK, that's what I'll do, Reinhold. I'll try asking Cilly.'

Franz reflects on the trade in women, and suddenly he's had enough, and wants something else

'Cilly, don't sit on my lap just yet. And don't hit me neither, you're my honeybunch. But guess who I've just seen.' 'I don't care.' 'Go on, Cilly Billy, guess? I saw – Reinhold.' That makes the girl suspicious, wonder why: 'Uh, Reinhold. So what did he have to say for himself?' 'That's just it, plenty.' 'I see. So you sit there, and listen, and you believe every word, I suppose.' 'Oh, Cilly, don't be like that.' 'Well, I think I'll just go. First I wait for you to come home for three hours, and then you want to tell me a lot of rubbish.' 'No, no, Christ (she's loopy), I want *you* to tell me something. Not him.' 'What's going on? Now I don't understand anything any more.' And then it got going. Cilly, the little brunette, got in a bate and was sometimes unable to go on, so she would let off steam, and Franz was snogging her while she talked, because she looked so pretty, such a shining little cherry-red honeybird, and on top of that she started crying because of stuff she was remembering. 'That man, Reinhold, he's not a lover and he's not a pimp, he's not a man at all, just a thug. He walks around like a sparrow, going pick pick pick, and he picks up the girls. There's dozens who could tell you about it. You're not thinking I'm his first or his tenth? I might be his hundredth. If you ask him, he won't have a clue how many he's had. And had how. So, Franz, if you're denouncing the crook, you won't get nothing from me, I got nothing, but you could go to the police HQ and pick up a reward. He's nothing to look at, sitting there ever so thoughtful over his chicory decaf. And then he gets interested in a girl.' 'That's just what he said.' 'First of all you're thinking what does he think he wants, he should go packing, and start again. Then he comes back, cheeky, nicely done-up, I tell you, Franz, you scratch your head, what happened with him, did he get the monkey gland treatment or something. So, he starts to talk, and he can dance a bit . . .' 'What, dance, Reinhold?' 'Why ever not. Where'd you spose I met him. On the dance floor, Chausseestrasse.' 'My

God, does he have moves.' 'He'll find you, Franz, wherever you are. Even if you're married, he won't let up, he'll work you round.' 'Swanky geezer.' Franz laughed and laughed. Promises, promises don't make me any promises, because over time everyone's tempted. Hot hearts never stop beating, always on the lookout for a meeting. Make me no promises, because I'm seeking diversion – no different from you. 'How can you laugh. Are you like that as well then?' 'No, Heavens, Cilly, he's weird, he goes wailing to me about how he can't keep his fingers off women.' I can't keep my fingers off, you can't keep your fingers off, he can't keep his fingers off. Franz unpeeled his jacket. 'Now he's with that blonde Trude, and have you heard the latest? He wants me to take her off him.' Does the woman scream? Can that woman ever scream. Cilly screams like a tigress. Rips the jacket away from Franz, hurls it to the floor, careful, it didn't come with a guarantee, she'll make a rip in it, I bet she could and all. 'Christ, Franz, they must have dipped you in chocolate. Tell me what's so great about Trude if you can.' She screams like a rabid tigress. If she keeps it up much longer the police will turn up, thinking I'm turning off the gas. Keep cool, Franz. 'Cilly, whatever you do, not me clothes, OK. They're valuable these days and not easily come by. There, give it to me. I haven't bitten you, have I?' 'No, but you're such an innocent, Franz.' 'Fine, then I'm an innocent. But if Reinhold's my mate, and he's in trouble, and he even legs it over to the Salvation Army in Dresdener Strasse and starts praying to the Almighty, what about that, then I have to stand by him if I'm his friend. Should I not take Trude off him?' 'What about me?' With you, well, with you I'd like to go fishing. 'We can talk it over, then, we can discuss it over a drink or somefink. By the way, have you seen my boots anywhere, the big ones? Look at them.' 'Leave it aht.' 'I just want to show you my boots, Cilly. Because, you know, I got them from him too. You remember – you brought me the fur collar that time. Well. And before that there was a girl brought me those boots.' Tell it straight out, why not, don't keep shtum about it, it's better in the open.

She sits down on the stool and stares at him. Then she starts crying, without a word. 'So that's it. It's the way he is. I helped him out. He's my friend. I'm not keeping nothing from you.' The way she's glaring at me. The fury: 'You dirty rotten bastard, you rotten so-and-so. You know if Reinhold's a bastard, you're worse – you're worse than the lowest pimp.' 'No, that's not true.' 'If I was a man . . .' 'Well, I'm happy you're not. But no need to get all het up about it, Cilly. I've told you everything that transpired. Just looking at you now, I've had a rethink. I've decided I'm not going to take Trude off his hands, I want you to stay where you are.' Franz gets up, picks up his boots, tosses them on the chest of drawers. It's not gonna happen, I'm not doing it, he wastes people, I'm not doing it. Something needs to be done about him. 'Cilly, you stay with me tonight. Tomorrow, when Reinhold's out, you can go and see his Trude and have a word with her. I'll help her, she can rely on me. Tell her, hang on, get her to come up, and we can both of us talk to her.'

And the next day when blonde Trude is up with Franz and Cilly, she's already very pale and sad-looking, and Cilly is telling her to her face about how Reinhold is just a drag and not doing anything for her. Which is all true. When Trude starts howling, without knowing what the two want her to do, Franz declares: 'The man's not a villain, though. He's my friend, I won't have anything said against him. But what he does is cruelty to dumb animals. It's torture.' She's not to allow herself to be turned against him, and anyway, he, Franz . . . well, we'll see.

That night, Reinhold comes to pick up Franz from his news-paper pitch, it's effing cold, Franz is happy to be treated to a hot toddy, he ignores Reinhold's preamble, then sure enough Reinhold starts in on Trude, and how she was too much for him, and he wanted to get shot of her tonight.

'Reinhold, I'm thinking you've got another girl already lined up?' He does, and doesn't mind saying so. Then Franz says he's not about to give Cilly the boot, she's settled in nicely with him and his ways, and she's a proper bit of woman, and he, Reinhold, needs to take his foot off the gas as befits a proper man, that's no way to carry on. Reinhold doesn't get it, and wants to know who give him the collar, the fur collar. Why, Trude might be good for a silver watch, or a fur hat with flaps, surely Franz could use something like that. No, nothing doing, just enough chit-chat. I can get it meself. Franz wanted a friendly word in Reinhold's ear. And then tells him what he's been thinking, today and yesterday as well. Reinhold was to hang on to Trude for the foreseeable. He's to get used to her, then it won't be such a problem. A person's a person, same with a woman, and then he can always go and buy himself a bird for 3 marks, she'll be happy to be allowed to trot off afterwards. But first ensnaring a woman with love and feeling, and then giving her the heave-ho, serially, that wasn't on.

Reinhold hears him out, in his way. He sips his coffee, and seems to be in a drowse. He says quietly that if Franz won't take Trude off his hands, so be it. He's managed without his help in the past. Then he pushes off, he's got stuff he needs to do.

In the night Franz wakes up and doesn't get off to sleep again. It's freezing. Cilly beside him is asleep and snoring. Why can he not sleep? The vegetable carts are trundling on their way to the market hall. I wouldn't want to be a horse, not in this weather, at this hour. Stables is warm, I'll be bound. My God, that woman can sleep. Can she ever sleep. Not me. My toes are frozen, I can feel the itch and tickle. There's something inside of him, his heart, his lungs, his inner self, it's there and it's being buffeted and bent, who by? It doesn't know, the mystery thing don't, who by. All it can say for sure is that it's not asleep.

A bird sits up in a tree, a snake just slipped by while it was asleep, the rustle it made woke the bird, and now it's sitting there with its feathers all fluffed up, it didn't register there was a snake. Keep breathing, draw even breaths, one after the other. Reinhold's hatred is weighing on him and attacking him. It makes its way through wooden doors, and has woken him up. Reinhold too is lying there. He is lying fast asleep, in his dream he is a murderer, in his dream he is making room for himself to breathe.

Local news

It was the second week of April in Berlin, the weather could be balmy at times, and, as the press unanimously proclaimed, the gorgeous Easter weather was bringing people out of doors. In Berlin at that time a Russian student, Alex Fränkel, shot his fiancée, the twenty-two-year-old arts and crafts worker Vera Kaminskaya, in her digs. The same-aged au pair, Tatiana Sanftleben, who had been in on the suicide pact, got scared at the very last moment, and slipped off as her friend was already lying lifeless on the floor. She ran into a police foot patrol, told them the terrible details of the past few months, and led the officials to the place where Vera and Alex lay dying. The serious crime squad was alerted, and murder detectives despatched to the site. Alex and Vera had wanted to marry, but their economic circumstances would not allow it.

In other news, the investigations over responsibility for the tram accident on Heerstrasse are still unconcluded. Eyewitnesses and the driver, one Redlich, are being questioned. Technical reports are not yet completed. Only when they have come in will it be possible to decide whether the catastrophe was due to human error (driver slow to apply the brakes) or a tragic combination of circumstances.

The stock exchange was largely quiet: in the open market, prices were a little firmer, in view of a recently published Reichsbank report that took a positive view of the disposal of 400 million in obligations and another 350 million in credit notes. In individual shares, as of 11 a.m. on 18 April, I. G. Farben traded over a narrow range from 260.5 to 267, Siemens & Halske 297.5 to 299; Dessau Gas 202 to 203, Waldhof Cellulose 295. German Petroleum steady at 134.5.

To return to the tram accident on Heerstrasse, all the injured passengers were said to be improving in hospital.

On 11 April, editor Braun mounted an armed escape from Moabit prison. In scenes reminiscent of the Wild West, a pursuit was staged, the prosecution reported to justice department officials. Eyewitnesses and law enforcement officers are still being questioned.

Public media in Berlin were less exercised at this time by one of the leading American auto manufacturers inviting offers from established German partners for exclusive rights to sell six- to eight-cylinder models across Northern Germany.

Cultural news now – and this is of particular interest to inhabitants of the Steinplatz telephone exchange – the drama *Knave of Hearts*, coupling exuberant comedy with deeper significance, is extending its run to 100 performances at the Renaissance Theatre on Hardenberg Strasse. Berliners are called upon by a poster campaign to help the piece attain still higher levels of popularity. Several things need to be borne in mind here: while Berliners may be called upon, they may be kept by a plethora of factors from hearing the call. They may have left town already, and be ignorant of the play's existence. They may be in Berlin without having seen the postings on advertising pillars, because they are ill, for instance, and in bed. In a city of 4 million inhabitants, such a number may be quite sizeable. They may have been alerted by radio advertisements on the six o'clock news that the charming French drama *Knave of Hearts*, coupling exuberant comedy with deeper significance, is extending its run at the Renaissance Theatre. Such news, though, could only move them to regret that they are unable to betake themselves to Hardenberg Strasse, because if they are indeed bed-bound, they cannot possibly get there. Sources close to the Renaissance Theatre have confirmed that there are no arrangements in hand for the accommodation of bedridden spectators, perhaps to be delivered by ambulances.

A further factor: there could well be people in Berlin – doubtless there are – who read the Renaissance Theatre's posting, but question its veracity, not in the sense that they doubt the existence of the poster, but the truthfulness and pertinence of its contents. They might read with distaste, with annoyance and irritation, the claim that the comedy *Knave of Hearts* is 'charming', charming whom, charming what, charming insomuch as what, how can they think of charming me, did I ask to be charmed. They might set their lips in a frown on reading of a play pairing exuberant comedy with deeper moments. They don't care for exuberant comedy, they take life seriously, their attitude is melancholy and grave, some recent fatalities have taken place in their family. Nor do they believe the claim that deeper seriousness is paired with the lamentable exuberant humour. For it is their opinion that a cancellation or neutralization of exuberant humour is not actually possible. Deeper meaning must and can only stand alone. Exuberant humour should be got rid of, the way Carthage was got rid of by the Romans, or various other cities in various ways they don't presently recall. Other people again don't believe in the deeper meaning that inheres in the play *Knave of Hearts* that is being celebrated on the advertising pillars. A deeper meaning – deeper than what? Is deeper supposed to be deeper than merely deep? So they carp and carp away.

It's fair enough: in a big city like Berlin, there will always be a lot of people doubting, finding fault and questioning a lot of things and, among them, every word of the director's expensively produced poster. They have no use for theatre. And even if they didn't knock it, even if they adored the theatre, and especially the Renaissance Theatre on Hardenberg Strasse, and admitted that this piece successfully combined delicious humour with deeper sense, they still wouldn't end up going there, simply because they had something else planned for tonight. With that, the number of persons streaming to the Hardenberg Strasse and extending the run of the play *Knave of Hearts* would be considerably reduced.

Following this instructive excursus on public and private events in Berlin in spring 1928, we return to the matter of Franz Biberkopf, Reinhold and his plague of women. It is to be expected that interest in their story is moderate at best. Let us not enquire into the reasons for this. I for my part will not be put off my dogged pursuit of the footsteps of my ordinary man in Berlin Mitte and east, in the end everyone does what he has to do.

Franz takes a calamitous decision. He fails to realize he is sitting in a nettle patch

Reinhold did not feel happy after his conversation with Franz Biberkopf. It was not in Reinhold's nature, at least thus far, to be rough with women, as Franz was. He needed someone to help him, and in this instance he was beached. They were all after him, Trude, the incumbent, Cilly his ex, and her predecessor whose name had escaped him. They were all snooping on him, partly out of anxiety (the latest model), partly out of vengeance (the second last model), partly newly in love with him (antepenultimate model). The very latest to have appeared on the horizon, a certain Nelly from the Central Market, a widow, had lost interest when Trude, Cilly and last of all a man, a sworn witness, one Franz Biberkopf, friend to Reinhold, had gone up to her and warned her. It's quite true, he did. 'Frau Labschinsky – which was Nelly's name, of course – I'm not doing this to get in with you, or to blacken the name of my friend or whatever. Not on your, whoops, nelly. I don't like to get involved in other people's dirty laundry. But what's right is right. To push a woman out on the street, that's not on where I'm concerned. And that's not love neither.'

Frau Labschinsky gave a contemptuous huff of the bosom: Reinhold'd better not try anything with *her*. She weren't born yesterday, you know. Continued Franz: 'I'm happy to hear that, that's good enough for me. Then I spect you'll know the ropes. Because you'll be doing a good thing, and that's my mission to you. I'm sorry for womenfolk, which are human beings like us, and Reinhold too. It does his head in. That's why he can't drink beer or schnapps, only watery coffee. He can't stand a drop. So he needs to get his act together. He's got a good heart.' 'Oh, he does, he does,' wailed Frau Labschinsky. Franz nodded earnestly: 'And that's why I'm here for him, he's been through a lot already, but he can't go on this way, and we need to hold up our hand and say enough's enough.'

Frau Labschinsky offered Herr Biberkopf her powerful mitt when he left: 'Well, I'm relying on you, Herr Biberkopf.' She was absolutely right to. Reinhold did not move out. He was a man of habits settled, but opaque. He was already three weeks past the deadline with Trude, every day Franz was summoned for consultations. Franz was jubilant: the next one's getting about due. Best look out. And indeed: one day a trembling Trude tells him Reinhold's been out for two nights running in his good suit. The following day she found out who it was: one Rosa, who sewed buttonholes, early thirties, she hadn't got her last name, but she knew the address. Well, then everything's as it should be, thought Franz. But there is no accommodation to be made with the Fates. And destiny moves fast. It's time to step out. Step out in Leiser's shoes. Leiser's is the biggest shoe shop on the square. And if you don't want to foot it, then why not drive: NSU invite you to take a spin in their new six-cylinder. That very day, a Thursday, Franz was once more walking up Prenzlauer Strasse, alone, because it had occurred to him to look up his friend Mack, he hadn't seen him in a while, and he wanted to tell him about Reinhold and the women, and Mack was to listen and marvel at the way he, Franz, set about taming such a fellow, and how he could get him under control, and get him used to stability and all.

And lo, when Franz walks into the bar with his column of newspapers, who do mine eyes see but Mack. Sitting there with a couple of others, troughing. So Franz up and joins the company, and when the other two are gone they take a couple of big ones at Franz's invitation, and now Franz is gleefully and gulpingly telling the story, and a startled and awed Mack is gleefully and gulpingly listening to it, some mothers do ave em. Mack promises to keep it under his hat, but it is an amazing yarn. Franz beams and tells him what steps he's taken in the matter, how he kept Nelly, what used to be Frau Labschinsky, out of Reinhold's clutches, and forced him to keep with Trude three weeks past due, and now there's a certain Rosa on the scene, what sews buttonholes, but we're not going to let him open those buttons. And Franz is sitting there well set with his beer and all, in clover. Praise ye, o tonsils, ye youthful choirs, there is a song arising up around our table, widdeboom, there is a song arising up. Three threes are nine, we drink like swine, three times three and one is ten, or men, we have another one, two, three, four, six, seven.

Who's standing at the bar, the place of refreshment, the place of song and shongsong, who's shmiling in the shmoke? Numero uno, Mijnheer von and zu Pums, if you please. He smiles, if you could call it a smile, but his little piggy eyes are searching. The fug in here, the brume, is so thick you'd need a broom to clear it. Here's three lads making their way towards him. They're the lads who always trade with him, good lads. Same types, same identical caps. Hanged early beats scavenging butts old. The four of them scratch their heads together, whinny together, look around together. It'd take a broom to see anything in here, or a ventilator would do at a pinch. Mack gives Franz a nudge: 'You know, they're not booked out yet. They're still looking for men to hire, the fat man can't find enough workers.' 'He's come knocking on my door before now. But will I get involved with him. What do I care about fruit and veg? Has he got a lot to sell?' 'Who knows what he's got. Fruit and veg, is all I know. Don't ask too many questions, Franz. But it's not bad advice to make up to him, something is bound to come your way. He's an old reprobate, and the other fellows are too.'

At 8:23:17 another man steps up to the bar, the place of refreshment, one – one, two, three, four, five, six, seven, my old mum, she cooks beets – who will it be? They say it's the King of England. No, it's not the King of England, on his way to the state opening of Parliament, to bear witness to the independence of the English government. Not him. So who is it? Is it the delegates of the nations, assembled in Paris to sign the Kellogg Pact, ringed by fifty photographers, the original inkwell could not be used because of its great size, so they had to make do with a set from Sèvres? No, not them either. It's just, shuffling up, bellying up, grey woollen socks round his ankles, Reinhold, unimposing, grey mouse in mouse-grey. All five scratch their heads, look about them in the bar. You'd need a broom to see something in here, or a ventilator might do the trick. Franz and Mack eye the five lads, watch what they do, and how they start off by occupying a table together.

After a quarter of an hour, Reinhold will get himself a cup of coffee and a fizzy lemonade, and take the opportunity of scanning the bar. And who will beam at him from the back wall, and give him a cheery wave? Not Dr Luppe, Mayor of Nuremberg, because he is giving the opening address today on Dürer Day, followed by the Minister of the Interior Dr Keudell and the Bavarian Culture Minister Dr Goldenberger, and the last-named gentlemen are similarly unable to be here. Wrigley P. R. chewing gum promotes healthy teeth, sweet breath and improved digestion. It's only Franz Biberkopf, grinning all over his face. He's thrilled to bits that Reinhold is coming over. Here's his pupil, his apprentice, he can show him off to his friend Mack. Well, look what the cat brought in. I've got him on a leash, seems. Reinhold putters up with coffee and fizz, collapses into himself, and stammers a bit. Franz feels like giving him an affectionate and curious quizzing in front of Mack: 'How's everything at home, Reinhold, all well?' 'Well, Trude's there . . . Getting used to it.' He says it by instalments, it's like listening to a leaky pipe drip. Well, and is Franz ever pleased to hear it. He almost leaps up in the air for joy. He's made it. All on his lonesome. And he beams at his mate Mack, who doesn't deny him a measure of admiration. 'Hear that, Mack, we're setting the world to rights, see if we ain't.' Franz pats Reinhold on the back, causing him to twitch: 'See, mate, a man pulls himself together a bit, then the world makes sense. I always says: pull together and pull through.' And Franz can't get enough of his joy about Reinhold. One repentant sinner is better than 999 righteous men.

'And what about Trude, she astonished how well everything's going? And you, mate, aren't you happy to be through that bit of bother? You know, women are a bit of all right, and fun. But if you ask me for my opinion of em, then I say: not too little of them, and not too much neither. If it's too much, then lay off of em. Just ask me, I know.' The lay of Ida, Paradiesgarten, Treptow, canvas shoes and Tegel to follow. The echo of triumph has drained away in the drink. 'I'll help you out, Reinhold, get you nicely set up. What do you need the Sally Army for, we'll get it sorted. Cheers Reinhold, old son, mebbe you'll have a beer with us now.' He silently bumped his glass against the coffee cup: 'What can you get sorted, Franz, and why?'

Christ, I almost shot me mouth off. 'Oh, just that you can always rely on me, schnapps is a bit of an acquired taste, but kummel's nice and easy on the system.' The other, insistently: 'You wanting to play doctor with me, is that it?' 'Why not. I know about these kind of things. You remember I helped you out before, Reinhold, with

Cilly, and all. Don't you trust me to stand by you now? Franz the philanthropist. The one who knows the way to go.'

Reinhold looks up, fixes him with his sad expression: 'I see, so you know that, do you?' Franz doesn't look away, won't be disturbed in his own joy and pride, let the other guy see, it'll do him good if he notices people standing up for themselves. 'Yeah, Mack here can confirm that we have been through certain grave experiences, and that's what gives us our authority. And then about the schnapps; Reinhold, once you can stomach some, then I'd like to throw a party for you here, at my expense, I'll pay the whole shebang.' Reinhold is still fixing Franz, who has his chest thrust out, and little Mack, who is eyeing him curiously. Reinhold lowers his regard and starts staring into his coffee: 'I expect you want to make half a married cripple out of me, then.' 'Cheers, Reinhold, here's to married cripples everywhere, three threes are nine, we drink like swine, sing along, Reinhold, beginnings is tricky, it's the endings are sticky.'

The whole lot. In formation. By the rate, quick, march. Reinhold climbs out of his cup of coffee. Pums, the one with the red feisty face, is whispering something in his ear, Reinhold shrugs. Then Pums parps through the fug: 'I've asked you once before, Biberkopf, what about you, are you still happy in the newspaper trade? What do you make, tuppence a copy, five pfennigs an hour, something like that?' And then there's a little back and forth, Franz is to take over a fruit or veg stand, Pums will supply the wares, the expected earnings are impressive. Franz is in favour and against, he doesn't really like Pums's set-up, they're bound to swindle me. Reinhold the stammerer keeps silent. When Franz turns to ask him what he thinks of it, he notices he's been watching him all along, and has just turned to seek refuge in his cup. 'Well, what do you reckon, Reinhold.' He stammers back: 'Well, I'm in, inni.' And when Mack chips in, why not, Franz, then Franz promises to think it over, he doesn't want to say yes or no right away, but he'll come by tomorrow or the day after and talk it over with Pums, and about the goods, and picking them up, and what area would be best suited to him.

Everyone's gone home, the pub is almost empty, Pums is gone, Mack and Biberkopf are gone, a tram driver is standing at the bar, getting into the question of wage stoppages with the landlord, he thinks they're on the high side. The stammerer Reinhold is still in his chair. There are three empty lemonade bottles in front of him, a half-full glass and the cup of coffee. He's not going home. At home is blonde Trude. He ponders and thinks. He gets up, shuffles across the pub, his woollen socks are round his ankles. The man looks wretched, deep furrows either side of his mouth, the terrible creases across his forehead. He buys himself another coffee and another lemonade.

Cursed be the man, saith Jeremiah, that trusteth in man, and maketh flesh his arm, and whose heart departeth from the Lord. For he shall be like the heath in the desert, and shall not see when good cometh; but shall inhabit the parched places in the wilderness, in a salt land and not inhabited. Blessed is the man that trusteth in the Lord, and whose hope the Lord is. For he shall be as a tree planted by the waters, and that spreadeth out her roots by the river, and shall not see when heat cometh, but her leaf shall be green; and shall not be careful in the year of drought, neither shall cease from yielding fruit. The heart is deceitful above all things, and desperately wicked: who can know it?

Water in the thick dark woods, terrible black water, you are so quiet. You lie there quiet and terrible. Your surface is not moved, no, not when the forest is hit by storm and the pines begin to bend and the spiders' webs between their branches tear and the branches themselves begin to crack. Then you lie down in the hollow, you black waters, and the boughs fall.

The wind tugs at the trees, but you the storm does not reach. You have no dragons in your beds, the time of mammoths is gone, nothing is there that might frighten anyone, plants moulder away in you, fishes and snails bestir themselves. Nothing more. But even then, even though you are nothing but water, you are eerie, black water, terrible, quiet water.

Sunday, 8 April 1928

'Will there be one more snowfall, one more white-out in April?' Franz Biberkopf sat by the window in his little digs, propped his left elbow on the sill, leant his head on his hand. It was Sunday afternoon, the room warm and snug. Cilly had heated the room, now she was asleep in the alcove with her little pussycat. 'Is there going to be snow? The sky's so grey. I wouldn't mind if there was.'

And as Franz closed his eyes, he heard the bells ringing. He sat there for minutes, listening to the ringing: boom, bim bim boom, bim bam, boom boom bim. Until he lifted his head off his hand, and listened: there were two tenor bells and one treble. They stopped.

Why are they ringing now, he wondered. Then all of a sudden they began again, authoritative, greedy, turbulent. It was a terrible din, and all at once it was over.

Franz took his elbow off the sill and turned to face the room. Cilly was sitting on the bed, hand-mirror in her hand, hairpins between her lips, humming as Franz approached. 'What's goin on, Cilly babes. Is it a holiday?' She fiddled with her hair. 'Well, t's a Sunday, innit.' 'Not a holiday?' 'Maybe Cathlick, I dunno.' 'Coz the way the bells was going.' 'Where?' 'Juss now.' 'Didn't hear nuffink. Did you hear em, Franz?' 'Well, they was loud enough.' 'I reckon you must of bin dreaming.' Alarm. 'Nah, I wasn't dreaming, I was sitting there.' 'Dropped off, mebbe.' 'Nah,' he insisted, was adamant, moved slowly, sat down at his place at the table. 'You can't dream summing like that. Heard it, dinni.' He poured a swallow of beer. His alarm remained.

He looked over to Cilly, who was already looking a bit tearful: 'Who knows what's just happened, Cilly.' And he asked about the paper. She could laugh. 'Not now, man, it's a Sunday.'

He looked at the morning paper, scanning the headlines: 'Loads of small fry. No, it's not in there. Nothing.' 'If you can hear bells, Franz, then you'll go to church.' 'Ah, leave the priests out of it. I got no use for them. Just it's so queer, you hear someink, and you go and see, and it weren't nothing.' He stopped and thought, she by his side, stroking him. 'I'm going out for a breath of air, Cilly. Just an hour or so. I wanna find out if anything's happened. *Die Welt* or *Montag Morgen* will be out, I gotta go see.' 'Oh, Franz, you and your pondering. It will say: Garbage truck breaks down at Prenzlauer Tor, and sheds its load. Or, how about this one: Newspaper seller gives correct change.'

Franz laughed: 'Well, that's my cue. Bye, Cilly.'

'Bye, Franz.'

And thereupon Franz slowly walked down four flights of steps, and never saw his Cilly again.

She waited in the room till five o'clock. When he didn't show up, she went out and asked after him in the bars as far as the corner of Prenzlauer Strasse. He hadn't been seen in any of them. But he was going to read up in the paper about that silly thing he probably dreamt. So he must have gone somewhere. On the corner of Prenzlauer, the landlady said: 'No, he's not been seen in here. But Herr Pums was asking for him. And then I tells him Herr Biberkopf's address, and he'll have gone to look for him there.' 'No, no one's been round.' 'Perhaps he didn't find him.' 'Maybe.' 'Or bumped into him going out.'

Then Cilly sat there till late at night. The bar filled up. She kept looking in the direction of the door. Once, she ran home and came back. Mack showed up, he comforted her and made her laugh for a quarter of an hour. He said: 'Oh, he'll be back. The lad's used to getting his meals. Don't you worry about him, Cilly.' But even as he said it, he remembered how Lina had sat next to him that other time, how she'd been out looking for Franz, during the business with Lüders and the bootlaces. And he almost accompanied Cilly out onto the dark mucky street; but he didn't want to alarm her, because it might all be a fuss about nothing.

In a temper, Cilly suddenly took it into her head to go looking for Reinhold; maybe he'd talked Franz into some other cow, and Franz was dumping her. Reinhold's place was locked, no one home, not even Trude.

She drifted back to the bar. It was snowing, but the snow didn't stick around. On the Alex the newspaper sellers were crying

Montag Morgen and *Welt am Montag*. She bought a paper from one of them, to take a look herself. To see if something had happened, to see if he was right this afternoon. Well, there was a train crash in the United States, in Ohio somewhere, and there was a clash between Communists and swastikas, no, that's not Franz's scene, and a fire in Wilmersdorf. That's nothing to do with me. She dawdled past the brightly lit Tietz's, then crossed over to unlit Prenzlauer Strasse. She was getting soaked, she'd forgotten her umbrella. Outside the little café on Prenzlauer Strasse was a little clutch of tarts under umbrellas, blocking the way. Just past them a hatless fat man accosted her as he stepped out of a doorway. She hurried by. But I'll go with the next man, what does he think he's playing at. I've not had such a mean thing done to me as that.

It was quarter to ten. A ghastly Sunday. At that time Franz was lying in another part of town with his legs on the pavement and his head in the gutter.

Franz goes down the stairs. One step, then another and another and another, four floors, down and down and down and down. A man feels tired, jumbled in his brain. Cooking soup, Miss Stein, got a spoon, Miss Stein, gotta spoon, Miss Stein, cooking soup, Miss Stein. No, that's no help, my, I was just boiling in there. I had to get some fresh air. The light's so dim, hang onto the balustrade, it'd be so easy to catch on a nail or something.

A door opens on the second floor, a man slowly follows him down. He must be carrying some weight, to hear him puffing like that, downstairs and all. Franz Biberkopf stops at the foot of the stairs, the sky is soft and grey, it really does look like snow. The man goes puffing past him, the man on the stairs, a little plump fellow, with a puffy white face; wearing a green felt hat. 'You're a bit short of breath, ain't ya, neighbour.' 'Yes, I'm overweight, and all those steps.' They walk along the street together. The short-breathed man puffs: 'Today I've been five times up and down four flights. Work it out, twenty flights, each of thirty steps or so, spiral stairs are shorter but harder, so say thirty steps, five flights, a hundred and fifty steps. All the way up and all the way down.' 'Makes three hundred all told.

Coz going down is a strain as well, as I've had occasion to notice.'
'You're right there.' 'I should look for a new job for myself.'

It is snowing heavy flakes, they twirl prettily in the air. 'Yes, I'm
in the ads business. Not every day, mind. Sunday's best. More
people buy space on Sundays, they think that's most likely to bring
results.' 'Sure, because that's the day people have time to read the
paper. I don't need glasses to understand that. It's my metier.' 'Do
you advertise as well?' 'Nah, I just sell papers. I'm on my way to
read one now.' 'Ha, coz I've read them all. What about this
weather, eh. Have you ever known the like.' 'Typical April, innit.
Yesterday was beautiful. Mark my words, tomorrow'll be fine
again. Wanna bet?' The fellow gets his breath back, the street lights
are on, under one he pulls out a small looseleaf jotter, holding it out
a long way away from himself to read. Franz volunteers: 'It's getting wet, you know.' The man doesn't hear him, stashes his jotter
away, the conversation is finished, thinks Franz, I'll take my leave.
Then the little man looks at him from under his green hat: 'Tell
me, neighbour, what is it you do, again?' 'Me? I'm a newspaper
seller, self-employed newspaper seller.' 'I see. And that gets you by,
does it.' 'Well, it's all right.' Wonder what's he after, queer fish. 'I
always wanted to be self-employed meself. Must be nice, you're
your own boss, and if you work hard, you get by.' 'Yeah. Or not. But
you do enough walking as it is, neighbour. Today, on a Sunday, and
with this weather, there's not many out and about.' 'You're right,
you're right. I spend half the day on my feet. And if nothing comes
in, then nothing comes in. People nowadays are strapped.' 'What is
it you sell, neighbour, if I might ask?' 'I've got my little pension. I
just wanted to, you know, be a free man, work, earn a living. So I've
had my pension for three years, that's how long I used to work for
the post office, and now I'm walking and walking. It's like this: I
look in the paper and then I go see what people are advertising.'
'Furniture, stuff like that?' 'Whatever there is, used office furniture, Bechstein pianos, old Persian rugs, pianolas, stamp collections,
coins, old clothes.' 'There's people dying all the time.' 'A whole
bunch. Well, and so I go up and take a look, and sometimes I buys.'
'And then you sell them on, I get it.'

Thereupon the asthmatic fell silent once more and pulled his coat around him, and they strolled on through the gently falling snow. At the next street light the fat asthmatic pulled a bunch of postcards out of his pocket, looked gloomily at Franz and pressed a couple into his hand: 'Read this, neighbour.' On the card he read: 'Dated as postmarked. To my regret I am forced by adverse circumstance to go back on the agreement we came to yesterday. Respectfully, Bernhard Kauer.' 'That's you is it, Kauer?' 'Yes, I had it printed on a copy machine I bought once. That's the only thing I bought meself. I do my own printing with it. You can make fifty copies in an hour.' 'You don't say. Well, but what's it in aid of.' The fellow's not right upstairs, his eyes wobble and all. 'Just read it, will you: forced by adverse circumstance to go back on the agreement? I'm buying something, and then I can't manage to pay for it. People don't hand stuff over without payment. Who can blame them either. And I keep running up and buying and agreeing, and the people are pleased because it all passed off so easily, and I'm thinking to myself I'm in luck, all these nice things, wonderful coin collections, I could tell you a thing or two, people who all've a sudden 've got no money, and then I walks up, look at everything and they tell me straight off what the position is, the misery people live in, if they could only manage to lay their hands on a few pennies, I bought something in your building too, people are so needy, a mangle and a small icebox, they were glad to be rid of em. And then I go down, see, I'd like to take everything off their hands, but downstairs I start to get worried: no money, no money.' 'But you must have already got someone lined up to take the stuff off your hands.' 'In your dreams. I bought the copy machine that I turn out the postcards on. Each of em costs me five pfennigs, those are my overheads, and that's it, end of story.'

Franz made big eyes: 'I can't believe what you're telling me there, neighbour. You're not serious.' 'My expenses – and sometimes I save five pfennigs, and drop the card in the box on my way out.' 'And you walk your legs off, and are short-winded, and all in aid of what?'

They had reached Alexanderplatz.

There was a crowd, and they joined it. The little man glowered up at Franz: 'You try living on eighty-five marks a month and your native wit.' 'But for God's sake, man, you need to give some thought to flogging the merchandise. If you want, I can ask around, I know some people.' 'Get away with you, I never asked you for help, I'm in business by myself, I don't work for a company.' They were in the middle of the crowd, there was some kind of commotion going on. Franz looked for the little man, but he was gone, stomped off. So he's run off, wondered Franz, you could have knocked me over with a. What got him going? He walked into a bar, ordered a kummel, leafed through a copy of *Vorwärts*, local advertiscr. There's more in there than in the rotten *Mottenpost*, a big horse race in England, and another one in Paris, mebbe; could be they had a huge payout. It might have been a great stroke of good fortune that I've got ringing in my cais.

And he's in the process of turning on his heel and going home. Then he just needs to go over the way and see what the kerfuffle is all about. Frankfurters'n'potato salad! Here, young man, try our whopping franks. *Montag Morgen, Welt, Welt am Montag*!

What do you say to those two, they've been pummelling each other for the past half-hour, for no reason. Think I'll stay here till tomorrow morning. You, you must have paid for a standing place, the way you're set there. Nah, a little flea can't exactly take up space. Ooh, look at that, isn't he just giving him what for.

When Franz has managed to push his way through to the front, who is it who's fighting? Two lads he knows, two of Pums's boys. Well, how about that. Smack, the tall one's got the other in a grip, smack, he's dropped him in the slush. My, how you let someone like that boss you about, you weakling. Hey, what's all the shoving about. Uh-oh, it's the filth. Scarper. Under rain-capes, two cops push their way through the mob. Hupp, the one Greco-Roman wrestler is up again, barging his way through the crowd. The other one, the tall geezer, it takes him a while to get up, he's winded from a pop in the ribs. Then Franz pushes his way through to the very front. I'm not about to leave the feller lying there, what kind of pcople are these, no one lending a hand. And Franz has picked him up and is hauling him away through the crowd. The police are looking. 'What's going on here then?' 'A couple of boys was having a fight.' 'All right then, nothing to see, move along.' Always plenty to say for themselves, and always a day late. We're doing our best, ossifer, keep your hair on.

Franz and the lanky geezer are sitting in a dimly lit entryway on Prenzlauer Strasse; two doors from the building where in another four hours a hatless fat man will accost Cilly; she walks on by, but she'll go with the next man for sure, how can that rotter Franz be so mean to her.

Now Franz is sitting in the entryway, giving lazy Emil a shake: 'Come on, man, let's get up and have a drink. Don't take on so, you can take more punishment than that. You need to wash the tarmac off you.' They walk over the road. 'Now I'm gonna drop you off at the next bar, right, Emil, I need to go home, I got my sweetheart waiting for me.' Franz is shaking him by the hand, when the fellow up and says: 'Say, Franz, could you do us a favour. I'm supposed to collect goods from Pums. Would you run by there for me, it's only a few steps. Be a good lad.' 'What are you on about, I ain't got time.' 'Just let him know I can't make it today, he's waiting. He'll be stuck otherwise.'

Cursing, Franz trots off, the weather, and always do this do that, Christ, I wanna get home, I can't keep Cilly waiting. Idiot, my time's not my own. He runs off. By a lamp-post stands a small man, reading a book. Who's that again, I know him, donni. Then he looks up and sees Franz right off: 'Oh, it's you, neighbour. You live in that house that had the mangle and the icebox, don't you. Here, will you deliver this card, later, when you go home, it'll save me the postage.' And he presses the postcard into Franz's hand, adverse circumstance compels me. Whereupon Franz Biberkopf wanders calmly on, he'll show Cilly the postcard first, it's not like it's urgent. He's happy about the loopy fellow, running around and making his purchases though he's got no money, but he's mad, and not just mad, he's got a full-blown mental condition that can feed a family. Or not.

'Evening to you, Herr Pums. Surprised to see me, are you, eh? Listen up and I'll tell you. I was crossing the Alex. Saw a brawl on the corner of Landsberger. I'm thinking I'll stop and take a look. So who is it who's fighting? Well? Your man, Emil, the lanky geezer, and a little guy who's called Franz, same as me. You'll know.' Whereupon Herr Pums replies: he had been thinking of Franz Biberkopf anyway, he had noticed at lunchtime that there was some bad blood between those other two. 'So the lanky man's not coming. What about stepping in for him, Biberkopf?' 'Me what?' 'It's getting on for six o'clock. We need to collect the goods at nine. Come on, Biberkopf, it's a Sunday, it's not as though you're doing anything else, I'll pay your expenses, and give you some money on top of that – let's say five marks an hour.' Franz is uncertain: 'Five marks, eh.' 'Well, you know, I'm up against it, those two have left me in a spot.' 'Oh, the little fellow'll show up all right.' 'So five marks plus your expenses, call it five-fifty, I'm feeling generous.'

Franz is laughing inwardly as he follows Pums down the stairs. This kind of thing doesn't happen every day, it really is his lucky Sunday, so there is something in it after all, all those bells ringing, I'm quids in, I stand to make 15 or 20 marks on a Sunday, and what are my expenses. And he's happy, the postcard from that ex-mailman is rustling in his pocket, he will just take his leave of Pums at the door. Pums is astounded: 'What's all this, Biberkopf, I thought we had an agreement.' 'Oh, we do, and you can count on me. I just need to pop home, you know, I've got a sweetheart, er, Cilly, maybe you remember her from when she used to step out with Reinhold. I can't leave her stuck at home for all of Sunday without word from me.' 'Oh no, Biberkopf, that's out of the question, I can't let you go now, you'll change your mind, and then I'll be back in a jam. No, leave the woman out of it, Biberkopf, that won't wash, I'm not about to go bust for her sake. She's not going anywhere.' 'I know, you're right, I trust her. And that's why. I don't want to leave her stranded, and her hearing nothing and seeing nothing and knowing nothing. About what I'm up to.' 'Now come along, man, we'll find some way.'

'What will I do?' thinks Franz. They walked on. Back on the corner of Prenzlauer Strasse. Here and there were ladies of the night standing about already, the ones Cilly will see in a few hours' time, when she's looking for Franz and looking and looking and wandering around. Time moves on, all sorts of things will happen to Franz; he will be in a car, people will lay hands on him. And what is preoccupying him now is how he'll manage to deliver the postcard on behalf of that mad chap, and get word to Cilly, because the girl's waiting for him.

He walks with Pums to a building on Alte Schönhauser Strasse, side entrance, that's where his premises are, says Pums. And there is a light up there, and the room looks just like a proper office, with a telephone and typewriters. A sour-faced elderly woman keeps walking into the room where Franz and Pums are sitting together: 'This is my wife, this is Herr Franz Biberkopf who is helping us out today.' She leaves as if she hadn't heard a dicky bird. In a newspaper that's lying out, Franz reads, while Pums is turning his desk upside down looking for summat: 3,000 nautical miles in a nutshell by Günther Plüschow, holidays and shipping routes, Leo Lania's *Conjuncture* at the Piscatorbühne in the Lessing Theatre. Piscator himself to direct. What is Piscator, what is Lania? What is envelope, and what is content, or drama? No more child brides in India, a cemetery for award-winning animals. Cultural news: Bruno Walter will take the rostrum for the season's final concert on Sunday, 15 April, at the Städtische Oper. The programme to include Mozart's Symphony in E flat major, the takings will go to the Gustav Mahler Memorial in Vienna. Truck driver, thirty-two, married, 2a and 3b licence, seeks work in privately owned business as deliveryman.

Herr Pums is looking all over his desk for matches for his cigar. Then the elderly woman opens a portière, and three men slowly walk in. Pums doesn't look up. So these are all Pums's chaps, Franz shakes hands with them. The woman is on her way out when Pums beckons Franz over: 'Biberkopf, you wanted a letter delivered, isn't that right. Now, Klara, will you look to it.' 'That's nice of you, Herr Pums, do you really mean it? Well, it's not a letter, just a postcard, and it's to my sweetheart.' – And then he tells her where exactly he lives, and he writes it down on one of Pums's business envelopes, and he tells Cilly not to worry about him, he'll be back around ten, and then there's the postcard –

So everything's sorted, and he's one relieved man. The scrawny bitch reads the envelope in the kitchen, and chucks it in the fire; she crumples up the note, throws it in the rubbish. Then she cosies up to the stove, goes back to her coffee, doesn't think about anything, sits, drinks coffee, feels warm. And Biberkopf feels a furious joy when who should come in in a cloth cap and his thick green army gear – well, who? Who else has such deep trenches in his face? Who walks as though he always had to pull one foot after another out of marshland? Well, Reinhold. Franz starts to feel properly at home. Isn't that nice? We'll be working together, Reinhold, you and me, I don't care about anything else. 'What, are you in then?' Reinhold whines, pads around. 'There's a turn-up.' And then Franz gets to talking about the shindig on the Alex, and how he helped lanky Emil. The other four are all ears, Pums is still writing at his desk, they nudge each other in the ribs, then two start whispering. One is always left to look after Franz, though.

At eight o'clock they head off. All of them are bundled up warm, Franz gets given a coat and all. He says with a beam he wouldn't mind hanging on to it, and the fur cap too, gollygosh. 'Why not,' they say, 'if you earn em.'

They're on their way, outside it's pitch-black and awful slush underfoot. 'What's the plan then?' asks Franz once they're standing around on the street.' They say: 'First we need a vehicle or two. And then we collect the goods, apples or whatever.' A lot of vehicles are allowed to pass, finally there's a couple parked on Metzer Strasse, and they bundle into them, and off they go.

The two cars drive in convoy for upward of half an hour, in the gloom you can't really make out where you are, it might be Weissensee or Friedrichsfelde. The boys say: the old man probably needs to set up the deal first. And then they stop in front of a house, there's a wide tree-lined avenue, it might be Tempelhof, the others say they don't know either, they're smoking to beat the band.

Reinhold's with Biberkopf in one car. How different Reinhold sounds now! No stammer, a loud confident voice, upright as a captain: he's even laughing, and the others in the car, they're all listening to him. Franz has thrown an arm round his shoulder:

'Well, Reinhold, old son (he whispers into his neck, under the cap), well, what do you say? Didn't I give you good advice about the women? Didn't I just?' 'Oh, and how, it's all good now, it's all good.' Reinhold gives him a bang on the knee, my God, he has some strength, there's some fist there. Franz gurgles: 'We're not about to get our knickers in a twist about a girl. She's not born yet, the one who could do that.'

Life in the desert is fraught with difficulty and danger. The camels seek and seek and fail to find, until one day you find their bleached bones.

Pums has climbed back in with a suitcase, and the two cars are once again driving in convoy through the city. It's just turned nine when they stop on Bülowplatz. Now they're on foot, and in pairs. They walk through the arch under the S-Bahn. Franz says: 'We'll soon be at the market.' 'That's right, but first we pick up the goods, then we deliver them.'

Suddenly the first two are no longer there, they're on Kaiser-Wilhelm-Strasse, hard by the S-Bahn, and then Franz and his companion turn into a dark open doorway. 'We're there,' says the fellow, 'now lose the cigar.' 'What for?' He squeezes his arm, rips the cigar out of his mouth: ''Cause I says so.' He's over the other side of the courtyard before Franz can do anything. What's going on here, what are they doing, leaving me standing here in the dark? And as Franz is feeling his way across the courtyard, a torch lights up in front of him, he's dazzled, and it's Pums. 'What are you doing here? You get out of here, Biberkopf, I want you out front, keeping watch. Get back there.' 'Oh, and I'm thinking I'm to collect goods.' 'Nonsense, go back there, didn't any of them tell you.'

The light goes out, and Franz feels his way back. There's a trembling in him, he gulps: 'What is all this, what's their game?' He's already back outside the gate when two men come out through the house – cripes, they're stealing, breaking into people's houses, let me out of here, far away, a chute, and off in a high arc back to the Alex – they grab hold of him, one of them is Reinhold, he has a steel grip: 'Didn't they tell you nothink? You're to stand here and keep watch.' 'Who, who says so?' 'Christ, man, shut up, we're under the cosh. Haven't you got any brains; stop fannying about. Stay put and whistle if there's trouble.' 'I . . .' 'Shut it', and he thumped Franz's right arm so hard that he bent double.

Franz is standing all alone in the dark entryway. He's actually trembling. What am I doing here? They made a monkey of me. That bastard whacked me. They're thieves, God only knows what they're stealing, they're not fruit and veg at all, they're breaking and entering. The long avenue with black trees, the iron gates, after lights out all prisoners are required to go to their cells, in summertime it is permitted to stay up till dark. This is a gang of criminals, with Pums in command of it. Do I run, do I not run, what do I do. They lured me under false pretences, the rascals. I'm their lookout.

Franz stood there, trembling, feeling his bruised arm. Prisoners may not keep medical conditions secret, but neither are they to invent false maladies, both are offences. The building is dead silent, from Bülowplatz car horns. A creaking and whispering from the back yard, the occasional flash of a torch, swiftly someone went down into the basement with a dark lantern. They've locked me up here, I'd rather live on bread and taters than stand here for those crooks. Several torches flashed in the yard, Franz thought of the man with the postcard, strange fellow, strange fellow all right. And he didn't leave the spot, he was rooted; ever since Reinhold had hit him, he felt he'd been nailed down. He tried, he thought he'd better, but he couldn't, it didn't let go of him. The world is iron, there's nothing you can do, it rolls up to you like a steamroller, there's nothing you can do, here it comes, there it goes, they're sitting on the inside, it's like a tank, a devil is driving it with horns and glowing eyes, they tear you limb from limb, they sit there with their chains and teeth and tear you into bits. And it runs on, and there's no getting out of the way of it. It quivers in the dark; when it gets light, then you'll be able to see the lie of the land, how it happened.

Let me go, let me go, the lowlifes, the bastards, I want no part of this. He tugged at his legs, wouldn't it be funny if I couldn't get away from here. He moved. As if someone threw me in a mixing bowl of dough and I couldn't get out. But he did it, he did it. It was hard, but he did it. I'm making headway, let them steal to their hearts' content,

I'm out of here. He pulled the coat off, went back into the yard, slowly, timidly, but he wanted to throw the coat in their faces, and in the dark he threw the coat in the direction of the back house. Then more lights came, two men ran past him, with coats, great bundles of them, both cars stopped in front of the gateway; as he ran by one of the men struck Franz on the arm again, an iron blow: 'Everything all right, then?' That was Reinhold. Now two more men ran by with baskets and another two, back and forth, without lights, past Franz, who could do nothing but grit his teeth and clench his fists. They were crazy busy, in the yard and in the passageway, back and forth in the dark, otherwise they'd have got a shock from Franz. Because it was no longer Franz who was standing there. No coat, no cap, his eyes popping, his hands in his pockets, peering to see if he can recognize a face, and if so whose, who's this now, who's this, no knife, you wait, maybe in my jacket, boys, you don't know Franz Biberkopf, you're in for a shock if you try and mess with him. Then all four came running out laden, and a little round fellow grabs Franz by the arm: 'All right, Biberkopf, we're done here, let's go.'

And Franz and some others stowed in a big motor, Reinhold next to him, pressing hard against Franz, that's the other Reinhold. They're driving without headlights. 'What are you pressing me like that for,' whispers Franz; no knife.

'Put a sock in it, man; not a squeak out of anyone.' The front car is speeding; the driver of the second is looking behind him, floors it, calls over his shoulder through the open window, 'We've got company.'

Reinhold sticks his head out of the window: 'Hurry, hurry, take the turn.' The other car always coming on. Then by the light of a street lamp, Reinhold sees Franz's face: he's beaming, he's happy as a sandboy. 'What are you laughing at, you idiot, you must be out of your mind.' 'I can laugh if I want to, it's nothing to do with you.' 'Cut it out.' What a waste of time, a layabout. And suddenly it dawns on Reinhold, something he's not thought about all evening: that this is Biberkopf who let him down, who keeps the women away, there's proof, that cheeky fat pig, and I told him all about me once. Suddenly Reinhold is no longer thinking of the pursuit.

Water in the black woods, you are so quiet. Terribly quiet you lie there. Your surface is unmoved, when the wood storms and the pines bend their branches and the spiders' webs between the boughs tear and the splintering begins. The storm doesn't reach down as far as you.

This lad, Reinhold is thinking, is in the full flush of it, and he's probably thinking the car behind us is gonna catch us, and I'm sitting here, and he's been speechifying to me about women, the damn fool, about how I need to get a grip on myself.

Franz is still laughing silently to himself, he cranes round to see the road behind out of the little back window, yes, the car is following them, they are discovered; just you wait, it's your punishment, even if it should cost me too, they're not to think they can do that to me, the wretches, the criminal scum.

Cursed be the man, saith Jeremiah, that trusteth in man. For he shall be like the heath in the desert, and shall not see when good cometh; but shall inhabit the parched places in the wilderness, in a salt land and not inhabited. The heart is deceitful above all things, and desperately wicked: who can know it?

Reinhold tips the man opposite the wink, in the car light and darkness alternate, they are in a chase. Reinhold has got his hand on the door handle by Franz. They turn into a wide avenue. Franz is still craning round to see behind them. Suddenly he feels himself grabbed by the scruff and pulled forward. He tries to get up, he hits out at Reinhold's face. But Reinhold is implacable. The wind whistles into the car, snowflakes fly in. Franz is shoved sideways over the bales of stuff towards the open door, with a scream he makes a grab for Reinhold's throat. He catches a blow from a stick against his arm. The other fellow is shoving against his left hip. From on top of the bundle of material a prone Franz is pushed through the open door; he tries to brace himself with his feet. His arms grip the running board for all he is worth.

Then he catches another blow from the stick, this time on the back of the head. Standing stooped over him, Reinhold scoops the body onto the street. The door slams to. The pursuing vehicle runs over him. The chase continues through the blizzard.

*

Let's be pleased when the sun goes up and kindly light returns. The gas and electrics can be turned off. People get up, alarm clocks purr, a new day begins. If it was 8 April before, it's now the 9th, if it was a Sunday, now it's a Monday. The year hasn't changed, nor the month, but something is different. The world has gone on turning. The sun has risen. We don't exactly know what this sun is. Astronomers busy their heads with it. It is, so they tell us, the central body of our solar system, because our earth is just a minor planet, and what are we really? If the sun rises, and we are pleased, we should really be depressed, because what does that make us, the sun is some 300,000 times as big as the earth, and there are lots and lots of other numbers and zeroes that go to tell us how null and void we are. We shouldn't really be pleased at all.

And for all that, we are pleased when kindly light returns, white and powerful, and it shines down on the roads, and in the rooms the colours come to life, and the faces and their features are all there. It is a good thing to feel shapes with your hands, but it is a boon to see colours and outlines. And we can be happy and show what we are and do and feel. Even in April we are happy about the marginal increase in warmth, and how happy are the flowers to be allowed to grow. There must be some mistake, some miscalculation in those terrible numbers with all the zeroes.

So go on and rise, sun, you don't scare us. All those miles are a matter of indifference to us, the diameter and volume. Warm sun, climb, bright light, rise. You are neither big nor small, you are a joy.

She has just alighted from the Paris express, the little discreet person in fur-trimmed coat, with her enormous eyes, and her two little Pekinese, Black and China, in her arms. Photographers and whir of film. Softly smiling, Raquil allows it all to happen, what makes her happiest is a bunch of yellow roses from the Spanish colony, ivory is her favourite colour. With the words, 'I can't wait to see Berlin', the famous woman climbs into her car and disappears from the waving crowds in the morning city.

Chapter Six

Now you don't see Franz Biberkopf boozing or hiding himself away. Now you see him laugh: baffling. He is furious at having been violated, no one, not even the strongest man, may defy his will. He brandishes his fist against the dark force, but he can't see it, something still needs to happen, the hammer must come down.

There are no grounds for despair. As I continue my story, and follow it through to its rough, awful, bitter conclusion, I will often have cause to repeat: there are no grounds for despair. For while the man whose story I am telling is no ordinary man, he is at least ordinary inasmuch as we exactly understand him, and sometimes tell ourselves. we would have done the same as he did at each point and put ourselves through what he did. I promise, although this is not customary, not to keep silent during the story.

It is the grisly truth that I tell about Franz Biberkopf, who left home in all innocence, against his will took part in a break-in, and was thrown under the wheels of a car. There he lies, under the wheels, having unquestionably tried his hardest to keep to the strait way. But is precisely this not cause for despair, where is the sense in this criminal, repulsive and pitiable nonsense, what twisted meaning can be imputed here, maybe even to become the fate of Franz Biberkopf?

I say again: no cause for despair. I have the odd surprise still up my sleeve, perhaps some readers can already sense something. A slow revelation is in progress, you will see Franz undergo it, and finally everything will be made clear.

Crime pays

Once having started, Reinhold carried on in the same way. He got home at lunchtime on Monday. Let us, my dear brethren and sustren, spread a charitable veil ten metres square over the intervening time. We unfortunately can't lift it. Let us content ourselves with establishing that once the sun had risen punctually on Monday morning, and the familiar bustle of Berlin was getting under way – on the dot of one p.m. Reinhold threw out of his apartment the long-overdue Trude, who was living there and didn't want to go. How well is me at the weekend, tirra lirra, when the billy goat runs to the nanny, tirra lirra. A different author would probably have come up with some punishment for Reinhold at this point, but – I'm terribly sorry – there was none offering. Reinhold was cheery and indicated his cheeriness by evicting Trude to the purpose of heightened cheeriness, though she was settled there and didn't want to go. He himself didn't really want to do it either, the thing came about by itself in spite of his not wanting it, which is to say it happened principally through the agency of his midbrain: for he was rather drunk. In this way, destiny assisted the man. The taking of strong drink was one of those things we have omitted from our account of the past night, now, in order to go forward, we must clear up a few things. Reinhold, the weakling, so laughable to Franz, incapable of saying a rough or a harsh word to a woman, could at one in the afternoon give Trude a terrible beating, tear out her hair, smash a mirror over her head, and finally, to stop her wailing, he could beat her mouth so bloody that when she showed it to the doctor in the evening it was still grotesquely swollen. In the space of a few hours the girl had lost all her beauty, and all through the vigorous measures of Reinhold, against whom she wanted to press charges. For the moment she could only apply ointment to her lips and keep shtum. All this, as I say, Reinhold could do because several glasses of schnapps had narcotized his cerebrum, leaving in charge his midbrain, which was, by and large, the more active in him anyway.

When he came round in the late afternoon, feeling a little under the weather, he noted to his surprise some excellent changes in his domestic situation. Evidently Trude was gone. Completely gone. Her things as well. Furthermore, the mirror was broken, and someone had rather vulgarly and bloodily spat on the floor. Reinhold inspected the damage. His own mouth was intact, so it was

Trude who had spat, and he had smashed her in the kisser. Which gave rise to such a surge of exaltation and self-respect in him that he laughed out loud. He picked up a shard of the mirror and looked at himself in it: whoa Reinhold, you did it, I'd never have thought it of you! Little Reinhold, Reinhold babes! Was he ever happy. He patted himself on both cheeks.

He reflected: or perhaps did someone else throw her out, maybe Franz? The events of the previous evening and night were not yet clear in his mind. Doubtfully, he brought in his landlady, the old madam, and gave her a prompt: 'Must have been a lot of noise here, eh?' But then she let loose: he had been completely in the right with Trude who was a lazy slut, incapable even of ironing a petticoat. What, she wore petticoats, that was almost enough for him. So it was all his own work. How happy Reinhold felt to hear that. And then all at once the events of the previous evening and night swam into his mind. A neat job, a bumper crop of merchandise, put one over on fat Franz Biberkopf, and let's hope they ran him over. And Trude thrown out. My God, what a list!

What do we do now? First of all gussy himself up for the evening. Don't anyone talk to me about schnapps. That I didn't and couldn't and all that crap. All that energy saved, and now all the things we accomplished.

While he's getting changed, one of Pums's boys runs up whispering and hissing and fearfully het up, and shuffling from one foot to the other, and Reinhold is to go down to the bar right away. But it takes a good further hour before our Reinhold is downstairs. Tonight is all about girls, tonight Pums can just be Pums. Down in the bar they're all shitting themselves, because of what Reinhold done to Biberkopf. He'll shop us if he's not dead. And if he is dead, then we're really in the soup. They're bound to investigate, and who knows what'll come out.

But Reinhold is happy, and happiness stands by him. You can't touch him. It's the happiest day he can remember. He's got schnapps and he's got girls and he can move them on as much as he likes. He can get rid of the lot of them, that's really the wonder of it. He fancies going off on a pub crawl, but Pums's boys won't let him go till he's promised to spend two three days lying low out in Weissensee with them. They need to establish what's happened to Franz, and what the damage is. Well, and so Reinhold promises to do that.

But that same night he's already forgotten all about it and has charged off. And nothing happens to him. They're all cowering out in Weissensee, trembling in their safe house. The next day they venture out to haul him in, but, no, he has to go see a certain Karla he's met the night before.

And Reinhold is borne out. There's no news of Biberkopf, neither squeak nor squat. The man seems to have vanished off the face of the planet. Well, see if we care. And they all pop out again and return merrily to their old haunts.

In Reinhold's pad, meanwhile, is Karla, smoking, a straw-blonde, who's brung him three big bottles. He sips at them now and again, she sips at them a bit more, sometimes even a whole lot more. He's thinking: go on you, drink, I'm only going to drink when it's my time, and that'll be sayonara for you.

There will be some readers who are worried about Cilly. What will become of the poor girl when Franz isn't there, when Franz is either gone or dead and gone? Oh, she'll get by, don't you worry your heads about her, she's really not someone you need to worry about, her sort always lands on their feet. Cilly has money for two days, and no later than Tuesday she runs into Reinhold, as I imagined she might, fancy-free, the nattiest gent in Berlin Mitte, in a knockout silk shirt. And Cilly is confused, she's not sure when she sees him whether she's still in love with the fellow or if she'd rather settle his hash once and for all.

She's already, with a nod to Schiller, carrying a dagger in her blouse. Technically speaking it's only a kitchen knife, but she wants to stick it to Reinhold for his cruelty, and she doesn't much mind where. So there she is standing outside his front door with him, and he's all friendly, two red roses and a peck on the cheek. And she thinks: you talk away till morning, then I'll let you have it. But where? That confuses her again. You surely can't cut through such nice material, the man is so exquisitely dressed, and it looks great on him. He's supposed to have, she says, as she staggers down the street with him, he's supposed to have took her Franz away from her. How does she know? Franz hasn't come home, he's still not home, and there's no news of him, plus Reinhold's Trude is on the loose again. So it stands to reason, and there's nothing he can say different, that Franz is off with Trude, because Reinhold egged him into it, and that's the limit.

Reinhold is astonished by how much she knows and so quickly. Well, it so happened she's been upstairs and the landlady spills the beans about the row with Trude. You rotter, Cilly scolds, she is trying to get in the mood to pull the knife on him, you've got someone else again, I can tell from looking at you.

Reinhold in turn can tell at a dozen paces: 1. she's got no money. 2. she's furious with Franz, and 3. she's got the hots for me, the dandy Reinhold. When he's in his glad rags he's irresistible to all women, especially those with previous, so-called second-timers. Therefore on heading 1. he slips her 10 marks. On 2. he badmouths Franz Biberkopf. He wouldn't mind knowing himself where the fellow's keeping. (Pricks of conscience, where are pricks of conscience, Orestes and Clytemnestra, Reinhold doesn't even know their names, he simply and sincerely desires Franz to be dead and disappeared.) But Cilly doesn't know where Franz is either, and that's an argument, argues Reinhold passionately, for the man's being six feet under. And so to point 3. Reinhold says kindly, where a reprise is concerned: I'm tied up just for the moment, but you might try again in May. You're barking, she scolds, and she's almost beside herself with joy. Everything's possible with me, he beams, takes his leave and strolls on. Reinhold, oh Reinhold, you're my darling, Reinhold, oh Reinhold, you're my only one.

He thanks his Creator at every bar that there is such a thing as schnapps. What if all the bars were to close down, or Germany went dry, what do I do then? Well, then I just have to be sure to lay in a supply at home in time. No time like the present. I really am a sharp lad, he thinks, as he stands in the shop, investing in a bit of this and a bit of that. He knows he has his cerebrum, and if need be his midbrain as well.

And so, at least for now, the night from Sunday to Monday was over for Reinhold. And anyone who still wants to ask if there's such a thing as justice in the world, the bad news is: for the moment, no, at least not this week.

The night of Sunday–Monday, 9 April

The big private automobile in which Franz Biberkopf is laid – unconscious, he has been given camphor and scopolamine – races for two hours. At the end of that time, it's in Magdeburg. He is taken out near a church, the two men bang on the doors of the clinic. He is operated on that same night. His right arm is taken off at the shoulder, part of the shoulder joint is reset, the bruising on chest and right thigh, is, for the moment, nothing to worry about. Internal injuries remain a possibility, a minor liver rupture, but probably not much. Wait and see. Has he lost a lot of blood? Where did you find him? On X-Y avenue, that's where his motorbike was, he must have been struck from behind. You didn't see the car that did it? No. We saw him lying there, we parted ways in Z, he took the left fork. We know, it's very dark there. Yes, that's where it happened. Will the gentlemen be staying in the area? Yes, for a couple of days more; he's my brother-in-law, his wife is coming down today or tomorrow. We're staying opposite, in case we're needed. Outside the operating room one of the gentlemen stops to address the clinicians once more: I know this is an awful business, but we would like word not to get out from your side. Let's wait till he comes round, and then see what he thinks. He's not a litigious type. If you must know, he once struck someone himself, so you know, his nerves. – Whatever you say. For now, let's just hope he pulls through.

At eleven his bandages are changed. It's Monday morning – the ones who caused the accident are in their cups, roister-boister, out in Weissensee at their fence's – Franz is conscious, lying in a nice bed, in a nice room, his chest feels pressed tight, he asks the sister where he is. She tells him what she heard from the night nurse and has managed to glean from conversation. He is awake. Understands everything, feels for his right arm. The sister takes his hand away: there now, lie still. In the slush on the road, blood had come out of his right sleeve – he had felt it. Then there were people next to him, and at that moment something happened in him. What had happened to Franz at that moment? He had come to a decision. When Reinhold had struck him those iron blows in the passage in the house in Bülowplatz he had trembled, the ground trembled under him. Franz didn't get it.

When the car drove him away, the ground was still trembling. Franz didn't want to acknowledge it, but it was.

But when he lay there in the slush, just five minutes later, there was a movement in him. Something tore free, broke through and gonged, gonged. Franz is stone, he feels it, I've been run over, he is cool and quiet. Franz realizes, I've had it – and he issues commands. Maybe I'm done for, never mind, I'm not done for. On, on. They make a tourniquet from one of his braces. Then they want to drive him to hospital in Pankow. But he's like a pointer alert to every move: no, no hospital, and he gives them an address. What address? Elsasser Strasse, Herbert Wischow, a colleague from another life, a life before Tegel! The address is present in a moment. That's what comes to life in him as he lies there in the slush, rips through, breaks through, and gongs, gongs. Instantaneously, without a moment's doubt or hesitation.

They mustn't catch me. He is certain Herbert is still living there, and will be in. They dash into the pub on Elsasser Strasse, asking for Herbert Wischow. A slimly built young man gets up next to a beautiful dark-haired woman, what is it, outside in the car, he runs out to the car with them, the girl too, followed by half the pub. Franz knows who's coming. He gives commands to time.

Franz and Herbert recognize one another, Franz whispers ten words in Herbert's ear, they make room for him in the back, Franz is carried in, laid down in a bed, a doctor is called, Eva, the dark-haired beauty, brings money. They put him into different clothes. An hour after the attack he is being driven by private automobile from Berlin to Magdeburg.

At noon Herbert visits the clinic, and is able to talk to Franz. Franz doesn't want to spend so much as a day needlessly in the clinic, in a week Wischow will be back, for now Eva will stay in Magdeburg. Franz lies there stock-still. He has a grip on himself. He forbids all reflection. Only when at 2 p.m. after visiting hours, the lady is announced and Eva walks in with a bunch of tulips, does he cry helplessly, cries and sobs and Eva has to wipe his face with a towel. He moistens his lips, squinches his eyes shut, grits his teeth. But his jaw is still trembling, he starts sobbing again, so that the nurse outside hears it, and knocks and tells Eva that's enough for today, the visits were taking too much out of the patient.

The next day he is perfectly calm, and smiles at Eva. At the end of two weeks they come for him. He is back in Berlin, breathing Berlin again. When he sees Elsasser Strasse something stirs in him, but he doesn't sob. He's thinking of the Sunday afternoon with Cilly, the bells, the bells, this is my home and something is in store for me, I have to do something, something will happen. Franz Biberkopf knows that for sure, and allows himself to be carried quietly from the car.

I have a duty, something will happen, I'm not leaving, I'm Franz Biberkopf. So they carry him inside, into the flat of his friend Herbert Wischow, who calls himself the commissioner. It's the same instinctive certainty that surfaced in him after the fall from the car.

Boomtime in the abattoir, boomboomtime: pigs 11,543, cattle 2,016, calves 920, sheep 14,450. One blow, bop, they lie there.

The pigs, the cattle, the calves, they are all slaughtered. There's no call to think about them. Now where were we? Eh?

Eva is sitting at Franz's bedside, Wischow keeps popping in: what happened, man, how did that happen? Franz doesn't tell. He has erected an iron box around himself, and he sits there and won't let anyone in.

Eva, Herbert and Herbert's friend Emil are sitting together. Ever since Franz turned up in the night having been run over, they are stumped. He wasn't just hit by a car, there was something else going on, what's he doing up in the north of the city at ten at night when no one's around. Herbert concludes: Franz must have done a job that went wrong, and now he's ashamed because his little paper business didn't work out, and there's other people involved who he doesn't want to betray. Eva agrees, he tried to do a job but something went wrong, and now he's a cripple. We'll worm it out of him one way or another.

It emerges when Franz tells Eva his latest address and asks her to pick up his stuff, but without saying where she's taking it. Herbert and Emil are sworn in, first the landlady won't surrender it, but for 5 marks she finally does, and then she goes back to her lamentations: every other day people come asking after Franz, who is she referring to, well, Pums and Reinhold and so on and so on. Pums, now they know. The Pums gang. Eva is beside herself, and Wischow is furious as well: if he's in business again, why with Pums? But of course, once the accident's happened he goes back to us; he's done work for Pums, well, he's a cripple now, half dead, else I'd talk to him differently.

Eva has with difficulty managed to be present when Herbert Wischow and Franz settle their accounts, and Emil is also present, the whole thing set them back an even thousand.

'Well, Franz,' begins Herbert, 'now you're out of the woods. Now you can get up and – what will you do? Did you give it any thought?' Franz turns his stubbly face in Herbert's direction: 'Just let me get on my own two feet first, won't you.' 'Oh, we're not hurrying you along, don't think that. You're still in good with me. But why didn't you come back to us in the first place. You've been out of Tegel for a whole bloody year.' 'It's not that long.' 'Well, then half a year. Through with us, were you?'

The buildings, the sliding roofs, a tall, lightless courtyard, 'Es braust ein Ruf wie Donnerhall', juvivallerallera, that's how it all began.

Franz lies back, looks up at the ceiling: 'I was flogging papers. I'm no good to you.'

Emil gets involved, pipes up: 'Jesus Christ, you were not flogging newspapers.' The liar. Eva calms him down, Franz can sense there's something afoot, they know something, what is it they know. 'I was flogging papers. Ask Mack.' Wischow: 'I can imagine what Mack would say. You sold papers. The way Pums's people sell fruit, some. Also wet fish. You know that.' 'Yeah, but I didn't, see. I sold newspapers. I earned my money. Then ask Cilly, we were together all day, ask her what I did.' 'For two marks a day, or three.' 'Or more, sometimes. It were enough for me, Herbert.'

The three of them are uncertain. Eva sits down beside Franz: 'You knew Pums, didn't you, Franz?' 'Yes.' Franz is no longer thinking they're quizzing me, Franz is reminiscing, he feels alive. 'Well?' Eva strokes him: 'Why not tell us what happened with Pums?' Herbert beside her weighs in: 'Go on, spit it out. I know what happened with Pums. Where you were that night. Don't think I don't know. Sure, you joined in. I don't care. It's your lookout. They're who you go to, they're the ones you know, the old crook, we don't hear a dicky bird.' Emil yells: 'See. We're only good when—' Herbert motions to him. Franz is weeping. It's not quite as bad as it was in the clinic, but it's pretty bad. He sobs and cries and throws his head from side to side. He got a blow on the head, he got a bang in the chest, and then he was thrown out in front of a car. Which ran over him. His arm is gone. He's a cripple. The two men leave. He goes on sobbing. Eva keeps wiping his face with the towel. Then Franz lies there quietly, eyes shut. She watches him, thinks he's sleeping. Then he opens his eyes, is all awake, says: 'Tell Herbert and Emil to come in, won't you.'

They walk in with eyes lowered. Then Franz asks: 'What do you know about Pums? Do you know the first thing about him?' The three of them exchange looks of incomprehension. Eva pats him on the arm: 'Come on, Franz, you know him too.' 'Well, I want to hear what you know about him.' Emil: 'That he's a hard-core swindler who's done five years in Sonnenburg, and it could easily have been fifteen or life. Him and his fruit cart.' Franz: 'He doesn't even live off his fruit cart.' 'No, he eats steak and plenty of it.' Herbert: 'For Christ's sake, Franz, you weren't born yesterday, you must have known that, can't you tell from just looking at the feller?' Franz: 'I thought he lived off fruit and greens.' 'Well, and what were you doing the Sunday you took off with him?' 'We were going to collect fruit for the market.' Franz lies there perfectly still. Herbert bends down over him to see his expression: 'And you believed that?'

Franz starts crying again, very quietly, his mouth is shut. He went downstairs, a man was looking up addresses in his notebook, then he was in Pums's flat, and Frau Pums was supposed to send Cilly a note. 'Of course I believed it. Then I noticed there was something fishy, when they told me to be lookout, and then—'

The three don't know where to look. What Franz is saying is the truth, but they can't believe it. Eva touches his arm: 'Well, what happened then?' Franz has his mouth open, say it now, then it'll be out, and over and done with. And he says: 'Then I didn't want to, and they threw me out the car because there was another car coming after them.'

Silence, no more words, no: I was run over, I might have been killed, they wanted to kill me. He doesn't sob, he keeps contained, teeth gritted, legs tensed.

The other three hear him. Now he's said it. It's God's truth. All three of them sense it instantly. There is a reaper, Death yclept, by Almighty God employed.

Herbert asks: 'Now just tell me this, Franz, we'll leave you in a minute: the reason you didn't come to us is because you wanted to flog newspapers, right?'

He can't speak, he thinks: yes, I wanted to go straight. I was straight till the end. Don't be put out that I didn't come to you. You remained my friends, I never give any of you away. He lies there in silence, they troop out.

Then – Franz has taken his sleeping pills again – they're all sitting down the pub, and can't think what to say. They don't look at each other. Eva is shaking like a leaf. She had the hots for Franz when he was going out with Ida, but he wouldn't give Ida up, even though she had already taken up with the Breslau boy. She's with Herbert, he gives her everything she needs, but she still has a soft spot for Franz.

Wischow orders a round of grog, and all three of them knock it back. Wischow orders another. Their throats remain tight. Eva has icy hands and feet, she keeps on feeling cold shudders going down the back of her head and neck, even her thighs feel icy, so she crosses her legs. Emil has his head in his hands, he's chewing away, sucking his tongue, swallowing his spittle, then he has to spit on the floor. Young Herbert Wischow sits upright on his chair as on horseback; he looks like a lieutenant leading his troop, impassive. None of them are present in the bar, they are not in their own skins, Eva is not Eva, Wischow is not Wischow, Emil not Emil. A wall around them has been breached, darkness is streaming in, different air. They are still at Franz's bedside. There is an unbroken shudder that connects them to Franz's bed.

There is a reaper, Death yclept, by Almighty God employed. His blade he whets, it cuts much better, soon he will cut, and we must suffer.

Herbert turns to face the table, he says in a hoarse voice: 'Who do you think it was?' Emil: 'Who what?' Herbert: 'Who threw him out?' Eva: 'Will you promise, Herbert, that if you get hold of him.' 'No need to ask. To think that a creature like that walks the earth. But, but.' Emil: 'Christ, Herbert, I can't get my head around it.'

Not wanting to hear, not having to think. Eva's knees are shaking, she implores: 'Herbert, Emil, do something.' To get out of that atmosphere. There is a reaper, Death yclept. Herbert concludes: 'What can we do, if we dunno who it was. The first step is to establish who it was. Maybe it means gettin the whole Pums gang.' Eva: 'And Franz with them?' 'I said maybe. Maybe that's what we'll do. Franz was no part of it, not really, a blind man'd see that, any judge would believe him. And here's the proof: they threw him out in front of the car. They'd hardly have done that otherwise.' He shudders: bastards. Think of it. Eva: 'Maybe he'll tell me who it was.'

But the man lying there like a lump of wood and giving no information is Franz. Let be, let be. The arm's gone, it'll not grow back. They threw me out of the car, they left my head on, we need to get along, we need to move forward, gotta pull the wagon out of the mud. First crawl.

*

The weather turns warm, and the patient improves with surprising speed. He's not supposed to get up yet, but he does, and it's all right. Herbert and Emil, who are flush, don't mind buying him whatever he wants and whatever the doctor says he needs. And Franz wants to get up and about, he eats and drinks what he's given, and he doesn't ask where they get the money from.

By now there are conversations between him and the others, but nothing consequential, nothing regarding the Pums affair. They talk about Tegel and they talk about Ida a lot. They talk about her frankly, and with sadness that it should have come to that, she was so young, but Eva agrees, the girl was a lowlife. Everything between them is as it was before Tegel, and no one knows or makes mention of the fact that since then the buildings have shaken, and the roofs made to slide off, and Franz has sung in back yards, and sworn, as his name is Franz Biberkopf, that he wants to remain on the straight and narrow, and the things of before are over and finished.

Franz sits and lies easily in their company. A lot of old acquaintances come along as well, bringing wives and girlfriends. They don't touch the subject, they talk with Franz as if he'd only just got out of Tegel and been in a hacksident. The boys don't ask what happened. They know what an occupational accident is, they can imagine. You get into a contretemps, and you come away with a bullet in your shoulder, or a broken leg. Well, it beats dying on bread and water or TB in Sonnenburg any day of the week. Innit.

In the meantime, the Pums mob have got a whiff of Franz's whereabouts. Who was it picked up Franz's trunk? They established that pretty quick, and it's someone they know. And before Wischow realizes anything, they've worked out that Franz is at his place, they were friends back in the day after all, and he got away with losing an arm, lucky bleeder, nothing worse than that, so the boy's still in circulation, and, who knows, in a position to grass them up. They have half a mind to set about Reinhold, who had the daft idea of inviting the likes of Franz Biberkopf into their gang in the first place. But it would take a lot to undertake anything against Reinhold, not before, and not now, even old Pums doesn't want to know. The way the lad so much as looks at you is terrifying, with his yellow face and the deep creases in it. He's not a well geezer, he'll not make fifty, and the frail ones you don't want to mess around with. You wouldn't put it past him to reach into his pocket and smirk and blow you away. The thing with Franz and the fact that he survived remains a danger. But Reinhold just shakes his head and says: stay calm. He's not about to grass. If one arm isn't enough for him, then he might grass. Well, I don't care. He might want to lose his head and all.

There is no call for them to fear Franz. Once, admittedly, Eva and Emil get together and try and get Franz to tell them where it happened and who done it, and if he can't do anything against them all by himself, then there'll be others to help, there are enough of the right sort in Berlin. But he clams up, and says: oh, leave be. Then he turns pale, gulps, so long as he doesn't start crying again: there's no point in talking about it, what's the use, it won't make my arm grow back, if I could I think I'd leave Berlin altogether, but what's a cripple to do? Eva: 'It's not on account of that, Franz, you aren't a cripple, but that can't be allowed, what they did to you, throwing you out of a car.' 'It won't make my arm grow back.' 'But they should pay for it.' 'What?'

Emil puts his oar in: 'Either we beat the bloke's brains in, or we make his firm pay if he's in one. We'll settle it with them. Either others will pay for him, or Pums and the firm will throw him out, and we'll see where he manages to join after, and what happens to him. The arm wants paying for. It's your right arm, innit. They gorra pay you a invalidity pension.' Franz shakes his head. 'You shake your head all you like. We'll catch up with them, it's a crime, and either we bring em to justice, or we take care of it ourselves.' Eva: 'You know Franz wasn't in a gang, Emil. He didn't have anything to do with the rest of them, that's why they did that to him.' 'He's perfectly entitled, he don't need to. Since when can you force a man to do something he don't wanna do? We're not savidges here. They can take those views and try them out on the Injuns.'

Franz shakes his head: 'What you've shelled out for me, you're going to get it repaid, every last penny.' 'You don't have to do that.

But goddamnit, this thing needs sorting. Can't just sweep that under the carpet.'

Eva chips in: 'No, Franz, we're not going to let this rest, they've destroyed your nerve, that's why you can't just say yes to us. But you can put your faith in us: Pums hasn't broken our nerve. You should listen to what Herbert says: there'll be a bloodbath in Berlin that will make people sit up and take notice.' Emil grimly nods: 'You betcha.'

Franz Biberkopf looks straight ahead, thinks: what they're talking about is no concern of mine. And if they go through with it, it's still no concern of mine. It won't make my arm grow back, and I've got no beef with my arm being gone neither. It had to go, there's no sense in yapping about it. And that's not all either.

And he thinks about everything that happened: how Reinhold was down on him because he wouldn't take the woman off his hands, and that's why he threw him out of the car, and there he is lying in the clinic in Magdeburg. He wanted to stay on the straight and narrow, and that's what happened. And he stretches out in bed, makes a fist: it's happened, that's all there is to it. We'll see. We will and all.

And Franz won't say who threw him in front of the car. His friends are calm. They think that one day he will.

Franz won't go down, and they can't make him go down

The Pums gang, now quids in, has disappeared from Berlin. A couple of them are down on the farm, somewhere in the Oranienburg area, Pums is taking the waters in Altheide on account of his asthma, getting his superb machine oiled. Reinhold is tippling a bit, one or two glasses a day, the man is enjoying himself, he's acquiring a taste for it, you might as well get something out of life, and he feels stupid for getting by without it for so long, just on coffee and lemonade, what kind of life was that. Well, Reinhold has a couple of thousand tucked away, which not a lot of people know.

He wants to spend them on something, but he doesn't know what. Not the farm, like the others. He's picked up a nice-looking bird who's been around the block, and he rents this nice pad for her on Nürnberger Strasse, and he can crawl in there whenever he wants to play the big feller, or when there's trouble brewing. So everything's hunky-dory, he has his pad out west, and of course kept on his old place with a girl in it, a different one every few weeks, the lad can't seem to kick the habit.

Well, when some of Pums's boys get together end of May time, in Berlin, what do they yatter about but Franz Biberkopf. Because on account of him, so they hear, there's been some talk in the fraternity. Herbert Wischow is turning people against us, he's saying we're scum, Biberkopf never wanted any part of the action, we forced him into it, and then to cap it all we tossed him out of a moving vehicle afterwards. But we countered like this: he was aiming to grass us up, there's nothing about any violence on our part, no one manhandled him, but when push came to shove, there was no other way of going about things. They sit there, shaking their heads, no one wants to be on the outs with the rest of the fraternity. Then your hands are tied, and you're out of a job. And so they say: we'd better show willing, pass the hat around for Franz, because he was decent after all, we can pay for him to convalesce somewhere, and settle his hospital bill and all. Not skimp.

Reinhold is adamant: the guy needs putting out of his misery. The others aren't really opposed, but no one steps forward, and in the end you might as well let the poor chump run around with just the one arm. They're not sure how things would end up either, if they got on his case again, because it seems the bloke enjoys astounding luck. Well, they get some money together, a coupla hundred, only Reinhold sticks to his guns and refuses to chip in, and someone is deputed to go up and see Biberkopf, sometime when Herbert Wischow's not around.

So here's Franz quietly reading the *Mottenpost* and then the *Grüne Post*, which is his personal favourite, because they go easy on the politics there. He's reading the edition of 27 November '27, it's a while ago, before Christmas, innit, there was Polish Lina, wonder what she's up to now? In the newspaper the new brother-in-law of the old Emperor is getting hitched, the Princess is sixty-one, the groom is just twenty-seven, it's costing her a bunch of money because he's missing out on a title. Bulletproof waistcoats for detectives, we've long since stopped believing in those.

Then all of a sudden Eva's arguing with somebody outside, hello, don't I know the voice. She doesn't want to let him come in, well I suppose I'd better see for myself what it's all about. And, *Grüne Post* in hand, Franz opens the door. It's one of Pums's lads, fellow by the name of Schreiber.

What's going on? Eva yells into the room: 'Franz, the only reason he's coming up is he knows Herbert's not here.' 'What do you want with me, Schreiber?' 'I told Eva, and she won't let me in. You a prisoner or something?' 'No, I'm not.' Eva: 'You're just afraid he'll grass you up. Franz, don't let him in.' Franz. 'So what have you come for, Schreiber? You can come on in, Eva, let him in.'

They're sitting in Franz's room. The *Grüne Post* is on the table, the new brother-in-law of the ex-Kaiser is getting married, two men are standing behind him holding the crown over his head. Lion hunt, rabbit hunt, whatever. 'What do you want to give me money for? I weren't no help to you.' 'For Chrissakes, you were lookout.' 'Nah, Schreiber, I weren't no lookout, I didn't know what I was doing when you stood me there, I had no idea what I was supposed to do.' Am I glad I'm out of it, I'm not going to stand around in that yard any more, I'd even pay not to have to stand there. 'Nah, that's rubbish, and there's no need to be afraid of me, I've never yet grassed anyone up.' Eva waves her fist at Schreiber: there are other people who are paying attention here. Christ, the risk you took in coming up. Herbert will have something to say to you.

Suddenly something terrible happens. Eva sees Schreiber reach into his pocket. He wants to take out the banknotes, and tempt Franz by the colour of the money. But Eva has misunderstood the gesture. She thinks he's pulling out a revolver to off him with so he doesn't squeal. And she's up and out of her chair, white as paint, her face contorted, screaming the whole time, spaghetti legs, getting up again. Franz jumps up, Schreiber jumps up, what's the matter, what's got into her, what's the matter with her, Jesus Christ. She runs round the table to Franz's side, hurry, oh, what am I doing, he'll shoot, death, the end of everything, you murderer, the world's over, I don't want to die, don't want to lose my head, finished with everything.

She stands, runs, falls, stands in front of Franz, white, yelling, trembling all over. 'Get behind the cabinet, murder, help, help!' She yells, her eyes as big as saucers: 'Help!' The two men are chilled to the bone. Franz has no idea what's going on, he just sees the gesture – then he gets it, Schreiber's right hand is in his trouser pocket. Then Franz starts to wobble. He feels the way he did looking out in the dingy yard, all that's about to start again. But he doesn't want it, I tell you, he won't have it, he won't let himself be thrown under the car. He groans. He manages to shake off Eva. On the ground is the *Grüne Post*, with the Bulgar marrying the Princess. Let me see, first I need to grab hold of the chair. He groans aloud. Since he has his eyes on Schreiber and not the chair, he knocks over the chair. We need to pick up the chair and turn and fight him off. We need – in the car to Magdeburg, banging on the door of the clinic, Eva keeps yelling, come on, we'll manage, we're getting somewhere, trouble ahead, but we'll push on through. He stoops for the chair. The terrified Schreiber dashes out of the room, everyone here is stark staring mad. Doors fly open along the corridor.

In the bar downstairs they've heard the shouting and crashing. Two men are up in a jiffy, they pass Schreiber on the stairs. He has his head up and is calling and gesturing: a doctor, quick, someone's had a seizure. And he's gone, the bold sonofabitch.

Upstairs Franz is lying next to the chair. Eva is cowering between the window and the cabinet, cowering and gibbering, as if she'd seen a ghost. They lay Franz cautiously on the bed. The landlady is already familiar with Eva's states. She pours some water over her head. Then Eva says quietly: 'A bread roll.' The men laugh. 'She says she wants a bread roll.' The landlady shrugs, they sit her down in a chair: 'She always says that when she gets one of these fits. But it's not a stroke. It's just her nerves, and looking after the invalid.

He must have collapsed in front of her. Don't see what he's doing up and about.' 'So what was the man shouting "Seizure!" for?' 'Who was?' 'The man who passed us on the stairs.' 'Well, because he's an eejit. I know my Eva, I've known her for years. Her mother's the same. When she gets to screeching, there's only water that will help.'

When Herbert gets home at night, he gives Eva a pistol just in case, and tells her not to let the others shoot first, because then it'll be too late. He gets going right away, makes inquiries after Schreiber, of course he's nowhere to be found. All of Pums's people are on holiday, and no one wants to get involved. He's pocketed Franz's money and gone off to Oranienburg and the farm. He even managed to put one over on Reinhold, saying Biberkopf wouldn't take any money, but Eva listened to reason, and he give it to her, and she'll come through. So, there.

In spite of everything June comes round. The Berlin weather continues warm and rainy. Lots of things are happening in the world. The blimp *Italia* crashed with General Nobile on board, and wired its inaccessible position somewhere north-east of Spitzbergen. Another aeroplane was more fortunate, in seventy-seven hours it flew non-stop from San Francisco to Australia and landed safely. Then the King of Spain has fallen out with his dictator Primo, well, let's hope they can sort out their differences. Royal romance, something to tug at your heartstrings, there's an engagement between Baden and Sweden: a princess from the home of the safety match has taken fire from a prince of Baden. If you think how far apart Sweden and Baden are, you'll be astounded how swiftly these things are worked out, sometimes. Yes, women are my weakness, they are the place where I am mortal, I kiss one, think of a second and eye up a third. Oh, women are my weakness, what can I do, I can't help it, and if one day I go broke on account of women, then I'll write Out of Stock on the door of my heart.

And Charlie Amberg adds: I'll pull out an eyelash and stab you dead with it. Then I'll take a lipstick and colour you red with it. And if you're still naughty, then I've only one more trick: I'll order a fried egg, and spatter you with spinach. Oh oh oh, I'll order eggs Florentine, and spatter you with spinach.

So: it continues warm and rainy, maximum temperature 72°F. It is in such an atmosphere that the murderer Rutowski appears before a jury to make a clean breast of things. Connected with this is the question: is the dead Else Arndt the runaway wife of a seminarian professor? Because he thinks it possible, perhaps even desirable, that the murdered Else Arndt is his wife. Should that be the case, he has an important statement to make to the court. There's objectivity in the air, there's objectivity in the air, oh, it's in the air, in the air, in the air. There's idiocy in the air, there's hypnotism in the air, it's in the air, it's in the air, and-it's-stay-ing-there.

The following Monday the electric S-Bahn is opened. The Railway Board uses the occasion to warn of the dangers, careful, do not board, stay back, you are committing an offence.

Get up, you feeble spirit, and stand on your own two feet

There is an exhaustion that is like living death. In his weakness Franz Biberkopf is put to bed, he lies there into the warm weather and realizes: I am close to dying, I can feel death near me. If you don't do something now, Franz, something real, final, dramatic, if you don't pick up a stick, a sword and lay about you, if you don't sally forth wielding something, whatever it might be, Franz, Franzeken, little BBK, old thing, then it's all up with you, for good. Then you can order Grieneisen to measure you up for your one-piece wood suit.

He moans: I don't want to die, and I'm not going to die. He looks round the room, the grandfather clock tocks, I'm still here, I'm still here, they were moving in on me, Schreiber almost shot me, but it won't happen. Franz raises his remaining arm: it won't happen.

And fear gets to work on him. He can't go on lying there. He'd rather die on the street, so he's got to get out of bed, he's got to.

Herbert Wischow has taken the lovely Eva to Sopot. She has an elderly gentleman who's interested in her, a stockbroker whom she's milking. Herbert Wischow has gone along for the ride, the girl is doing well, they see each other every day, step out together, sleep apart. In the fine summer season Franz Biberkopf may be seen out again on the street, all alone once more, the solitary Franz Biberkopf, wobbly, but on his pins. The cobra sees, it creeps, it runs, it is wounded. It is still the same old cobra, with black rings around the eyes, but the once-fat beast is lean and scrawny.

Some things are clearer now than they used to be to the old fellow who is now dragging his carcass through the streets so as not to die in his room, the old fellow who is on the run from death. Life has taught him something after all. He's sniffing the air, sniffing the streets, to see if they still belong to him, if they will still accept him. He stares at the advertising columns, as though they were an event. Yes, lad, now you're not walking as if you owned the place, you're clinging on, you're hanging in there with all your fingers and toes and teeth, holding on for dear life.

Life's hellish, isn't it? You knew that once before, in Henschke's pub, when they wanted to throw you out, you and your sash, and the guy laid into you, when you hadn't done a thing to hurt him. And I thought, the world is in order, and here, the way they're standing there so menacingly, is disorder. Wasn't that prophetic of me?

Come, you, I want to show you something. The harlot Babylon, the great harlot, that sitteth upon many waters. I saw a woman sit upon a scarlet-coloured beast, full of names of blasphemy, having seven heads and ten horns. And the woman was arrayed in purple and scarlet colour, and decked with gold and precious stones and pearls, having a golden cup in her hand full of abominations and filthiness of her fornication: And upon her forehead was a name written, Mystery, Babylon the Great, The Mother of Harlots and Abominations of the Earth. And I saw the woman drunken with the blood of the saints.

*

Franz Biberkopf drifts through the streets, trots his trot and doesn't stop, he's getting his strength back. It is warm summer weather, Franz schlepps himself from bar to bar.

He steers clear of the heat. In the bar they are just drawing the first beers.

The first beer says: I come from the cellar, from hops and malt. I am cool, how do I taste?

Franz says: Bitter, good, cool.

Yes, I'll cool you down. I cool the men, then I make them warm, and then I take away their superfluous thoughts.

Superfluous thoughts?

Yes, most thoughts are superfluous. Am I right or am I right? – Right.

A small schnapps stands bright yellow before Franz. Where did you spring from? – They burnt me, man. – You have a bite to you, fellow, you've got claws. – Well, that's what makes me a schnapps. Expect you haven't seen one in a while. – No, I was almost dead, little schnapps, I was almost dead and done for. Gone without a return ticket. – You look like it too. – Look like it, cut the cackle. Let's try you again, come here. Ah, you're good, good and fiery. – The schnapps trickles down the back of his throat: fire.

The smoke from the fire rises in Franz, it scorches his throat, he needs another beer: you're my second beer, I've already had one, what have you got to say to me? – Taste me first, fatso, then we can talk. – All right.

Then the beer says: now listen, you, if you drink another couple of beers, and another kummel, and another grog, then you'll swell up like dried peas. – So? – Yes, then you'll be fat again, and then what will that look like? Can you be seen among people like that? Have another swallow.

And Franz grabs his third: I'm swallowing. One after the other. All in nice order.

He asks the fourth: what do you know, darling? – She just growls back blissfully. Franz knocks her back: I believe yer. Whatever you say, my darling, I believe yer. You're my little sheep, and you and me are going up to the meadow together.

Third conquest of Berlin

And so it came to pass that Franz Biberkopf entered Berlin for the third time. The first time the roofs were sloping off, then the Jews took him in and he was saved. The second time Lüders cheated him, and he drank it off. Now, the third time, he's lost an arm, but he's happy to take his chances. The man's got guts, double and triple guts.

Herbert and Eva left him a nice nest egg of money, the barman downstairs is looking after it. But Franz just takes a few pennies and decides: I'm not going to take that money, I need to be independent. He goes to the welfare office and asks for support. 'We'll have to make some inquiries first.' 'And what do I do in the meantime?' 'Come back in a few days.' 'A man can starve in a few days.' 'That's what they all say; no one starves that fast in Berlin. Anyway there's no money, just tokens, and we pay your rent, you're happy with your accommodation aren't you?'

And with that Franz leaves the welfare office, and once he's gone, he loses his illusions: inquiries, ha, inquiries, they might inquire about what happened to my arm, how that came about. He stands in front of a tobacconist's, pondering: they'll ask what happened to my arm, who paid for it and where I was treated. They can ask all that. And then what I've been living on for the last few months. Hang on a minute.

He ponders and walks on: what to do? Who do I ask now, how am I going to go about it, given I don't want to scrounge off of their money.

He spends a couple of days between the Alex and Rosenthaler Platz, looking for Mack, to see if he can talk to him, and on the evening of the second day he runs into him on Rosenthaler Platz. Their eyes meet. Franz makes to shake him by the hand – the way they greeted each other back then, after the Lüders episode, the joy, and now – Mack reluctantly puts out his hand, doesn't squeeze. Franz wants to start shaking the left hand again, when little Mack makes such a serious face; what's the matter with the lad, what have I done to him? And they walk up Münzstrasse together, and walk and walk, and then go back to Rosenthaler Strasse, and Franz waits for Mack to ask what happened to his arm. But he doesn't even ask, and always looks the other way. Maybe I just look too shabby for him. Then Franz makes a merry start, and asks after Cilly, what's she up to.

Oh, she's fine, how wouldn't she be, and Mack goes into all kinds of detail about her. Franz is at pains to laugh. Mack still isn't asking him about his arm, and Franz suddenly gets it, and he asks: 'You still go to that bar on Prenzlauer?' And Mack goes, 'Mneh, some-times.' And then Franz knows, and he slows down and loiters behind Mack: that means Pums has told him about me, or Rein-hold or Schreiber did, and he takes me for a burglar. And if I want to speak to him now, I'd have to tell him everything, but he's got another think coming if he thinks I'm about to do that.

And Franz gets a grip on hisself and stands tall in front of Mack: 'Well, Gottlieb, I guess this is the parting of the ways, I've got to go home, we cripples like to hit the hay nice and early.' For the first time Mack looks him in the eye, takes the pipe out of his mouth, makes to ask him a question, but Franz motions, nothing doing, and they've shaken hands, and he's gone. Mack is left scratching his head, and thinking, I need to have a proper talk with him, and he feels dissatisfied with himself.

Franz Biberkopf crosses Rosenthaler Platz, feels good and says: what's the use of talking, I need to earn some money, why am I wasting my time with Mack, it's money I need.

Oh, you should have seen Franz Biberkopf as he set out on the hunt for money. There was something new and furious in him. Eva and Herbert had left him the use of their room, but Franz wants his own place, otherwise he can't really get going. The moment comes when Franz gets his place, and the landlady lays the registration forms on the table. Franz is sitting there, pondering again: so I'm to write down, name Biberkopf, and straight away they'll be able to look me up in their files, and then they can call the police, and then it's: come on over, and why can't we take a look at you, and what's the matter with your arm, where were you treated, who paid, and it's all one big mess.

And he rages over the table: welfare, do I need welfare and looking after. I don't want that, that's not fitting for a free man; and while he's still pondering and raging, he writes a name on the form, first Franz, and in his mind's eye he sees the police station and the prisoners welfare bureau on Grunerstrasse and the car they threw him out of. He feels the stump through his sleeve, they will ask him about his arm, well, let them, I don't care, goddamnit, I'll do it.

And thickly as with a burnt stick he inscribes the letters on the paper; I've never been a coward yet, and I'm not letting anyone tell me what my name is, this is who I am, this is who I was born as, and so I remain: Franz Biberkopf. One thick letter after another, Tegel Prison, the avenue of trees, the prisoners are sitting in there, glueing, planing, stitching. One more dip of the pen, a dot over the 'i'. I'm not scared of the police with their badges. I'm a free man or I'm nothing at all.

There is a reaper, Death yclept.

Franz hands the registration form to the landlady, there, that's that taken care of. Done. And now we hitch up our troos, stiffen our thews and we march into Berlin.

Clothes make people, and a new person gets a new set of eyes

On Brunnenstrasse, where they're digging a tunnel for the underground, a horse fell down a shaft. People have been standing around for half an hour, and here come the fire brigade with their truck. They run a strap under the horse's belly. It's standing on a bunch of electricity cables and gaspipes, who knows if it hasn't broken a leg, it's trembling and whinnying, from the street all you can see of it is its head. They winch it up, the animal lashing out in all directions.

Franz Biberkopf and Mack are in the crowd. Franz jumps into

the pit with the fireman, helps push the horse forward. Mack and everyone are astounded by what Franz can do with his one arm. They pat the sweating animal, which is unhurt.

'How do you do it, Franz, you're brave, and how do you get the strength in one arm?' 'Because I've got muscles, if I want to do something I can do it.' They slope off down Brunnenstrasse, they've just run into each other again. This time, Mack is all over Franz. 'Well, Gottlieb, it's from all that good food and drink. And shall I tell you what else I'm doing?' I'm going to snub him, Mack's not gonna talk to me like that again. I don't need friends like that. 'Listen, I've got gainful employment. I'm working as a barker in a circus on the fairground on Elbingerstrasse, and I shout horses, once around ladies and gents fifty pfennigs, and back on Elbinger-strasse I'm the strongest man in the world with one arm, but only since yesterday, and then you can get in the ring with me if you like.' 'Christ, one-armed boxing.' 'Turn up and see for yourself. Whatever I can't keep covered, I make up for with legwork.' Mack is astounded, Franz must be having a laff.

They walk their old beat down to the Alex, take a turn through Gipsstrasse, where Franz takes him to the Old Ballroom: 'It's all renovated, and you can watch me dance and see me at the bar.' Mack doesn't know what's going on: 'Hey, wassa matter with you?' 'You're right, I'm starting over. And why not. Got ny objections. Come on in, watch me dance with one arm.' 'No no, I'd sooner go to Münzhof.' 'Not a bad idea, they won't let us in dressed as we are, but try on a Thursday or Saturday. You probably take me for a eunuch, just because I've had one arm shot off.' 'Who shot yer?' 'I was involved in a shoot-out with the cops. It wasn't about nothing really, it was back of Bülowplatz, there were a couple of thieves, nice fellers, but they din't have a clue. So like I say, I'm walking along minding my business, and seeing what's going on, and right on the corner there are these two suspicious-looking characters with shaving brushes on their hats. So of course I go in the house, whisper something in the ear of the lad who's the lookout, but they're not about to quit, not on account of two policemen. They were just lads, looking to nick some gear. So then the two policemen roll up, and they go sniffing about. Must have smelt a rat, furs, women's stuff, handy when you're running low. So we mount an ambush, and when the police try and get in, do you follow, they can't manage to open the door. Of course the others are meanwhile making good their escape out the back. And then, while the police are buggering about with the lock, I let em have it through the keyhole. What do you say, Mack?' 'Where was all this?' He's incredulous. 'Round the corner, Kaiserallee.' 'You're having a laugh.' 'No, I shot blindly. But they shot back, through the door. They never catched me though. By the time they got the door open, we were long gone. Just my arm. As you see.' Mack whinnies. 'See what?' Franz magnificently shakes him by the hand. 'Well, be seeing you, Mack. And if you need anything, I'm living – ah, tell you later. Health and prosperity.'

And exit down Weinmeisterstrasse. Mack in his wake a broken man. Either the fellow's having me on – or I'll have to ask Pums. The version they told was different.

And Franz loops back up to the Alex.

The shield of Achilles, how armed and accoutred he went into battle, I can't exactly bring to mind, but I have a dim sense of forearm guards and greaves.

But how Franz looked, as he moved into his next engagement, that's something I am able to tell you. So, Franz Biberkopf is wearing his old and dusty, lightly horse-soiled gear, a seaman's peaked cap with a curved anchor on it, over-jacket and trousers of worn brown serge.

He goes in the Münzhof, and after ten minutes and a beer he walks out with someone stood up by someone else, still reasonably fresh, and because it's fuggy indoors and very nice out, though there's some drizzle in the air, he takes her for a gander along Weinmeisterstrasse and Rosenthaler Strasse.

And Franz, his heart turns over at the sight of so much swindling and deception. Crikey, it's everywhere! A new man and a new pair of eyes. As if he had just been given the gift of sight! He and the girl are laughing themselves silly about all the things they see. It's six o'clock, or a little after, and it's chucking it down, thank God the little chit has an umbrella.

The bar, they peer in at the window.

'Here's the landlord selling his beer. Watch the way he pours it. There, see that, Emmi: it's half foam!' 'So what?' 'Half foam? A swindle is what that is! A cheat! And he's right. A dab hand. I'm pleased for him.'

'Ooh you! Then he's a rascal!' 'No, a dab hand.'

Toyshop:

'Jesus, Emmi, the very sight of that stuff makes me unhappy. It's such trash, and those painted eggs, when we were little we used to make them with Mum. I don't want to know what they want for them.' 'Well.' 'They're pigs. Want their window smashing. Loot. Exploiting the poor is cruel.'

Ladies' coats. He's for fast-forwarding, but she applies the brakes. 'If you're interested, I can tell you a thing or two about them. Sewing ladies' coats. You. For fine ladies. What do you think you get paid for work like that?' 'Oh, come on, why would I care? If you let them get away with it.' 'Now, hang on a minute. What do you propose to do if you were in my shoes?'

'Well, I'd be a fool to accept a few pennies. Not if what I want's the silk coat, innit?' 'I hear you.' 'And so I'll see that I gets a silk coat. Otherwise I'm a fool, and they've every right to go on paying me their rubbish wages.' 'Sez you.' 'Just because my trousers are dirty. You know, Emmi, that was a horse what done that, that fell in the shaft of the U-Bahn. No, I've got no use for a few coppers, I reckon I need a thousand marks.' 'And you're going to get them?'

She eyed him. 'Haven't got them, I say, but – but I'm going to get them, and not a few coppers.' She hangs on his arm, startled and happy.

American steam-laundry, open window, two steaming irons, in the background several 'Americans' of doubtful authenticity sitting around, smoking, in the front, in shirtsleeves, the young black-haired tailor. Franz eyes the scene cursorily. He yelps: 'Emmi, little Emmi, I'm so glad I ran into yer today.' She doesn't understand yet, but she feels mighty flattered; oh, the other fellow, the one who stood her up, he'll be sorry. 'Emmi, Emmi, sweetheart, look in that shop.' 'Come on, he won't be earning much for just ironing.' 'Who won't?' 'The little tailor.' 'No, you're right, he won't, but the others will.' 'You mean them? How could you know. Who are they?' Franz whoops. 'I've not seen them before neither, but I know them all right. Take a look at them. And the owner; there he is ironing, and at the back – he's doing something different.' 'A dive?' 'Maybe and all, no, them's all crooks. Who do the suits belong to that are hanging up? I tell you, if I was a copper with a badge and walked in and popped the question, I'd see him take to his heels all right.' 'Really?' 'Course. It's all stolen goods parked in there. Good-looking boys, mind. See them smoking. Living life to the full.'

They walk on. 'You should do as they do, Emmi, you know. It's the only way. Not work. Forget about working. Working gives you calluses, but not money. At most a hole in your head. Working never made anyone rich, I tell you. Only cheating. As you see.'

'So what do you do?' She is full of hope. 'Keep going, Emmi, I'll tell yer.' They are back in the throng of Rosenthaler Strasse, follow Sophienstrasse into Münzstrasse. Franz walks. The trumpets at his side are playing a march. The battle has been fought, the field is ours, ratatata, ratatata, ratatata, we have won the town, and taken all the gold, bold, hold, sold, rolled, ratatata, tatata, tata!

They both laugh. The girl he's picked up is class. She may just be a common-or-garden Emmi, but she's already been through welfare and divorce. They're both feeling on top of the world. Emmi asks him: 'What happened to your other arm then?' 'It's at home with my sweetheart, she didn't want to let me go, so I left it with her as a deposit.' 'Well, I hope it's as good company as you are.' 'You bet it is. Haven't you heard, I opened a business with my arm, it stands behind a counter all day and intones: only them as works gets to eat. Don't work, and you can starve. My arm goes banging about like that all day, entrance is sixpence, and the proles come in and have a whale of a time.' She splits her sides, and he laughs as well: 'Jesus, you'll tear the other one off!'

A new person gets a new head as well

A strange little vehicle comes trundling through the city. On a wheeled structure is a cripple, cranking himself forward with his arms. The little cart is flying a whole lot of brightly coloured flags, and it goes down Schönhauser Allee, stopping every so often, people cluster round, and an assistant sells postcards for 10 pfennigs apiece.

'World traveller! Johann Kirbach, born 20 February 1874 at Mönchengladbach, a happy and busy character till the outbreak of the Great War, my ambition and industry were checked by a stroke that lamed the right side of my body. I recovered sufficiently so that I could walk unaided for hours at a time, to pursue my profession. My family was shielded from the gravest consequences. In November 1924 the whole population of the Rhineland cheered when the railway was freed of the oppressive Belgian occupation. Many German comrades got drunk, which was to have calamitous consequences for me. On that day I was on my way home, when I was knocked over not more than a quarter of a mile from my front door by a group of men discharged from a licensed premises. So unhappy was my fall that I was crippled for life and will never walk again. I draw no pension or other form of support. Johann Kirbach.'

In the bar where Franz Biberkopf is scouting around these fine days, looking for an opening, some new, solid and hopeful business, a young lad saw the cart with the cripple at the Danziger Strasse station. And then he starts a commotion about what happened to his father, who was shot in the chest and now can't breathe, but all of a sudden that's supposed to be just a nervous ailment, and they cut his war pension and before long he won't get any at all.

His gripes are listened to by another young fellow in an over-sized jockey cap, sitting on the same bench as Franz, but with no beer in front of him. The guy has a jaw on him like a boxer. He goes: 'Bah, cripples, they shouldn't get a penny!' 'You'd like that,

wouldn't you. Stick em in your war, and then not pay them.'
'That's the way it should be, Christ, man. If you do something idiotic, then you won't expect to be paid for it. If a small boy falls off
a roller and breaks his leg, he won't expect a penny neither. Why
should he, just for being stupid.' 'When there was a war on,
before your time by the look of you, you were still in nappies.'
'Rot, rot, the trouble with Germany is that they pay support. Thousands of people sitting around, no one doing anything, just
collecting.'

Others around the table weigh in: 'Think for a moment, Willi!
What work do you do?' 'None. And if they goes on paying me, I'll
not do anything then either. They've got no sense just paying me.'
The others laugh: 'He likes to talk.'

Franz Biberkopf is of the company. The boy in the jockey cap
keeps his hands cheekily tucked in his pockets, looks at him sitting
there with his one arm. A girl embraces Franz: 'What about you,
you've just got the one arm and all. What kind of benefit are you
on?' 'Who wants to know?' The girl gestures at the boy in the cap:
'Him. He's interested.' 'No, I'm not interested. I just says: anyone
stupid enough to go to war – forget it.' The girl to Franz: 'I think
he's scared.' 'Not of me he isn't. He's no call to be scared of me.
That's all I'm saying. Do you know where my arm is, this one here,
the one that's missing? I put it in a bottle of spirits, and now it sits
around on the sideboard at home, and lectures me all day long:
"Morning, Franz. You blimming idiot!"'

Ha ha! What a card. An old gent has unpacked some sandwiches
from a newspaper, cuts them up with his pocket knife, crams the
pieces in his mouth: 'I weren't in the war, I were locked up the whole
time in Siberier. Well, and now I'm back with my old lady, and I've
got roomatism. What if they come round to take my benefit, Jesus,
imagine.' The youth: 'Where'd you get your roomatism from, then?
From dealing out on the street, right? If your bones are sick, then
don't go work on the street.' 'Then maybe I'll become a pimp.' The
boy brings his hand down on the table, crumples up the newspaper:
'That's right. Yes. It's not a joke neither. You should see my brother's
wife, they're respectable people, a match for anyone, do you

suppose they were too proud to collect stamp money, dole, whatever. So he ran around looking for work, and she didn't know how to get by on the pittance he earns, and two little bairns at home. The woman can't go to work then, can she. So she met a man, and then she maybe met another one. Till my brother notices something's up. Then he gets hold of me and he says I'm to come and listen while he sorts her out. Well, he came to the right man. You should have heard it. She tore him off a strip for his few dirty bills, and left him shaking. Just let him try that again.' 'So, no more action?' 'Oh, he'd like to all right, but she doesn't want to go near such a flaming idiot, a fellow who goes on the state and lectures her for earning money.'

That converts most of the listeners. Franz Biberkopf, sitting next to the youth they call Willi, raises a glass to him: 'You know, you're probly ten or twelve years younger than what I am, but you're about a hundred years smarter. Jesus, if I talked like you when I was twenty. Respect, or what the Prussians used to say say: at-ten-*shun*.' 'We still say that. When we're not paying any.' Laughter.

The pub is full, the waiter opens a door, a little back room is free. The whole table decamps there, under the gaslight. It's very hot, the room is full of flies, a straw sack is on the floor, it's tipped up onto the windowsill to air. The talk goes on. Willi sits there in the midst of it, giving as good as he gets.

Then the young boy who went missing earlier sees the watch on Willi's wrist, and keeps remarking on the fact that it's gold: 'You must have bought that cheap.' 'Three marks.' 'Stolen goods.' 'Nothing to do with me. Do you want one?' 'No thanks. And have them pull me in and ask where d'you get that from?' Willi laughs in their faces: 'He's afraid of robbers.' 'Now that's enough.' Willi lays his arm across the table: 'He's got something against my watch. As far as I'm concerned it's a watch that keeps time and is made of gold.' 'Yes, for three marks.' 'Then I'll show you something else. Give me your beer mug. Now tell me, what is it?' 'It's a beer mug.' 'That's right. A mug to drink out of.' 'Right.' 'And this here?' 'That's your watch. Christ, you seem to like playing silly buggers.' 'That's a watch. It's not a boot and it's not a canary, but if you want you can call it a boot, well, suit yourself.' 'I don't follow. What are you getting at?' But Willi seems to know what he's about, he takes back his arm, and touches a girl, and says: 'Take a walk.' 'Waa? Why should I?' 'Oh, just go walk over to the wall.' She doesn't want to. The others call out to her, 'Oh, go on, do it.'

Then she gets up, gives Willi a look and walks over to the wall. 'Fascist!' 'Walk!' yells Willi. She sticks out her tongue at him and marches, swinging her hips. They laugh. 'Now come back! So: what did she do just now?' 'Stuck her tongue out at you!' 'What else?' 'Walked.' 'Right. She walked.' The girl puts her oar in: 'Nah, I didn't. That was dancing.' The old man over his sandwiches: 'That weren't no dancing. Since when is waggling your bum dancing.' The girl: 'Well, it wouldn't be if you did it.' A couple of calls: 'That were walking.' Willi laughs triumphantly to hear it: 'Well, then, and I say she marched.' The boy, irritably: 'What's all this in aid of, I'd like to know.'

'Nothing. But you see walked, danced, marched, whatever you like. You still don't get it, do you. I'll give it you in bite-size pieces. This was a mug before, but you can call it spittle, and then maybe everyone else will take to calling it spittle too, though people will still use them to drink out of. And when she marched, she was marching. Or walking or dancing. But what it was you could see for yourself, with your own eyes. It was what you saw. And if someone takes your watch off you, then that's not the same as stealing it, by a long chalk. See, now you get it. Maybe it came out of a pocket or a display, but stolen? Who's to say?' Willi leans back, thrusts his hands in his pocket: 'Not me, for sure.' 'And what do you say?' 'You heard me. I say taken away. I say change of ownership.' Freeze. Willi shoots his boxer's jaw and stops. The others are lost in thought. Something a little eerie has come over the group.

Suddenly Willi turns to Franz, the one-armed, with his harsh voice: 'You had to join the Prussians, you were in the war. For me that's the same as being deprived of liberty. But they had the courts and the police on their side, and because they had them, they could gag you, and now it's not called loss of liberty, as you, fool, think, but patriotic duty. And you sign up for it, just like you pay your taxes, and you don't know what happens to that money neither.'

The girl whines: 'Enough politics. I don't like it in the evenings.' The boy, muttering, withdraws: 'Load of rubbish. When it's so nice out.' Willi chases him off: 'Then away with you. You think politics is what's said indoors, and it's people like me. I'm just demonstrating it to you. Politics will shit on your head wherever you go. If you let it.' A shout of: 'I've had it, shut up now.'

Two new customers come in. The girl swings her hips cutely, slithers along the wall, waggles her bottom, scoots sweetly over to Willi. He leaps up, they dance a pert little number, then fall into a clinch, ten-minute snog, 'festgemauert in der Erden steht die Form aus Mehl gebrannt'.[7] No one looks. The one-armed Franz starts on his third drink, strokes his stump. The stump burns, burns, burns. Helluva boy, that Willi, helluva boy, helluva boy. The lads lug the table out, drop the straw sack out of the window, someone has showed up with an accordion, he's sitting on a stool by the door, noodling away. Andy can, oh Andy can, he's a handy man.

They chatter away, have taken off their jackets, are drinking, yacking, sweating. If no one can, then my handy Andy can. Franz Biberkopf gets up, pays and says to himself: I'm too old to dance, and I don't rightly feel like it either, I need to come into money, and I don't much care where I get it from.

Cap on and out.

A couple of fellows are sitting on Rosenthaler Strasse in the middle of the day, tucking into pea soup, one has the *Berliner Zeitung* open next to him, is pissing himself laughing: 'Horrifying family tragedy in Westphalia.' 'What's so funny?' 'Listen. Father drowns his three children. Three in one go. Desperate man.' 'Where was it?' 'Place called Hamm. That's making a clean breast of things. He must have had it up to here. But you can rely on a man like that. Wait, let's see what become of his missus. I spect he— No, it seems she took her own life first. Separately. What do you say to that then? Jolly family, Max, they know how to live. The wife's note: Cheat! The heading, with exclamation marks, that's a cry for help.

"I've had enough of this life, I'm going in the canal. Why don't you take a rope and hang yourself. Julie." Full stop.' He doubles over with laughter: 'There's real strife for you: she goes in the canal, and he's to reach for the rope. The wife says: hang yourself, and he throws the kids in the water. The man doesn't do as he's told. No wonder the marriage was a failure.'

They are two older men, construction workers from Rosenthaler Strasse. The one speaks, the other takes issue. 'But that's enough to break your heart. If you saw something like that in the theatre or read about it in a book, you'd cry over it.' 'You might, Max. But you shouldn't.' 'The woman, the three little ones, what more do you want?' 'The way I am, I think it's funny, I like the feller, sure I feel sorry for the kids, but all at one fell swoop, the entire family, that commands respect, and then—' He can't contain himself: 'I just think it's fucking hilarious, sorry, I think it's hilarious the way they fall out till the very end. The wife tells him to use a rope, and he says: sorry, Julie, old thing, no can do, and he drops the children overboard.'

The other puts on his steel-rimmed glasses and reads the story again. 'The man's alive. They've arrested him. Well, I wouldn't want to be in his shoes.' 'Who knows. How can you tell?' 'Oh, I know all right.' 'Oh, get away. I picture him like this. He's sitting in his cell, smoking his baccy, if he gets any, and he says: take a walk.' 'That's all you know. What about his conscience. He's crying, he's that eaten up about it. Can't sleep at night. My God, you're talking yourself into sin.' 'Oh, I'm not having that. If he's such a determined fellow as that, then he'll be sleeping soundly, and probably have better food and drink than outside. I bet.' The other gives him a serious look. 'In that case he's just an animal. If they want to hang someone like that, I'll give them my blessing.' 'You're right. Tell you what, though. He'd agree too. He'd say you're right.' 'Now stop your nonsense. I'm going to order a gherkin.' 'There's interesting stories in the paper. A rabid dog, but maybe he feels sorry for what he's done, you can overdo it.' 'I'm having a gherkin and brawn.' 'Now you're talking. Me too.'

A new man needs a new job or he needs none at all

When you notice those tell-tale shiny patches, you'll know the time has come to start thinking about a new suit. Try us first. In brand-new brightly lit premises amid contemporary displays, we'll show you on wide tables all the clothes you so badly need.

'I can't do nothing, say all you like, Frau Wegner: a man missing an arm, and his right at that, is done for.' 'I can't deny that, it's hard, Herr Biberkopf. But that's still no reason to wail and lament and pull long faces so that a person'd fear for you.' 'Well, what am I supposed to do, with one arm?' 'Go on the dole, or open a small business or something?' 'A small business?' 'Newspapers or flowers, or selling sock-suspenders or ties outside Tietz's.' 'A news-stand?' 'Or fruit and veg.' 'I'm past that, I'm too old.'

That's something I've done before, I'm through with that, that's over and done.

'You need a mate, Herr Biberkopf, who'll tell you what you need to do, and stand by your side when you need her. She can help pull the wagon, or sell at a stall, if you happen to be called away.'

Cap on, down, all nonsense, next of all I'll strap on a hurdy-gurdy and go busking. Where's Willi?

'Morning, Willi.' Afterwards, Willi says: 'Nah, there's not a lot you can do. But if you're smart about it, there is something. If I give you something to sell every day, or pass on under the counter, and you've got some good friends, and they stand by you, then you can flog it and earn a decent percentage.'

And that's what Franz sets himself to do. He is ambitious. He wants to stand on his own two feet. He wants whatever brings in money fast. Work is bullshit. He spits at newspapers, his blood boils when he sees those blockheads of vendors, and sometimes he is astonished to see how a man can be so stupid as to stand there slaving away while others careen past in their automobiles. I can just see myself doing that. Back in the day, lad. Tegel prison, the avenue of dark trees, the buildings wobbling, the roofs sliding off down on your head, and there's me going straight! Franz Biberkopf insists on respectability, oh, pull the other one! I must have had brain fever from prison, Manoli mania.[8] I want money, money makes money, a man needs money.

Now behold Franz Biberkopf as a fence, a criminal, a new man has a new profession, before long he'll take another turn to the bad.

There is a woman arrayed in purple and scarlet, and bedecked with jewels and pearls, holding in her hand a golden cup. She laughs. On her forehead her name is written, a name of mystery, great Babylon, the mother of harlots and of earth's abominations. She has drunk of the blood of saints, she is drunken with the blood of saints. There sits the harlot Babylon, she is drunken with the blood of saints.

What did Franz Biberkopf go around in when he was living at Herbert Wischow's?

What is he wearing now? On a table, purchased for 20 marks, a spotless summer suit. For special occasions, an Iron Cross on the left tit, by way of legitimation for his arm, enjoys the respect of passers-by and the fury of workers.

A well-fed pub landlord or master butcher is what he looks like, knife-sharp creases, glove, stiff derby. In case of trouble he carries papers, false papers, made out in the name of one Franz Räcker, who died during the troubles of 1922 and whose papers have already helped a good many others. Franz knows all the details off pat, where his parents are living, when they were born, how many brothers and sisters he has, what job he last worked at, all the kinds of things it might occur to a policeman to ask, and the rest can take care of itself.

This was in June. Glorious June, when the butterfly hatches, having gone through its pupation. And Franz is doing well for himself by the time Herbert and Eva return from the spa at Sopot. A lot had happened in the spa, there is much to be said about it, as Franz learns to his pleasure. Eva's old put was out of luck. He had success at the tables, but on the very day he drew 10,000 marks from the bank his hotel room is broken into while he is dining with Eva. How can such a thing be. The room was opened with a spare key, his gold watch is gone, plus another 5,000 marks he had loose in the bedside drawer. Of course that was remiss of the gentleman, but who would think of such a thing happening. That thieves can sneak into such a first-class hotel, why didn't the porter see anything, I will press charges, what's the matter with your security, we don't guarantee valuables in hotel rooms. The man is livid with Eva because she insisted that they have dinner, and what for, just so you can catch a glimpse of the Baron, what next, you'll be kissing his hands, sending him a box of chocolates, all paid for by me. Now that's not very nice of you, Ernst. What about the 5,000 marks? Is that my fault too? Oh, let's go home. The banker agrees furiously: not a bad idea, let's get the hell out of here.

So Herbert is back in Elsasser Strasse, and Eva moves into a swish pad in the west of the city, nothing new to her, she thinks pretty soon he'll have had his fill of me, and I'll be back in Elsasser.

Even in the first-class train compartment where she sits with her banker, accepting his caresses with boredom and a semblance of delight, she dreams: wonder what Franz is up to. And when the banker gets off a little before Berlin and leaves her alone in the compartment, she has a little crisis and panics: what if Franz is gone again. So picture the joy and surprise and gossip among Herbert and Eva and Emil when, on 4 July (a Wednesday), who should walk in, well, you'll have got there by yourselves. Trim and tidy, the Iron Cross on his hero's chest, the brown eyes as doggishly true as ever, warm fist and strong handshake: Franz Biberkopf. Now stand up straight. Now don't lose your balance. Emil is already familiar with the transformation, he pastures the little lambs of his gaze instead on Herbert and Eva. Franz is one slick dude. 'Boy, you look like you wash your legs in champagne!' is Herbert's gleeful welcome. Eva sits there, stunned. Franz has tucked his empty right sleeve in his pocket, the arm doesn't seem to have grown back. She hugs and kisses him. 'My God, Frankie, to think of how we sat there racking our brains about what you'll do, we were worried about you like you wouldn't believe.' Franz does the rounds, kisses Eva, kisses Herbert, even Emil gets a smacker: 'Silly, worrying your heads about me!' He blinks at them cannily. 'How'd you like me as a war hero, then, in my bomber jacket?' Eva crows: 'What's going on, what's going on, I'm so happy to see you looking like this.' 'Well, so am I as well.' 'And – and who are you seeing these days, Franz?' 'Seeing? Ah. No, no. Not the moment. I ain't got no one.' And he gets to talking and telling them how he's been, and promises Herbert he'll give him all his money back, every last penny, in a few months it should all be paid off. At that, Herbert and Eva laugh. Herbert waves a brown 1,000-mark note in front of Franz. 'This any good to you, Franz?' Eva implores him: 'Just take it, Frankie.' 'No chance. Don't need it. At the most, we can drink its health downstairs, that would do.'

A girl shows up, and now Franz is back to strength

They approve of everything Franz is doing. Eva, who still entertains tender feelings for the lad, would like to hook him up with a nice girl. He resists, no, I know the right girl, you don't, nor does Herbert neither, how would you know, she's new in Berlin, she's from Bernau, she used to hang around the Stettiner Bahnhof at night, and I met her there one time, and I told her: you'll get ground up in little pieces, sweetheart, unless you quit commuting, you can't make a go of things in Berlin that way. You see, Franz – Herbert knows the story already, and so does Emil – one time she's sitting in the café, and it's midnight. I go up to her and I says: why are you making a face like that, girl, don't take on so. Then she starts crying in front of me, she had to go to the police station, she's got no papers and she's under-age, she doesn't dare go home. She had a job, but she lost it, and now her mum's thrown her out as well. She says: and all because I wanted to have a bit of fun. Do you know what people do at night, in Bernau?

Emil, as ever, listens with his hands on his hips and puts in: 'The girl's right. I've been in Bernau. There's nothin going on.'

Eva: 'Well, so I take her under my wing; the Stettiner Bahnhof isn't a place for her in future.'

Herbert is smoking an imported cigar: 'If you're a man that understands how to go about things properly, Franz, then you'll be able to make something of that girl. I've seen her. She's got class.'

Emil backs him up: 'A bit young, but she's got class. Good bones.' They carry on tippling.

This girl, who promptly comes knocking on his door next day, delights Franz from the moment he first claps eyes on her. Eva has stimulated his imagination, and he would like to do her a good turn as well. But the girl really is a prime piece, sweet and charming, nothing like that has ever been on his bill of fare before. She is a small person, in her little white dress with bare arms she looks like a schoolgirl, she has slow gentle movements, she takes her place right away discreetly at his side. She's hardly been there half an hour, but already he can't imagine a time he didn't know the little minx. Emilie Parsunke is her real name, but she prefers to go by Sonia, and that's what Eva always called her, because of her high Russian cheekbones. 'Cos Eva,' says the girl reasonably, 'Eva's not her proper name neither, she's an Emilie same as what I am. She told me so herself.'

Franz rocks her on his lap, takes in the delicate but solidly built little miracle, and is amazed at the happiness the Almighty has sent to him. Life is ups and downs, no doubt about it. The man who gave Eva her name is known to him, because it was himself, she was his girl before Ida, if only he could of stayed with Eva. Well, now he's got this new one here.

She lasts only a single day with him as Sonia, though, then he begs her, he can't get along with strange names. If she's from Bernau, then it doesn't matter if she takes a different name. He's had a number of girls, as she will have imagined, but none yet by the name of Marie. He'd like one now. Whereupon he starts to call her 'Mitzi'.

And it doesn't take long – early July time – till something good happens to him with her. No, there isn't a baby, and she doesn't fall ill either. This is some other thing that shocks Franz to the core, but in the end it doesn't turn out too badly for him. It's the time Stresemann goes to Paris, or again perhaps he doesn't, in Weimar the telegraph office ceiling collapses, and perhaps an unemployed man takes off after his missus who has travelled to Graz with another man, and he shoots the pair of them before putting a bullet in his own brain. Such things happen in all weathers, the wholesale dying of fish in the Weisse Elster is another instance. Astounding to read about; if you happened to be there, not so great; every building has its own stories to relate.

Franz is often to be found standing outside the pawnshop in Alte Schönhauser Strasse; inside in the dining room he deals with the odd acquaintance, or he studies the section of the paper headed Items, For Sale and Wanted; at lunchtime he sees Mitzi. Then one time he notices Mitzi steaming into Aschinger's on the Alex, which is where they like to have lunch. She says she overslept – but something seems a bit off to him. He forgets about it by and by, the girl is tender like you wouldn't believe, everything in her room is so clean and tidy, with flowers and ribbons and knick-knacks, like with a little girl. And it's always so nicely aired, and sprayed with lavender water, that it's a proper delight for him when they arrive home together at night. And in bed she's as light as a feather, always so sweet and soft and happy, like the very first time. And with it, she's a bit serious, he really can't make her out at all. Is there anything on her mind as she sits there, not doing anything, and if so, what. When he asks her that, she always replies with a laugh: nothing at all. You can't spend all day thinking. Which stands to reason.

But on the door outside there's a letter box marked with Franz's name, the false one: Franz Räcker, because that's the one he likes to give for small ads and the mail. So one day Mitzi tells him she distinctly heard the postman drop something in the box and when she goes to look later, there's nothing there. Franz is surprised, and wonders what that's about. And Mitzi says someone must have fished out the letter; the people across the landing, they're always at the peephole, and they will have seen the postie walk up, and they must have helped themselves to his letter. Franz goes purple with rage, and thinks: what's this, people are after me, and that evening he goes round there. Knocks, there's a woman comes to the door, and she says she'll get her husband. There's an old man – the woman is younger, the man's about sixty, the woman half that. So Franz asks him whether a letter meant for him was mistakenly delivered there. The man looks at his wife: 'Was a letter delivered here? I've just got home.' 'No, not here.' 'When was this, Mitzi?' 'About eleven, he generally comes at around eleven.' The woman says: 'Yes, he's always here around eleven. But the young lady always takes in the mail in person, if there is any, because he always rings.' 'How do you know?' 'I've met him on the stairs sometimes, and then he's give it to me, and then I put it in the box.' 'I wouldn't know if you put it in the box, but I've seen him giving it to you. Well, what shall we do?' Franz: 'So you're saying there's no letter for me, Räcker?' 'Heaven forfend, what would I be doing, taking in letters addressed to other people. We haven't even got a letter box, that's how rarely the postie comes for us.' Franz slopes off unhappily with Mitzi, tips his cap: 'Scuse the disturbance. Good evening to yer.' 'Evening. Evening.'

Franz and Mitzi argue the ins and outs of the thing. Franz wonders if the people are maybe snooping on him, he wants to tell Herbert and Eva about them. He dins it into Mitzi to tell the postie to ring. 'I do, Franz, honey, but sometimes there's a new one, or a replacement.'

A couple of days later, when Franz unexpectedly comes home in the morning and Mitzi's already on her way to Aschinger's, he finds the answer, something entirely new – and that's the thing that strikes a chill into his bones, though finally it doesn't hurt him all that much. He walks into the living room, of course it's clean and empty, but there's a box of fine cigars out for him, Mitzi's stuck a piece of paper on them saying: 'For Franz', and a couple of bottles of Allasch. Franz feels happy, he thinks the way that girl runs my household, I ought to marry her really, and he's quite delirious, and what about that, she's gone and bought me a little bird as well, it's as if it was my birthday, well, you wait, my little mouse, I'm sweet on you too. And he's just took out his wallet to see how much money he has when there's a ring at the door, yes, it's the postie, but he's late today, it's past twelve, I'll tell him so myself.

And Franz goes out into the corridor, opens the front door, listens out, no postie. He waits, nothing, well, maybe he's just popped into one of the other flats. Franz takes the letter out and goes into the drawing room. The unsealed envelope contains a further, sealed letter, and next to it a note, with a scribbled 'Wrongly addressed' and an illegible signature. So that must have come from over the way, who are they spying on now. The sealed letter is addressed to 'Sonia Parsunke, c/o Herr Franz Räcker'. How peculiar, who's she getting letters from, it's postmarked Berlin, and it's a man's writing. And there's someone writing, and this is when Franz feels a chill to his heart: 'Dearly beloved, how long can you leave a fellow waiting for an answer—' he can't read on, he stops – and there are the cigars and the little birdcage.

And then Franz runs downstairs, not to Aschinger's, he goes straight to Herbert and he's all pale, to show him the letter. Herbert is whispering next door with Eva. Then in comes Eva, she gives Herbert a parting kiss, shoves him away and drapes herself round Franz's neck: 'Well, Frankie, don't I get a kiss?' He stares at her. 'Leave it out.' 'Oh, go on, Frankie, just a kiss. We're old friends.' 'What's got into you, behave yourself, what's Herbert going to think.' 'I've just thrown him out, come on, let's see if he's there.' She leads Franz through the rooms, Herbert is gone, well, so he's gone. Eva shuts the door: 'Now you can give me a proper kiss.' And she curls herself around him, she is in a strange passion.

'Steady on, girl,' pants Franz, 'you're mad, what's this all about?' But she is beside herself, there's nothing he can do about it, he's astonished, pushes her away. Then something in him switches. He doesn't know what it is with Eva, there's a rage and ardour in the two of them. Afterwards, with bites on arms and throat, they lie there crosswise, she with her back against his chest.

Franz grunts: 'Say, is Herbert really gone?' 'You don't believe me.' 'I feel rotten, doing this to my friend.' 'You're such a sweet man, Franz, I love you so.' 'Christ, and you'll have bite marks all over you.' 'I don't care, I could gobble you up. When you came in a moment ago, with the letter, I was this close to leaping at you in front of Herbert.' 'Eva, what's Herbert going to say when he sees those marks later on, they'll be blue and green for days.' 'He won't know. I'll go to my banker later, and I'll tell Herbert he did it.' 'Ah, that's good. You're a clever girl, Eva. I don't like going behind people's backs. But what will the banker say when he sees you like that?' 'Yes, and what will my aunt say, and my grandmother? You are a scaredy cat, aren't you.'

Then Eva has sorted herself out, grabs Franz by the ears, snogs him and presses her hot cheeks against his stump. And she takes the letter, gets dressed, puts her hat on: 'I'm going now. You know what I'm going to do, I'm going to Aschinger's, have a word with Mitzi.' 'Aw, Eva, why do that?' 'Cos I want to. Stay here. I'll be back soon. Let me do it my way. Trust me to look after a little girl with no experience, in Berlin for the first time. All right, Franz—' And she kisses him again, and they almost start all over again, but she pulls away and runs out. Franz doesn't get it.

This is at half past one; by half past two she's back, serious, calm, happy, helps Franz, who has dropped off, into his clothes, dabs his sweaty face with her scent. Then she gets going, perched on the bedside table, smoking: 'OK, Mitzi laughed, Franz. She's all right.' Franz is astounded. 'Forget the letter, Franz. She was sitting at Aschinger's, waiting for you. I showed her the letter. And then she asked if you weren't pleased about the canary and the schnapps.' 'Sure.' 'Now listen to me. I tell you she didn't bat an eyelid. I liked her so much. She's a good girl. I'd never put anything tawdry your way.' Franz is grim and impatient: what's it all about. Eva leans down, pats him on the knee: 'You're a sweetie, Franzeken. Don't you get it. A girl wants to do something for her feller as well. What's the good of you running around all day doing deals and so on, and all she can do for you is make coffee and keep the place tidy. She wants to give you presents, she wants to make you happy. That's why she does it.' 'That's why? You're letting her pull the wool over your eyes. She's cheating on me to make me happy?' Eva gets serious: 'Listen, there's no question of her cheating on you. She said that right out: no chance. If someone sends her a letter, so what, these things happen, some man gets stuck on her and writes her a letter, haven't you ever heard of that happening before, eh?'

Gradually it begins to dawn on Franz. Ah, so that's the game, is it? She notices that he's beginning to understand. 'Of course. So? She wants to earn money. Is that so wrong? I earn my own keep as well. It doesn't feel right to her to be kept by you, with you handicapped by your arm and all.' 'I see.' 'She told me so right out. Didn't bat an eyelid. She's a good girl, see, you can trust her. You need to take it easy, she says to me, after your having had such a year. And things weren't exactly wonderful for you before that, you know, in the big house, Tegel, and all. She would feel ashamed to have you labouring away for her. So she works for you. Just she doesn't quite dare tell you.'

'I see,' nods Franz, and his head slumps down onto his chest. 'You've no idea,' Eva is with him, rubs his back, 'how devoted that girl is to you. You don't want me. Or do you – want me, Franz?'

He takes her round the waist, she settles herself carefully on his lap, after all he's only got the one arm to hold her with, he presses her head against his chest, quietly says: 'You're a good woman, Eva, I want you to stay with Herbert, he needs you, he's a good fellow.' Before Ida, Eva used to be his girl, don't mess with that, don't start it over again: Eva understands. 'I want you to go to Aschinger's now, Franz. Mitzi'll either still be there, or waiting outside the door. She doesn't want to go home unless she knows you want her.'

Very quietly and tenderly, Franz says goodbye to Eva. He sees little Mitzi standing outside Aschinger's on the Alex, the side with the photo display case. Franz stands on the opposite side, in front of the construction fence, and watches her from behind for a long time. She walks over to the corner, Franz follows her with his eyes. It's a decision, a turning point. His feet start to move. He sees her in profile on the corner. How petite she is. She's wearing those little brown shoes with buckles at the sides. Watch out, someone will accost her any minute. The little turned-up nose. She's looking. Yes, I've come from over the way, from Tietz's, so she's not seen me. An Aschinger's bread van is in the way. Franz follows the construction fence to the corner where there are piles of sand for cement. Now she'll be able to see him, but she's looking the other way. An old gentleman is giving her the eye, she looks past him, wanders on in the direction of Loeser & Wolff. Franz crosses the road. He's still ten paces behind her, and keeps his distance. It's a sunny July day, a woman offers him a bunch of flowers, he gives her 20 pfennigs and takes the flowers and still doesn't approach. Still not. But the flowers smell nice, she put some out in the room this morning, along with the birdcage and the bottles.

She turns round. Sees him right away, the flowers, he came after all. And she flies at him, her face glows, for an instant it glows and flames as she sees the flowers in his hand. Then she pales, a few red splotches remain on her face.

His heart is thumping. She takes his arm, and they cross into Landsberger Strasse, not saying a word. She peeks at the wild-flowers he has in his hand, but Franz is walking along perfectly upright at her side. A yellow double-decker 19 rumbles past, completely chocka, on the construction fence there's an old poster. Reich Party of the German Middle Class, they can't get across the street, the cars coming from the Alex and the police headquarters have a green light. By the Persil pillar Franz realizes he's still holding the flowers, and wants to give them to her. And, looking down at his hand, he is still wondering, there's a heaviness in him, he still hasn't decided: do I give her the flowers or do I not. Ida, what's it got to do with Ida, Tegel, I love her so much.

And on the little island with the Persil column, he presses the bunch into her hand. She has looked up at him beseechingly so many times, he hasn't spoken a word, now she clasps his left fore-arm and lifts his hand, presses it to her face, which once again flushes. The heat from her cheek streams through him. And then she stops, drops his arm, her head seems to slump onto her left shoulder. She whispers to Franz, who in alarm clutches at her hip. 'It's all right, Franz. Let be.' And they walk across the road diagonally to where they're tearing down Hahn's, and past. Mitzi is now perfectly upright again. 'Why are you so upright, Mitzi?' She presses Franz's arm: 'I was so scared just now.' She turns her head to the side, tears have started up in her eyes, but she can start to laugh just as quickly, before he notices anything, they were terrible hours.

They are up in his room, the girl is sitting on the stool in front of him in her white dress, they've thrown open the windows because it's boiling hot, a dense and humid heat, and he's sitting in his shirtsleeve on the sofa, and he can't take his eyes off his girleen. How in love he is; I'm so happy she's there, look at your pretty little hands, child, I'll buy you some kid gloves, just you wait, and then I want to get you a blouse, I don't care what else you get up to, it's just so nice that you're there, I'm so happy you came back. Jesus. And he burrows his head in her lap. He pulls her over, can't get enough of looking at her and squeezing her, feeling the girl all over. Now I feel human again, now I feel human again, no, I won't leave you, I don't care what. He opens his mouth: 'Mitzi, my love, you can do what you like, I'll never leave you.'

How happy they are. Arm in arm, they stop and admire the new canary. Mitzi feels in her handbag, shows Franz the letter from today: 'And to think that you got all het up about that stuff?' She crumples it up, throws it over her shoulder: 'I could show you a whole box of those.'

Defensive war against bourgeois values

And over the next few days Franz Biberkopf goes for quiet walks. He's no longer so dogged about his shady deals, and going from fence to fence or fence to buyer. If something fails to work out, he shrugs. Franz has time, patience, quiet. If the weather were better, he would do what Mitzi and Eva suggest, namely go out to

Swinemünde and take a few days off; but the weather's useless, every day it's raining or drizzling or tipping it down, and it's cold as well, trees have blown over in Hoppegarten, it wouldn't be very pleasant up on the coast. Franz feels close to Mitzi and they are regular visitors at Herbert and Eva's. Mitzi has found a well-off gentleman of her own, Franz has met him, Franz is her 'husband', he gets together sometimes with the man and another fellow, and the three of them eat and drink amicably together.

How nicely our Franz Biberkopf is currently situated! How well off he is, how everything has changed for the better! He was close to death once, now he's picked himself up! What a well-fed critter he is, short of nothing, not food, not drink, not clothes. He's got a girl who makes him happy, he's got more money than he can spend, he's already paid off his entire debt to Herbert. Herbert, Emil and Eva are his friends, they look out for him. He spends whole days sitting around at Herbert and Eva's, waiting for Mitzi, going out to Müggelsee, where he rows with the other two: because by the day Franz is getting more adept and stronger with his left arm. He puts in an occasional appearance in the pawnshop on Münzstrasse, no more, just to see what's going down.

You swore, Franz Biberkopf, that you would keep to the straight and narrow. You had a squalid life, you got under the wheels, before that you killed Ida and did time for it, all that was terrible. And now? You're in the same situation, for Ida read Mitzi, you've lost an arm, careful you don't start drinking, because then everything will start all over again, only worse, and then it'll be all up with you.

– Nonsense, what can I do about it, did I ask to be a pimp? Bollocks. I did what I could, I did everything that was humanly possible, I let them take my arm, what more do you want. I've had it up to here. Didn't I trade, didn't I run around from morning till night? I've had it. No, I'm not decent, yes, I'm living off immoral earnings. No, I'm not ashamed. And what do you do, what do you live off, if not other people? Am I putting the squeeze on anyone?

– You'll finish up in prison, someone will stick a knife in your belly.

– Let him. He'll have had mine first.

The German Reich is now a Republeck, better believe it, or you'll get it in the neck. On the corner of Köpenicker Strasse and Michael-kirchstrasse there's a public meeting in progress, the hall is deep and narrow, workers, young men in open collars and blue overalls are sitting on ranks of chairs, women and girls, brochure sellers do their trade. On the stage behind the table, flanked by two others, sits a fat balding man, provoking, tempting, laughing, teasing.

'After all, we're not here to produce more hot air. They do enough of that in the Reichstag. Somebody asked one of our comrades once if he wouldn't like to sit in the Reichstag. The Reichstag, with the gold dome on top and the leather armchairs inside. Do you want to know what he said? He said, comrade, if I do that and go in the Reichstag, that would just mean one more sonofabitch in the world. We've not got the time to talk out the chimney, everything turns to vapour. The Communists without lists, they like to say: we will pursue a politics of disclosure. And we've seen the upshot for ourselves: the Communists have ended up being corrupted themselves, so much for their politics of disclosure. It's all a deception, and what is to be disclosed is something a blind man can see. We don't need to go into the Reichstag for that, and whoever can't see that is past help, Reichstag or no. Everybody understands that that talking shop is no good for anything except pulling the wool over the people's eyes – everybody except the so-called representatives of the working people.

'Our good Socialists! There are even some religious ones among them, and they're the cat's pyjamas: they can all run to Jesus for all I care. Because whether a man is a priest or a politician doesn't matter; main thing is, you obey him. (Call from the audience: and you believe him.) Yes, that in any case. The Socialists don't stand for anything, don't know anything, can't do anything. They always get the most votes in the Reichstag, but they don't know what to do with them, except for sitting in the leather armchairs and smoking cigars and drawing ministerial salaries. And these are the people that the workers have supported with their votes and their political contributions; it just means another fifty or hundred individuals getting fat at the expense of the workers. The Socialists will never take over the state, no chance – because the state has taken over the Socialists. You can live to be a cow's age, and still be learning, but there's never been a cow yet to match the German proletariat. They keep taking their ballots in their hands, and going to the polling booths and voting, and they think, that's it, all done. They say: we want to hear our voice in the Reichstag. I tell you, they'd be better advised to start a male voice choir.

'Comrades, we won't take a ballot in our hands, and we won't vote. We'd rather spend Sunday in the country. And why else? Because the voter commits himself to the rule of law. And the rule of law is the same thing as the state's monopoly on violence. Our democrats want us to put a good face on things, they want to hush us up, to keep us from understanding what the rule of law is. But we won't vote, because we understand all too well what the rule of law is, and what the state is, and there are no holes and no doors that would let us tunnel into the state. At best we prop up the state, we carry the state. And that's what the high priests of elections have in mind for us. They want to trap us and train us into being the state's beasts of burden. With most of the workers they have succeeded long ago. As Germans, we are raised in the spirit of obedience. But comrades, it is not possible to combine fire and water, as workers ought to understand.

'The Centrists and the Socialists and the Communists shout in one choir and are happy: all blessings come from above, they chant. From the state, from the law, from the powers of order. That's what it feels like too. For people who live in a state, freedoms are enshrined in a constitution. They are fixed. The freedom we need is given us by no one, we have to take it for ourselves. This constitution wants to rob sensible people of their sanity, but what do you do with paper freedoms, comrades, with freedoms that are pen and ink? If you take your freedom, a policeman comes along and bops you on the head; you shout: what are you playing at, in the constitution it says such and such, and he says: you hold your noise, mate, and he's right; the man doesn't know any constitution, he knows his rule book, and he's got his nightstick, so you'd better shut up.

'Before long it won't be legal for workers in any of the major industries to go on strike. They've slapped the guillotine of compulsory arbitration on you, but beneath that you can move freely.

'Comrades, people vote endlessly. They tell themselves, the next time will be better, pay attention, make an effort, organize at home, in the workplace, another five votes, another ten votes, another dozen votes, just you wait, then you'll be in for a surprise. Yes, you are in for a surprise. This is just an endless game of ring-a-ring-a-roses, and at the end of it nothing has changed. Parliamentary democracy merely prolongs the agony of the proletariat. There's talk about a crisis of justice, the need to reform the legal system root and branch, the judiciary needs to be refreshed, democratized, just, put at the service of the state. But we don't want any new judges. In place of their justice we want no justice at all. We aim to destroy all the institutions of state by direct action. We have the means: refusal of labour. The wheels grind to a halt. And that's not a form of words either. Comrades, we refuse to be lulled by parliament, welfare, that whole socio-political mumbo-jumbo. All we have to offer this state is our opposition – spontaneity and lawlessness.'

Franz walks round the room with canny Willi, listens, buys brochures, stuffs them in his pocket. He doesn't really care for politics, Willi hectors him, Franz listens, he pokes it with his fingers, it moves him, then it doesn't. But he sticks close to Willi.

– The existing social order is founded on the economic, political and social enslavement of working people. It finds expression in the property laws, in various monopolies, and in the state, with its monopoly of power. Not the satisfying of natural human needs, but the prospect of gain is the basis of production today. All technical innovation serves to increase the wealth of the propertied class to infinity, in shameless contrast to the wretchedness of broad swathes of society. The state serves to protect and perpetuate the privileges of the owning class and the oppression of the masses, it works with every means of cunning and power to preserve the monopoly and the class divides. The creation of the state marks the beginning of an artificial organization, from the top down. The individual becomes a puppet, a dead cog in a vast mechanism. Wake up! We don't aspire to take political power, the way all the other parties do, we want its removal. Don't co-operate with the so-called legal institutions: all they do is put the seal of law on the enslavement of the slave, nothing more. We reject all arbitrary national and political boundaries. Nationalism is the creed of the modern state. We reject all national units: they only camouflage the rule of the propertied classes. Wake up! –

Franz Biberkopf gulps down what Willi gives him. Following one of these meetings there is a debate, where they stay in the hall and argue the toss with an old worker. Willi knows the man already, and the man takes Willi for a worker in his factory, and wants to get him to do more agitating. But Willi laughs in his face: 'Christ, man, since when am I your comrade. I don't work for the factory barons.' 'Well then, do something in your place of work.' 'I don't need to do anything there. Where I work, everyone knows what they have to do.' Willi falls over the table laughing. Rubbish, he gives Franz a pinch in the leg, next someone will run around with a pot of glue and a brush and put up posters. He laughs at the worker, who has long iron-grey hair and an open shirt: 'You know, you sell the publications, the *Pfaffenspiegel*, *Black Flag*, *Atheist*; have you ever opened one and looked inside?' 'Listen, comrade, you open your mouth way too far. I'll show you something I've written myself.' 'I suppose that makes you an authority. Don't bother. But what about this: read whatever it is you wrote, and abide by it. See this: Culture and Technology. Now listen: "Egyptian slaves worked for decades without any machines on a king's tomb, European workers spend years working with machines on an individual's private fortune. Is that progress? Perhaps. But for whom?" Well. Soon I'm going to work myself, so that Krupp in Essen or Borsig has another thousand marks a month, one of those Berlin kings. Christ, comrade, when I look at you, what do I see? You claim to be a man of direct action. Where? I don't see any. Do you, Franz?' 'Oh, leave him be, Willi.' 'No, tell me, do you see the least difference between our man here and the SPD?'

The worker sits doughtily in his chair. Willi: 'For me there's no difference, comrade. Just on paper, in the publications. All right, imagine you get your way. But then what will you do, that's what I'm wondering. Well, I'll tell you: the same as someone in the SPD. The same, exactly the same; stand at your lathe, cart your lousy wage packet home on Fridays, and the company pays dividends on your labour. European workers toil at their machines to build private fortunes for wealthy individuals. Maybe that's even one of yours.'

The greying worker looks from Franz to Willi and back again, he looks around, there are still a few people at the beer table at the back of the room, the worker leans forward, whispers: 'Well, so what do you do?' Willi prompts Franz: 'You tell him.' But Franz is reluctant, he says he doesn't like these political discussions. The grizzled anarchist persists: 'This isn't a political discussion. We're just having a chat. What job do you do?'

Franz sits up on his chair and reaches for his beer mug, he fixes the anarchist with a look. There is a reaper, Death yclept, I must go up on the hills and weep and wail and lament with the herds in the desert, because they are so ravaged that none wander there, both the birds of the heavens and the beasts of the field are gone.

'I'll tell you what I do, colleague, because I'm not your comrade. I go around, I do odd things, but I don't work, I let other people work for me.'

What's he on about, is he having me on. 'Then that makes you an entrepreneur, have you got employees, and how many? What arc you doing here with us, if you're a capitalist?' I will make Jerusalem a ruin, and a den of dragons; and I will lay the cities of Judah desolate, so that none shall dwell in them.

'Christ's sake, man, can't you see, I've only got one arm. I lost the other. That's what I got from working. That's why I've had it with work, understand?' Understand, understand, you've got eyes to see, shall I buy you a pair of glasses, the way you're staring at me. 'No, I don't understand, colleague. What line of work are you in? If it's not regular work, then it must be irregular.' Franz bangs on the table, points at the anarchist, lowers his head: 'See, he's understood. That's just what it is. Irregular work. Your regular work is slavery, because that's what regular work is, you said so yourself. I remembered.' Without your help, I don't need you for that, you soft-soap scribbler and chatterbox.

The anarchist has white tapered hands, he is a precision-tool manufacturer, he inspects his fingertips and thinks: it's good to unmask these bastards, they'd only compromise me otherwise. I'll get someone else along to listen with me. He gets to his feet, but Willi holds him back: 'Where are you off to, colleague? Are we done already? Why don't you settle things with your brother here, surely you won't duck out of it?' 'I'm just getting someone else to listen. There's two of you against me.' 'What's that about you getting someone, I don't want anyone else. You can say what you want to Franz here.' The anarchist sits down again, in that case we'll do it by ourselves: 'OK, then. He's no comrade, and he's no colleague neither. Because he doesn't work. Doesn't seem like he goes on the dole either.'

Franz's face hardens, his eyes blaze out: 'No, that he doesn't.' 'Then he's not my comrade and not my colleague and not unemployed either. Then I'm just asking, and nothing else concerns me: who is he and what's he doing here?' Franz puts on his most resolute expression: 'I was just waiting for you to say that: what are you doing here. Here is where you sell leaflets and brochures and newspapers, and when I ask you about them, and what they say, then you say: who are you to ask? What are you doing here? Didn't you write and talk about wage slavery and that we're victims and can't move freely?' Wake up, damned of the earth, who are still forced to starve. 'Well, then you weren't listening very closely. I was talking about the workers' movement. To be part of that, a man's gotta work.' 'Well, I refused to.' 'That's no good to us. You might as well stay in bed. I was talking about industrial action, collective action, the strike weapon.'

Franz raises his arm and laughs, he is enraged. 'So what you do goes by the name of direct action, right: going round, putting up pieces of paper, making speeches? But for the time being you keep going to work, and strengthening the capitalists? Comrade idiot, you're screwing together grenades for them to kill you with. Who do you think you are, preaching to me? Willi, say something! I'm floored.' 'Same question: what work do you do?' 'I'll repeat myself: None! Shit! None at all. What's the matter with you. I can't. By your own theory. I'm not going to support any capitalist. And I shit on your moaning and your strikes and your little people who are supposed to be organized. Self-reliance. I see to what I need. I'm self-sufficient. Amen.'

The worker gulps his lemonade, nods: 'Well, just try getting by on your own.' Franz laughs and laughs. The worker: 'I've told you this umpteen times: you won't get by on your own. We need a fighting organization. We need to educate the masses about the state's rule through force and economic monopoly.' And Franz laughs and laughs. No higher being will come to our rescue, no god or emperor, no tribune to relieve us from misery, we can only do it ourselves.

They sit and face each other in silence. The old worker in his boiler suit stares at Franz, who scowls back, what are you staring at me for, sonny boy, you'll not outstare me. The worker opens his mouth: 'You know, I can see from your face, my words are wasted on you. You're obstinate. You're banging your head against a brick wall. You don't know what the main thing is with the proletariat: solidarity. You don't know.' 'You know what, colleague, I'm minded to take my hat and go. What do you say, Willi. I've had enough. You keep on saying the same thing over and over again.' 'Yes, so I do. You can go in the basement for all I care, and bury yourselves. But I don't want you at our political meetings.' 'Excuse me, sir. We just happened to have half an hour to spare. And now we'd like to say thank you very much. Landlord, the bill please. Now watch this: three beers and two shorts, one mark ten, there, I paid for em, direct action.'

'What is your story, mate?' He won't let up. Franz pockets his change: 'Me? I'm a pimp. Can't you tell?' 'Well, it's not a complete

surprise.' 'Me. Pimp. Got it. Did I say so or didn't I? All right, Willi,
your turn.' 'It's none of his business.' Those bastards were making
a fool of me, the wretches were riling me up. 'You scum of the capitalist swamp. Get lost you, you're not even proletarians. The word
for you is parasites.' Franz is already up on his feet: 'We're not going
to the homeless shelter though. Good day to you, Mr Direct Action.
I hope the capitalists grow fat on your labour. Back to the grind-
stone tomorrow at seven sharp, there's fifty pfennigs in it for the
missus.' 'Don't ever show your faces here again.' 'No chance of
that, direct hot air, we don't hang around with capitalist lackeys.'

Calmly sauntered out. On the dusty street, the two link
arms. Willi takes a deep breath: 'You sorted his hash, Franz.' He's
surprised that Franz is so taciturn. Franz is livid, odd. Franz has left
the hall boiling with rage and hatred, he couldn't say why.

They meet Mitzi in the Mokka-fix on Münzstrasse, where there's
a huge commotion. Franz is keen to take Mitzi home, he wants to
sit her down and talk to her. He tells her about the conversation
with the old worker. Mitzi is very gentle with him, but all he cares
about is if he said the right thing. She smiles, doesn't get it, strokes
his hands, their bird wakes up, Franz sighs, she is unable to calm
him down.

Conspiracy of females, our dear ladies take the floor, the heart of Europe is unchanged

Franz can't get away from politics. (Why? What's tormenting you?
What are you protecting yourself against?) He sees something, he
sees something, he feels like smacking them in the face, they pro-
voke him continually, he reads the *Red Flag* and the *Unwaged*. He
often turns up at Herbert and Eva's with Willi in tow, but they
don't like him. Franz doesn't much like him either, but he's interesting to talk to, he knows more about politics than the rest of
them put together. When Eva asks Franz to stop seeing Willi, who
just costs him money and is nothing but a drain on him, then Franz
completely agrees with her; Franz really has no use for politics,

never did. But one day he promises to let Willi go, and the next he strolls up with the louse, and brings him rowing.

Eva says to Herbert: 'If it wasn't Franz, and if he hadn't had that accident with his arm, then I'd know how to straighten him out.' 'Well?' 'He wouldn't be seeing that wretched boy all the time who just exploits him. Who're his real friends anyway. If I was Mitzi, I'd let him go.' 'Who, Willi?' 'Willi, or Franz. I wouldn't care. But he needs to understand. If someone's been locked up, they've surely had a chance to think about what's right and what's wrong.' 'You're upset with him aren't you, Eva.' 'Well, why did I play Mitzi to him, and set her up with the two fellers – just so Franz can go sounding off? No, it's time our Franz listened a bit. Now he's down one arm, where's it going to end? He's getting into politics, and he's annoying the girl.' 'Yes, she's fed up all right. She said as much last night. Sits around waiting for him to show. Not much of a life for a girl like that.' Eva gives him a kiss: 'And it's no different for me either. Just you try staying away and doing stupid things like going to meetings! Herbert!' 'Well, sweetie, and what if I did?'

'First I'd scratch your eyes out, and then you can come visit me by moonlight.' 'I'd like that, sweetie.' She clips him across the mouth, laughs, gives him a shaking: 'I'm not going to let my Sonia be ruined like that, she deserves better. As if the girl hasn't had her fingers burnt already, and she's bringing in money.' 'Well, you'd better take steps with our Franz. For as long as I've known him, he's been a good and dear man, but talking to him is like talking to a brick wall, he doesn't listen.' Eva remembers how she wooed him when Ida turned up, and after, how she warned him, what the man has put her through, and she still isn't happy.

'Tell you what I don't get,' she says, standing in the middle of the room, 'the man's had his run-in with Pums, and they were flat out of order, and he won't lift a finger. He's all right now, but an arm is still an arm.' 'Agreed.' 'He won't talk about it, you know that. But I'll tell you something, Herbert. Of course Mitzi knows all about the business with the arm. Everything except who done it and why, she doesn't know that. I tried asking her. Doesn't know and doesn't want to get into it. She's a bit soppy, our Mitzi.

Well, maybe she might get to thinking about it a bit, while she's sitting there on her own waiting and wondering what's keeping Franz, and of course he'll be vulnerable then. Mitzi cries a lot anyway, only not in front of him. The man's heading for misfortune. He needs to keep his end up. Mitzi needs to start him thinking about that Pums business.' 'Oh dear.' 'No, trust me. I know. That's what Franz needs to think about. And if he takes a knife or a pistol, hasn't he got right on his side?' 'As far as I'm concerned, of course. I've done enough asking around. The Pums gang is tight: no one's saying anything.' 'Someone will know something.' 'Well, so what do you want?' 'Franz to start thinking about that, instead of Willi and his Communists and anarchists and all that worthless stuff that's not good for nothing.' 'Mind you don't get your fingers burnt, Eva.'

Eva's gentleman is off to Brussels, so she can have Mitzi round and show her how very elegant people live. Because Mitzi has never seen anything like that. So besotted with Eva is the gentleman that he has even furnished a little nursery room for her, with two little monkeys. 'I expect you think this is for the monkeys, Sonia? Not a bit of it! I just put them in there because it's such a nice little room, and Herbert loves the monkeys and he always gets such a kick out of them when he comes.' 'Oh, so you bring him here too?' 'Of course, why wouldn't I? The old man knows him, and he's jealous as hell, which is lovely. I think if he wasn't so jealous he'd probably have let me go long ago. The man wants a baby with me, that's what the nursery room is for!' They laugh, it's a plush, colourful, beribboned room with a low children's crib. The monkeys clamber up and down the bars of the crib; Eva picks one up and holds it to her breast, with a dreamy expression: 'I'd have humoured him over the baby too, only I don't want one with him. Not from him.' 'And I guess Herbert doesn't want one.' 'Oh, I'd have one with Herbert all right. Or Franz. – Are you upset, Sonia?'

Sonia's reaction is unexpected. She squeals, her face cracks open, she pushes the monkey away from Eva's bosom, and vehemently, happily, blissfully, ecstatically embraces Eva, who doesn't understand and turns away, because Sonia keeps trying to kiss her. 'Oh, Eva. No, I'm not angry, I'm happy you like him. Tell me how much do you love him? If you want his baby, why'n't you tell him?' Finally, finally, Eva manages to push the girl away. 'Are you crazy?! What's the matter with you, Sonia. Tell me truthfully: do you want to palm him off on me?' 'No, why would I, I want to keep him, he's my Franz, isn't he. But you're my Eva too.' 'What did you say?' 'My Eva, my Eva.'

And Eva can't keep her off. Sonia covers her with kisses – mouth, nose, ears, throat. Eva keeps still; then, as Sonia buries her face in Eva's breast, she pulls her head up: 'I never knew you were that way.' 'Not at all,' stammers Sonia, frees her head, and presses it to Eva's face, 'I like you, I didn't know that about you. The thing you said just now, about wanting a baby with him—' 'So? That makes you jealous?' 'No, Eva, I had no idea. And Sonia's face is beet-red, and she looks up at Eva: 'Do you really want his baby?' 'What's the matter with you?' 'Do you?' 'No, it was just something I said.' 'No, now you're just saying that. I know you do, I know you do.' And again, Sonia burrows into Eva's bosom and hums delightedly: 'That's so lovely, you wanting a baby with him, oh, that's so lovely, it makes me so, so happy.'

Then Eva takes Sonia into the other room and lays her down on the couch: 'You're queer, girl.' 'No, I'm not queer, I've never touched a girl before.' 'But you want to touch me, don't you.' 'Yes, because I like you so much, and because you want his baby. You should have it too.' 'You're mad, girl.' She is completely carried away, holding Eva's hands, keeping her from getting up: 'Oh, don't deny it now, you want it, don't you, you must promise me you will. Promise me you'll have a baby with him.' Eva has to break free from Sonia, who lies there all floppy, eyes closed, her mouth making smacking noises.

Then Sonia gets up, sits down at the table next to Eva, where the maid serves them lunch with wine. For Sonia she brings coffee and cigarettes, Sonia is still dreaming away to herself confusedly. As always, she is wearing a plain white dress; Eva is in a black silk kimono. 'Now, Sonia, can I talk to you properly?' 'Sure.' 'Well, how do you like all this here?' 'Love it.' 'You see. And you like Franz, don't you?' 'Yes.' 'Well, if you like him, then you need to look after him a bit. He goes places that aren't good for him, and always in the company of that dratted Willi.' 'He likes him, don't he.' 'What about you?' 'Me? He likes me too.' 'That's so typical of you, you've got no eyes to see, you're too young. It's the wrong company for Franz, I'm telling you, and Herbert agrees. He's no good. He'll lead Franz off the straight and narrow. Don't you think his losing one arm is bad enough?'

Instantly, Sonia goes pale, the cigarette sags in the corner of her mouth, she puts it down, asks quietly: 'What's the matter? For goodness sake?' 'Who knows what the matter is. I don't go around looking after Franz, and it seems you don't either. I know, I know, you're busy. But does he tell you where he goes? What's he say?' 'Ooh, it's just politics, I don't understand any of it.' 'And you see, that's what he's occupying himself with, politics and nothing but politics, with Communists and anarchists and scum like that that don't have a decent pair of trousers to cover themselves with. And that's the kind of person your Franz is running around with. And you're happy about it, and you work to support it?' 'I can't tell Franz what to do. Go here, go there – I can't do it, Eva.' 'If you weren't so small and not yet twenty, I'd smack you. Suddenly you've got no say in what he does. Do you want him to finish up under the wheels again?' 'He won't, Eva. I'll keep an eye on him.' Odd, little Sonia has tears in her eyes now, and holds her head in her hands, Eva looks at her and can't make her out; does she love him so much? 'Here, have some wine, Sonia, my gentleman likes claret, here you are.'

She pours her half a glass, while a tear rolls down the girl's cheek, and her face looks terribly sad. 'Have another sip, Sonia.' Eva sets the glass down, strokes Sonia's face and thinks, she'll get excited again. But no, she keeps staring into space, gets up, walks over to the window and looks out. Eva ups and stands beside her, I can't make any sense of her. 'Don't take it to heart so about Franz, Sonia, you know, the thing I said, I didn't mean it that way. Just don't let him run around with that idiot Willi, Franz is too easy-going, he should be thinking what to do about Pums, and whoever took his arm off, and undertake something in that regard.' 'I'll keep an eye on him,' says little Sonia quietly, and, not lifting her head, slips her arm around Eva's shoulder, and they stand there like that for almost five minutes. Eva thinks: I don't mind her having Franz, but no one else.

Afterwards they go rampaging around the rooms with the little monkeys, Eva gives her a tour of everything, Sonia is dumbfounded by so much splendour: Eva's wardrobe, the furniture, the beds, the carpets. Are you dreaming of the hour when you are crowned Pixavon Queen? Is it all right to smoke here? You bet. I'm astonished at the way you've been able to sell this quality cigarette for so many years at such a low low price; I must admit I'm overjoyed. Ah, the aroma. The wonderful scent of white roses, classical, as the German lady demands, and yet strong enough to develop a full range. Ah, the life of the American screen goddess is different than the legends would have you believe. Coffee is served. Sonia sings a song:

'Once there roved at Abrudpanta Brigands wild and daring too. But their chief whose name was Guito Had a noble heart and true. Once he met in darkling forests Count von Marschan's little maid. Soon there echoes through the branches: I am yours till life shall fade.

'But they are too soon awakened, Hunters come with loud halloo. They are startled from their raptures, And they ask, what shall we do? And her sire doth curse the maiden, Curses loud the chieftain grim, Oh, have pity, father dearest, I shall go to death with him.

'Soon Guito lies in darkness, Fearful is his woe and pain! Isabella seeks to shatter Her dear sweetheart's heavy chain. She succeeds – and no oh wonder, He is once more safe and free, Yet scarce rid from ghastly shackles, He must stop a villainy.

'To the castle next he hastens, There he sees his sweetheart now, But already she is kneeling, Ready for the wedding vow. Forced to say "yes" to the union Which she loathes with all her might, But the crime's denounced by Guito, And his lips are pale and tight.

'Swoon of death grips Isabella, And she lies so sweet and pale.

Ah, there is no kiss can wake her, Nobly then he tells his tale. To her father now he turns: Yours the guilt that she is dead, You alone her heart have broken. You made pale those cheeks so red.

'When the chief once more beholds her Lying on the silent bier, He bends down to see her better, She still lives, Death is not near. Off he bears her, on his saddle, Struck with fear the people stand, And she wakes up from her swooning, He and she go hand in hand.

'And they flee by love's wind carried, Peace and quiet have left them now, Hunted and pursued by justice, Solemnly they take this vow: Freely let us both surrender. When the poison cup we've drained, God his judgment then will render, Up in heaven our love we've gained.'9

Sonia and Eva know it's just a market ballad, cranked out against a painted background, but they are both reduced to tears, and when it's over it takes them a little while to lay their hands on their cigarettes and get them lit.

Enough politics, idleness is much more dangerous

Franz Biberkopf stays bogged down in politics a little longer. The dashing Willi doesn't have much in the way of money, he's a quick thinker and a bright fellow, but a beginner among pickpockets, and that's why he's leeching off Franz. He was once in a home, and someone there told him about Communism, and that it wasn't up to much, and that a sensible person follows his own bent and believes in Nietzsche and Stirner: everything else is just so much bullshit. And now the bold sarcastic fellow takes great relish in going to political meetings, and making trouble from the floor. He gets hold of people to do business with, or else just to take the mickey out of.

Franz doesn't go around with him much any more. He's through with politics, even without Mitzi and Eva intervening.

Late one evening he's sitting at a table with an elderly carpenter they've run into; Willi is at the bar, talking to someone else. Franz has his elbow propped on the table, his head in his hand, and he's listening to what the carpenter has to say, which is: 'You know mate, the only reason I came to the meeting was because my wife's ill, and's got no use for me at home in the evenings, she needs her peace and quiet, on the dot of eight she takes her sleeping pill and her tea, and I need to turn out the lights, so what is there for me to do up there. It's enough to give a man a taste for pub life, if he's got a sick wife at home.'

'Stick her in a hospital, mate. Keeping her at home's no good.'

'She's tried hospital. I got her out of there. She didn't like the food, and she didn't get any better either.'

'Is she very ill then, your wife?'

'Her womb's got fused with her gut or something like that. They tried operating, but it didn't solve the problem. Not physically. And now the doctor's saying it's just a nervous condition, and there's nothing really the matter with her. But she's still in pain, and cries all day long.'

'Jesus.'

'He'll discharge her, mark my words. She was supposed to go back to the company doctor, but she didn't. He'll discharge her. If someone's got a nervous ailment, then they're well, by his book.'

Franz listens, he was ill as well, his arm was run over, he was in hospital in Magdeburg. But he doesn't need all that now, the world has moved on. 'Want another beer?' 'Sure.' 'A beer.' The carpenter looks at Franz. 'You're not in the party, are ya, mate.'

'Used to be. Not 'ny more. Don't see the point in it.'

The landlord joins them, greets the carpenter with an 'Evening, Eddy', and asks after the kids, and then he whispers: 'Christ, you're not going to get all political again, are you.'

'We wuz just talking about that. No chance.' 'That's as well, Eddy, I tell you, and my boy would bear me out, you won't make anything out of politics, it ain't no good for us, just other people.'

The carpenter looks at him through narrowed eyes: 'I see, so your nipper August is saying that already, at his age.'

'He's a good boy, you'll not pull the wool over his eyes, whoever you are. We just want to get by. And – well, it's not going too badly. Just don't complain.'

'Cheers, Fritz. I'm happy for you.'

'I don't give a stuff for Marxism, and Lenin and Stalin and the rest of the crew. If someone gives me credit, and how much and how long for – that's what it's about.'

'Well, you've made something of yourself.' Thereupon Franz and the carpenter sit there in silence. The landlord is burbling away about something, but the carpenter talks over him:

'I don't know the first thing about Marxism. But listen, Fritz, it's not as simple as you might imagine it to be. What do I need Marxism for or the rest of them, the Roosians, or Willi here, and his man Stirner. They can all be mistaken. What I need I can count off on my fingers any day of the week. If someone gives me a thrashing, I understand that. Or if I gotta job one day, and am out on my ear the next, there's no orders, the foreman stays, the boss too, of course, but I'm on my bike. And – if I got three kids and they go to the local school, the oldest girl has crooked legs from rickets, and I can't send her away, maybe she'll get a chance at school. Maybe my wife can run along to the social service place, but right now she's sick and has her hands full with herself, she's a good woman, she sells herrings, and the kids learn about as much as we did, you get the picture. See. And I can understand it too if other people teach their kids foreign langwidges, and go to the seaside in summer, and we can't afford for them even to go out to Tegel. Posh kids probably don't even get rickets. When I need to see the doctor for my rheumatism, then there's about thirty of us perched together in the waiting room, and when it's my turn he asks me, I expect you've had your condition for a while, and how long have you been working, and have you got your forms with you: he doesn't believe me, and then I go to the company doctor, and if you're hoping to get a rest cure prescribed, they always make deductions, I tell you you'll be carrying your head in your hands by the time they agree. I don't need spectacles to understand all that. You'd have to be a camel in the zoo not to understand that. And you certainly don't need Karl Marx. But Fritz, listen to me, tell me I'm wrong.'

And the carpenter raises his grey head and looks at the landlord with his big eyes. He puts his pipe back in his mouth, draws at it, and waits to hear what the reply will be. The landlord growls, pulls a face, looks unhappy: 'No, you're right. My girl's got rickets too, and I can't afford to send her out into the countryside to get well. But then there's always been rich and poor. There's no way you and me will fix that.'

The carpenter smokes phlegmatically: 'Just let them be poor as wants to be. Sooner someone else than me, I don't feel like it. It grates on me.'

They talk very calmly, sip at their beer. Franz is still listening. Willi comes over from the bar. Hurriedly Franz gets up, takes his hat and goes: 'Oh, Willi, I want to get to bed early tonight. We had a late night yesterday.'

And Franz stomps off alone down the hot dusty street, room dee boom dee dummel dee boo dee dummel dee day. Just wait a minute and then Hopper will come to you, with his little chopper he'll make mincemeat out of you, wait, wait a minute and Hopper will come to you. Damn, where am I going, damn, where am I going. And he stops, and can't cross the street, then he turns on his heel and retraces his steps, past the bar where they are all still sitting, the carpenter over his beer. I'm not going back in there. What the carpenter said was true. He was right. What am I doing with politics, all that garbage. No good to me. No good to me.

And Franz stomps back along the hot, dusty, unquiet streets. August. There are more people on Rosenthaler Platz, one man stands there with newspapers, the *Berliner Arbeiter-Zeitung*, Marxists at it again, a Czech Jew child abuser, had his way with twenty lads in his time and still not arrested, I used to sell that too. Terribly hot out today. And Franz stands there, buys the paper off the man, the green swastika on the masthead, the one-eyed invalid of the Neue Welt, drink, drink, little brother drink, leave your worries at home, no more trouble, no more pain, then life is a jest, no more trouble, no more pain, then life is a jest.

And he carries on round the square, into Elsasser Strasse, bootlaces, Lüders, no more trouble, no more pain, then life is a jest. Remember that, it were last Christmas, Christ, that's a long time ago, I used to stand here outside Fabisch's and shout, those crappy things for ties, tie-holders, and Lina, fat, Polish Lina would pick me up.

And, not knowing what to do with himself, Franz stomps back to Rosenthaler Platz and stands outside Fabisch's by the bus stop, opposite Aschinger's. And waits. Yes, that's what he wants. He stands there waiting, and he feels like a needle on a compass – pointing north. To Tegel, the prison, the walls! That's where he wants to go. That's where he has to be.

And it so happens that the 41 comes along, stops, and Franz hops on. This is right, he feels, let's go, and he takes the 41 tram out to Tegel. He pays his 20 pfennigs, he buys his ticket, everything goes tickety-boo, he's off to Tegel, this is it! He feels so good. He's on his way now, Brunnenstrasse, Uferstrasse, the avenues, Reinickendorf, it's true, it all exists, that's where he's going, he's on his way to find it. And this is the way. And the longer he sits there, the larger it looms, the more real, the more powerful. He feels such satisfaction, such strong and compelling pleasure, that as he sits he closes his eyes and is swallowed up by a mighty sleep.

The tram has passed the Rathaus in the dark. Berliner Strasse, Reinickendorf West, Tegel, everybody out. The conductor wakes him, helps him to his feet. 'This is as far as we go. Where are you headed?' Franz staggers out: 'Tegel.' 'Well, then you've come to the right place.' Clearly he's sloshed, the way those veterans drink away their pension money.

Franz is so seized by a need for sleep that he crosses the square and makes straight for the first bench under a lantern. A policeman wakes him, it's three in the morning, he doesn't book him, the man looks respectable, he's not sober, but someone might come along and rob him. 'You can't sleep here, sir, haven't you got somewhere to go?'

Franz has had enough. He yawns. He wants to go to beddy-byes. Yes, so this is Tegel, what did I come out here for, did I want anything, his thoughts run into each other, I need to go to bed, that's all there is for it. He drifts sadly: yes, this is Tegel, he doesn't know why, yes, he was locked up there once. A cab. What was it again, what was I doing here. You, will you wake me if I drop off.

And sleep returns and tears his eyes open, and Franz knows everything.

And there are mountains, and the old man gets up and says to his son: come with me. Come with me, says the old man to his son, and he goes and his son goes with him, and they walk together into the mountains, up and down, mountains and valleys. How much further, Father? I don't know, we are walking uphill, downhill, into the mountains, come with me. Are you tired, son, don't you want to come with me. Oh, I'm not tired, if you want me to come, I'll come. Yes, come. Up, down, valleys, it's a long way, it's midday, we've arrived. Look about you, son, is that an altar. Father, I am afraid. Why are you afraid, son? You woke me, we went out early, and we forgot the sheep we meant to sacrifice. Yes, we forgot it. Up and down, the long valleys, we forgot it, the sheep is not with us, there is the altar, I am afraid. I must take off my coat, are you afraid, my son. Yes, Father, I am afraid. I am afraid too, son, come closer, don't be afraid, we must do it. What must we do? Up and down, the long valleys, I got up so early. Fear not, son, do it willingly, come closer to me, I have taken off my coat, so as not to bloody the sleeves. I am afraid, because you have the knife. Yes, I have the knife, I must slaughter you, I must sacrifice you, the Lord commands it, do it gladly, my son.

No, I cannot do it, I will scream, don't touch me, I don't want to be slaughtered. Now you are on your knees, do not scream, my son. Yes, I am screaming. Do not scream; if you don't want, then I can't do it, you must want it. Up and down, why should I not go home again. What will you do at home, is not the Lord more than a home. I cannot, yes I can, no I cannot. Move closer, see, I have the knife here, look at it, it is very sharp, it will touch your throat. Will it cut my throat? Yes. Then the blood will bubble forth? Yes. The Lord wills it. Do you want it? I cannot yet, Father. Come quickly, I must not slay you; if I do it, then it must be as though you did it unto yourself. I unto myself? Ah. Yes, and be not afraid. Ah. And not live life, not live your life, because you will give it unto the Lord. Move closer. The Lord our God wills it? Up, down, I got up so early. You surely will not be cowardly. I know, I know, I know! What do you know, my son? Apply the knife to me, wait, let me turn down my collar so that my neck is open. You seem to know something. You must only will it, and I must will it, we will both do it, then the Lord will call, we will both hear Him call: yes, come here, give me your throat. There. I am not afraid, I do it willingly. Up and down, the long valleys, there put the knife to me, and cut, I will not scream.

And the son throws his head back, his father steps behind him, clasps his forehead, and shows him the butcher's knife in his right hand. The son wills it. The Lord calls. They both fall on their faces.

What calls the voice of the Lord. Hallelujah. Through the mountains, through the valleys. You are obedient unto me, halle-lujah. You shall live. Hallelujah. Stop, throw the knife away. Hallelujah. I am the Lord whom you obey, and whom alone you always must obey. Hallelujah. Hallelujah. Hallelujah. Hallelujah. Hallelujah. Hallelujah. Hallelujah. Hallelujah, lujah, lujah, lujah, hallelujah, lujah, hallelujah.

'Mitzi babes, little Mitzi, will you give me a proper ticking off.' Franz tries to pull Mitzi down onto his lap. 'Say something. What was I doing, to make myself so late last night?' 'Oh, Franz, you're making me so unhappy by the company you keep.' 'What do you mean?' 'The driver had to help you up the stairs. And not a squeak out of you because you're lying there fast asleep.' 'I told you, I went to Tegel, all by myself, right, all by myself.' 'Be truthful, Franz.' 'All by myself. I once had to do time there.' 'Was there nothing else?' 'No, it was all served, every last day of it. I just wanted to have another look at it, there's no need for you to be cross, Mitzi.'

Then she sits by him, looks at him tenderly the way she always does: 'Oh, won't you give up politics.' 'I don't do politics.' 'And not go to political meetings neither.' 'I think I'll stop going.' 'Then tell me.' 'Yes.'

With that, Mitzi lays her arm round Franz's shoulder, presses her head to his, and they don't say anything.

And once again, there is nothing so contented as our Franz Biberkopf, who tells politics to go get lost. As if he'd bang his head against a wall. There he is in the bars, moping, playing cards, and Mitzi has already made the acquaintance of a gentleman who is almost as rich as Eva's, but he's married, which is even better, and he'll set her up in a nice two-bedroom flat.

And what Mitzi wants, Franz is helpless to avoid. One day Eva surprises him in his room, and why not, if Mitzi wants it too, but Eva, if you really had a little one, Christ, if I have a little one, my feller will build me ten castles, he'd be that made up

The fly clambers up, shaking the sand from its wings; before long it will buzz some more

There's really not much to say about Franz Biberkopf, we know the fellow already. We can predict what a pig will do when it reaches the sty. Only, a pig is better off than a human being, because it's put together from meat and lard and not much more can happen to it so long as it gets enough to eat: at most it might throw another litter, and at the end of its life there's the knife, which isn't particularly bad or upsetting either: before it notices anything – and what does an animal notice anyway – it's already kaput. Whereas a man, he's got eyes, and there's a lot going on inside him, and all of it mixed up together: he's capable of thinking God knows what and he will think (his head is terrible) about what will happen to him.

So sweet, chubby, one-armed Biberkopf, our little beaverhead, lives on into the month of August, and feels reasonably good about things. He's become quite adept at rowing with his left arm, and he doesn't hear anything from the police either, even though he's failed to report to them, they're having their summer holidays at

the station, my God, they're only officials with two legs, and they'll
hardly pull one out for the pittance they're paid, and why should
someone run around and make inquiries: what's the story with
Franz Biberkopf, what kind of name is that, Biberkopf, and why has
he got one arm when he used to have two; let him rot in the files,
we've got other worries.

But there are the streets where you can see and hear various
things, you remember things from before, even if you didn't want
to, and life goes on, day after day, something happens one day, and
you blink and miss it, then something else happens the next, you
forget that too, in short something's always happening. Life will
turn out, he daydreams. On a warm day you can trap a fly on the
windowsill and put it in a flowerpot and dribble sand over it: if it's
a proper healthy fly, it will crawl out again, and all your dribbling
won't have made the least bit of difference in the long run. That's
what Franz thinks sometimes, when he sees one thing and another,
I'm all right, what do I care, and if I do care, politics has got nothing
to do with me, and if people are stupid enough to allow themselves
to be exploited, then it's no fault of mine. Why should I go around
racking my brains on their behalf.

Only Mitzi has her work cut out keeping him off the booze,
that's a weak point with Franz. He has a powerful inclination to
drink, it's in him, and keeps popping out. He says: it makes a man
put on weight, and keeps him from thinking too much. But Herbert says to Franz: 'Christ, man, don't drink such a lot. You're a
lucky sod. Look at what you used to be. A newspaper seller. Now
you're short one arm, but you've got Mitzi, you've got your living,
you surely won't start drinking again, like when you were with
Ida.' 'Of course not, Herbert. When I drinks now, it's only to pass
the time. You're sitting there, doing nothing, so what do you do:
you have a drink, and then you have another, and another. And
anyway, look at me, I can handle it.' 'Well, you may say so. I say
you've gotten pretty fat. Take a look at your eyes in the mirror.'
'Wassa matter with my eyes?' 'Well, touch them, you've got bags
there like an old man; how old are you, you make yourself old
drinking, drinking ages yer.'

'Oh, leave it out. You got any news? What are you up to, Herbert?' 'We're almost ready to go again, we've got a couple of new lads, good lads, they're doing well. Remember Knopp, what used to swallow fire? See, he recruited those lads. He says to em: well, so you want to join us? Let's see what you can do. Eighteen-, nineteen-year-olds. So Knopp stands over on the corner of Danziger, to see what they're made of. They've got an old woman in view, they watched her collect money from the bank. They come after her. Knopp imagines they'll give her a little push somewhere along the line and reach in, and thank you ma'am. Not a bit of it, they're patient, and follow her to where she lives, and there they are, standing there as she totters along, the old biddy, and look her in the eye. Are you Frau Müller, because that's her real name, and then they talk to her till the tram comes along, and then it's pepper in her face, grab the bag, slam the door, and over the road. Knopp is cross and says the whole thing with the tram was unnecessary; before she had the door open and anyone knowing anything, they'd be calmly back in the pub. Just drawing suspicion to themselves by running.' 'Did they at least jump off early?' 'Yes, and then, as Knopp went on to lament, they did something else: they took Knopp with them, and picked up a brick, this is nine at night, and smashed the window of a jeweller's on Romintener Strasse, reached in, and ran away. And not took anything. These boys are brazen as Oskar, stopped in the middle of the crowd. We could use their sort all right.' Franz's head drops: 'Cheeky fellers.' 'Well, it's not something you need to be doing.' 'No, I don't – need it. And I won't worry my head too much about what to do later.' 'Just lay off the booze, Franz.'

Franz's face judders: 'Get off my case, Herbert, why shouldn't I drink. I can't do anything else, what can I do, I'm a hundred per cent invalid.' He looks Herbert in the eye, the corners of his mouth are drawn down: 'You know, you're all having a go at me the whole time, one says I'm not to drink, the next one says not to go around with Willi, the other says, Christ, leave the politics out.' 'I never said anything about that, you can keep the politics for all I care.'

And then Franz leans back in his chair and looks at his friend Herbert, and Herbert thinks: his face is going every which way, and he's a dangerous man, however cheerful he may be the rest of the time. Franz whispers, nudges him with his outstretched arm: 'They made a cripple of me, Herbert, look at me, I'm no good for nothing.' 'Get over it, can't you. Tell it to Eva, or Mitzi.' 'Oh, I can loaf around in bed, I'm good for that. But you, you can do things, you and the boys, you're working.' 'If you really want to, you can go back into business with your one arm and all.' 'They didn't want me. Mitzi didn't want me to neither, and I had to give in.' 'Then go on, just start up again.' 'Oh, so it's called start now. Stop this, start that. As if I was a little dog on the table, get down off the table, get up on the table.'

Herbert pours a couple of cognacs; it's time I had a word with Mitzi, the boy's not sound in the head, she needs to look out, else he'll get in a temper and she'll wind up like Ida. Franz knocks his back: 'I'm a cripple, Herbert: see this sleeve, well, there's nothing in it. You can't imagine how my shoulder hurts at night; I can't sleep.' 'Then see the doctor.' 'I don't want to, I won't do it, I don't want to see any doctor, Magdeburg was plenty for me.' 'In that case I'll tell Mitzi to take you away somewhere, you need to get out of Berlin, have a change of scene.' 'Just let me drink, Herbert.' Herbert whispers something in his ear: 'Mitzi's going to end up the same way as Ida!' Franz listens: 'What?' 'Yes.' See, that got your attention. Now look at me. I reckon four years wasn't enough for you. Franz brandishes his fist in Herbert's face: 'Christ, are you stark staring mad?' 'Me? No, you are!'

Eva was standing listening at the door, she's about to go out, she walks in in a smart tan suit and gives Herbert a little jab: 'Lay off him, man, let him drink.' 'Can't you see what's going to happen. Don't you remember last time?' 'You're crazy, shut yer mouth.'

Franz stares across at Eva.

Half an hour later he's back in his room, asking Mitzi: 'What do you say, do I have permission to drink?' 'Yes, but not too much. Not too much.' 'Would you like to get drunk with me?' 'With you, yes.'

Franz is jubilant: 'Wow, Mitzi, you want to get drunk, I bet you've never been drunk?' 'Yes. Come on, let's get drunk. Right away.'

Just a moment ago he was sad, and now Franz can see her burning, just like she was not long ago, with Eva, and the talk of the baby. And Franz is standing next to her, his girl, his dear girl, his best girl so small next to him, he can tuck her in his jacket, she is clinging onto him, he holds her hip with his left arm, and then – and then –

And then Franz is gone, only for a second. His arm is round her hip, perfectly stiff. But in his mind Franz performed a movement with the arm. All the time his face remains stony. In his mind there was a little wooden instrument he was holding in his hand and he brought it down on her from above, and he struck Mitzi, struck her ribcage, one time, two times. And he broke her ribs. Hospital, cemetery, the boy from Breslau.

Franz lets go of Mitzi, and she doesn't know what's come over him, she is lying next to him on the ground, and he is muttering and chattering and crying and kissing her and crying, and she is crying with him, and she doesn't know why. And then she brings in two bottles of schnapps and he keeps saying, 'No, no', but it makes him blissful, my God, the two of them are having such fun. Mitzi is supposed to be with her gentleman, but what's the girl to do, she stays with Franz, he's armless, she's legless, she can't stand up, much less run. She drinks schnapps out of Franz's mouth, and he tries to fish it back, but already it's running out of her nose. And then they giggle, and he snores stertorously into the day.

Why is my shoulder hurting me so, they cut my arm off.

Why is my shoulder hurting me like that, my shoulder is so sore. Where has Mitzi got to. She left me lying here alone.

They cut my arm off, it's gone, my shoulder hurts, bastards, my arm is gone, they did it, the bastards, it was them, those bastards, the arm's gone, and they left me lying there. My shoulder, my shoulder hurts, they left me the stump, if they could have done they would have taken it off as well. Why didn't they tear that off as well, then it wouldn't hurt so much, dammit. They didn't kill me, the bastards, they failed, they were unlucky, the brutes, but it's still not good, I can lie there and no one is with me and who will listen to me yell: my arm, my shoulder, I wish the bastards had run me over properly and killed me. Now I'm just half a man. My shoulder, my shoulder, I can't stand it any more. Brutes, they've made a mess of me the brutes, what am I supposed to do, where's Mitzi got to, she's gone and left me lying here. Oh, oh, oh, ow, ow, oh.

The fly scrambles and scrambles, it's in the flowerpot, the sand is trickling off it, it doesn't bother it, it shakes it off, it sticks out its black head, it crawls up.

There by the water sits the great Babylon, mother of harlots and of earth's abominations. How she sits on a scarlet-coloured beast, having seven heads and ten horns, visible, you must see it. She is happy about every step you take towards her. She is drunken with the blood of saints, whom she has torn to pieces. There are the horns with which she butts, she comes from the abyss and leads to perdition, there look at her, the pearls, the scarlet, the purple, the teeth, the way she shows them, the thick fat lips, blood has flowed over them, she used them to drink with. The whore Babylon. Golden yellow poisonous eyes, bulbous throat. She is giving you the glad eye.

Forward, in step, drum roll and battalions

Careful, man, where there are shells, there's dirt, advance, lift your legs, push on through, I gotta get out, advance, I can't get more than my bones broken, dummdrummdumm, in step, one two, one two, left right, left right, left right.

Here comes Franz Biberkopf marching through the streets, with firm stride, left right, left right, not feigning tiredness, no bar, no drink, let's see, a bullet came flying, let's see it, if I get it, I lie, left right, left right. Beating of drums and battalions. Finally he draws a deep breath.

They're marching through Berlin. When the soldiers march

through the city, oh for wherefore, oh for therefore, oh just on account of the tarara-boom di-ay, oh just on account of the tatara-toom.

The buildings are standing still, the wind blows where it wills. Oh wherefore, oh therefore, oh just on account of the tatara-toom.

In his dull and dirty building – dirty building, oh wherefore, oh therefore, oh just on account of the tatara-toom – sits Reinhold, big wheel in the Pums gang, when the soldiers march through the city, the girls look out at windows and doors, he reads the newspaper, left right, left right, is she mine or is she thine, reads about the Olympic Games, one two, and the fact that pumpkin seeds are a sovereign remedy for tapeworm. He reads very slowly, aloud, to help his stammer. When he's on his own, it's better anyway. He cuts out the pumpkin seed article, when the soldiers march through town, because he had a tapeworm once, maybe he's still got one, perhaps it's the same one, perhaps it's a new one, the old one had babies, he should try the thing with the pumpkin seeds, it's import-ant to eat the husks as well, not peel them. The houses stand still, the wind blows where it wills. Skat congress in Altenburg, not my game. Round the world trip, all expenses paid, only 30 pfennigs per week, pull the other one. When the soldiers march through the city, the girls look out at windows and doors, oh wherefore, oh therefore, oh just on account of the tarara-boom di-ay oom. A knock, come in.

Jump up, march, march. Reinhold straight away reaches into his pocket, revolver. A bullet came flying, is she mine or is she thine. She took him away, he lies now at my feet, as if it were a piece of me, as if it were a piece of me. There he stands: Franz Biberkopf. Lost an arm, war veteran, the fellow's drunk, yes no. One move and I'll blow him away.

'Who let you in?' 'Your landlady,' offensive, offensive. 'The bitch is out of her mind!' Reinhold in the doorway. 'Frau Tietsch! Frau Tietsch! What's all this about? Am I at home or am I not at home? When I tell you I'm not at home, I'm not at home.' 'Sorry, Herr Reinhold, no one said anything to me.' 'Then I'm not at home, for

Christ Almighty. That means you don't let any Tom Dick and
Harry in.' 'You must of told my daughter, but she just come downstairs, and never told me nothing.'

He slams the door, revolver present and correct. The soldiers.
'What are you doing here? What have you got to s-s-say to me.'
He stammers. Which Franz is it. You'll know soon. The man lost
his arm to a car recently, he used to be a law-abiding citizen, it
can be sworn on oath, now he's living on immoral earnings, we
will look into the reason why. Drum roll, battalions, now he's
standing there. 'Christ, Reinhold, you got a six-shooter.' 'So?' 'What
do you need it for?' 'Me? Nothing.' 'Well, then you can put it
away, can't you.' Reinhold lays the revolver on the table in front
of him. 'What have you come here for?' There he stands, there
he is, he hit me in the passageway, he threw me out of the speeding car, before that there was nothing, there was Cilly, I went down
the stairs. All that swims into his ken. Moon over water, brighter,
more dazzling in the evening, ringing of bells. Now he's got a
six-shooter.

'Sit down, Franz, say, you must have been tippling?' Because he's
staring straight in front of him, he must be drunk, he can't lay off
the booze. That'll be it, he's juiced, but I've got my little friend. Oh
just on account of the tarara-boom di-ay, di-ay oom. Franz sits
down. Sits there. The bright moon, the water, gleams. He's sitting
at Reinhold's. That's the man he helped out with his woman problem, taking them off him one after another, then he tried to get me
to be lookout, though I never agreed, and now I'm a pimp, and God
knows what will happen with Mitzi, that's the situation. But that's
all just in the mind. Only one thing is happening, which is Reinhold. Reinhold sits there.

'I just wanted to see you, Reinhold.' That's all I wanted, to look
at him, just look at him and me sitting there. 'You wanted to put the
squeeze on me, eh, spot of blackmail, eh, because of what happened?' Keep still, no twitch, boy, march on, it's just light shelling.
'Blackmail, eh? How much you want? We're expecting it. We knew
you was a pimp now.' 'That's what I am. What else am I going to
do, with one arm?' 'So whaddaya want?' 'Oh, nothing, nothing.'

Just sit up straight, hold on, that's Reinhold, that's the way he likes to slink around, don't let meself be knocked over.

But there is a trembling in Franz. There were three Kings from Orient, they had incense and they shook it, they kept on shaking it. Before long they are swathed in smoke. Reinhold ponders: either the fellow's drunk, in which case he'll leave soon and there's nothing the matter, or he's after something. He's after something, but what, it's not blackmail, but what is it. Reinhold gets schnapps, and thinks I'll draw him out with this. So long as Herbert hasn't sent him to scout us out, and then wreck us. The instant he sets out the two little blue glasses, he sees that Franz is trembling. The moon, the pale moon, it is climbing loonimously over the water, no one can look at it, I'm blind, what's the matter with me. Look, he's all in. He's sitting upright, but he's all in. And then Reinhold feels joyful, and he slowly takes the revolver off the table, and puts it in his pocket, and he pours and he looks up again; the fellow's mitts are shaking, he's got the shakes, he's a quitter, the big-mouthed so-and-so, he's afraid of the revolver, or of me, well, I'm not about to harm him. And Reinhold is very calm and friendly, oh yes indeedy. The bliss of seeing him trembling, no he's not drunk, Franz, he's just scared, he's falling apart, he's shitting himself, he so badly wanted to come and talk big.

And Reinhold starts to talk about Cilly, as if we had seen each other only yesterday, she came by not long ago, a couple of weeks, yes, that happens sometimes, a woman I haven't seen in a few months, then I don't mind taking her back, a reprise, funny thing. And he gets out cigarettes and a bunch of dirty postcards, and there's Cilly on them, with Reinhold.

Franz is incapable of saying anything, he just keeps looking at Reinhold's hands, Reinhold has two hands and two arms, while he's down to one, with those two hands Reinhold threw him under the car, oh wherefore, oh therefore, shouldn't I have to kill him for that, oh just on account of the tarara-boom di-ay. Herbert thinks so, but I don't think so, what do I think. I must do something, I gotta, oh just on account of the tarara-boom di-ay – I'm not a man, just a sadsack. He slumps and then trembles up again, he gulps his cognac and then another, it doesn't help, and then softly softly Reinhold says: 'What I'd like, Franz, I'd like very much to see your injury.' Oh just on account of the tarara-boom di-ay. Thereupon Franz Biberkopf – for it is he – opens his jacket, produces the stump from the shirtsleeve, Reinhold pulls a face: disgusting, Franz shuts the jacket: 'Used to look worse.' And then Reinhold goes back to looking at Franz, who says nothing and is capable of nothing and is as fat as a pig and can't even open his mouth, and Reinhold breaks into his grin again, and doesn't stop.

'Hey, do you always keep your sleeve tucked into your pocket like that? Is it sewn in place, or do you have to keep putting it there?' 'No, I keep putting it there.' 'With your other hand? I guess before you put the jacket on?' 'Well, sometimes one and sometimes the other; but once I'm already in the jacket, 's not so easy.' Reinhold stands next to Franz, tweaks at his sleeve. 'You have to remember not to put anything in your right pocket. It'd be too easy to steal.' 'Not with me.' Reinhold is still exercised: 'Say, what do you do with an overcoat, that must be tricky. Two empty sleeves.' 'It's summer. That's a problem for winter.' 'You'll be in for a surprise then, I tell you. Shouldn't you maybe get an artificial arm, I mean when someone loses a leg, they get an artificial one.' 'Yes, because he couldn't walk otherwise.' 'You could strap on an artificial arm, it would look better.' 'No, no, I think it would just press.' 'I would, you know, or at least pad the sleeve with something. Come on, let's give it a go.' 'What's the point, I don't want to.' 'So you wouldn't be running around with an empty sleeve, it would look better, no one would have to know.' 'What would be the point. I don't feel like it.' 'Come on, I can see wood is wrong. Look, just stuff in a few socks or shirts, here.'

And Reinhold gets going, he untucks the empty sleeve, reaches in, goes across to his dresser and starts padding it with socks and handkerchiefs. Franz resists. 'What are you doing, there's nothing to secure it, it'd just hang there like a sausage, leave off.' 'No. I think you should get something professionally made, like by a tailor, nice and tight, it'd look really good, your hand in your pocket, you wouldn't even look like you're a cripple.' The socks fall out: 'See, it's

a job for a tailor. I don't like cripples, in my eyes a cripple is a worthless person. When I see a cripple, I say: get rid of him.'
And Franz listens and listens, and nods. The tremor comes over him, without him being able to do anything about it. He's somewhere on the Alex at the break-in, all of him is gone, it must be to do with the accident, it's his nerves, let's see. But it goes on tugging and shaking him. All right, up, out, adieu Reinhold, I gotta go, put my feet down, right, left, right, left, tarara-boom di-ay.

Then fat old Franz Biberkopf gets home, having been to see Reinhold, and his hand and his arm are still shaking, the cigarette falls out of his mouth when he walks in. And there is Mitzi up in his room with her gentleman, waiting for Franz, because she wants to go away with her gentleman for a couple of days.
He pulls her aside: 'What good are you to me?' 'What shall I do, Franz? God, Franz, what's the matter?' 'Nothing, get lost.' 'I'll be back tonight.' 'Get lost,' he almost roars. She looks over at her gentleman, quickly gives Franz a kiss on the neck and she's off. And downstairs she gives Eva a ring: 'If you've got a moment, go and see Franz. What the matter is? Search me. Come if you can.' But then Eva can't make it, Herbert's been cross with her all day, she can't get away.
In the meantime, our Franz Biberkopf, the cobra snake, the iron wrestler, is sitting alone, all alone, sitting in front of his window, gripping the windowsill with his hand and wondering if it wasn't stupid, if it wasn't fucking moronic of him to go up to Reinhold's room, and the devil take it, it's stupid when the soldiers go marching through the town, stupid, obstinacy, and I need to get out, I need to do something different. And meanwhile he's already thinking, I will do it, I've got to go there, things can't go on like this, he humiliated me, he stuffed my jacket with handkerchiefs and socks, I can't tell anyone about it, that anything like that happened to me.
And Franz presses his head hard against the sill, and digs himself in and feels shame, feels bitterly ashamed of himself: that's what I did, that's what I stood for, I am such an idiot to tremble in

front of that feller. And his shame is so great and so strong. Franz grits his teeth, he feels like tearing himself in pieces, I didn't want that, I'm no coward, even if I just have one arm. I need to go see him. And he gets into it. By the time Franz has reached this point it's already evening, and he gets up off his chair. He looks around the room, there's the schnapps, Mitzi put it there, I'm not going to drink it. I don't want to be ashamed of myself. Let people look into Franz's eyes. I – I'm going to go see him. Rum di bum. Tucket, fuck it. Forward, downstairs, jacket on, that he wanted to stuff for me, I'm going to plonk myself down in front of him, no one's face trembles when they see me.

Berlin! Berlin! Berlin! Tragedy on the seabed, submarine sunk. Crew drownded. And when they're drownded, they're dead, no cock will crow over them, then it's over, then it's finished. Nuff said. March, march, two military planes downed. Then they're down, then they're dead, no cock to crow over them, what's dead is dead. 'Evening, Reinhold. Yup, it's me again.' He stares at Franz: 'Who let you in?' 'Me? No one. The door was open, so I walked in.' 'I see, ringing the bell is too much trouble, is it.' 'I don't have to ring the bell when I want to see you, I'm not plastered.'

And then the two of them sit facing one another, smoking, and Franz Biberkopf isn't trembling, and he sits upright and is happy to be alive, and this is his best day since he fell under the car, and the best thing he has done since that time: to be sitting here, damn, it feels good. And it's better than the political meetings and almost better – better than Mitzi. Yes, it's the best of everything: he'll not throw me out.

It's eight in the evening. Reinhold looks Franz in the face: 'Franz, you know what you and I have to sort out between us. Tell me if you want anything from me, just put it out in the open.' 'What do I have to sort out with you?' 'With the car.' 'There's no point, it'll not make my arm grow back. And then—' Franz hits the table with his fist: 'It was good. I couldn't go on like that. It had to happen.' Oh ho, so that's as far as we've got, we've been there for a while. Reinhold considers: 'You mean with the street vending.'

'Yes, that too. I had a bee in my bonnet. Now it's gone.' 'And your arm is too.' 'Well, I've still got the other one, and then I've got a head and two legs and all.' 'What will you do? Turn tricks by yourself, or with Herbert?' 'What, with one arm? I can't do anything.' 'But you know, just pimping, that's a bit boring.'

And Reinhold thinks and looks at him, sitting there so fat and strong: I fancy playing this lad. He'll sit up and beg. He likes getting his bones broken. One arm's not enough for him.

And they get on to the subject of women, and Franz is telling Reinhold about Mitzi, who used to be called Sonia, who's earning well, and is a good girl. Then Reinhold thinks to hisself: that's well and good, I'll take her off him, and that'll throw him in the dirt for good.

Because when worms eat soil and make more, they always eat the same stuff. The creatures can't stop once they've had a healthy breakfast, they need to stuff themselves the next day as well. And it's the same way with people, and with fire: it's hungry if it's burning, and when it can't eat, it goes out, that's the way of it.

Franz Biberkopf is pleased with himself for being able to sit there, perfectly quiet and not tremble, and cheerful as a newborn. And when he goes downstairs with Reinhold, he feels the same thing: when the soldiers march through the town, right, left, it's good to be alive, these are all my friends walking beside me, no one will throw me over, just let them try. Oh wherefore, oh therefore, the girls are looking at windows and at doors.

'I'm going dancing,' he says to Reinhold. Who asks: 'Will your Mitzi be there?' 'She's gone away with a patron for a coupla days.' 'When she's back, I'll go with you.' 'That's nice, she'll be happy then.' 'Well, so how about it?' 'I tell you, she won't bite.'

Franz is in an exhilarated mood, he has danced away the night, the newborn, the happy, first in the old ballroom, then in the pub at Herbert's, and everyone's happy for him, but not as much as he is for himself. And furthest inside himself, while he's dancing with Eva, he loves these two people: the one is his Mitzi, whom he misses, and the other is – Reinhold. But he doesn't dare say so out loud. All through the whole wonderful night where he's dancing with this and that broad, he's in love with those two who're not there, and he's happy with them.

The fist on the table

Here everyone who has read thus far can see the turn that has been taken; the turn back, and we're where we started, with Franz. Franz Biberkopf, the strong, the cobra snake, has reappeared on the scene. It wasn't easy, but he's back.

He seemed to be there already when he became Mitzi's pimp and wandered around with a gold cigarette case and a natty yachting cap. But now he's all back, whooping it up and not afraid of anything. Now the roofs have stopped wobbling for him, and his arm, well, that was the price of admission. The screw that was loose in his head has been tightened up. He is a pimp now, and will shortly turn to crime again, but all that doesn't bother him, quite the opposite.

And everything is the way it was at the beginning. But the reader will understand that this is not the old cobra. Our old Franz Biberkopf, clearly, is not that. The first time it was his friend Lüders who cheated him, and he threw a wobbly. The second time he was supposed to stand watch, but he didn't want to, and then Reinhold threw him out of the car and ran him over. Franz has had enough now, it would be enough for any normal fellow too. He doesn't enter a monastery, he doesn't tear himself in pieces, he goes on the warpath, he won't be just a pimp and a criminal, and high time too. Now you will see Franz, not skidooing and filling his belly by himself, but in a dance, a rattling dance with something else, which wants to see how strong it is, and who is the stronger, it, this other thing, or Franz.

Franz Biberkopf made a vow when he came out of Tegel and could walk freely again: I will be decent. That vow he was unable to keep. Now he wants to know what he has it in him to be. He wants to ask whether and why his arm had to be run over. Or perhaps, who knows what someone's head looks like from the inside, perhaps Franz wants to reclaim his arm from Reinhold.

Chapter Seven

In which the hammer, the hammer comes down on Franz Biberkopf.

Pussi Uhl, the flood of American visitors, and do you write Wilma with a V or a W?

On Alexanderplatz they're going on and on. On the corner of Königstrasse and Neue Friedrichstrasse they want to knock down the building over the Salamander shoe shop, they've already started on the building next door. The route under the S-Bahn arches on the Alex is severely complicated: new supports for the railway bridge are being put in; you can look down into a neatly bricked-in shaft, where the pillars will set their feet.

Anyone who wants the S-Bahn station has to go up and down a little flight of wooden steps. The weather has got cooler too, it's raining a lot, to the detriment of cars and motorcycles, which often slip and crash, there are suits for damages and so forth, people fall and break various bones, all attributable to the weather. Do you know the tragedy of the aviator Beese-Arnim? Today he was questioned by the police, he is the principal in the shooting incident that took place in the flat of the clapped-out old whore Pussi Uhl, may she rest in peace. Edgar Beese was shooting wildly in Uhl's place, he was feeling, so the detectives say, rather peculiar. Once during the war he was shot down a mile up in the air, hence the tragedy of the aviator Beese-Arnim, shot down a mile high, cheated of his inheritance, in prison under an assumed name; the last act was still ahead of him. Once he was shot down, he went home, where an insurance director relieves him of his money. Only he was a crook, and so the airman's money went very straightforwardly to the crook, and the airman has no money left. From that moment forth,

Beese takes to calling himself Auclaire. He is ashamed in front of his family, because he is so hard up. This was all ascertained and written up by the police at the station this morning. It also says that is when he was set on the path of crime. Once, he was put away for thirty months, and because he was calling himself Krachtovil at the time, he was repatriated to Poland at the end of them. Later on, in Berlin, there was a particularly murky entanglement with this Pussi Uhl. Amid a ceremonial we don't care to describe in detail, Pussi Uhl baptized him as 'von Arnim', and his subsequent crimes were committed under that moniker. On Tuesday, 14 August 1928 von Arnim planted a bullet in the body of Pussi Uhl, how and why the rabble won't say, they don't speak out of turn, not even at the foot of the scaffold. Why would they tell the police, who are their enemies? All that is known is that the boxer Hein was also involved in some capacity, and amateur psychologists wrongly presume jealousy. I myself would bet there was no jealousy involved. Or if jealousy, then jealousy beefed up by money, but with money the main element. Beese, the police tell us, suffered a complete psychological collapse; you can believe that if you like. I think the lad will have collapsed – if collapse he did – because the police were onto him, and he's annoyed with himself for shooting the Uhl woman. Because what's he going to live off now; he's thinking: pray god the bitch doesn't die on me. And herewith enough of the tragedy of the aviator Beese-Arnim, shot down a mile high, cheated of his inheritance, and now in prison under an assumed name.

The flood of Americans visiting Berlin continues. Among the many thousands visiting the German metropolis are prominent individuals who have come to Berlin for professional or personal reasons. Thus the Secretary of the American delegation of the Inter-Parliamentary Union, Dr Call from Washington, is currently in town (Hotel Esplanade) in advance of a group of American senators. Also in the course of the next few days we are expecting the head of the New York fire brigade, John Keylon; like the ex-Secretary of Labor Davis before him, he is staying in the Hotel Adlon.

From London, the President of the World Union of Religious

Liberal Jews, whose conference is scheduled to take place in Berlin from 18 to 21 August, Claude Montefiore, has arrived; he is staying at the Esplanade, along with his assistant, Lady Lilly Montague, who is travelling with him.

The weather being so dismal, it seems a good idea to get out of the rain, perhaps into the Zentralmarkthalle, but there's a huge commotion, we are almost run over by trolleys, and the porters don't even give a warning shout. So let's instead pop into the Industrial Court on Zimmerstrasse and breakfast there. Whoever has occupied himself with small lives – and let's face it, Franz Biberkopf is no household name – likes to take the occasional trip west, and check things out there.

Room 60, Industrial Claims Court, cafeteria; a fairly small space with a bar and coffee machine; there's a board with 'lunch menu: rice soup, rissoles (all the r's) 1 mark'. A fat young man in horn-rims is sitting on a chair, eating his lunch. You look at him and see: in front of him is a steaming plate with rissoles, gravy and potatoes, and he is polishing it off in short order. His eyes rove around his plate, even though no one's threatening to take anything away from him, no one is sitting anywhere near him, he is all alone at his table, but he is still worried, he slices and squashes and shovels, quick, one two, one, one, and while he works, one in, one out, one in, one out, while he slices and squashes and bolts and snuffles and gulps and swallows, his eyes are wide open, his eyes are watching the diminishing quantity of food on his plate, guarding him like two Alsatians, alert to his surroundings. Another one in, one out. Full stop. Finished, now he gets to his feet, flobby and fat, the fellow has eaten it all up, now he can pay for it. He reaches into his inside pocket and smacks his lips: 'What's the damage, Fräulein?' Then the fat fellow walks out, puffs, adjusts his waistband to make room for his belly. He must have three pounds of lunch in there. Now his stomach gets to work. The guts wobble and lurch, there are twistings and windings like earthworms, the glands do what is in their power, they hose their juice into the stuff, like firemen, from up top spittle drenches down, the man swallows, it flows into the guts, there's a rush to the kidneys like the assault of shoppers in the New Year's sales, and easy does it, drip by drip, the drops fall into the bladder. Wait, laddie, soon you'll be headed back this same way, to the door labelled: gentlemen. That's the way of the world.

Behind closed doors they are hearing cases. Domestic employee Wilma, how do you spell that, I thought it was with a V, it is here, well, we'll try it with a W. She was impertinent, she cheeked us, all right, pack your things and get out, that's why we have witnesses. She refuses, she has too much of a sense of honour. All right, I am prepared to pay you up until the 6th, three days' notice, that's a further 10 marks, my wife is in hospital. You may claim, Fräulein, that 22.75 is the sum at issue, but there are things I won't stand for. 'Mean bitch,' and so forth, we can call my wife as witness once she is up and about, the plaintiff expects to be rewarded for her insolence. The parties come to the following agreement.

Papke the chauffeur and the film distributor Wilhelm Totzke. What's this one about, someone has just put it down on the table. Please write down: film distributor Wilhelm Totzke appeared in person, no, I've just got power of attorney from him, all right, and you were working for him as his driver, for a relatively short period, yes, I hit it, give me the keys, so you were involved in a motor vehicle accident, what do you have to say for yourself? It was Friday the 28th, he was to collect the boss's wife from the Admiralsbad, it was in Viktoriastrasse, there are witnesses who can confirm that he was blind drunk. He's widely known as a drunkard. I don't drink bad beer; the car was a German make, the repairs came to 387.20. Can you describe the collision? I'm creeping forward, don't have four-wheel brakes, graze his rear wheel with my front wheel. How much did you have to drink that day, you will have had something with your lunch, I went to the office and got given lunch, the boss looks after us very well because he's such a nice fellow. We're not pinning the damages on him either, just want to be allowed to sack him; because of his habitual drunkenness, he's often been involved in collisions. Pick up your uniform; it's in Viktoriastrasse in the dirt. And then the boss said over the phone: that big ape, he made a mess of my car. You couldn't have heard that, oh yes, it was loud enough, the boss is uncouth; anyway he also claimed I'd stolen the spare wheel, I'd like to call witnesses. I wouldn't dream of it, you are both equally to blame, your boss called you fool or ape, with your first name, you should agree to settle for 35 marks, it's a quarter to twelve now, there's plenty of time, you can call him, if need be he can be here for a quarter to one.

Outside the door down on Zimmerstrasse stands a girl who was just passing, she raises her umbrella and pops a letter in the box. The letter says: Dear Ferdinand, thanks for both of yours. I see I was mistaken about you, I never thought you would turn out like that. Well, you must admit yourself that we're both very young to consider such a step. Maybe you thought I was like all the others, but then you made a mistake. Or did you think I was a good match? Then you're mistaken too. I'm just a working-class girl. I'm telling you so you'll know better next time. If I'd known what was going to happen, I'd never have started writing to you in the first place. Well, that's what I think, take it on board, you'll know what's in your heart of hearts. Best wishes, Anna.

In the rear block at the same address, a girl is sitting in the kitchen; her mother's gone out to do the shopping, the girl is keeping a secret diary, she's twenty-six and unemployed. Her last entry of 10 July went: I felt a bit better in the afternoon, but the good days are so few and far between. There is no one I can talk to as I'd like to. That's why I decided to put everything down on paper. When my condition hits me, I'm incapable of anything, the least little thing is extremely difficult for me. Everything I see when I'm in that state provokes new thoughts which I am unable to shake off, and then I'm agitated and have difficulty making myself do anything. I get terribly wound up, and still I can't do anything. For instance: when I wake up early in the morning I don't feel like getting up at all; but I make myself and I try to encourage myself. Even getting dressed is an effort, because so many things are going through my mind. I am continually obsessed with the idea of doing something badly, and causing damage. Even, when I put a piece of coal in the fire and cause a spark to jump up, I take fright, and have to check and see that nothing has caught, in case I've ruined something and caused a conflagration. And that's how it is all day long: everything I am required to do seems terribly difficult, and when I make myself achieve it, in spite of trying to be quick about it, it seems to take for ever. So the day passes, and I don't do anything, because every little action demands so much thought. When, in spite of all my efforts, I still can't cope, then I fall into despair and cry. I have always suffered from this condition, the first time it appeared in my life I was only sixteen. My parents took it all for play-acting. When I was twenty-four I tried to end my life, but I was rescued. At that time I hadn't had sex yet, and I put all my faith in that, unfortunately. I have only had a little, and recently I've given it up, because I feel physically so weak.

14 August. For the past week I've been doing very badly again. I don't know what will become of me if it stays like this. I think if I was alone in the world I would turn on the gas tap without another thought, but I can't do that to my mother. I really hope I get a grave illness which will carry me off. I have written everything down the way I really feel it.

The duel begins! It continues rainy

But for whatever reason (I kiss your hand, madam, I do), for whatever reason, let me think, let me think, Herbert in felt slippers thinks in his room, and it's raining, plick plock plick plock, it's impossible to go outside, he's out of cigars and there's no cigar seller in the building, for whatever reason it only ever rains in August, the whole month is awash, it floats away from you, so for whatever reason Franz has taken to going to Reinhold and will talk about nothing else? (I kiss your hand, madam, and no less a person than Sigrid Onegin delighted listeners with her singing, till he gave up, bet his life and so won it back). He will know why, he will, and it's raining all the time, he can come here if he likes.

'Christ, Herbert, why are you racking your brains about that. Just be pleased he's left politics, maybe it's because he's got his friend back.' 'Come on, Eva, his friend. Start making sense, I know better than that. He wants something from him, he wants something—' (The sale has been approved by the board, so the price must be viewed as reasonable.) 'He wants something and whatever it is he wants and why, he goes round there, and keeps talking about it: he wants something from there! He wants to ingratiate himself, mark my words, Eva, and once he's in there, he'll go "bang bang" and no one will know it was him.' 'D'you reckon?' 'Don't you?' The thing is clear, I kiss your hand, madam, shame about the rain. 'Of course, sugar, of course.' 'Do you really think so, Herbert? It seems a bit weird to me, him getting his arm took off, and then going up to see him.' 'Sure. We got it.' I kiss. 'Herbert, are you sure, do you think we shouldn't say a word to him, just as though we were completely blind and hadn't noticed anything?' 'We're like camels, you can do anything with us.' 'Yes, Herbert. That's the right way to be with him, we'll do that, we've got to. He's such a strange man.' The purchase, admittedly by the government, so that the price achieved, for whatever reason, think, think, the rain.

'Listen, Eva, keeping shtum is one thing, but we still need to pay attention. What if Pums's people smell a rat? Well?' 'That's what I've been saying, oh Lord, how can he go there with one good arm?' 'Because it's good. But we need to keep our eyes peeled, and Mitzi's too.' 'I'll tell her. What can we do?' 'Not let Franz out of our sight.' 'Just hope her gentleman gives her a moment.' 'In that case she'd do better getting rid of him.' 'He's talking about marriage.' 'Hahaha. I need to catch my breath. What does he want? What about Franz?' 'It's nonsense, of course, she lets him run his mouth, why not.' 'She'd be better advised to watch Franz. He's going to track down the gang member responsible, and mark my words, someone will be driven up here in a dead condition.' 'Oh, Herbert, how can you.' 'Christ, Eva, I'm not saying it's Franz. But Mitzi needs to keep an eye on him.' 'I'll see to it. But you know something, this seems much worse to me than politics ever was.' 'You don't get it. Women don't get these things. Eva, I tell you, Franz is getting going. He's on the way.'

I kiss your hand, madam, forced his life, won his life by

gambling it, have you ever known an August like it, look at it, pissing down all the time.

'What's he want here? He's mad, I told him he's barking, if you've just got one arm, and you turn up here, and you want to be a player. And he.' Pums: 'Well, what did he say?' 'What he says? Oh, he's laughing and grinning, he's not all there, I think he must have taken some brain damage as well. First off, I can't believe what I'm hearing. Really, I ask him. With one arm? Well why not, he grins, there's enough strength in the one he's got, I should try him, he can lift weights and shoot and even climb with it if he has to.' 'So it's true?' 'See if I care. I don't like him. Do we really want someone like that? Someone like you, Pums, you need workers. But when I see his ox's head, I think I've had enough.' 'Well, if you say so. Fine by me. I gotta go now, Reinhold. Get hold of a ladder.' 'But make it a good strong one. Steel or something. Adjustable, folding, kind of thing. And not here in Berlin.' 'Suck eggs.' 'And the burner. From Hamburg or Leipzig.' 'I'll get on to it.' 'And how are we going to get it here?' 'Let that be my concern.' 'I'm not having him, Franz, all right?' 'Reinhold, where Franz is concerned, I think he's just a bur-den on us, but we're not bothered either way, do what you want.' 'Now hold on a minute, do you think his face fits? Picture it: I throw him out of the car, and then he climbs the stairs to see me, and I'm thinking: there's something not right in that man's head, he's stand-ing there, imagine, what a camel, and he's shaking, and what possesses that camel to climb my stairs. And then he starts gurning at me, and he's mad keen to be in the group.' 'Sort it out with him. Whatever you decide is fine. Gotta go.' 'Maybe he wants to turn us in?' 'Could be. Could be. You know, then the best thing is to keep the guy away, that's best. Evening.' 'He'll turn us in. Or sometime when it's nice and dark, he'll shoot us.' 'Evening, Reinhold, like I say, I gotta go. The ladder.'

Biberkopf is a muttonhead, but he's after something. He's play-ing the innocent. Wants to tangle with me. But you're mistaken if you think I'll stand by and let you. I'll trip you up. Schnapps, schnapps, schnabus, schnabus is good for giving you hot hands, it's as well Aunt Paula is in bed eating tomatoes. A friend advised her. If he thinks I'm obliged to look after him, we're not an insurance company here. If he's got one arm, then let him go and cut coupons for all I care. (Pads around and looks at the flowers.) So I got flowerpots and the woman gets 2 marks on the first of the month to water them, just look at the state of them, blooming Sahara. Silly cow, bitch, only good for swallowing money. I'm gonna have to pull the worms out of her nose. Another – don't mind if I do. That's something he taught me. Maybe I'll take his girl, hey, that's not a bad idea. Probably thinks I'm afraid of him. You'd like that. Oh, I'll have him. It's not about the money, no chance of that, he's got his Mitzi, and then there's his mate Herbert, the old windbag, the ram, he's sitting pretty in their sty over there. Where're my boots, I'll break his legs. Let me give you a hug, mate. Closer, closer, to the penitent form, I've got a penitent form here where you can repent.

And he pads around his flat, pushes his finger in a flowerpot, 2 marks and the baggage doesn't even water the flars. In the penitent form, sunshine, let's have you. Salvation Army, I'll have him go there and all, he needs to go round Dresdener Strasse, the penitent form there, that pig with his big staring eyes, the pimp, the animal, animal is what he is, up the front, praying, and me pissing myself watching.

And why shouldn't Franz Biberkopf go to the penitent form? Is the penitent form not the very place for him? Who says?

What can you say against the Salvation Army, and what's Reinhold doing, speaking out against it, when the man himself has been round the Dresdener Strasse, oh, five times at least, and in an indescribable state, and they helped him out. His tongue was hanging out his throat, and they fixed him up, of course not so that he could pursue his life of villainy.

Hallelujah, hallelujah, Franz has heard it, the song, the call. The knife was pressed against his throat, Franz, hallelujah. He offers his throat, he wants to seek his life, his blood. My blood, my innermost, at last it's coming out, it was a long journey till it came, God, it was difficult, there it is, I've got you now, why did I not want to go in the penitent form, if only I'd been there earlier, ah, here I am arrived at last.

Why shouldn't Franz go in the penitent form, when will the blest moment come when he throws himself down before his terrible death and opens his mouth and sings with the many flanking him:

Come, o sinner, come to Jesus, do not hesitate, wake up, tethered victim, come to the light, thou shalt know complete salvation, even today, o believe, and then light and joy will come. Chorus: For the victorious saviour, he breaks every band and leads to victory with mighty hand, and leads to victory with mighty hand. Music! Blare, crash, chingdaradada: He breaks every band and leads to victory with mighty hand. Tara, tari, tara! Boom! Chingdaradada.

Franz doesn't give up, gets no peace, he's philosophizing like a drunk. He slinks around Reinhold's pad with the rest of the Pums gang, who are unhappy about him being there. But Franz lashes out, brandishes his one remaining fist and yells: 'If you don't believe me, if you think I'm here to cheat you and deliver you to justice, then forget it. What do I need you for if that's what I have in mind? I can go back to Herbert or whoever any time I like.' 'Well go on then.' 'Go on then! You ape, telling me to "go on then". Take a look at my arm, you. Reinhold, over there, projected me out of the car. I survived that and now I'm here and it's not for you to say "go on then". If I'm here with you and I say: I'm in, then you need to understand who Franz Biberkopf is. He's never cheated anyone in his life, ask around. I don't give a shit about what happened, the arm's gone, I know you, this is where I work, and this is the reason why, so you understand.' The little plumber still doesn't get it. 'Then explain why you want to be in, because back then you were flogging papers on the Alex, and nothing would induce you to join us.'

Franz settles himself in his chair and for a long time says nothing, and nor do they either. He has sworn to be decent, and you saw he stayed decent for weeks, but that was just a period of grace. He is involved in criminality, he doesn't want to be, he resists it, it passes over his head, he has to do it. For a long time they sit there and don't speak.

Then Franz says: 'If you want to find out who Franz Biberkopf is, then go to the Landsberger Allee, there's a woman's grave in the cemetery there. I did four years for her sake. That was my good arm what did it. Then I went to flogging papers. I thought I'd go straight.'

And Franz moans softly, gulps: 'My object lesson, see. When that happens to you, you have to give up newspapers and this and that and the other thing as well. That's why I'm here.' 'So we're expected to fix your arm coz we broke it.' 'That's not in your power. It's enough for me to be sitting here, Max, instead of trotting around on the Alex. I don't make any reproaches to Reinhold, I never breathed a word, ask him When I'm sitting in the car, and there's a suspicious party sitting next to me, I know what I have to do. There's to be no more talk of my foolishness. If you should do something stupid yourself, Max, then I hope you learn from it.' With that Franz takes his hat and slopes off. That's the way it is.

Inside, Reinhold is pouring himself a drink from his hip flask and saying: 'Well, this whole thing is settled, so far as I'm concerned. I dealt with him the first time, I'll deal with him next time as well. I know it's taking a chance, getting involved with him. But first of all, he's already in it up to here: he's a pimp, he says so himself, he's not going straight anytime soon. There's just the question: why's he joining us, and not Herbert, who's his friend. I dunno. I have a few ideas though. Any road, we'd be pathetic if we couldn't manage to cope with Franz fucking Biberkopf. Let him join. If he plays up, he'll get one on the noddle. I say right out: let him have a go.' And so Franz has a go.

Franz breaking and entering, Franz not under the wheels, he's in the box seat now, he's made it

At the beginning of August the criminal classes are still enjoying rest and recreation, busy with holidays and what have you. If the weather is anything like, you wouldn't take it upon yourself to break in or strain yourself – not if you know what you're doing. Those are the things of winter, when a man's gotta get out and about. Take Franz Kirsch, for instance, the celebrated safe-cracker, he and an accomplice broke out of Sonnenburg eight weeks ago, at the beginning of July. Sonnenburg sounds ever so nice, but it's no use for r. and r., so instead he's taken a nice holiday in Berlin, rested up for eight weeks, and his thoughts are maybe beginning to turn to the next job. Then there's a complication, life's like that. The fellow has to take the tram. The police show up, end of August time, in Reinickendorf West, pull him off the tram, and his holiday's over, there's no help for it. But there's plenty of other fish in the sea, and they're about to get busy.

I'd better supply the official weather forecast for Berlin. General atmospheric conditions: a high pressure zone to the west has now spread over central Germany, and brought about an improvement in the outlook. The southern edge of the high pressure area is already fraying. So we anticipate that the improvement will not last. But up until Saturday the high will dominate the weather, and we will have it pretty fine. Then a depression currently over the Iberian peninsula will move north-east and begin to affect German conditions on Sunday.

Berlin and surrounding area: partly cloudy, partly bright, winds mild, temperatures slowly rising. In the rest of Germany: cloudy in the south and west, elsewhere sunny intervals, windy in the north-east, temperatures gradually warming.

With conditions thus favouring work, the Pums gang, our Franz included, slowly gets moving; the ladies associated with the gang are also in favour of the gang getting moving again, because otherwise they will be out on the street, and no lady likes to do that unless she has to. But really, it's a question of knowing the market and finding buyers, if the clothes are wrong then switch into fur, the ladies think it's pretty straightforward too, there's not much in the way of variations, quickly mastered, but the fine points, the adjustments necessary when the general economy is slow, that's something of which they have no conception.

Pums has got to know a plumber who is something of an expert on oxy-acetylene, so he's in, and there's a troublesome geezer who looks sharp, though he's bone-idle, which is why his old lady threw him out, but he's useful in a tight spot, and he knows businesses, and you can send him anywhere to case a joint. Pums tells the senior partners in his outfit: 'Basically we don't need to factor in competition. It exists as it exists everywhere, but we don't get in each other's way. But if we don't make sure to hire good people who know their tools and the trade, then of course we'll be disadvantaged. Then we might as well go into theft pure and simple, and for that we don't need six or eight people, everyone can do that for himself.'

Because they're in the tailoring and furs sector, everything with legs has to trot off and locate businesses that sell goods that you can fence without lots of questions being asked, and without the police coming calling. It can all be altered, you sew it differently, and of course you can start off by simply storing it. Well, find those first.

Pums has trouble with his fence in Weissensee all the time. If you work the way that fellow does, you won't ever do any business. Live and let live. Of course. But because he claims to have made losses over the past winter – he says! – because he over-extended himself and got in debt, and we took the summer off, coming to us with a sob story and asking us for a refund: he's just made some bad investments! He's made some bad investments because he's a fool, bad geezer, just doesn't understand the trade, he's wrong for us. We just better find someone else. Of course, easier said than done, but it has to be, and the only member of the gang who's thinking about it is old Pums. It's a funny thing, wherever you listen out, the other boys take an interest in what happens with the goods, because plain stealing never made anyone rich: it still needs to be turned into money, but as I say: in Pums's lot they all stretch out on their bearskins and say: 'Pums will fix it.' He will too, he's on the case. But what if Pums can't fix it? Eh? Pums can't do it every time, he's only human. Then you'll see, well, what do we do with the staff, and all that breaking and entering won't have done a blind bit of good. Nowadays the world isn't settled with breaking irons and explosives, today every thief needs to be his own business manager as well.

Which is why Pums isn't just concerned with an oxygen explosion set for early September, but with who's going to take the merchandise off my hands. He began in early August. And if you want to know who Pums is: he's the sleeping partner in at least five small fur businesses – never you mind where – plus he's invested money in a couple of American-style launderettes, with ironing boards in the windows, and a tailor standing there in shirtsleeves, and the suits are hanging at the back, the suits, oh, yes indeedy. That's what matters and where you've got them from, well, you just say: oh, from the customers, who brought them along yesterday to get them pressed and altered, here are the addresses if a pig comes in to check it's all on the level. So fatty Pums has already planned ahead for the winter, and we would have to say, bring it on. If something happens, well, there's always contingencies and surprises; you need a bit of luck, but beyond that we don't want to bother our pretty little heads.

Next thing. All right, it's early September and our smartypants villain who also does animal imitations – that doesn't belong here – Waldemar Heller the fellow calls himself, and he is a bright fellow as the name suggests, he's sniffed around the big outfitters on Kronenstrasse and Neue Wallstrasse, and where you go for what. He knows the entrances and exits, the front and back doors, who lives upstairs, who lives downstairs, who locks up, where the clocks are, etc. Pums pays his expenses. Sometimes Heller is the buyer for a start-up firm in Posen; someone wants to make some inquiries about the firm in Posen, sure, go ahead, I just wanted to see how high your ceilings are, the next time someone comes abseiling down.

It's at this show, Saturday night, that Franz participates for the first time. He's cracked it. Franz Biberkopf is sitting in the car, they all know what they have to do, and he has his part as much as they do. It's on a strictly business basis, someone else is standing watch, though in fact it's not literally that, the night before three lads crept up into the printworks on the floor above, they carried up the ladder and the explosive in crates and hid them behind bales of paper, someone drove the car away, at eleven they unlock the doors to let the others in, no one in the building hears a dicky bird, after all it's just offices and warehouses. Then they sit there working away, one is always at the window looking out, someone else is watching the yard, then the blasting gets going on the floor, half a yard square, the plumber does it with protective goggles. Once they're through the wood floor there's some crashing and banging, but it's nothing much, bits of stucco falling down, the ceiling is cracked from the heat, they push a silk parasol through the hole they've made, and the later pieces are caught in that, mostly, some of them aren't. But nothing happens, downstairs everything is dark and silent.

At ten they climb down, natty Waldemar first, because he knows his way around the store. Climbs down a rope ladder like a cat, he's never done it before, not a trace of nerves, those are the greyhounds, they are the lucky ones, at least until something goes wrong. And then someone else needs to go down, the steel ladder is only eight feet, it won't reach as far as the ceiling, not by some way, downstairs they stack a few tables, then they slowly lower the ladder on to the topmost table, and bob's your uncle. Franz stays upstairs, lying on his front beside the hole, like a fisherman he hauls in the bales of cloth they pass up to him, swings them behind him where someone else is positioned. Franz is strong. Reinhold, who is downstairs with the plumber, is astounded by his strength. Funny, doing a job with a one-armed bandit. He has a grip like a crane, it's really something else, a bomb, a freak. Afterwards they lug the baskets downstairs. Even though they've got a man posted down in the yard, Reinhold patrols as well. Two hours, and it's all over, the nightwatchman does his rounds, don't hurt the fellow, he'll not notice anything, you'd have to be pretty stupid to allow yourself to be shot for the pittance he gets paid, there, he's gone, punctual fellow, we'll leave him a big blue note next to the time-clock. By now it's two o'clock, the car's due at half past. They eat a snack upstairs, easy on the schnapps, keep the noise down, and then it's half past. Two debutants are with the gang today, Franz and Waldemar.

They toss a coin, natty Waldemar wins, it's for him to set the seal on the job, so he shimmies down the ladder once more into the dark plundered storehouse, squats down, trousers off, and it's 'roses are red, violets are blue' onto the floor.

Then once the rest of them have unloaded their goods and it's half past three, they quickly do another job, because we'll not get together as young as we are again, and who knows when we'll next meet on the green banks of the Spree. Everything passes off easily enough. Just on the way home they run over a dog, had to happen, and Pums gets terrifically het up about it because he likes dogs, and he tears into the plumber who's driving, couldn't he have hooted, they put their dog out on the street because they can't afford the tax, and now you come along and kill the brute. Reinhold and Franz piss themselves laughing at the way the old fellow is so excited over a dog, he must be getting a bit soft in the head. The dog must have been deaf, I did hoot, yeah, once, and since when are there deaf dogs, well, shall I turn round and take him to hospital, oh, don't be stupid, watch where you're going, I hate this sort of thing, it's bad luck, innit. Thereupon Franz nudges the plumber in the ribs: I think he's thinking of cats. Everyone explodes with laughter.

For two days Franz Biberkopf doesn't say a word at home about what happened. Only when Pums gives him a couple of hundreds, and if he doesn't need them he can always give em back, and at that Franz laughs, he can always use them, even if I give them to Herbert for Magdeburg. And who will he go to, whose eyes will he look into at home, who do you think, eh, eh, who? For who, or rather for whom did I keep a pure heart? For who, if not for you, for you alone, tonight I meet my happiness, so I invite you my princess, tonight I will urgently beseech you, all others to, what is it again, eschew. Mitzi, Mieze, my golden Mieze looks like a marzipan/Mitzipan bride in golden slippers, and there you are standing waiting for me to see what your Franz will do with his magic wallet. He jams it between his knees, and then he gets out his money, a couple of big ones, and he holds them out to her, lays them on the table, beams at her, and is as tender to her as can be, big boy that he is, and he squeezes her fingers tight, her sweet frail little fingerkins.

'Well, Mitzi, little Mitzi?' 'What's the matter, Franz?' 'Nothing; I'm just pleased you're there.' 'Franzeken.' Oh, can she look, and can she ever say your name. 'I'm happy, that's all. Look, Mitzi, it's the funny thing about life. Things with me are so back to front. Everyone else is fine, and they run around and earn money and throw their weight around. And me – I can't do what they do. I got to look at my skin, my jacket, my sleeve, my arm is missing.' 'Oh, Franzeken, my dear Franzeken.' 'See, Mitzi, it is as it is, and I won't be able to change it, no one can change it, but if you carry it around with you like that, and it's like an open wound.' 'Oh, what is it, Franz, I'm here, everything's all right, and don't start on that again.' 'I'm not. That's just it, I'm not.' And he smiles up into her face, the taut pretty face and the pretty mobile eyes: 'See, look what's on the table. – I earned it, Mitzi – I'm givin it to yer.' Now what is it, what's that face she's making, why's she looking at the money like that, it's not gonna bite her, it's good money. 'Did you earn it?' 'Yes, girl, I earned it. I've got to work, otherwise I'm no good. I'll go to pieces. Don't tell anyone about it, I was with Pums and Reinhold, Saturday night. Don't tell Herbert, and don't tell Eva neither. Christ, if they ever get to hear about it, then I'm finished for them.' 'Where d'ya get it from?' 'We did a job, just a little one, I told you, with Pums, so what about it, Mitzi? And it's all for you. Well, what do you say? Don't I get a kiss?'

Her head slumps down on her chest, then she presses her cheek against his, kisses him, holds him to her, doesn't say anything. Doesn't look at him: 'Is that really for me?' 'Well, who else?' My, what a girl, and what a performance. 'Why – why do you want to give me money?' 'What is it, don't you want it?' She moves her lips, frees herself, now Franz sees: she's looking the way she did that time on the Alex, when they were coming from Aschinger's, she's gone pale, she's doesn't look well. Sitting in her chair again, staring at the blue tablecloth. What is it now, I defy anyone to make sense of women. 'Don't you want it then, girl, I was so looking forward to it, look at it, we can go somewhere nice, don't you want to.' 'Is that really true, Franz.'

And she lays her head on the table and she cries, the girl is crying, what on earth is the matter with her. Franz strokes her neck and is so sweet and kind to her, so darling, for who, for who did I keep my heart pure, for who, for her alone. 'Mitzi, girl, if we can go somewhere, would you want to go with me?' 'Yes', and then she raises her head, her sweet little face and all the powder turned to porridge with the tears, and she throws her arm round Franz's neck, and presses her face to his, and then she hurriedly lets him go, as if something was biting her, and she's back to crying on the table-top, but he can't see that, the girl is keeping entirely still, she's not giving anything away. What's the matter, what have I done this time, she doesn't want me to work. 'Come on, lift your little head, come along, little head, what are you crying for?' 'Do you want to, do you want to,' I'll sort her out, 'do you want to get rid of me, Franz?' 'Good gracious, girl.' 'Do you want to, Franzeken?' 'Good gracious, no.' 'So why are you running around; don't I earn enough money; I earn enough, don't I.' 'Mitzi, I just want to be able to make you a present.' 'No, I don't want it.' And she lays her head down on the table edge again. 'Now, Mitzi, can't I do anything for you at all? I can't live that way.' 'I'm not saying that, but you don't need to go out to earn money. I don't want you to.'

And Mitzi sits up, hugs her Franz and looks rapturously in his face, and babbles all sorts of silly nonsense and begs him and begs him: 'I don't want it, I don't want it.' And why doesn't he just tell her if there's something he wants, but girl, I've got enough, I don't need anything. 'Shouldn't I do anything then?' 'I do, though, Franz, what am I there for, Franz.' 'But I – I . . .' She hugs him. 'Oh, don't leave me.' She babbles and kisses and beckons to him: 'Give it away, give it to Herbert, Franz.' Franz is so happy with the girl, her skin is beyond soft, he can't say anything, it was stupid of him to bring up Pums, of course, she won't understand that. 'Will you promise me, Franz, not to do that ever again.' 'I'm not doing it for the money, Mitzi.' And it's only then that she remembers what Eva said to her, and how she needed to keep an eye on him.

Then a little light goes on inside her, he's really not doing it on account of money, and the thing with his arm before, he's always thinking about his arm. And it's true what he says to her about money, it really doesn't matter to him, because he gets plenty from her, as much as he needs. She is thinking and thinking and holding him in her arms.

Love's weal and woe

And once Franz has loved her up, she's back out on the street and over to see Eva. 'Guess what, Franz brung me two hundred marks. Guess where from? From them, you know who I mean.' 'Pums?' 'Yes, he told me hisself. What shall I do?'

Eva calls Herbert, Franz was out on Saturday with Pums. 'Did he say where?' 'No, but what shall I do?' Herbert is stunned: 'Well, well, so he's gone and joined them.' Eva: 'Do you understand it, Herbert?' 'No. Mad.' 'What do we do?' 'Let him be. Don't suppose it's for the money?! Nah, it's like I said. He's in a hurry, I think he's about to take steps.' Eva is standing facing Mitzi, the little whey-faced whore she picked up on Invalidenstrasse; they are both remembering the time they first met; in the bar of the Baltic Hotel. Eva is sitting with a man from the provinces, she doesn't need to do it, but she likes her extras, and then there are lots of other girls, and three or four boys. And at ten o'clock a police patrol from Mitte walks in, and they're all called over to the station at the Stettiner Bahnhof, marched over in goosestep, cigarettes in their snoots, cheeky as you like. The police are marching front and back, drunken old Wanda Hubrich of course leads the women, and the fuss there was, and Mitzi, Sonia as was, in floods of tears with Eva, because now everything will come out in Bernau, and then one of the police smacks the cigarette out of drunken Wanda's hand, and she stomps off on her own into the cell and slams the door and chunters away to herself.

Eva and Mitzi look at each other, Eva prompts her: 'You'll have to watch yourself now, Mitzi.' Mitzi implores her: 'But what shall I do?' 'He's your feller, a woman has to know what she's about.' 'But I don't know.' 'Well, whatever you do, don't cry.' Herbert is beaming: 'I'm telling you, this is a good lad, I'm pleased with the way he's going about things, he's got a plan, he's a wily fellow all right.' 'Oh God, Eva.' 'Don't cry, stop crying, girl, I'll watch him too.' You don't deserve Franz. Not if you carry on like that you don't. Listen to that silly bitch howling. I'll smack her one if she don't stop.

Tucket! The battle is in progress, the regiments are advancing, tara, tari, tara, the artillery and the cavalry, and the cavalry and the infantry, and the infantry and the air squadron, tari, tara, we're moving into enemy tara-terrain. Whereupon Napoleon said: advance, advance, without interruption, up is dry and down is wet. But when down is dry, we take Milan, and you'll get a medallian, tari, tara, tari, tara, we're moving in, we're almost there, o the joy of being a soldier boy.

Mitzi doesn't need to cry and ponder for long. The answer presents itself to her. Sitting in some establishment is Reinhold with his dolled-up girlfriend, going over the businesses that Pums has in mind for fencing, and with a little time left to himself. Actually, the fellow is bored like you wouldn't believe, it's not good for him. When he has money, that's no good for him either, and nor is drink, what's better for him is when he's pacing around the bar, listening and working and drinking coffee. And now, each time Pums comes in or he does himself, there's Franz in his eyeline, the fool, the brazen so and so, with his one arm, all hail fellow, well met, and he's still not had enough, wall-to-wall sanctimoniousness, as if the donkey wouldn't hurt a fly. And it's certain, like twice two is four, that the wretch is after something. He's always jolly as fuck, and wherever I'm working and trying to think, there he is. Well, we need to clear ourselves a little space. A little space for ourselves.

And what of Franz? Eh? What do you suppose? He's wandering round, full of peace on earth and goodwill to all men. You can do what you like to the boy, he'll always land on his feet. There are people like that, not a lot, but some.

In Potsdam, you know in Potsdam there was a fellow they

later called the living corpse. He was that ilk. This fellow, one Bornemann, he did a bunk when he was almost at the end of his time, and he was doing fifteen years' hard, so, the fellow escapes, and by the way it wasn't Potsdam at all, it was somewhere near Anklam, Gorke was the name of the place. So our man Bornemann on his way out of Neugard runs into this dead body in the river, in the Spree, and Neugard, or rather Bornemann from Neugard, says to hisself: 'I'm as good as dead meself', and he walks up to the corpse and slips it his papers, and now he is dead. And Frau Bornemann: 'What shall I do? There's nothing I can do, he's dead, and is it really my husband, I almost hope it is, because what have I lost, what's a man like that good for, he spends half his life behind bars, away with him.' My little Otto, oh God, my little Otto, he's not dead a lot-to, or even a little-o. He reaches Anklam, and because he's just had occasion to note that water is something nice, he now has a liking for it, and so he sets up as a fishmonger, sells wet fish in Anklam, and goes by the name of Finke. No more Bornemann. But they managed to nab him anyway. If you want to learn how, then hang onto your chairs.

A stepdaughter of his, as luck would have it, came to Anklam in service, what are the odds on that, in the whole world, but no, she moves to Anklam, and she runs into the redivived fish who's been living there for a hundred years and has left Neugard, and the girl is all growed up, and has fled her coop, and of course he fails to recognize her, but she recognizes him. She says to him: 'Ain't you my old man?' He replies: 'I never, you must have a screw loose.' And because she still doesn't believe him, he calls his wife and his one-two-three-four-five children, and they bear him out: 'That's Finke the fishmonger.' Otto Finke, everyone in the village knows. Everyone knows, Herr Finke's the man, and it's the other fellow, Herr Bornemann, who died.

But she, not that he done anything to her, she doesn't see it that way. The girl leaves, who knows what goes on in a female soul, she's got bees in her bonnet. She writes a letter to the police in Berlin, dept. 4 A: 'I made several purchases from Herr Finke, but seeing as I am his stepdaughter, he doesn't see himself as my father, and is cheating my mother, and has five children with another woman.' The children are allowed to keep their given names, but where everything else is concerned, they've lost. They're called Hundt, with a dt at the end, which is their mother's name, and all of a sudden they're illegitimate, the relevant paragraph goes: an illegitimate child and its father are not related in law.

And no different than the aforementioned Finke, Franz Biberkopf is the embodiment of serenity. The man was once set upon by a beast that took his arm off, but then he's beat her, leaving her fuming and looming behind him. No one who sees Franz, except for one person, has seen him beat her, her fuming and dooming behind him. Franz walks stiff-legged, he carries his thick skull upright. Even though like the others he does nothing, he has such bright eyes. But the one – the one to whom he has done less than nothing – he asks: 'What's he want? He's after something.' He sees everything the others don't see, and he understands everything. It shouldn't be any skin off his nose, Franz's muscular neck, his stiff legs, his sound sleep. But they bother him, he can't keep quiet about them. He has to come up with some sort of answer. What?

Just as a gate opens sometimes to a puff of wind, and a mob of cattle runs out of a paddock. Or a fly torments a lion into lashing out and roaring hideously.

Or as a guard might take out a small key, fiddle an iron bolt, and a bevy of criminals can wander out, with murder, grievous bodily harm, breaking and entering, robbery with violence and statutory rape finding themselves at large.

Reinhold walks up and down in his room, and in his bar at Prenzlauer Tor, thinks back, thinks forward, thinks left and thinks right. And one day, when he knows Franz is with the plumber and they're working on a new plan, wonder what that'll come to, he decides he'll pay Mitzi a little call.

And she catches her first sight of the man. There's nothing to him very much, Mitzi, you're quite right, not bad-looking, the fellow, a bit sad, a bit floppy, perhaps a bit ill, a touch liverish maybe. But not bad.

Now take a closer look at him, give him your hand and take a look at his face when you do it. That face, little Mitzi, is more important to you than every other face in the world, more important than Eva's, more important even than your dearly beloved Franz's. He's coming up the stairs now, it's a nothing sort of day, Thursday, 3 September, take a look, you don't feel anything, don't know anything, no premonition of anything.

What is in store for you anyway, little Mitzi from Bernau? You're in good health, earning money, you love your Franz, and that's why coming up the stairs now and standing in front of you and fiddling with your hand is Franz's destiny and – now – yours as well. Actually, you don't need to take a close look at his face, just his hands, his two hands, two nothing hands in grey kid gloves.

Reinhold is all togged up, and first of all Mitzi doesn't know how to behave with him, whether Franz maybe sent him along, or it could be Franz setting a trap for her, but that can't really be. Then he out and tells her that Franz is not to know he came calling, that's something Franz is very sensitive about. It's because he Reinhold wants to have a word with her, and that's a little difficult with Franz around, with his arm out of commission, and whether he needs to work, that's the question that's on everybody's mind. Now Mitzi is not slow, and she knows what Herbert said Franz is about, and she says: no, earning money for the sake of it, no, that's not something he has to do, there are people who will help him out. But maybe that's not enough for him, after all a man wants to make something of himself. Reinhold says: that's quite right, so he does. Just it's not easy to do what they do, it's no ordinary work, people with two good arms find it hard. And so the conversation goes back and forth, Mitzi's not really sure what he wants, then Reinhold up and asks her to pour him a drink after all: he just wanted to ascertain what their financial circumstances were, and if that's the way it is, then they'll surely look out for him, of course they will. And then he has another, and he asks: 'Do you know about me, miss? Did he never tell you about me?' 'No,' she says, now what's he up to, I wish

Eva was here, she's better at these kind of conversations than I am. 'You see, we palled around together for a long time, Franz and me, it was before you showed up, and there were other girls, you know, like Cilly.' Perhaps that's what he's doing, he wants me to think badly of Franz with his one arm: 'Well, why shouldn't he have been out with other girls. I had a different feller too, but I'm with Franz now.'

They sit facing each other, Mitzi on the chair, Reinhold on the sofa, and they're both nicely at ease: 'Oh, of course you're wi him now, miss, you surely don't think I'm trying to oust him in your affections, I'd do no such thing. But there were funny things transpired between him and me, did he never tell you?' 'Funny? What do you mean funny?' 'Oh, very funny things, miss. I'll be open with you: if Franz is in our gang, you know, it's purely on my account, just for that and our history together; because you know we always kept together, through thick and thin. I could tell you some stories.' 'I daresay. Now, don't you have a job to go to, that you can just sit here and talk to me all day?' 'Now miss, don't you know even the Almighty sometimes took a day off, and that means we humans are allowed at least two.' 'It wouldn't surprise me if you took three.' They both laugh. 'Ah, you may be right; I like to save my strength, laziness lengthens life, other times you need too much strength.' Then she smiles at him. 'In that case, you'd better economize.' 'You understand, miss. One man is one way, another is another. So here's the thing, miss, Franz and I, we always swapped our women. What do you say to that?' And he tilts his head to one side, sips at his drink, and waits to hear what the little thing replies. She's a nice-looking bit, we'll have her soon enough, and then won't I just pinch her little bottom.

'You should tell your gran that one about swapping women. Someone told me one time that they like to do that in Russia. You must be from there, because we don't have that kind of carry-on here.' 'But I'm telling you.' 'Well, I think it's a load of nonsense.' 'You should ask Franz about it.' 'Must have been nice women, I must say, maybe fifty-pfennig hussies, from the shelter or something.' 'Now, miss, watch your tongue, that's really not our style.' 'So what kind of stunt are you trying to pull here? What exactly do you have in mind?' Oh, look at her. But she's nice, she's sticking by him, sweet. 'Oh no, miss, no intentions. Just wanted to pass on some information (sweet thing, hanky-panky Pankow punk), Pums gave me some instructions, well, and so I guess I'll be cutting along now, perhaps you'd like to come by see us one evening, our mob?' 'Well, if you like to tell stories like that.' 'No harm, miss, I thought you knew all that anyway. Oh, and there's one other piece of business. Pums said that if I go up and see you and you ask me about money and so on, where Franz is sensitive on account of his arm, then you're not to tell him. Franz doesn't need to know. I could have asked around in the house and so on, but I thought why go sneaking around. You're here, and I'll just go straight up and see you and ask.' 'You want me not to tell him?' 'Yes, it's best you don't. Mind you, if you really want to, there's nothing we can do about it. Up to you. Well, be seeing you. The door's on the right.' she's a nice piece, we'll have her all right, tata.

So little Mitzi in the room by the table, didn't see anything, didn't notice anything, and thinks, when she sees the glass standing there – well, what does she think, something or other, all right, and she tidies the glass away and she doesn't know anything about anything. I'm so wrought up, that fellow got me so wrought up, I'm just shaking all over. He's full of it. What did he want, what did he want. Looks at the glass in the cupboard, it's the one at the back, I'm shaking, I'm going to sit down, no, not on the sofa, he's set there. I'm so wrought up, what's the matter with me, both arms and my bosom, I'm shaking like a leaf. Franz isn't that sort of lowlife, swapping women. Wouldn't surprise me with that fellow Reinhold, but Franz – if there's anything to it at all, I expect they just let him be the mug.

She bites her nails. If there's anything to it: yes, but Franz is a bit slow, he's someone to be taken advantage of. That's why they threw him out of the car. That's the sort they are. Those are the people he thinks are his friends.

She bites and bites her nails. Tell Eva? I'm not sure. Tell Franz? Not sure either. I'll not tell anyone. No one's been here.

She feels ashamed, puts her hands down on the table, bites her knuckle. It doesn't help, there's still the burning feeling in her throat. After, they'll do what they want with me anyway, they'll sell me too.

A hurdy-gurdy man sets up in the courtyard: I lost my heart in Heidelberg. I've gone and lost mine too, and now it's wrecked, and she sits hunched over and wails, it's all broken, I haven't got another one, I'm helpless, and if they decide to drag me through the dirt, there's nothing I can do about it. But my Franz won't do that, he's no Russkie wife-swapper, all that's just so much nonsense.

She is standing in front of the open window in a blue-check dressing gown, and joins in the hurdy-gurdy man's rendition: I lost my heart in Heidelberg (it's a false society, he's quite right to want to smoke them out) one balmy summer night (why doesn't he come home, I'll run downstairs to meet him). I was head over heels in love. (I won't say a word to him, I won't confront him with so much vileness, not one word, not one word. I love him so much. Well, I'd best put on my blouse then.) And like a rosebud the smile on her mouth. And when we said goodbye outside the gates, on the occation of our farewell kiss, then I recognized it (and it's true too what Herbert and Eva like to say: the Pumses have twigged that something's going on, and they just want to go to me to check if there's anything to it or not, well, they can listen for as long as they like, they'd better find some other woman), that I lost my heart in Heidelberg, my heart, it beats on the shores of the Neckar.

Dazzling harvest in prospect, but miscalculations have been known to happen

Goes around, goes around, keeps going round, the fullest calm and peaceableness to you. You can do what you like with the boy, he'll always land on his feet. There's some that are like that. There was one in Potsdam, in Gorke near Anklam, name of Bornemann, escapes from prison, gets to the River Spree. There's someone bobbing about in the water.

'Scoot up, Franz. So what about it, what's your girl's name

anyway?' 'She's Mitzi, as you know perfectly well, Reinhold, used to go by Sonia.' 'And I guess you won't bring her round. Too good for us, is she.' 'Come on, I don't have a menagerie, I don't need to show her off. She walks the streets. She's got her admirer, and she brings home a good bit of money.' 'Just you don't like for us to see her.' 'What are you talking about, Reinhold. The girl's got work to do.' 'You could bring her along sometime. She's supposed to be a looker.' 'They say.' 'I wouldn't mind seeing her. You got anything against it?' 'Ach, Reinhold, we used to do stuff like that in the past, you know, over boots and fur collars and whatnot.' 'So that's finished, is it?' 'Yes, that's finished. I'm not interested in swinishness like that any more.' 'It's all right, don't get het up, I was only asking.' (The bastard, the way he still refers to swinish this and that. You wait, boy.)

So, as Bornemann's approaching the water, there was this fresh corpse bobbing about. And light-bulbs went on in Bornemann's head. Out of his pocket he pulled his papers, and reassigned them. It's been written about already, but it's a useful aide-mem. Then he tied the body to a tree, it would have floated free and you might have had trouble finding it. For his part, he hopped on the local to Stettin, got a ticket, and when he gets into Berlin he calls his old lady from a bar, she's to come quick, there was someone waiting for her. She came with money and a change of clothes, he whispered something to her, then he had to leave again, oh no. She promised to have someone identify the stiff, he would send her money as and when he had any, as if. Then he had to hurry away, otherwise someone else'll find the boday.

'That's all I wanted to know, Franz. I guess you're very fond of her.' 'Now leave off this talk of girls and such nonsense.' 'I'm just establishing some ground rules here, don't bite my head off.' 'I'm not biting yer head off, Reinhold, just, you know, you're a bit of no good.' Franz laughs, and so does the other man. 'Now what about your little lady, Franz. Can you really not see your way to showing her me.' (What a wag you are, Reinhold, you threw me out of the car, but now you're all over me.) 'Now, what is it you want, Reinhold?' 'Nothink. Just have a look at her.' 'You wanna see if she likes me? I tell you, her heart beats for me from head to toe, that girl. It's all she's got room for, liking and sweetness. You know, Reinhold, you can't imagine how besotted she is. You remember Eva, don't you?' 'Course. Come on.' 'See, and what Mitzi wants . . . ach, what's the use.' 'What? Tell me.' 'No, I couldn't possibly, but that's the way she is, you've never come across the like, Reinhold, I've not come across it in all my born days.' 'What's this thing you're not saying. With Eva?' 'All right, but keep it under your hat, what she wants, Mitzi, is for Eva to have a baby wiv me.'

Boom boom. They sit there and look at each other. Franz smacks his thigh and bursts out laughing. Reinhold smiles, or begins to smile and gets stuck part-way.

So then our man, Finke, he goes to Gorke and enters the wet fish business. One fine day along comes his stepdaughter, she's in service in Anklam, and she wants to buy some fish, she walks up to Finke with her shopping bag in her hand and says.

Reinhold smiles, or begins to smile and gets stuck part-way: 'Is she queer or something?' Franz smacks his thigh some more and giggles. 'No, she just loves me.' 'I'm sure that's not the case.' (Such a thing exists, and the fool has it, and makes a joke of it.) 'What does Eva say about it?' 'Well, they know each other, they're friends, in fact it's through Eva that I met Mitzi.' 'Now, you've whetted my appetite, Franz. Tell me if I can't get to see Mitzi, maybe at a range of twenty yards, or through a grille, if you're that nervous about it.' 'I'm not the least bit nervous! She is so true and golden, you have no idea. You remember I told you once that you need to stop seeing all those girls, it's not good for your health, even if you have nerves of steel it's too much. You'll end up getting a stroke. You need to pull yourself together, it'd do you the world of good. You should see how right I am, Reinhold. All right, I'll show her to you sometime.' 'But she's not to see me?' 'Why not?' 'No, I don't want her to. Just point her out to me.' 'OK, we'll do it. Oh, I'm looking forward to it. It'll do you good.'

And then it's three in the afternoon, Franz and Reinhold are walking down the street, enamel signs of every type, enamelware,

German and genuine Persian rugs, in twelve monthly payments, floorings, sofa and table coverings, quilts, curtains, blinds, Leisner & Co., do you subscribe to *Fashion*, if not, demand your copy, completely free, delivered by next post, beware, danger, high tension. They walk into Franz's house. Now you're walking into my house: I'm all right, nothing can touch me, you can see the way I stand there, my name is Franz Biberkopf.

'Tread softly, I'll just open the door and see if she's in. No. Anyway, here is where I live, and she'll be back any minute. Oh, you should see us, it's like summin at the theatre, but keep nice and quiet.' 'You bet I will.' 'The best thing is, you lie down in the bed, Reinhold, it's not in use during the day, I'll be sure she doesn't go in there, and then you can peep out through the net curtain. Lie down there. Can you see?' 'Sure I can. But I ought to take me boots off.' 'Good idea. I'll put them out in the corridor for you, and you can pick them up later, when you go.' 'Oh Franz, I hope everything works out.' 'Are you worried? You know, I'm not even worried if she does see you, heck, let her.' 'No, I don't want to meet her.' 'Well, lie down anyway. She'll be along any minute.'

Enamel signs, enamel wares of every type, German and echt Persian rugs, Persians and Persian rugs, get your free copy now.

Then detective Blum in Stettin said: 'Where do you know the man from? How did you come to recognize him?' 'He's me stepfather, inne.' 'Well, then let's you and me go out to Gorke. And if you're right, I'll book him straight away.'

A key turns in the door. And Franz in the corridor: 'Surprise, Mitzi! It's me, sweetheart. Come on in. Don't go in the bedroom though. There's a little surprise for you there.' 'Oh, I'd better go and have a look right away.' 'Hold on a minute. First I want you to swear, cross your heart, stand up, say after me: I swear.' 'I swear.' 'I swear not to go in the bedroom.' 'Not to go in the bedroom.' 'Until I say.' 'Until I run in there.' 'You stay right here. Now swear properly: I swear.' 'I swear I won't go in the bedroom.' 'Until I drag you in there myself.'

Then she comes over all serious, drapes herself round his neck and hangs there for a long time. He can tell something's up with her, and he wants to push her out the door into the corridor, today's not a good day for this thing he's planned. But she stays right where she is. 'I won't go in the bedroom, let me go.' 'What's the matter with my little Mitzi, Mitzi cat, Mitzi babes?'

She barges onto the sofa, and there they sit side by side, arms round each other, she not saying anything. Then she murmurs something under him, and tugs at his tie, and then it all begins. 'Franz, can I talk to you?' 'Of course you can, Mitzikitten.' 'Something happened with my feller.' 'Well?' 'There.' 'Well, tell me, Mitzi babes.' Working away at his tie, what's the matter with the girl today of all days, with Reinhold laying there.

The detective says: 'So your name's Finke, is it? Any papers?' 'You just need to ask in the registry.' 'I don't care what they've got in the registry.' 'Well, I got papers too.' 'Very good. We'll take those for a start. And outside there's an officer from Neugard who used to have someone called Bornemann on his wing, let me introduce the pair of you.'

'You see, Franz, my feller always had his nephew there the last few times we met, that is, he never invited him, he just came.' Franz mumbles something and feels a chill: 'I see.' She doesn't take her eyes off his: 'Do you know him, Franz?' 'How could I?' 'I just wondered. Well, he was always around, and then he would go out with us too.' Franz trembles, his eyes go dark: 'Why din't you say anything. Jesus.' 'I thought I'd manage to get rid of him. And why the trouble, if all he's doing is just keeping us company.' 'So now . . .' The quivering of her mouth at his throat is getting stronger, then suddenly something's wet, she's clasped onto him, the girl's holding onto me, that's her stubborn way, she doesn't say a word, and now why's she in floods of tears, and with him laying there, I feel like grabbing a stick and whacking the bed so hard he never gets up again, fucking bitch, showing me up in front of him. But he's still trembling. 'So wassa matter?' 'Nothing, Franzeken, don't worry, but please don't hurt me, it wasn't nothing. He came along this last time, hung around all morning, till I leave the old geezer, and then I have to ride with him, and he keeps insisting.' 'And of course you have to do it, don't you.' 'Yes, I do, what else am I to do?

Franz, imagine a feller coming onto you like that. And he's such a young man. And then . . .' 'Where was this?' 'We were in Berlin, Grunewald somewhere, I don't know, then we walked, and I keep telling him to go. And he's crying and pleading like a baby, he's so young, engineer I think he is.' 'Well then, why doesn't he work, the lazy sod, instead of running around the whole time.' 'I don't know. Oh Franz, don't be angry.' 'I still don't know what's going on. Why are you even crying?' She doesn't reply, just presses herself against him, and plays with his tie. 'Don't be cross, Franz.' 'Are you in love with him, is that it?' No answer. How frightened he feels, a chill down to his toes. He whispers into her hair, he's forgotten all about Reinhold: 'Are you in love with him then?' She is pressed against him body to body, he can feel all of her, out of her mouth it comes: 'Yes.' Ah, but he's heard it. He should let her go, I oughtta smack her, Ida and the Breslau boy, here it comes, but his arm feels feeble, he is lamed, she is clutching hold of him like an animal, what does she want, doesn't speak, holds onto him, her face against his throat, he looks stonily past her out the window.

Franz shakes her, yells: 'What is it? Put me out of my misery.' What am I doing with the bitch. 'I'm here, Franzeken. I haven't left you, I'm still here.' 'Why don't you go then, I don't want you.' 'Please don't shout, oh God, what have I done.' 'Run off to the man you love, bitch.' 'Don't call me that, oh Franz, be nice to me, won't you, I've told him I can't and that I belong to you.' 'I don't want you. I don't want anyone like you.' 'But I belong to you I said, and then I left him, and I want you to comfort me.' 'I can't believe it. Let go of me. You're mad. I'm to comfort you because you're in love with him.' 'Yes, you should and all, Franzeken, I'm your Mitzi, inni, and you loves me, oh dear, and now the lad's running around . . .' 'Give over, Mitzi! Go to your man, he's yours.' At that Mitzi screeches, and he can't shake her off. 'Yes, go to him, and leave me alone.' 'No, I won't do that. You don't love me, you don't want me, what have I done.'

Franz manages to free his arm and break away, she runs after him, at that moment Franz spins round, hits her in the face, sending her reeling, then he smashes her on the shoulder. She falls down, him on top of her, hitting her with his one hand anywhere he can. She whimpers and writhes, oh oh, he's hitting her, he's hitting her, she rolls over onto her front. When he stops to draw breath the room is spinning round him, she turns round and gets to her feet: 'No stick, Franz, this'll do, please no stick.'

She's sitting there with her blouse ripped, one eye sealed, blood from her nose smeared across her chin and left cheek.

But Franz Biberkopf – Beaverhead, Thieverhead, Leverhead, who has no name – the room is spinning round him, there are the beds, he grabs hold of one of them to stop himself. There's Reinhold lying in it, the fellow laying there in his boots, dirtying up his sheets. What's he doing there? He's got his own room and all. I'm going to get him out, turf him out, if it's the last thing. And Franz Biberkopf, Beaverhead, Heaverhead, Reaverhead hops up to the bed, reaches through the covers for the head, it moves, the sheets come off, Reinhold sits up.

'Get outta here, Reinhold, take a look at her, and then get lost.'

Mitzi's ripped mouth, earthquake, lightning, thunder, the rails broken, warped, the station, the stationmaster's hut all thrown hither and yon, roaring, crashing, smoke, zero visibility, everything busted to smithereens, broke.

'What is it, is something broken?'

Screams, incessant screams from her mouth, through the smoke screams of anguish at the thing in the bed, a wall of cries, lance of cries against it, higher, stones of screams.

'Shut yer mouth, what's the matter, ssh, everyone'll think something's the matter.'

Gurgling screams, massed screams, against the thing. No time, no hour, no year.

And now Franz is gripped by the wave of screaming. An epileptic. From the side of the bed he grabs at a chair that slips from his grasp. Then across to Mitzi who is sitting upright and screaming without interruption, screaming and wailing and howling, and he holds his hand across her mouth from behind, spills her onto her back, kneels across her, presses his chest against her face. I'm going to fucking kill her.

The screeching stops, she's still kicking out with both feet. Reinhold drags Franz aside: 'Christ, man, you're strangling her.' 'Get lost, you.' 'Get up. Up.' He succeeds in hauling Franz off, the girl is lying on her front, tossing her head from side to side, whimpering and gurgling, thrashing her arms. Franz stammers: 'Look at the bitch. The bitch. Who is it you want to hit, bitch.' 'Take a walk, Franz, get your coat on, and don't come back till you've cleared your head.' Mitzi is whimpering on the floor, opens her eyes, the right eyelid is swollen shut and red. 'Push off, mate, you're killing her. Get yer coat on. Here.'

Franz snorts, gasps, allows himself to be helped into his coat.

Then Mitzi picks herself up, spits mucus, tries to speak, pulls herself up, sits, gurgles: 'Franz.' He's got his coat on. 'Your hat.' 'Tranz . . .' she's not screaming any more, she has a voice, she spits. 'Lemme . . . go with you.' 'No, no, you stay here, miss, I ll help you.' 'Franz, please, lemme . . . go with you.'

He's upright, crushes his hat on his head, smacks his lips, hawks and spits, walks reeling to the door. Crash. Shut.

Mitzi moans, stands up, pushes Reinhold away, struggles through the bedroom door. She gets as far as the front door. Franz is already down the stairs. Reinhold drags her back inside. As soon as he lays her out on the bed she gurgles, struggles to get upright, spits blood, tries to get her feet down. 'Out, out.' She persists: 'Go away, go away.' Her one open eye is fixed on him. Her legs are hanging down. The drool. The drool disgusts him, I'm not hanging around here, people will think I did this. What's this got to do with me. Good day, miss. Hat on, exit.

Downstairs he wipes the blood off his left hand, that drool, laughs harshly to himself: that's what he took me up for, to put on a show like that, the wretch. Lays me in his bed wi' me boots on, to watch. Then he gets stir-crazy. He's not got a full deck, where's he running around now.

And saunters off. Enamel signs, enamel wares of every kind. It was fun up there. The wretch. You did well, my son, carry on, in your own time. I could laugh.

Thereupon Bornemann found himself back in police hands in Stettin. They produced his wife, the real one. Detective, leave my wife out of it, I made her help. Put another couple years on my sentence, I don't care.

And then there's an evening up in Franz's room. They laugh, they hug, they kiss, they are spoony on each other. 'I almost killed yer, Mitzi. What have I done to you, oh my god.' 'Never mind that. Just having you back is all I mind about.' 'Did Reinhold skedaddle right away?' 'Yes.' 'You didn't even ask me what he was doing up there.' 'No.' 'Aren't you curious?' 'No.' 'Oh, Mitzi.' 'It's not true anyway.' 'What's not true?' 'That you want to sell me to him.' 'What?' 'It's not true, is it?' 'But Mitzi.' 'I know it's not, so that's fine.' 'He's my friend, Mitzi, but he's a pig around women. I wanted to show him what a decent woman was like. That's what I brought him up to see.' 'Well then.' 'Do you still love me then. Or just that new geezer.' 'I'm yours, Franz.'

Wednesday, 29 August

And she leaves her put of a patron without her for two whole days, and does nothing but be with her beloved Franz, take trips with him out to Erkner and Potsdam, and be spoony with him. She's all lovey-dovey with him, even more than before, the little wretch, and she's not the least bit worried about what her beloved Franz will do with Pums's people: she's doing something herself. She's decided she's going to take a good look around herself and see what's what, at a dance or a bowling evening. Franz never takes her along to those, Herbert takes his Eva, but Franz says: that's no place for you, I don't want you mingling with filth like that.

But Sonia – Mitzi – wants to do something for Franz, our little pusspuss wants to do something that's nicer than just earning money for him. She wants to find out about everything, and protect him.

The next time the Pums boys and their significant others have a ball out Rahnsdorf way, private party, there's a lady in attendance that none of them know, the plumber brought her along, she's his bird, she's masked, and one time she even dances with Franz, but just the once, he can smell the perfume afterwards. This is in Müggelhort, in the evening the fairy lights come on in the garden, a paddle-wheel steamer sets off, full to bursting, the band plays a farewell tune as it sets off, but they carry on drinking and dancing till three.

And there's Mitzi bobbing about with her plumber who's showing off to everyone what a nice bird he's got; she sees Pums and his lady, and Reinhold sitting there in a mood – something always seems to get his goat – the sharp geezer. At two in the morning she and the plumber get in the car; she lets him snog her in the car, why not, she knows more already, it's not the first time. So what is it Mitzi knows? What all the Pums boys look like, that by itself buys snogging rights, she is and remains Franz's bird, it's gotten late, it was on a night like this that the boys threw Franz out of the car, and now he's going to get his own back, he'll know who it was all right, and they're all terrified of him, why else would Reinhold have agreed to go up, he's a cheekie chappie all right, my Franz is a golden boy, I could kiss the plumber to death, oh, I love Franz so, yes, go on, snog me, I'll swallow your tongue, Jesus, where's he going, we'll both end up in the ditch, hurrah, it was so lovely the evening with your mob, do I go right or left, drive, just drive, you're a sweet thing, you know, Mitzi, like the taste do you, sugar, then you should take me out more regularly, whoopsie, the idiot, he must have had a skinful, he'll drive us into the river.

That can't be, because then I'd drown, and I've a lot of plans yet, I want to follow my dear Franz, I don't know what's on his mind, he don't know what's on my mind, and that's the way it should remain between the two of us, as long as he wants and as long as I want, we both want the same thing, oh that feels good, kissamme more, hold me, boy, I'm melting, can you feel me melt.

Karl, Karl, you're to be my fancy boy, on the avenue the black oaks shoot by, I'll give you 128 days a year, each of them with a morning, and a noon, and a night.

*

But in the cemetery two blue policemen were walking. They sat down on a tombstone and asked passers-by if they happened to have seen a certain Kasimir Brodowicz. He had done something some thirty years before, but they couldn't exactly say what it was, and something will probably have to be done about it, you never know with the criminal fraternity, and now they want to take his fingerprints and measure his collar, and ideally they would nab him for that, show us who he is, trari trara.

Reinhold hitches up his trousers, prowls back and forth in his pad, too much peace and quiet don't seem to agree with him, let alone having all that spending money. He sent his last bird packing, and he doesn't like the new toffee-nosed one any more.

It's time for a change. He wants to do something involving Franz. The old camel is doing the rounds and beaming and show-ing off his dolly bird; as if there was anything to it. Maybe I will take her off him after all. Though the scene with all that slobber and crying turned his stomach.

The plumber, right name Matter, though known to the police as Oskar Fischer, don't half look bemused when Reinhold asks him about Sonia. He asks right out about Sonia, and Matter concedes, well, if you know then you know. At that, Reinhold puts his arm round Matter and asks whether Matter would mind loaning her to him for a little outing. Then it turns out that Sonia's Franz's bird, and not Matter's to dispose of at all. Well, maybe Matter could bring the girl round for a little drive to Freienwalde.

'You need to ask Franz that, not me.' 'I can't ask Franz, there's bad blood between us, and I don't think she likes me. I think I'm right in saying!' 'Well, but I don't see why I should. What if I want to keep her for myself.' 'Well, you can. It's just for a little drive.' 'You can have all the women you want, Reinhold, so far as I care, including her, but where do you get them without stealing.' 'Well, she goes around with you. If you want a brown note, I'm good for one.' 'Let's have it then.'

Two blue policemen sat down on a stone and asked everyone who went by, and stopped every car: if they hadn't happened to see someone with a yellow face and black hair. They were looking for him. They don't know what he's supposed to have done or is about to do, it's all in the files. But no one has seen him or admits to having seen him. So the two policemen have to start walking along the avenue, and a couple more policemen join them.

On Wednesday, 29 August 1928, by which time the year has already shed 242 days and has precious few left to lose – and they are irrevocably gone, along with the ride to Magdeburg, the operation and the convalescence, with Reinhold's new brandy habit, Mitzi's appearance on the scene, and they are doing their first job of the year, and Franz is all serenity again and fullest peaceableness – on that day the plumber cruises off into the green belt with little Mitzi. She's told him, which is to say Franz, that she's out with her fancy man. She doesn't know what it's about. She just wants to help Franz, but doesn't know how. That night she dreamt: her bed and Franz's are in their landlady's living room under the lamp, and the curtain by the door starts to move, and something grey and ghostly slowly unwraps itself and moves into the room. Oh, she sighed, and she sat up in bed, with Franz fast asleep by her side. I'll help him, nothing bad's going to happen to him. And with that she lay down again, funny, the way our beds trundled into her living room.

Then hup they're out in Freienwalde, beautiful Freienwalde, it's a resort, has a pretty spa garden laid out on yellow gravel, with people strolling up and down on it. Who will they run into there after they've lunched, on the terrace beside the spa garden.

Earthquake, lightning, lightning, thunder, torn-up tracks, the station topsy-turvy, wheels, smoke, smoke, swathes of it, nothing to see, swathes of smoke, piercing screams . . . I'm yours, I belong to you.

Let him approach, let him sit down, I'm not scared of him, him least of all, I can look him coolly in the eye. 'May I introduce you: Mitzi; Reinhold? Oh, you know each other?' 'Fleetingly. Glad to make your acquaintance, miss.'

So there they are sitting in the public park in Freienwalde, in the restaurant someone is playing the piano. I'm sitting in Freienwalde, and he's sitting opposite.

Earthquake, lightning, thunderbolt, swathes, all done in, but it's nice that we ran into him, I'll worm it out of him, everything that happened with Pums's mob, and what Franz is up to, I can get it out of him with a bit of teasing; let him dangle, and he'll come across. Mitzi dreams of fortune's favour. The piano player sings: Say oui, little girl, that's French. Yes, yes, na and Chinese as well, it doesn't matter what you want, love is internationa'. Tell me in Chinese whispers, or through the nose, tell me softly or in ecstasies, say oui, yes, ja. – And everything else is there!

Glasses are brought out, and all partake. Mitzi lets it be known that she was at the ball, and a wonderful conversation begins. The maestro at the piano takes requests: 'In Switzerland and in Tyrol', words by Fritz Roller and Otto Stransky, music by Anton Profes. In Switzerland and in Tyrol, there you feel so terribly swoll. Cos in Tyrol there's warm milk straight from the udder, and in Switzerland there's a little dudder of a liddle mudder. We have nothing to compare, let's be honest, it's just not there, and that's why I find it so beyond compare, Switzerland and Tyrol as woll. Holoroidi. Available from music shops everywhere. Holoroidi, laughs Mitzi, there's my sweet Franz thinking I'm with my feller – when I'm all about Franz, and he don't even know.

Now they propose to take a drive round the countryside, in the motor. That's what Karl, Reinhold and Mitzi want to do, or arsy-versy Mitzi, Reinhold and Karl, or again Reinhold, Karl and Mitzi, every man and woman jack of them want to take a drive. And just then the telephone is brought, and a waiter calls out: telephone for Herr Matter, didn't you wink your eye at me a moment ago, Reinhold my lad, well I won't say anything, Mitzi is smiling and all, it seems you two have no objection, we'll have a lovely afternoon. Here's Karlchen back again, oh Karelein, Karelein, you, you must be mine, does something hurt, no, it's just I have to dash back to Berlin, you stay here, though, Mitzi, I've got to go, no one must know, and he gives Mitzi a kiss, every man, when he can, likes a little something off the plan, be seeing you Reinhold, happy Easter, happy Whitsun, plucks his hat off the hatstand and he's off.

So here we are, just the two of us. 'What do you say to that then.'

'Now miss, there was no call for you to scream like that the other time.' 'It was just the shock of it.' 'I mean, not in front of me.' 'I need time to get used to people.' 'Not exactly flattering.' The way the little minx rolls her eyes, sweet fine carcass, bet I put one over on her today; you wait, boy, I just want to leave you wriggling, and tell me everything you know. My god, look at his eyes. He must have eaten a tree full of celery.

Then the piano player has sung his lot and the piano is tired, and wants to go beddy-byes, and Reinhold and Mitzi traipse off up the hill and into the woods. And they talk about this and that, and they link elbows, and the boy's really not so bad. And when they're back in the spa gardens at six Karl is waiting for her, he's back in the car already. Do we have to go home, there's a moon, we can go for a walk in the woods, it's so lovely there, yes, let's. And so at eight the three of them go walking up to the woods, and Karl quickly has to go and book rooms for them at the hotel, and see to the car. We'll meet up later in the spa gardens.

The wood is full of trees, and many people are walking there arm in arm, and there are a few paths that are more secluded too. They walk along dreamily side by side. Mitzi has questions she wants to ask, but she doesn't know how, it's so nice walking arm in arm with him, I'll ask him another time, why spoil the beautiful evening. God, what must Franz be thinking, I'd better go soon, but it's so pretty here. Reinhold has his arm round her waist, he has a right arm, the man is walking at her left, funny, Franz of course is always on her right, he has a strong arm, what a fellow he is. They walk among trees, the forest floor is soft and yielding, Franz has good taste, I'll take her off him, I'll have her for a month, willy-nilly. Else I'll sock him so hard on our next job that he'll forget which way is up, a beautiful bird, a spirited bird, who's true to him.

They walk and they talk about this and that. It gets dark. It's better to speak; Mitzi sighs, it's so dangerous to walk in silence and only to feel the man at her side. She keeps her eyes on the path in front of her. I don't know what I'm doing with him; God, what am I doing with him. They walk in a circle. Secretly, Mitzi has led them back to the main drag. Open your eyes, you're back.

It's eight o'clock. He takes out his torch, they're on their way up to the hotel, the woods are behind them, the little birds, oh, the little birds, they all sang so merrily so merrily. He's trembling. It was a strangely silent walk. His eyes are light. He walks quietly along at her side. The plumber is waiting for them, all alone on the terrace. 'Did you get us rooms?' Reinhold looks round for Mitzi; she's gone. 'Where did the lady get to?' 'She's up in her room.' He knocks on the door. 'The lady says to say she's gone to bed.'

He's trembling. It was so wonderful. The darksome woods, the birds. What do I want from the girl. A nice girlfriend Franz has got; I want her. Reinhold sits with Karl on the terrace; they light up a couple of thick cigars. They exchange smiles: what are we doing here exactly when we could be asleep in our own beds at home. – Reinhold is still breathing deeply and slowly, draws on his cigar, the dark woods, the circular walk, she leads me back: 'If you like, Karl. I'll spend the night here.'

And then they both march out to the edge of the woods, and sit there, and watch the passing cars. There are many trees in these woods, you walk on soft ground, many people walk there arm in arm, why am I such a bastard.

Saturday, 1 September

This was all on Wednesday, 29 August 1928.

Three days later they do it all again. The plumber drives up in a car, Mitzi – Mitzi said yes right away when he suggested going out to Freienwalde again, and Reinhold wants to come too. This time I'll be tougher, she thinks, as she sits down in the car, I'll not go with him into the woods. She said yes right away, because Franz was such a misery all day, and he won't say what the matter is, and I need to find out. I give him money, he's got everything, he's not short of anything, I want to know what's upsetting the man.

Reinhold sits beside her in the car, his hand wastes no time finding her hip. Everything's planned this time: today's the day you're leaving your beloved Franz for the last time, today you'll be staying with me, and for as long as I say. You're my five hundredth or thousandth woman, so far I've had no complaints, and this'll be fine too. She's sitting there and has no idea, but I know and that's all that matters.

They park the car outside the inn at Freienwalde, Karl Matter takes Mitzi walking through Freienwalde unaccompanied, it's four o'clock on Saturday, 1 September. Reinhold wants to have a little nap in the hotel. Sometime after six he shakes himself awake, tinkers with the car for a bit, downs a swift half, and he's on his way.

In the woods Mitzi is happy. Karl is so nice and all the things he knows to talk about, he's the inventor of a patent that the company he used to work for took off him, employees are always being rooked like that, they should take care to have everything put in writing, and the company's made millions, and the only reason he's helping out at Pums's is because he's at work now on a different design that will make the other one, the one that the company stole, obsolete. A design like that costs a lot of money, he can't say much about it to Mitzi, it's very hush-hush, the whole world will change when he pulls it off, all the trams and fire engines and waste removal, everything, it applies to everything, everything you can think of. They reminisce about their drive back from the masked ball, on the avenue the oaks shoot past, I'll give you 128 days of the year, each with morning, noon and night.

'Yoohoo,' Reinhold calls through the woods. That's Reinhold calling, and they call back: 'Yoohoo, yoohoo.' Karl hides away somewhere, but Mitzi gets serious when she sees Reinhold approach.

Then the two policemen got up from their stone. And said the observation had been an exercise in futility and they disappeared, there was nothing we could do about it, only inconsequential things happened, we'll make a written report to the authorities. And if anything should happen, then we'll know soon enough, it'll be posted on the information board.

In the woods, though, there were Mitzi and Reinhold walking alone together, a couple of birds whistled and squeaked softly. The tops of the trees started to sing.

One tree sang, then another, then they sang together, then they both stopped, then they sang over the heads of our two.

There is a reaper, Death yclept, by Almighty God employed. His blade he whets, it cuts much better.

'Oh, I'm so glad to be back in Freienwalde, Reinhold. Do you know, the day before yesterday, that was such a lovely day, wasn't that a lovely day.' 'Just a bit curtailed, miss. You were probably tired, I went knocking on your door, and you never answered.' 'The fresh air takes it out of you so, and the drive and everything.' 'Well, and wasn't it a little bit nice as well?' 'Of course it was, what do you mean?' 'Oh, I mean walking along together side by side. With such an attractive young lady and all.' 'Attractive young lady, give it a rest. I don't call you an attractive young gentleman, do I?' 'The fact that you're walking here with me—' 'What about it?' 'Well, I'm thinking maybe it doesn't show in me. But believe me, miss, the fact that we're stepping out makes me very happy.' A decent fellow. 'Don't you have a girlfriend?' 'Girlfriend, who doesn't call herself your girlfriend nowadays?' 'Oh.' 'Well. There's all sorts. You're not to know. You've got a boyfriend who's a solid type, and he cares about you. But girls, girls just want to have fun, they've no heart.' 'You must be out of luck.' 'You see, miss, that's how he came to be thinking of – you know – of swapping. But you don't want to hear about that.' 'Oh, you can tell me. What happened.' 'I can tell you all about it, and you'll understand me too. How can you keep a woman for longer than a couple of months or maybe weeks, if there's nothing to her? Well? Maybe she plays the field, or there's just nothing to her, she doesn't understand nothing, sticks her nose in everywhere, or maybe she's on the sauce?' 'Sounds awful.' 'You see, Mitzi, and that's what happened to me. That's what you get. That's what's out there, trash, rubbish, dreck. All got out of the garbage. Can you imagine being married to something like that? Me, not for one hour. Well, so you stick it out a little while, maybe a week or two, and that's about as much as you can take, and after that she gets her marching orders, and I'm all on my lonesome. It's not nice. This is, though.' 'A bit of a change too, wouldn't you say.' Reinhold laughs: 'What do you mean by that, Mitzi?' 'Well, just maybe you feel like someone else once in a while.' 'Why not, hey, they're all human.'

They laugh, they walk with linked arms, it's 1 September. The trees won't stop singing. It's one long sermon.

To every thing there is a season, and a time to every purpose under heaven: A time to be born, and a time to die; a time to plant, and a time to pluck up that which is planted; A time to kill, and a time to heal; a time to break down, and a time to build up; A time to weep, and a time to laugh; a time to mourn, and a time to dance; A time to cast away stones, and a time to gather stones together; a time to embrace, and a time to refrain from embracing; A time to get, and a time to lose; a time to keep, and a time to cast away; A time to rend, and a time to sew; a time to keep silence, and a time to speak. To every thing there is a season. I know that there is nothing better for a man than to be happy and enjoy himself. Better than enjoying himself. Enjoy ourselves, therefore let us enjoy ourselves. There is nothing better under the sun than laughing and rejoicing.

Reinhold has taken Mitzi by the hand, he is walking at her side, ooh, the strength there is in his arm. 'You know, Mitzi, I didn't trust myself to ask you out, back then, you remember.' And now we've been walking for half an hour, hardly talking. It's dangerous to walk for a long time without talking. But feel his right arm.

Where will I set the sweet dish down, she's a class act all right, and maybe I'll tuck her behind my ear for later, I mean to have her, maybe I'll drag her back to the hotel, and in the night, in the night, when the moon is shining bright. 'You've got loads of scars on your hand, and you've got tattoos and all. Have you got tattoos on your chest?' 'Sure. Wanna look?' 'What possesses you to get a tattoo?' 'That depends on the place, miss.' Mitzi giggles, pulls on his arm: 'I can imagine. I had a fellow before Franz, he was painted all over, more places than I could tell you.' 'It hurts, but it looks nice. Have a look, why don't you.' He lets go of her arm, quickly unbuttons his shirt, shows off his chest. There's an anvil, and a laurel wreath around it. 'Now put it away, Reinhold.' 'Take a good look.' The flame in him, the naked desire, he grabs hold of her head, forces it against his chest. 'Kiss it, you. Kiss. I want you to kiss it.' She doesn't kiss him, her head remains pressed down by his hands: 'Let me go.' He lets go of her: 'Don't take on, girl.' 'I've had enough.' The cunt, I'll grab her by the throat, that's no way to talk to me. He pulls his shirt down. I'll have her, she gives herself all those airs, easy does it, boy, easy. 'I didn't hurt you, now do me up, will you. Come on, you'll have seen a man before now.'

What am I doing with this fellow here, he's messed up my hair, he's a brute, I'm going. Everything in its own time. Everything, everything.

'Don't you take on like that, it was just an instant. A little moment, you know, you get them in the course of a lifetime.' 'That's still no need to grab my head like that.' 'Don't be cross, Mitzi.' You don't know where I mean to grab you next. The wild heat is upon him again. Oh, to get my hands on her. 'Now, Mitzi, shall we make peace?' 'Well, you'd better behave, is all I can say.' 'There's a deal.' Arm in arm. He smiles at her, she smiles down at the grass. 'Wasn't so bad, Mitzi, eh? We just bark a little, we don't bite.' 'I'm thinking, why have you got an anvil there? Some have got a picture of a woman or a heart or summink, but an anvil?' 'Now why do you think, Mitzi?' 'No idea. Search me.' 'It's my emblem.' 'An anvil?' 'Yeah. Someone has to lie down on it, get banged.' He gives her a grin. 'You're filthy. You should have had a bed there.' 'Na, nanvil's better.' 'You a blacksmith, then?' 'A bit of one. Jack of all trades, you know. But I don't think you understand about the anvil, Mitzi. No one's to get too close to me, else there'll be a blaze. But you're not to think I bite, least of all you. We're walking along and it's so nice and I feel like a little sit-down in a dell.' 'Are they all like that then, Pums's boys?' 'That depends, Mitzi, we're not the kind you can eat cherries with.' 'Well, so what things do you get up to?' How do I get her in a dell, and no one by. 'Oh, Mitzi, you'd best ask your Franz about that, he knows as much as I do.' 'But he won't tell me.' 'That's good. He's no fool. Best say nothing.' 'But you can tell me.' 'Whaddaya wanna know?' 'The stuff you do?' 'Will I get a kiss if I do?' 'If you tell me.'

Then she's in his arms. The fellow has two. And the way he can squeeze her in them. To every thing there is a season, planting and weeding, seeking and losing. I can't breathe. He won't let me go. Oh, it's so hot. Let me go. If he does that to me twice more, I'll be done for. Oh, but he needs to tell me first what it is with Franz, and what Franz wants and what happened and what they're thinking. 'Let go of me now, Reinhold.' 'All right.' And he lets go of her, and he stands there, then he drops to the ground, starts kissing her shoes, he must be mad, kisses her stockings, further up her, her dress, her hands, everything in its season, right the way up to her throat. She laughs, and flaps her hands at him: 'Stop that, stop it, you silly.' The glow of him, he needs to be stood under the cold tap. He is breathing hard and panting, he is trying to scrabble into her throat, he stammers, but she doesn't understand what he's trying to say, he lays off her for a minute, he's like a bull. His arm is pushed through hers, they are walking again, the trees are singing. 'Look, Mitzi, here's a nice dell, it might have been made for us – look. A weekend dell. Someone's been cooking in here. Let's tidy up. I don't want to get me trousers dirtied in there.' 'I'll sit down. Maybe he'll start talking a bit. 'Well, all right then. A coat'd be nicer.' 'Hang on, Mitzi, I'll take my jacket off.' 'That's nice of you.'

There are they, lying diagonally in a grassy hollow, she kicks away a tin can, plops down on her tummy, casually puts out an arm across his chest. There we are. She smiles at him. He pushes his weskit aside, and there's a little shimmer of the anvil again, and she doesn't pull her head away. 'Now tell me something, Reinhold.' He presses her against his chest, there we are, hunky-dory, here's the girl, everything's working out, nice girl, I'll say, I'll keep hold of her, I don't care what Franz says, he's not getting her back until I'm good and ready. And Reinhold slithers down, pulling Mitzi on top of him, wraps her in his arms, and kisses her on the mouth. He sucks himself full, no thought in him, just pleasure, greed, wildness and every move is predetermined, and no one better get in his way. Then it breaks and splinters and no hurricane or avalanche can stop it, it's like something shot out of a gun, a shell flying. Whatever gets in its way is blown to smithereens, knocked aside, and it goes on and on.

'Don't be so rough, Reinhold.' He's making me weak. If I don't pull myself together, he'll have me. 'Mitzi.' He blinks up at her, not letting go. 'Well, Mitzi.' 'Well, Reinhold.' 'What are you looking like that for?' 'It's not a nice thing you're about here. How long have you known Franz for?' 'You mean your Franz?' 'Yes.' 'Your Franz? Is he still yours then?' 'Who else's?' 'Well, who am I then?' 'What do you mean?' She tries to bury her head in his chest, but he pulls her up: 'Now who am I?' She throws herself against him, presses his mouth, he flickers into flame again, I do like him a bit, the way he stretches and glows. There is no amount of water, no firemen's hose can quench the fire, the flames flare out of the windows, press up inside. 'There, now let go of me.' 'What do you want, girl?' 'Nothing, just be with you.' 'Well then. I'm yours too, inni. Did you have a row with Franz then?' 'No.' 'Did you have a row, Mitzi?' 'No. Why don't you tell me about him, you've known him for much longer.' 'I can't tell you about him.' 'Oh.' 'I'm not going to, Mitzi.' He grabs hold of her, throws her aside, she tussles with him: 'No, I don't want to.' 'Don't be that way, girl.' 'I need to get up, I'm getting all dirty here.' 'And what if I tell you something?' 'That'd be nice.' 'What will you give me in return, Mitzi?' 'Whatever you want.' 'Everything?' 'Well – we'll see.' 'Everything?' Their faces are pressed together, burning; she doesn't say anything, I don't even know what I'll do, the impulse shoots through him, no thinking, beyond thinking, insensate.

He gets up to wipe his face, it's filthy in the woods. 'I'll tell you about your Franz then. I've known him for a long time, see. You know, he's an odd bird all right. I met him in a bar on Prenzlauer Allee. Last winter. He was flogging papers, he must have known someone in that line, yes that's right, Mack. That was when I met him. Then we sat together, and I told you about the girls.' 'Is that all true then?' 'You bet it is. But he's a fool, Biberkopf, airhead, he can hardly brag about that, it was all my idea, you think it was him palming off his women on me? Jesus, those women. No, if it'd been up to him, we'd have been round the Salvation Army, for me to better meself.' 'But you didn't better yourself, did you, Reinhold?' 'No. As you see. There's nothing to be done with me. You have to take me as I am. It's as sure as eggs is eggs, and there's nothing to be done about it. But that fellow, Mitzi, you can certainly change him. He's pimping you, Mitzi, and you're such a pretty piece. How can you dig up a man like that, with one arm, a pretty girl like you, you can get ten on each finger?' 'Stop talking nonsense.' 'I know love is blind in both eyes, but that's doing it some. You know what his game is now, in the gang, your pimp? He wants to play the bigshot. With us. First he wanted to send me to the penitent form, Salvation Army, he didn't quite pull that off. And now.' 'Oh, don't scold him so. I can't stand to hear it.' 'Ootchie kootchie, I know, he's still your sweetheart, Franz? Eh?' 'It doesn't affect you, Reinhold.'

Everything in its season, everything, everything. Terrible man, wish he'd let me go, I don't want anything to do with him, I don't want him to tell me anything. 'No, no, doesn't affect me, I'd like to see him try. But you've got yourself a fine man there, Mitzi. Did he ever tell you the story of his arm? What? I thought you're his squeeze, or used to be. Come here, Mitzi, honey, don't take on.' What am I doing here, I don't want him. A time to plant, and a time to pluck up that which is planted, a time to rend, and a time to sew, a time to mourn, and a time to dance, a time to complain and a time to laugh. 'Come on, Mitzi, what are you doing with a numbskull like that. You're my sweetheart. Don't fuss. Just because you're with him, doesn't make you a duchess. You should be glad to be rid of him.' Be glad, why should I be glad. 'And now he can howl, now he's lost his Mitzi.' 'Now, there's an end, and stop crushing me, I'm not made of iron.' 'I know, you're flesh and blood, lovely flesh and blood, Mitzi, give me your mouth.' 'What are you doing, stop squeezing me. Don't imagine you're getting anywhere. How am I your Mitzi?'

Out of the dell. Left my hat down the bottom. He'll smack me, I'm running. And already – he's not up out of the dell yet – she's calling for Franz, and running. Now he's up and running and in a couple of bounds he's caught up with her, in his shirtsleeves. Both sprawled at the foot of a tree. She's lashing out, he's on top of her, holding her mouth shut: 'Will you stop shouting, you cunt, you're shouting again, what are you shouting about, am I hurting you, will you be quiet now. He left you in one piece the other day. You watch yourself, I take a different approach.' He takes his hand off her mouth. 'I won't shout.' 'All right. There, there. And now I want you to get up, and go and get your hat. I'm not one to attack a woman. I never have yet in all my born days. But you'd best not get me in a bate. That's the way.'

He walks along behind her.

'It's hardly something to be proud of, being Franz's bit on the side.' 'I've had enough of this, I'm going.' 'What do you mean, you're going, do you know who you're talking to, it may do for him but it won't wash wi' me.' 'What do you want anyway.' 'Go in the dell and put up.'

To slaughter a veal calf, tie a rope round its neck, and take it to the slaughtering bench. Then pick it up, lay it across the bench, and tie it fast.

They march back to the dell. He says: 'Lie down.' 'Me?' 'Don't you try yelling. Listen, I like you, otherwise I'd never have brought you here, I tell you: if you're his whore, you're no duchess. Don't pull a scene. That's no good to anyone. I don't mind if it's a man or woman or child, it's never done them any good wi me. Ask your ponce if you want to know. He'll tell you. Unless he's embarrassed to. I'll tell you myself just as well, then you'll know who he is. And I'll tell you where you get off with me. He had something in mind that he wanted to do. Maybe he wanted to shop us to the police. One time he was standing guard, while we were doing a job. Then he says he doesn't want to be involved, he's a law-abiding citizen. He's all talk and no cider. So I tells him, you have to. So he goes along in the car and I have no idea what I'm going to do with the guy, he always had a big mouth on him, and then there's this car following us and I think, now see what happens, my lad, acting big with us. And I get him out the car. There. Now you know where he left his arm.'

An icy feeling in her hands and feet, so it was him. 'Now lie down, and put up, like a good girl.' He's a murderer. 'You cruel bastard, you wretch.' He beams: 'You see. Now you've got something to shout about.' You'll behave yourself. She yells and cries: 'You bastard, you tried to kill him, you made him miserable, and now you want to have me as well, you bastard.' 'Yes, I do and all.' 'You bastard. I spit in your face.' He covers her mouth: 'And now?' She goes blue, tugs at his hand: 'Murder, help, Franz, darling, help.'

His time! His season! Everything its season. To kill and to heal, a time to break down, and a time to build up, a time to rend and a time to sew, everything in its season. She throws herself to the ground to escape. They wrestle together in the dell. Help, Franz.

We'll take care of you all right, we'll play a little joke on Franz that will keep him occupied all week. 'Let me go.' 'You try. You won't be the first.'

He is kneeling over her back, his hands round her throat, the thumbs at her neck, her body draws itself together. It's time, to be born and to die, to be born and to die, each thing.

Murderer you say, and you trap me here and maybe you want to lead me by the nose, girl. You don't know what you're about with Reinhold.

Violence, violence is a reaper, by Almighty God employed. Let me go. She wriggles and tries to get up and lashes out behind her. We'll see you there, the dogs will come and eat what's left of you.

Her body knits together, Mitzi's, knits together Mitzi's body. Murderer, she says, well, she'll see, maybe he sent you here, your darling Franz.

Thereupon strike the animal on the back of the head with a wooden mallet, and open the veins on either side of the neck with a knife. Collect the blood in a metal basin.

It's eight o'clock, the woods are getting dark. The trees sough and sway. Hard work. What's she got to say for herself now? She's stopped yapping, the bitch. That's what you get for taking a cunt like that on an outing.

Covered her over with foliage, hung a handkerchief on the nearest tree so you can find the place, that's me done with her, where's Karl now, I need his help. After a good hour he's back with Karl, what a sadsack, he's shaking all over, knock knees, how can a man work with beginners like that. It's pitch-black, they pull out their torches, there's the handkerchief. They've brought shovels with them from the car. The body is buried, cover it with sand, cover it with foliage, careful not to leave any footprints, stay upright, Karl, it's as though you're the one we're burying.

'So you've got my passport, my legal passport, Karl, and now here's some money, and keep out of sight as long as the hue and cry's on. I'll see that you get money, don't you worry. Apply to Pums. I'm going back to the city. No one's seen me, and no one can do anything to you, you've got your alibi. OK. Let's go.'

The trees sough and sway. Each thing, season.

It's pitch-black. Her face is pulp, her teeth are pulp, her eyes are pulp, her mouth, her lips, her tongue, her throat, her trunk, her legs, her crotch, I'm yours, please comfort me, police station Stettiner Bahnhof, Aschinger's, I feel sick, come along, we'll be home in a minute, I'm yours.

The trees pitch and toss, a wind gets up. Woo-woo-woo-a-woo. The night continues. Her trunk a pulp, her tongue, her mouth, come on, we'll be home in a minute, I'm yours. A tree crashes at the wood's edge. Woo-woo-a-ah-woo, here's the storm coming with its pipes and drums, now it's directly over the wood, now it drops down, when it howls like that it's down. The whimpering comes from the bushes. It sounds as though something's being slashed, it howls like a shut-in mastiff, and wails and whimpers, listen to it whimpering, someone must have really put the boot in, now it's stopped again.

Hoo-hoo-a-hoo-oo-oo, the storm returns, it's night, the woods are calm, tree ranked by tree. They've grown tall in peace, they stand together like a herd, when they are packed tight like that the storm can't get at them so easily, and it's only the ones on the periphery and the weaklings that need worry. But we stay put, we stick together, it's night time, the sun is gone, hoo-hoo-ah-oo-hoo, it starts again, there it is, it's down among us and up and all round. Yellowish-red light in the sky and night again, thunderlight and night, the whimpering and whistling get louder. The ones on the outside know what's coming, they whimper, and the rushes, but they can bend, they can flutter, what can thick trees do. And suddenly the wind stops, it's given up, it won't do that any more, they're still squeaking in fear, what will it do now.

If you want to knock over a building you don't do it by hand, you need to take a wrecking-ball to it or plant some dynamite. The wind doesn't do any more than puff out its chest. Watch this, it fills its lungs, then it blows, hoo-hoo-ah-oo-hoo, then it breathes in, then blows out, hoo-hoo-ah-oo-hoo. Each breath is as heavy as a mountain, when it blows out, hoo-hoo-ah-oo-hoo, the mountain comes trundling up, it rolls away again, exhales, hoo-hoo-ah-oo-hoo. Back and forth. Breath is a weight, a ball that is thrown against the woods. And when the woods stand on the slopes like a herd, then the wind runs around the herd and whooshes through the middle.

Now we have the boom-boom, without drums and fifes. The trees swing left and right. Boom-boom. But they can't keep time. When the trees are just leaning left, then it's boom-by-the-left, they bend over, crack, clatter, burst, shear, clump down. Timing. Boom goes the storm, you go left. Hoo-hoo-ah-oo-hoo, back, that's over, it's gone, you just need to catch the right moment. Boom, here it is back again, watch out, boom, boom, boom, those are bombs, the fighter plane wants to knock over the wood, it wants to bomb the whole forest.

The trees drag and sway, there's a rustle, they break, a clatter, boom, life is at stake, boom-boom, the sun is gone, weights crash, night, boom-boom.

I'm yours, come to me, we're nearly there, I'm yours. Boom-boom.

Chapter Eight

It was no use. It still wasn't any use. Franz Biberkopf receives a hammer-blow, he knows he is done for, though he still doesn't know why.

Franz notices nothing, and the world goes on its way

September 2nd. Franz goes around as normal, takes a trip out to the Wannsee baths with the natty geezer. On the 3rd, the Monday, he's surprised his little Mitzi's not showed up, she hasn't said anything to him, the landlady can't remember her phoning either. Well, perhaps she's gone on an outing with her distinguished friend and benefactor and he'll be dropping her off soon. Let's wait till tonight.

It's noon, Franz is sitting at home, there's a ring, pneumatique, for Mitzi from her benefactor. Oh, what's this about, I thought she was with him, what can it be. I open it: 'and I'm surprised you didn't even call, Sonia. Yesterday and the day before I waited in the office, as we'd agreed.' So what's going on, where is she.

Franz ups, looks for his hat, don't understand, go and see the gentleman, taxi. 'She's not been with you? When was she last here then? Friday? I see.' The two men look at each other. 'You have a nephew, could it be she's with him?' The gentleman loses his rag, what, I want to see him, you stick around. They sip wine together. The nephew turns up. 'This is Sonia's fiancé, do you know where she is?' 'Me, why?' 'When did you see her last?' 'Oh, it must have been two weeks ago.' 'That's right. That's what she said to me. And not since?' 'Nope.' 'And heard nothing?' 'Not a thing, why, is something the matter?' 'The gentleman will tell you himself.' 'She's been gone since Saturday, not a dicky bird, not a syllabubble.' The benefactor: 'Could she have made a new acquaintance?' 'Don't

343

think so.' They quaff wine, the three of them. Franz sits quietly: 'Perhaps we'd better wait a bit.'

Her face pulp, her teeth pulp, her eyes pulp, her lips, her tongue, her throat, her trunk, her legs, her crotch, all pulp.

She's not there the next day. Not there. Everything the way she left it. She's not there. Does Eva know? 'Did you have a fight with her, Franz?' 'Two weeks ago, but it's all settled.' 'An acquaintance?' 'No, she told me that her gentleman had a nephew, but he's around, I've seen him.' 'Maybe keep an eye on him, maybe she is with him.' 'Do you think so?' 'Should keep an eye out. You never know with Mitzi. She has her moods.'

She's not there. For two days Franz does nothing, thinks, I'm not going to chase her. Then he hears nothing, nothing at all, and he spends all day walking around on the trail of the nephew, and midday the following day, when the nephew's landlady's popped out, Franz and the dapper geezer barge into the flat, the door's no problem with a crowbar, no one in at all, loads of books, no sign of a woman, nice pictures on the walls, more books, she's not here, I know her powder, I can't smell it here, come on, let's go, let's not take anything, leave the poor woman be, she needs to let rooms to live.

What's the matter. Franz sits up in his room for hours on end. Where's Mitzi. Gone, without a word. What can you say. Plucked everything to pieces in the room, dismantled the bed, put it back together. She's dumped me. Not possible. Not possible. Dumped me. Did I do anything to her, I never did nuffink. She's forgiven me for the fuss over the nephew.

Who's this? Eva. 'Sitting in the dark, Franz, put the gaslight on.' 'Mitzi's gone and dumped me. Do you believe it?' 'Ooh, I don't think so. She'll be back. She's fond of you, she won't run off, I know people.' 'I know. I know. I'm not really worried about her either. She'll be back.' 'See. Something's up with that girl, she's met someone from way back, gone for a little drive, I've known her for a long time, before you ever met her, that's the kind of thing she does, she gets funny ideas sometimes.' 'I still think it's odd. I dunno.' 'But she

loves yer. Now open your eyes, touch me on the stomach, Franz.'
'What is it?' 'Well, it's yours, you know, your little one. Mitzi
wanted it.' 'What?' ''S true.'

Franz presses his head against Eva's belly: 'From Mitzi. I need to
sit down. I don't believe this.' 'Now listen up, Franz, when she gets
back, she's gonna make a face about this.' Eva herself starts crying.
'See who's wound up about this, Eva? It's you.' 'Oh, it's doing me in.
I don't understand that girl.' 'So I need to comfort you, is that it?'
'No, it's just my nerves, perhaps from carrying the baby.' 'Listen,
when she comes back, don't think she won't make a fuss then.' She
doesn't stop crying: 'What are we going to do, Franz, it's not like
her at all.' 'First you say she'll have gone off for a trip with someone,
and now you say it's not like her at all.' 'I don't know what to say,
Franz.'

Eva holds Franz's head in her arms. She looks down at Franz's
head: the clinic in Magdeburg, the arm they severed, him killing
Ida, what is it with that man. He's cursed. Mitzi will be dead. Something is after him. Something's happened to Mitzi. She flops onto a
chair. She lifts her hands in front of her face. Franz is mystified. She
is sobbing and sobbing. She knows something's up, something
must have happened to Mitzi.

He presses her, but she won't say what it is. After a while she
pulls herself together: 'I'm not going to let them take away my
baby. I don't care what Herbert says.' 'Will he say anything?' Over-
leaping six miles of thinking. 'No, he'll think it's his. But I'm going
to keep it anyway.' 'That's fine, Eva. I can be its godfather.' 'I don't
understand why you're in such a good mood, Franz.' 'Because no
one can do anything to me. Cheer up, Eva. And I know my Mitzi,
don't I. She's not fallen under a bus, it'll all be sorted.' 'You're right,
Franz. Bye-bye now.' 'Don't I get a kiss then?' 'I don't understand
why you're in such a good mood.'

We've got legs, we've got teeth, we've got eyes, we've got arms, so
just someone try and bite us, bite Franz, let him just try. He's got
two arms and two legs, he's got muscles, he can chop everything
into kindling. If you know Franz, he's no weakling. Whatever we

have behind us, whatever lies ahead of us, we'll have someone along the way, we'll lift a glass to that, no two, no nine.

We have no legs, o woe, we have no teeth, we have no eyes, we have no arms, anyone can turn up to bite Franz, he is a weakling, he's incapable of sticking up for himself, all he does is drink.

'I'll do something, Herbert, I can't stand to watch it.' 'What will you do, girl?' 'I can't stand to watch it, the man doesn't get it, he sits there and tells hisself, she'll be back, she'll be back, while I'm scanning the papers every day and there's never anything about her. Did you hear anything?' 'Nope.' 'Couldn't you listen out, in case someone's happened to hear summink.' 'It's all nonsense, Eva, everything you say is nonsense. The mystery isn't a mystery at all. What's happened? The girl's gone. So why do yourself in about it. Find another one.' 'Is that what you'd say if it was me?' 'Now hang on, Eva. I'm talking about those sort of girls.' 'That's where you're wrong. I introduced them to each other, I've been round the morgue to look, mark my words, Herbert, something's happened. There's something awfully wrong with Franz, Herbert. Something's up. Haven't you heard anything at all?' 'I dunno what you mean.' 'Well, sometimes somebody says something, in the group. Has anyone seen her? She can't have just disappeared. I tell you, if she doesn't turn up soon, I'll go to the police.' 'As if! I can just see you doing that.' 'Don't laugh, I'm serious. I have to find her, Herbert, something's happened, she hasn't just disappeared by herself, she wouldn't leave me like that, and she wouldn't leave Franz like that either. And he doesn't get it.' 'I don't want to hear any more about it, it's all crap, and now we're going to the cinema, Eva.'

In the cinema they see a film.

When in the third act the hero is apparently mown down by a bandit, Eva gives a sigh. And out of the corner of his eye Herbert sees her slip down off her seat and pass out. Afterwards they walk silently arm in arm through the streets. Herbert is astounded: 'Your fancy man isn't going to like it if you're like this.' 'He shot him, didn't you see, Herbert?' 'That was just a trick, he didn't really, you missed it when they set it up. And you're still shaking.' 'You've got to do something, Herbert, it can't go on this way.' 'You're supposed to be going abroad, tell your gentleman you're ill.' 'No, I mean do something. Do something, Herbert. You helped Franz when he lost his arm, you need to do something for him again now. Please!' 'I can't, Eva. What am I supposed to do?' She cries. He has to sit her down in the car.

Franz doesn't have to beg, Eva helps him out, he's on the Pums payroll, something is being lined up for the end of September. At the end of September the plumber Matter returns. He was abroad, on some plumbing job or something. When he sees Franz he says it was to recuperate, something with his lungs. He looks terrible, and not at all recuperated. Franz says Mitzi's gone, did he remember her; but he's not to tell anyone about it, there are vindictive people who just laugh when they hear about someone's bird walking out on them. 'So not a squeak to Reinhold, we used to share women in the past sometimes, he would laugh himself silly if he got wind of something like that. Besides,' Franz smiles, 'I haven't got around to replacing her yet.' He looks sad about the mouth, across the forehead. But then he throws his head back and presses his lips together.

There's a lot going on in the city. Tunney has successfully defended his title, but the Yanks aren't too pleased, he's not very popular there. In the seventh he took a count of nine. Then it was Dempsey's turn to wobble. Turned out, that was his last big punch, and it was all over by 4.58 a.m., 23 September 1928. You can read all about it, and the flight record from Cologne to Leipzig, and then there's supposed to be an economic war between oranges and bananas. But that's in the inside pages.

How does a plant protect itself against the cold? There are many species that are quite defenceless, even against a slight frost. Others have something in their chemistry that allows them to look after themselves. The most significant is the conversion of starch to sugar. Not all food crops benefit by this process – e.g. the increased sweetness in frost-affected potatoes. But there are other instances where it takes the heightened sugar content of a plant or fruit through refrigeration to make said plant or fruit palatable, as in the case of wild fruits. If such fruits are left on the bough until the first frost, they will make so much sugar that their taste is transformed and greatly improved. Rose-hips are an example here.

Does it matter that a couple of Berlin kayakers were drowned in the Danube, or that Nungesser crashed off the Irish coast in his *White Bird*. They cry the headlines out on the street, you buy the paper for 10 pfennigs, throw it away somewhere. They tried to lynch the Hungarian Prime Minister because he ran over a farm lad in his car. If they had succeeded, the headline would have read: 'Hungarian Prime Minister lynched outside Kaposvar', and there would have been a great hoo-ha about it, a few cultivated people would have read 'Lunched' and just laughed, the other 80 per cent would have said: too bad, or what do I care, pity it didn't happen here.

People like to laugh in Berlin. At Dobrin's, on the corner of Kaiser-Wilhelm-Strasse, there are three people sitting at a table, a fat lump, a merry grig and his bird, if only she didn't screech like that when she laughed, and then another fellow, a kind of non-entity, he's the fat guy's friend, who is paid for, his job is to listen to the fat guy and laugh at his jokes. The chubby tart snogs her loudmouth every five minutes and croons: 'Ooh, whatever will he come up with next!' Then he will nibble her neck, which takes up another two minutes. She doesn't care what the other guy thinks, watching them. The loudmouth is saying: 'So she says to him, she says: what was that thing you did to me just now? What was that thing you did just now? The third thing I could say would be boom-boom.' The third man smirks: 'You really are a hard-boiled piece of work.' The loudmouth, with delight: 'Not so hard-boiled as you are a twerp.' They sip their soup, next story.

'An angler walks up to a lake, and there's a girl sitting there, and he says, "Well, Fräulein Fischer, what about you and me going fishing together?" She says, "Me name's not Fischer, it's Fokker." "So much the better."' The three of them roar with laughter. The fat man explains: 'Because today we happen to have soupe du jour.' The bint: 'What will the man come up with next!' 'All right, all right, what about this one? A woman says: "Tell me, do you know what a propos means?" "A propos, that means, while we're on the subject." "You see," she says, "I knew it was filthy. Kchch!" ' It's very nice and cosy, the little lady needs to step out six times to powder her nose. 'Then the hen says to the cock, oh when will it be my turn. Waiter, bill please, that's three cognacs, two bread and cheese, three bouillons with three rubber soles.' 'Rubber soles, that were zwieback.' 'Well, you say zwieback, I say rubber soles. Haven't you got any change? There's a wee one at home, and when I go out, I like to leave him ten pfennigs to suck on. Right, that's it. Come along, honey. Comedy hour's over, time to go home.'

A few girls and women cross Alexanderplatz and Alexanderstrasse with a foetus on board, which is protected by law. And while the women and girls are sweating because of the heat, the foetus is sitting quietly in his temperature-controlled womb-room, he walks over the Alexanderplatz, but there's trouble in store for some foetuses, and it wouldn't do to laugh too readily.

Then there are others wandering around stealing anything they can lay their hands on, some have got their guts full, others are thinking how they might achieve such a state of affairs. Hahn's department store is on the skids, but all the other firms are doing good business, though it just looks as if they are businesses, in actual fact they are calls, halloos, twitterings, crick crack, a twittering without a forest.

So I returned, and considered all the oppressions that are done under the sun: and behold the tears of such as were oppressed, and they had no comforter; and on the side of their oppressors there was power; but they had no comforter. Wherefore I praised the dead which are already dead more than the living which are yet alive.

I praised the dead. Each in his season, to rend, and a time to sew, a time to keep, and a time to cast away. I praised the dead who lay under trees, sleeping.

*

And once more Eva starts in: 'Franz, won't you do something at last? Three weeks are up, you know, imagine if you were mine, and you didn't care.' 'There's no one I can talk to about it, Eva, you know that, I can talk to you and Herbert and the plumber, but that's all. I can't tell anyone, they'd all laugh in my face. And I can't go to the police. If you don't want to give me any more money, Eva, then that's fine. I – I'll go to work again.' 'I don't understand how you're so unmoved, I never seen you cry – I feel like giving you a good shaking, but that wouldn't change anything.' 'I can't help you.'

A few bonds are loosened, the criminals fall out among themselves

Early October time there's the internal dispute within the firm that Pums was dreading. It's about money. As ever, Pums takes the resale of goods for the principal concern of a criminal outfit, whereas to Reinhold and the others, Franz included, it's their acquisition. It's the acquisition, not the resale value, that should determine the distribution of rewards, Pums's cut is quite disproportionate, the man is taking advantage of his monopoly in relation to the fences, the better fences won't do business with anyone but Pums. The gang can see that, even though Pums has relented a bit and offered various concessions, something still needs to be done. They tend to favour a more co-operative arrangement. To which he says: that's what we've got. But the point is they don't think so.

There is the break-in on Stralauer Strasse. Even though Pums no longer plays an active part in jobs, he goes along this time. It's a bandage factory in a back building on Stralauer Strasse. They've managed to ascertain that there's money in the office safe. It's partly intended as a blow against Pums: no more dodgy goods, just straight cash. No question of a swindle when they divvy up the money. Which is also what moved Pums to participate. They climb up the fire escape in twos, and calmly unscrew the lock on the office door. Then the plumber gets to work. They break open all the office storage facilities, there's nothing beyond a few marks, stamps, a couple of petrol canisters in the corridor, they'll come in. So they have to wait while Karlchen the plumber gets to work. Then, wouldn't you know it, he burns his hand so badly while he's messing about with the safe that he can't go on. Reinhold has a shot at it, but he's had no practice, Pums takes the oxy-acetylene torch from him, but he can't do it either. Things are getting tense. They need to knock off, the security guard will be along any minute.

In their rage they take the petrol canisters, empty them over the furniture, including the wretched safe, and chuck in matches. Won't Pums just crow, but they've had enough. So someone's a bit previous with the matches and Pums gets a little bit singed, big deal! What's he doing there anyway. His back is scorched, they run down the stairs, wave: 'Guard', Pums just barely makes it into the car. He'll have to wear his longon, you would think. But what are they going to do for money.

Pums can laugh. Goods always were the better option. You need to be a specialist. Do something. Pums is denounced as an exploiter, a cheat. But you can't be sure, overdo things with him and he'll take his connections and start a new firm. In the sports club on Thursday he will say, I did my best for you, I can show you written accounts if you like, that's just it, you can't prove anything against the man, and if we don't want in, then the club will say it's none of our doing, you baled, the man does his best, and if he does slightly better out of it than you guys, don't get sore, you've still got your girls on the game while he's got his old lady and fuck all. So they decide to persevere with him, the lousy exploiter and entrepreneur.

It's the plumber who cops their full rage. We can't use a bungler like that. He's burnt his hand, is trying to heal it, has always done good work so far, and now all he hears is gripes.

Listen to them, he thinks, scowling. I was cheated out of my business when I still had one; I have a tipple and my wife yells at me, and then it's New Year's Eve, and I come home, and who's not there. The bitch. Gets in at seven in the morning, slept with some fellow, cheated on me. So there's me with no trade and no missus. And little Mitzi and that bugger Reinhold. She was mine, she didn't want him, it was me she went with to the party, driving down the avenue, she wrote the book about kissing, and then he took her off me because I'm just a poor scab. And that fucker, he did her in, he's a killer, because she wanted no part of him, and now he's throwing his weight around, and I burnt my hand, and I even helped him carry the body. He's a big villain, a proper killer. And I was supposed to take the whole thing on myself, for a wretch like that. What kind of eejit am I.

Keep your eyes on Karl the plumber: something's going on with him

Karl the plumber is looking for someone to confide in. He's in the Alexander-Quelle opposite Tietz's, a couple of borstal boys with him, and then a mystery man, you can't say what it is he does, he's in various trades, what he studied back in the day was wheelwright. He's a classy draughtsman all right, they're sitting round the table together tucking into frankfurters, and the young wheelwright is drawing all kinds of saucy pictures, men and girls and Christ knows what all else. The welfare boys are having a time of it, and Karl moves in and takes a dekko and thinks: he's a good draughtsman all right. The three of them can't stop laughing, the two welfare boys are exhilarated because they've just come from Rückerstrasse, and there was a raid, and they managed to get out round the back. And at that moment Karl the plumber goes up to the bar.

Just then two fellows are slowly making their way through the joint, looking left and right, talking to a man who pulls out his papers, and they take a look at them, say a word or two, and suddenly the two men are standing at their table, they're surprised all right but they don't let on, they don't say anything. They keep talking calmly away, of course the two are cops, they're the ones from the Rückerdiele, they've seen us. And the wheelwright goes on making his filthy drawings, and one of the policemen whispers in his shell-like: 'Police', peels back his lapel to show the badge on his weskit. His partner in crime does the same thing with the two boys. Who've got no papers, while mystery wheelwright has got a doctor's certificate and a letter from some girl, and all three of them are to report to the station on Kaiser-Wilhelm-Strasse. The boys say right out what's on their minds, but to their astonishment the police say they never saw them in Rücker-strasse, it was pure coincidence that they ran into them later in the Alexander-Quelle. Well, then we shouldn't have volunteered that we skipped out, and all of them laugh. The policeman pats them on the back: 'Well, the warden will be all the more pleased to have you back.' 'Oh, him, he's on holiday.' The wheelwright is standing in the office with the constables, he can talk his way out, his address is correct, just he's got such soft hands for a wheelwright, one of the cops can't get his head around that, he keeps turning them over and over, but I've been out of work for the past year, shall I tell you what I think, I think you're a nance, I don't even know what that is, a queer.

An hour later he's back in the bar. Karl the plumber is still there, the wheelwright runs up to him.

'What do you do for a living?' It's twelve o'clock as Karl asks the question. 'What do you do?' 'I take what comes.' 'Are you afraid to tell me?' 'Well, you're no wheelwright neither.' 'I'm as much a wheelwright as you are a plumber.' 'You never. Look at my hand, the burns on that, that was from doing electrical work.' 'Some shady business, more like.' 'Shady business! Wasn't good for any-thing, I'll tell you that much.' 'Who d'you work for then?' 'Little villain, asking the questions.' Karl asks the wheelwright: 'Whose outfit are you in?' 'Schönhauser local.' 'Oh yeah, the bowls club.' 'So you've heard of us.' 'Why wouldn't I have heard of the bowls club? Try asking there if they know about me, plumber Karl, and is Paule the mason not with you as well.' 'Oh sure, he's a mate of mine.' 'We were together in Brandenburg back in the day.' 'Well. Listen, then maybe you'll loan me five marks, I'm skint, my landlady will throw me out, and I won't go in the August shelter, there's always trouble there.' 'Five marks, all right. But no more 'n'at.' 'Ta. Well, maybe talk about business?'

The wheelwright is a windbag, sometimes it's women, sometimes it's boys. When he's in a fix, he borrows or steals. He, the plumber, and someone else from the Schönhauser group go freelance, and pull a couple of quick jobs. Someone in the wheelwright's mob tips them the wink about where to go. First off, they get a hold of some motorbikes, which gives them some mobility and access to the countryside. That way they're not dependent on Berlin, in case there's something worth having in the environs.

They do one job which is really neat. There's a tailor's on Elsasser Strasse, and the union has a couple of tailors who are good for fencing goods like that. So one morning finds the three of them standing outside, it's 3 a.m., and there's the security guard watching the premises. The wheelwright asks what business it is, and they all get talking, and the subject turns to break-ins, and how this is a dangerous time, because a lot of customers have started packing, and if a thief is caught he'll as likely as not be blown away. Well, the three of them protest, we'd never do anything like that; but was there anything worth taking in the outfitter's anyway? Lord, it's chock-full of gear, gents' suitings, overcoats, whatever you wanted. Well, in that case it must be worth going up and taking a look and maybe acquiring a new wardrobe. 'You must be mad, you wouldn't make trouble for our friend here.' 'Trouble, who said anything about trouble. Our neighbour here is only human, he's probably not earning a whole hell of a lot himself, what does the security industry pay?' 'It's barely worth asking. If you're past sixty and you're retired and can't really work any more, then they've got you over a barrel.' 'That's just what I'm saying, here's this old man standing around all night, getting rheumatism, I expect you were in the war and all?' 'Territorials, in Poland, but no digging, we never had to go in no trenches.' 'Tell me about it! Except with us it was, get in the trenches, unless you're carrying your head in your hands, that's why you're standing here now, brother, making sure that no one steals anything from the fine gentleman up there. What do you say, brother, shall we do something? You got a cubbyhole?' 'Oh no, that's too scary for me, the gentleman sleeps next door, and if he hears a sound he's got ever such a light sleep.' 'Well then we'll tiptoe. Come on, give us a coffee and talk to us, I bet you've got a water boiler. No need to look after him, fat pig like that.'

So there's the four of them at the watchman's, in his office, drinking coffee, the wheelwright is the cutest of them, he's quietly having a chat with the watchman, and in the meantime the other two sneak off and fill their bags. The watchman keeps wanting to get up, he has to do his rounds, he wants no part of this, and finally the wheelwright says: 'Oh, why don't we just leave the two of them to it, if you don't notice anything, then no one can break in.' 'What do you mean: not notice.' 'You know what we can do: I'll tie you up, there's been a break-in, you're an old man, you can't be expected to put up much of a fight, if I throw a blanket over your head then before you know it you've been gagged and your ankles tied.' 'Oh.' 'So, don't fuss. You'll not risk your skull for a fat pig of a boss, will you? Finish your coffee, and then we'll work something out, where do you live, write it down, we'll do accounts fair and square, shake on it.' 'What's in it for me then?' 'Depends what we find. Hundred marks for sure.' 'Two hundred.' 'Orright.' They smoke, finish their coffee, and it's as good as done, get hold of a vehicle, the plumber telephones for one and they're in luck, half an hour later the car is at the door.

Next comes the fun part: the old guard sits down in his comfy chair, the wheelwright takes some copper wire and ties his legs together, but not too tight. The man has varicose veins, and he feels it. He wraps up his arms with phone wire, and now they're starting to rib him a bit, the old fellow, how much is it exactly he wants, was it 300 or 350. And then they pick up a couple of pairs of boys' trousers and a summer duster. With the trouser legs they tie the man to his chair, and him saying, I've had just about enough of this. But they go on ribbing him, he kicks up a fuss and they slap him around a bit, and before he can shout, there he is with the coat over his head and a towel tied round his chest just in case. The wheelwright writes out a couple of signs: 'Caution! Freshly trussed fowl!' And hangs those over the guard, front and back. Then they push off. They haven't had such easy pickings in a long time.

The guard meanwhile, he's getting anxious, and he's boiling

with rage in his trussage. How am I going to get out of here, and then they've gone and left the doors open so people can walk in off the streets and help themselves. He's not able to free his hands, but he can part the wire around his legs, if only he was able to see. Then the old man lurches forward and, taking tiny tippling steps, he shuffles blindly through the office, the chair tethered to his back, like a snail, his hands tied to his body, he can't manage to free them nor can he get the coat off his head. By butting his head forward he manages to grope his way out to the corridor door, which of course he can't open, and then he gets in a towering rage, he turns round and rams his chair against the door, front and sideways. He doesn't succeed in dislodging the chair but the door splinters, and you can hear it all over the building. The blindfolded guard keeps backing up and charging, crashing and banging against the door, someone must surely come, I need to see, those bastards are going to catch it, get that coat off my head, he cries for help, but the coat does its stuff. After about two minutes of this the proprietor is awake, and people are on their way down from the second floor. The old man is just then slumping back into his chair, unconscious. All that noise, and the break-in, and they tethered the old man, what are they doing hiring an old geezer like that for anyway, just to save a bit of money. False economy, I say.

The little gang is jubilant.

Christ what were we doing with Pums and Reinhold and that whole bother anyway.

Then things come to a head, but not in the way they had in mind.

Things come to a head, plumber Karl gets caught and spills some beans

Reinhold walks up to the plumber in the bar on Prenzlauer and asks to have a word, they've been looking for a locksmith, and not found anyone, they want to talk to Karl. They go into the back room, Reinhold says: 'Why aren't you in? Wotcher been doing with yourself anyway? We've been hearing things.' 'I'm not about to let myself be bossed about by you.' 'It seems you've found something else.' 'It's none of your beeswax what I'm doing.' 'I can see you're flush, but working and earning for us one day, and then sayonara the next, that's not on.' 'That's not on, that's not on! First it's: you useless git, then it's: oh, Karl, come back, we need you.' 'We do and all, we don't have anyone, or else give us back the money we give you. We don't use casual labour.' 'I dunno where you're going to get it from, Reinhold, because I ain't got it any more.' 'Then you'd better get back in with us.' 'I'm not doing that neither, as I've already explained.' 'Now, Karl, you know we'll break every bone in your body, and let you starve to death, if that's what you want.' 'Oh sure. You're not thinking straight. You're mistaking me for a little pig that will do whatever you tell it.' 'I see. Now, push off. I don't care if you're a pig or not. Think it over. We'll talk.' 'Sure we will.' There is a reaper.

Reinhold thinks things over with the others. Without a locksmith they're stymied, and conditions are favourable just now, Reinhold has orders from a couple of fences he's managed to prise away from Pums. They're all of one mind, the fear of God needs to be put into plumber Karl, he's a two-timer, and he stands to be thrown out of the gang.

The plumber can sense certain moves are afoot. He looks up Franz, who just then is spending a lot of time up in his room, he wants Franz to support him or clue him into their thinking. Franz says: 'First you duped us with the Stralauer Strasse job, and then you leave us in the lurch, that's about enough.' 'It's coz I want nothing to do with Reinhold. The man's an evil bastard, as you know well enough.' 'He's all right.' 'You're a fool, you don't understand anything, you've got no eyes.' 'Don't fill my head with your talk, Karl, I've got enough on my plate, we've got work to do, and you leave us in the lurch. I'd look out if I was you, you're not in a good way.' 'Because of Reinhold? Don't make me laugh. See me laugh. That's how wide I can open my mouth. This is my belly wobbling. I'm as strong as he is. He takes me for his little porker, well, I'm not saying anything. Let him come.' 'Push off, but I tell you, watch yourself.'

And then, as luck would have it, two days later the plumber and his two accomplices do a job on Friedenstrasse that goes wrong. The wheelwright is nabbed too, only the third man, who was posted as lookout, managed to get away. In short order the detectives establish that Karl was also involved in the Elsasser Strasse job, it's his fingerprints all over the coffee cups.

How come I got caught, thinks Karl, how did the cops get wind of this job. It must have been cunt Reinhold who tipped them off. The malice! Because I wouldn't go back to them. The bastard wants to see me off, a wretch catching me in his trap. Was there ever such a louse. He sends a secret message to the wheelwright, Reinhold's to blame, he's a nark, I tell you, he's part of it. The wheelwright gives him a nod in the corridor. Karl asks to see the magistrate, and in the police station he says: 'Reinhold was in on the job, but he baled beforehand.'

They bring in Reinhold that afternoon. He denies everything, he's got an alibi. He is pale with fury when he sees the other two at the magistrate's and confronts them both, and the two cunts claiming he was in on the suit job. The magistrate listens to them all, looks at the faces, something's amiss here, the two sides are that furious with each other. Sure enough, two days later Reinhold's alibi is confirmed, he's a ponce, but he's got nothing to do with this.

It's the beginning of October.

Reinhold is freed, the police know he's up to something, they will keep an eye on him. Meanwhile the two others, the wheelwright and Karl, are laid into by the magistrate, they're to stop lying, Reinhold has had his alibi confirmed. Thereupon the two of them are mum.

Karl sits in his cell, boiling with rage. His brother-in-law, the brother of his ex-wife, who he's kept up with, comes by to visit him in prison. He hooks him up with a lawyer, he insists on a lawyer, an expert in criminal law. He sounds him out for a bit, and then he asks him what the situation is if you've helped bury a dead person. 'Why, how come?' 'What if you run into someone, and they happen to be dead, and you help bury them?' 'Maybe someone you want to hide, shot by the police, something like that?' 'Well, anyway, if you haven't killed them yourself, and you don't want the body to be found. Is that serious?' 'Well, were you acquainted with the dead party, do you stand to gain any advantage from burying them?' 'Not exactly an advantage, but it's out of friendship, you're helping out, the dead person's lying there, sure you knew them, you don't want them to be found.' 'Found by the police? Actually that's just suppressing information. But how did he meet his death?' 'I dunno. Wasn't there. It's to do with someone else. Nothing to do wi me. Didn't even know about it, notta thing. Corpse lying there. And then it's, all right, lend a hand, let's get him buried.' 'Who says so?' 'To bury him? Oh, never mind, someone or other. I just want to know what my situation is. Have I broken the law if I helped bury them?' 'You know, the way you're telling me, not really, not in a substantial way. If you weren't involved in the death, had no interest in it. Just remains the question why you helped?' 'I lent a hand, didn't I, friendship, I suppose, but that doesn't matter, any road, I wasn't involved, had no interest in him either way.' 'An honour killing, something like that? ' 'Mebbe.' 'Man, stay out of it. I still don't know what you were doing.' 'That's all right, Your Honour, I've found out as much as I needed to know.' 'Sure you don't want to tell me about it in greater detail?' 'I'll sleep on it.'

And then Karl the plumber lies in his cot all night, trying vainly to sleep, and not able to, and he's furious with himself for being the biggest fool in the world, I tried to squeal on Reinhold, he couldn't help noticing, and now he's not around any more, he will have done one. I'm a fool. A hard bastard like that, he won't lift a finger for me, but I swear I'm going to get him.

For Karl the night is never-ending, when is the first bell going to ring, it's all the same to me, there's no punishment for just assisting in a burial, and even if I get a month or two this guy's going to get life, he's not going to walk out, that is, if they don't go all the way and knock his block off. When is the magistrate coming, how late is it going to get, and in the meantime Reinhold will have hopped on a train and gone. There's never been another bastard like that, I can't believe Biberkopf is his friend, what's he going to live off, with one arm, shameful the way they treat invalids these days.

Eventually the panopticon comes to life, Karl pokes out his tin flag right away, by eleven he's with the magistrate. Who pulls a face. 'You really don't like him, do you. Happy to have him charged a second time. Well I hope for your sake you haven't misjudged it.' But this time Karl's information is so detailed that by noon he's in a car, the magistrate in the front seat, and a couple of strongly built detectives in the back, flanking Karl, who has his hands cuffed. Their destination is Freienwalde.

There they are, driving the old roads. It feels good to be driving again. Damn, if only he could get out of the car. The bastards have braceleted him, though, so nothing doing. They've got pistols as well. Nothing doing, nothing doing. Driving, driving, shooting down the avenue. I'll give you 180 days, Mitzi, on my lap, sweet child, he's a bastard, Reinhold, walks over corpses, you wait, sunshine. Think about Mitzi again, biting her in the tongue, she knew how to kiss all right, which way shall we go, left or right, I don't mind, my darling, sweet child.

They go over the hill and enter the woods.

It's pretty in Freienwalde, it's a bathing spa, a little holiday spot. The little spa gardens are freshly sprinkled with yellow gravel, there at the back is the inn with the terrace, that's where the three of us sat together. In Switzerland and in Tyrol, that's where a man feels swoll, in Tyrol there's warm milk straight from the odder, and in Switzerland there's a little dodder of a little modder, yodelay-ihay. Then he bunked off with her, I got a couple of bills and minded my own business, I sold him that poor girl, and I'm doing time for him right now.

Here are the woods, autumnal now, it's a sunny day, nothing moving in the tree tops. 'It's along here somewhere, he had a torch with him, it won't be easy to find, but I'll recognize the spot if I see it, it was in the open, and there was a crooked pine and a dell.' 'There's no shortage of dells here.' 'Sorry, Inspector. We've gone too far. It was only twenty or twenty-five minutes from the inn. Not this far.' 'But you told us you were running.' 'Yes, but only in the woods, not on the road, that would have attracted notice.'

And then there's the open spot, the crooked pine there, and

everything as it was on that day. I am yours, her heart to pulp, her eyes to pulp, her mouth to pulp, let's go a bit further, don't press me so hard. 'There's the black pine, you're right.'

Men came on horseback over the land, they were mounted on little brown horses, they came from far away. They kept asking where the highway was, then they got to the water, the great lake, where they dismounted. They made the horses fast to an oak tree, they said prayers by the water, they threw themselves to the ground, then they took a boat and sailed over the water. They sang to the lake, they spoke to the lake. They weren't looking for treasure in the lake, they wanted to pay their respects to the great lake, a chieftain of theirs lay at the bottom. Hence, hence these men.

The police had shovels and picks with them, plumber Karl went around and showed them the place. They dug their shovels into the ground, and from the first moment the ground was loose, then they dug deeper, threw the sandy soil up in the air, the ground had been churned up, there were pine cones under the ground, the plumber Karl stands there and watches and watches and waits. It was here, this is the place, this is where they buried the girl. 'But how deep was it?' 'Not more than a foot.' 'We're past that already.' 'But this is the place all right, keep digging.' 'Keep digging, keep digging, but there's nothing there.' The ground is churned up, they shovel up green grass from the depths, somebody must have been digging here as recently as this morning or last night. She must turn up soon, he's already holding his sleeve in front of his nose, she must have been gone, how many months is it now, and there's been rain too. The one digging down below calls up: 'Do you remember what she was wearing?' 'A dark skirt, pink blouse.' 'Silk?' 'Could have been, but it was pale pink anyway.' 'Something like this?' And one of the men has a lacy border in his hand, it's soiled and mucky-looking, but it's pink all right. He shows it to the magistrate: 'Could be a bit off the sleeve.' They go on digging. It's pretty clear: something's happened here. Dug up maybe yesterday or this morning. Karl stands by; so he was right, Reinhold sensed something was up, dug her up, maybe threw her in the river or something, what a piece of work. Off to the side, the magistrate is in conversation with the detective, it's a lengthy conversation, the detective takes notes. Then three of them walk back to the car; one man is left to guard the spot.

As they walk, the magistrate asks Karl: 'So when you came along, I suppose the girl was already dead?' 'Yes.' 'Can you prove it?' 'Why?' 'Well, if Reinhold says you killed her, or helped kill her?' 'I helped carry her. What would I have killed her for?' 'For the same reason he killed her or is said to have killed her.' 'But I wasn't even with her that evening.' 'But you were in the afternoon.' 'But not after. She was still alive then.' 'It's not an easy case to make.'

In the car, the magistrate asks Karl: 'Where were you then in the evening and the night after the business with Reinhold?' Fuck, I'll tell him. 'I left. He gave me his papers, I scarpered, so that, if anything came to light, I'd be able to prove my alibi.' 'Curious. And what possessed you to do it, were you so tight with him?' 'Ach. I'm just a poor bugger, and he paid me for it.' 'And now he's not your friend any more, or he's run out of money?' 'My friend? No, Your Honour, he's never my friend. You know what I'm in for, the break-in with the security guard and that. He shopped me.'

The magistrate and detective exchange glances, the car flies on its way, dips into potholes, bounces up again, the avenue shoots by, this is where I drove with him, 180 days I give you. 'I expect something cropped up that damaged your friendship?' 'Well, the way it is (he's trying to sound me out, no, stop right there, we're not falling for that one). It's like this, Your Honour: Reinhold is a madman, and the latest thing is he wanted to rub me out.' 'Oh, so he made an attempt on your life?' 'Not as such. But he made remarks.' 'Nothing more?' 'No.' 'Well, let's see.'

Mitzi's body is found a couple of days later, half a mile away in the same woods. Following early newspaper reports, two assistant gardeners came forward who had seen a man in the area lugging a heavy suitcase. They wondered what he might be carrying, later they saw him taking a breather, sitting in the dell. When they went back that way half an hour later he was still sitting there, in his shirtsleeves. This time the suitcase was gone, it was probably in the hole. They had an excellent description of the man. About five foot ten, broad shoulders, black stiff hat, light-coloured summer clothes in dove-grey, houndstooth jacket, drags his legs as though he's walking with a limp, very high forehead with horizontal creases. In the vicinity of the area the two gardeners were talking about, there are a lot of dells, police dogs come up with nothing, then all traces of recent activity are examined. In one of them, after a couple of spits, they struck a large brown cardboard box, tied with string. When the officers open it they find women's clothing, a torn chemise, long, flesh-coloured stockings, an old brown wool dress, used handkerchiefs, a couple of toothbrushes. The cardboard is wet, but not sodden; the whole thing looks as though it's not been there very long. Strange. The deceased had a pink blouse.

And shortly afterwards in another dell they find the suitcase, and the body curled up inside it. It's tightly secured with venetian-blind straps. By evening there are reports buzzing round all the stations in the country, descriptions of a man the police would like to interview, and so on and so forth.

Reinhold knows what's coming from the moment he was questioned at the station. And he decides to get Franz involved. Why couldn't he have done it. What can Karl the plumber prove. Doubtful that anyone saw me in Freienwalde. And if someone saw me in the inn, on the way, that's no matter, I'll try it anyway, Franz has got to go, it'll look as though he was in on this.

The afternoon he gets out, Reinhold is up at Franz's, Karl the plumber has squealed, you'd better get out of here. Franz does his packing in fifteen minutes, Reinhold helps him, both of them cursing Karl for a grass, then Eva takes Franz round to Toni's, an old girlfriend of hers in Wilmersdorf. Reinhold goes out to Wilmersdorf with them and they buy suitcases together, Reinhold wants to go abroad, he is in the market for something enormous, first a wardrobe trunk, then he decides in favour of a wooden seachest, the biggest one he can lift, I don't trust railway porters, they're nosy parkers, I'll send you my address, Franz, remember me to Eva.

The great disaster of Prague, twenty-one confirmed dead, 150 still missing. The pile of rubble that only moments earlier had been a seven-storey tenement, now many more dead and badly injured are buried there. The reinforced concrete structure, weighing 800 tonnes, collapsed onto its two subterranean storeys. A policeman on duty in the street outside warned pedestrians away when he heard the creaking. With great presence of mind he leapt in the path of an approaching tram and applied the brakes himself. Violent storms over the Atlantic. A succession of low-pressure ridges are advancing across the European mainland, while two highs are stuck fast, one in Central America and the other in the North Atlantic between Greenland and Ireland. The newspapers are bringing pages and pages about the *Graf Zeppelin* and its impending flight. Every detail of the airship's construction, the personality of the commander and the prospects for the enterprise are itemized, while lead articles hymn German efficiency in general and Zeppelin's airships in particular. In spite of all the propaganda for fixed-wing aeroplanes, it is thought that the future of flight lies squarely with the airship. But the *Zeppelin* isn't flying, Eckener is against putting it at unnecessary risk.

The trunk containing Mitzi is opened. She was the daughter of a tram conductor in Bernau. There were three kids at home, the mother walked out on the father, no one knows why. Mitzi is parked at home all alone, and given the household to run. In the evenings she sometimes hopped on the train to Berlin and went to dances, at Lestmann's and opposite, now and again a man took her back to a hotel, and then it got late, and she didn't dare go home, she stayed in Berlin, and then she met Eva, and things took their course. All in the vicinity of the Stettiner Bahnhof. Life smiled at Mitzi, who at the time was going by Sonia, she had a large circle of acquaintances and quite a few friends, but after a while she was regularly seen in the company of a powerfully built man with one arm, with whom Mitzi fell in love at first sight and to whom she remained devoted to the end. A bad end, a sad end that Mitzi came to in the end. Why, oh why, what did she do wrong, she came from

Bernau to the whirlpool metropolis of Berlin, she was no innocent, by no means, but she felt an inner, inextinguishable love for the man who was like a husband to her, and whom she tended like a child. She was shattered because she went there, as luck would have it, to stand by her man, and that was her life, hard though it is to contemplate. She went to Freienwalde to protect him, and there she was strangled, strangled, died, finished, and that was her life.

They take an impression of her face and neck, and she is just a murder file, a technical process not dissimilar to the laying of a telephone line, that's how far along she is. They make up a mask of her, paint everything in natural colours, it looks eerily real, like a kind of celluloid. And lo there is Mitzi, her face and neck in a filing cabinet, come to me, come to me, we'll be home soon, Aschinger's, comfort me, I'm yours. She is behind glass, her face a pulp, heart a pulp, crotch a pulp, smile a pulp, comfort me, please.

So I returned, and considered all the oppressions that are done under the sun

Dear Franz, what are you sighing for, why does Eva have to keep sidling up to you and ask you what you're thinking, and no answer, and sidle away again with no answer, why are you depressed, and now you're keeping your head down, down, down, little hole in corner, little curtain, just taking little tiny baby steps? You know something about life, it's not as though you got here yesterday from another planet, you have a nose for things and you notice them. And now you see nothing and hear nothing, but somehow you sense it, you don't dare level your eyes at it, you squinny away, but you don't run either, you're too resolute for that, you've got your teeth gritted, you're no coward, but you don't know what might happen, and whether you're up to it, whether your shoulders are broad enough to take it.

How much did Job, the man from the land of Uz, suffer before he learnt everything, before nothing more could befall him. From

Saba enemies fell upon him, and murdered his shepherds, the fire of God fell from the heavens and burnt up his flocks and herds, the Chaldeans slew his camels and their drovers, his sons and daughters were sat in the house of the oldest brother, when a wind blew out of the desert and smote the four corners of the house, and the children were all killed.

That was plenty, but it was not enough. Job rent his clothes, bit his hands, tore his hair, he heaped earth on himself. But it was not enough. Job was struck with a plague of boils, he had boils from the sole of his foot to the crown of his head, he sat in the sand, pus flowing down his body, he picked up a potsherd to scrape his skin withal.

His friends came to visit him, there was Eliphaz the Temanite, Bildad the Shuhite and Zophar the Naamathite, they all came from afar to comfort him, they cried and wept terribly. They didn't recognize Job, so terribly was he stricken, who had had seven sons and three daughters and 7,000 sheep, 3,000 camels, 500 yoke of cattle, 500 she-asses and a very great household.

You haven't lost as much as Job from the land of Uz, Franz Biberkopf, your woes are taking their time to descend on you. And step by step you drag your way to what has befallen you, you have a thousand kind words for yourself, you flatter yourself, because you want to take a chance, you are determined to come closer to yourself, to risk the ultimate, but oh woe, the very ultimate thing of all? Not that, oh not that. You buck yourself up, you coddle yourself: oh come, nothing will happen, we can't avoid it. But something in you won't have it. You sigh: where can I find protection, misfortune is descending on me, where is there something I can hold on to. It's coming ever closer. And you draw nearer, like a snail, you're no coward, you have more than just strong muscles, you are Franz Biberkopf, you are the cobra. Watch it coil, inch by inch, against the monstrous beast that stands there about to pounce.

You will lose no money, Franz, but you will be burnt to your innermost core. See the whore rejoicing! The whore of Babylon! And there came one of the seven angels which had the seven vials, and talked with me, saying unto me, Come hither; I will shew unto thee the judgment of the great whore that sitteth upon many waters: And the woman was arrayed in purple and scarlet colour, and decked with gold and precious stones and pearls, having a golden cup in her hand full of abominations and filthiness of her fornication: And upon her forehead was a name written, Mystery, Babylon the Great, the Mother of Harlots and Abominations of the Earth. The woman is drunken with the blood of saints.

You sense her now, you can feel her. Will you be strong, that you won't go under.

Franz Biberkopf sits and waits in the nice bright room in the garden house on Wilmersdorfer Strasse.

The cobra coils, lies in the sun, warming itself. It is bored, and it is full of strength, and it wants to do something, it is lying around, they haven't yet agreed as to where they will meet, and fat Toni has got him a pair of dark horn-rims, I need to buy myself a whole new wardrobe, maybe I'll get myself one of those duelling scars over the cheek. Down there someone is running across the courtyard. Is he ever in a hurry. Take your time, sunshine. If people weren't in such a rush, they'd live twice as long and achieve three times as much. It's the same thing with the six-day races, you go round and round, stay calm, patience, the saucepan won't boil over, it doesn't matter if the spectators boo, what do they know about it.

There's a knock on the door outside. What's this, why don't they use the bell. Damn it, I'm going to go outside, listen.

Step by little step you get closer, you brace yourself with a thousand comforting words, you flatter yourself, you bribe yourself, you're prepared for anything, if not for the most ultimate thing of all, oh, not for that.

Listen out. Who's this. I know her. I know that voice. Wailing, crying, crying. Let's have a peek. Oh Lord, oh my God, what's going through your mind? The things that go through a man's mind. I know her. That's Eva.

The door is open. Eva is outside, fat Toni is holding her in her arms. A whimpering and lamenting, something's up with the woman. All the things that go through your mind, all the things that have happened, Mitzi crying, Reinhold lying in bed. 'Hello, Eva. Don't take on so, woman, what's the matter, it may never happen.' 'Let me go.' Listen to her grunt, she must have had a beating, somebody's been laying into her. She's talked to Herbert, Herbert knows about the baby. 'Did Herbert beat you?' 'Let go of me, don't touch me.' The way she's looking at me. She doesn't want anything to do with me. When it was her idea. What can the matter be, what's got into her, people will come, I'd better bolt the door. There's Toni standing there, looking after Eva: 'There, there, Eva, it's all right, tell me what the trouble is, come in won't you, where's Herbert?' 'You won't get me to go in there, I'm not going in there.' 'Well, then stop here, sit down, I'll fix us some coffee. Franz, leave us alone.' 'Why should I leave you alone, I've not done anything.'

At that Eva makes big, round, terrible eyes, as though she wanted to eat him, and she screams, clutches at Franz's weskit: 'I want him there, I want him, he's to be there too, you come with me.' What's got into her, the woman's lost her marbles, somebody must have said something to her. Then she's on the sofa, gibbering away next to plump Toni. She looks all puffy and nervous, that's to do with her condition, although that was me that caused it, and I'm hardly going to hurt her. Then Eva puts her arms around fat Toni and whispers something in her ear, first she can't speak but finally she manages to get it out. Now Toni looks all shocked. She claps her hands together, and Eva is gibbering and pulling a crumpled sheet of newspaper out of her handbag, they've gone mad the pair of them, what's this performance they're putting on for me, what does it say in the newspaper, maybe it's something about the job on Stralauer Strasse, Franz gets to his feet and roars, these fucking stupid bitches. 'You idiots. Stop your show you're putting on for me, you think I'm your idiot.' 'For goodness' sake, for goodness' sake,' the fat one sitting there, Eva still gibbering away to herself not saying anything and whimpering and shaking. At that Franz reaches across the table and snatches the newspaper out of the fat one's hands.

There are two photos side by side, eh, eh, terrible, terrible gruesome horror, but, hey – that's me, what am I doing there, must be because of the Stralauer Strasse job, what for, gruesome horror, but that's me, and that's Reinhold, title: Murder, murder of a prostitute in Freienwalde, one Emilie Parsunke from Bernau. Mitzi! What's this all about. Me. Behind the stove sits a mouse, wants out.

His hand clutches the newspaper. He slowly lowers himself into his chair and sits there shrunkenly. What's it say then. Behind the stove sits a mouse.

So the two women are staring and crying and gawping at him, what's the matter with those two, murder, how can that be, Mitzi, I'm going mad, what's that, what have they written. His hand returns to the table, and there it says in the newspaper, here: my picture, me, and Reinhold, murder, Emilie Parsunke from Bernau, in Freienwalde, what's she doing out in Freienwalde. What newspaper is this anyway, oh, the *Morgenpost*. His hand rises with the paper, his hand falls with the paper. Eva, what's she doing, she's changed her expression, she's looking at him now, she's not howling any more: 'Well, Franz?' A voice, someone said my name, I have to reply, two women, a murder, what's murder, out in Freienwalde, I murdered her in Freienwalde, hang on, I've never been to Freienwalde, where the fuck is Freienwalde anyway. 'Go on, Franz, say something.'

Franz looks at her with his big eyes, he balances the newspaper on the palm of his hand, his head is trembling, he reads and speaks in jerks, he rumbles. Murder in Freienwalde, Emilie Parsunke from Bernau, born 12 June 1908. That's Mitzi, Eva. He scratches his jaw, looks at Eva with his open, empty expression, you can't see anything there. That's Mitzi, Eva. It is. What – say, Eva. She's dead. That's why we didn't find her. 'And that's you in the paper, Franz.' 'Me?'

He picks up the paper, looks into it. She's right. That's my picture.

His torso is rocking back and forth. For the love of God, for the love of God, Eva. She is more and more frightened, pushes a chair between them. He continues to rock. For the love of God, Eva, for the love of God, the love of God. And continues to rock. Now he starts to huff and blow. There's an expression on his face as though it was a joke. 'For the love of God, what are we going to do, Eva, what are we going to do.' 'So why did they have the picture of you for?' 'Where?' 'There.' 'Christ, I don't know. I've no idea, what is that, how did they come up with that, haha, that's funny.' And now he looks at her with a helpless expression, and trembles, and she's glad, because that's a human emotion, the tears spill from her eyes, and fat Toni starts to whimper too, then his arm goes round her back, his hand is on her shoulder, his face pressed against her throat, Franz whimpers: 'What's going on, Eva, what's happened to our wee Mitzi, what's happened, she's died, something's happened to her, that's it, she didn't leave me, someone killed her, Eva, someone killed our little Mitzi, my Mitzikins, what's the matter, can that be right, tell me it's not true.'

And he thinks of his little Mitzi, and something comes up in him, a kind of fear, terror beckons to him, there it is, there is a reaper, Death yclept, he comes with axes and rods, he blows a flute, then he cracks open his jaws and he takes a trombone, will he play the trombone, will he hit the cymbals, will the terrible black storm goat come, boom, always gently, boom-vroom.

Eva watches the slow grinding of his jaws. Eva holds Franz. His head trembles, his voice comes, the first note creaks, then it gets quieter. Not one word.

He was lying under the car, it felt like now, there is a mill, a stone quarry, which poured over me incessantly, I pull myself together, it doesn't matter what I do, nothing helps, it will break me, and if I'm a steel beam, it will still break me.

Franz churns and mutters. 'Something's coming.' 'What's coming?' What sort of mill was it, the works are churning, a windmill, a water-mill. 'Watch yourself, Franz, they're looking for you.' And I'm supposed to have done her in, me, he's back to trembling, his face is pulled into a grin, I smacked her once, they must think because I done Ida. 'Sit down, Franz, don't go out, where will you go, they'll spot you with your one arm.' 'They won't get me, Eva, not if I don't want, you can bet your bottom dollar they won't. I have to go out to the advertising column. I need to see it. I need to read about it in the bar, in the newspapers, the things they're writing, and what happened.' And then he's standing in front of Eva, staring at her, can't get a single word out, so long as he doesn't laugh: 'Look at me, Eva, is there something on me, look at me.' 'No, no,' she screams and holds him. 'Look at me, is there something about me, there must be something about me.'

No, no, she cries, and wails, and he goes to the door, smiles, takes down his hat from the hatstand, and walks out.

And behold the tears of such as were oppressed, and they had no comforter

Franz has an artificial arm, he doesn't wear it often, now he goes out on the street with it, the artificial hand in his coat pocket and in his left the cigar. He had trouble getting out of the flat. Eva yelled and threw herself in front of the door, he had to promise he wasn't leaving and that he would be careful, he said: 'I'll be back at tea-time,' and then he went downstairs.

Franz Biberkopf wasn't caught, not as long as he didn't want to be. He was flanked by two guardian angels that drew attention away from him.

By four o'clock he's back for tea. Herbert's there too. For the first time they hear a long speech from Franz. He read the paper while he was out, including about his friend Karl the plumber, who squealed on them. He's not sure why he did that. And Karl the plumber was also of the party in Freienwalde, where they dragged Mitzi off to. Reinhold did that by force. He got hold of a car and maybe he drove Mitzi a ways, then Karl got in and they held her down and dragged her off to Freienwalde, maybe at night. Maybe she was dead before they even got there. 'And why did Reinhold do it?' 'He threw me under the wheels, may as well tell you now, it was him, but never mind, I'm not upset with him, you learn as you go along, otherwise you'll never understand anything. Then you just run around like an ox and don't know the first thing about life, so no, I'm not upset with him. Then he wanted to do me down, thought he had me under his thumb which wasn't the case, and so he took Mitzi off me, and done this to her. It's not her fault.'

Therefore, oh wherefore, oh therefore. Thunder of drums, company, by the right, quick march. When the soldiers march through the town, oh wherefore, oh therefore, and all on account of the chingderada bumderada bum.

So I marched in on him, and so he replied, and it was accursed and wrong of me to march.

It was wrong of me to march, wrong, wrong.

But that doesn't matter, that doesn't matter any more.

Herbert is staring, Eva can't produce a squeak. Herbert: 'Why didn't you tell Mitzi anything about that?' 'It's not my fault, there's nothing you can do about it, he could equally well have shot me when I was up in his room. I tell you, there's no remedy.'

Seven heads and ten horns, in one hand a cup full of horrors. They'll get all of me now, there's nothing to be done about it.

'If only you'd let on, man, Mitzi would be alive now and someone else would be wandering about with his head under his arm.' 'It's not my fault. You never know what someone like that will do.' 'I would.' Eva begs him: 'Don't go round to him, Herbert, I'm scared too.' 'We'll be careful. First of all, find out where he's hiding, and then half an hour later the cops will have him.' Franz gestures: 'Leave off, Herbert, he's not yours. Shake on it, all right?' Eva: 'Go on, Herbert. And then what are you going to do, Franz?' 'Who cares? May as well put me out with the trash.'

And he walks over to the corner and turns his back on them.

And they hear a sobbing, sobbing, whimpering, he is crying for himself and Mitzi, they can hear it, Eva is crying and shouting across the table, the newspaper with 'Murder' on it is still lying there, Mitzi has been murdered, no one lifted a finger for her, that's what's happened here.

Then I praised the dead which are already dead

In the evening, Franz Biberkopf heads out again. Five sparrows fly across the Bayrischer Platz over his head. They are five murdered villains who have run into Franz Biberkopf many times before. They are considering what to do with him, what decision to come to in his regard, how to make him uncertain and apprehensive, what beam to have him stumble over.

One screams: there he goes. Look, he's got his falsie on, he's not given up yet, he wants to be incognito.

The second: all the crimes he's committed. He's a serious criminal, he should be put away, and for life. Killing one woman, thefts, break-ins, and now a second woman. What does he think he's playing at?

The third: he's puffing himself up. He's playing the innocent. The law-abiding citizen. Look at the wretch. If a policeman comes along, we'll knock his hat off.

The first one again: why should someone like that even be alive? I snuffed it in prison at the end of nine years. I was younger'n him and I was already gone, I couldn't cheep. Take your hat off, you ape, take your silly glasses off, you're not a journalist you bloody fool, you don't even know the times table, and you go putting on horn-rims like a scholar, we've got your number.

The fourth one: hush, not so loud. What do you want with him. Look at him, he's got a head, he's a biped. Us little sparrows, the most we can do is shit on his hat.

The fifth: yell at him. He's crazy, he's got a screw loose. He's out strolling with two angels, his sweetheart is a mock-up at the police station, we need to do something. Shout at him.

There they swoop, screech, yammer over his head. And Franz lifts his head, his thoughts are in pieces, the birds scold and argue away.

Autumn is here, in the Tauentzienpalast they're showing *The Last Days of Francisco*, fifty dance-hall beauties are in the Jägerkasino, you may kiss me for a bouquet of lilac. There Franz concludes: I'm finished, it's all up with me, I've had it.

The trams go barrelling down the streets, they're all on their way somewhere, where shall I go. The 51 to Nordend, Schillerstrasse, Pankow, Breitestrasse, Bahnhof Schönhauser Allee, Stettiner Bahnhof, Potsdamer Bahnhof, Nollendorfplatz,

Bayrischer Platz, Uhlandstrasse, Bahnhof Schmargendorf, Grune-wald, hop on shall I. Hello, I'm sitting here, take me wherever you're going. And Franz starts to look around at the city like a dog that's lost a scent. What a city, what a stonking great city, and what lives he once led when he was living there. He gets out at the Stettiner Bahnhof, then he walks down Invaliden-strasse, there's the Rosenthaler Tor. Fabisch Konfektion, that's where I used to stand selling me ties last Christmas. He goes to Tegel on the 41. And the instant the red walls surface, the red walls on the left, the great heavy iron gate, that settles him. That's part of my life too, and I need to take a good look at it, a good long look.

The walls are red, the avenue leading up to them long, the 41 takes you past the entrance, General-Pape-Strasse. West Reinicken-dorf, Tegel, the Borsig works. And Franz Biberkopf stands outside the red walls, and he crosses over to the other side, where there's a bar. And the red buildings behind the walls start to flutter and bulge and puff out their cheeks. At all the windows there are convicts, nutting themselves against the bars, their hair is shaved to half a millimetre, they look wretched, underfed, their faces are grey and stubbly, they roll their eyes and lament. There are the murderers, the break-ins, petty thefts, forgeries, rapes, the whole statute book, and all complaining with grey faces, sitting there, grey, now they've squeezed the life out of Mitzi.

And Franz Biberkopf wanders round the enormous prison that continues to tremble and to bulge and to call out to him, over the fields, through the wood and back onto the street with the trees.

Now he's on the tree-lined street again. I never killed Mitzi. I didn't do it. I've got no business here, that's history, there's nothing for me in Tegel, whatever happened, it's nothing to do with me.

It's six at night when Franz says to himself, I want to see Mitzi, I need to go to the cemetery they buried her in.

The five jailbirds, the sparrows, are with him again, they are sitting up on a telegraph pole, shouting down to him: go to her, you crook, have you got the neck, aren't you ashamed of going to see her? She called out to you when she was lying in the dell. Look her over in the cemetery.

May they all rest in peace. In Berlin in 1927, there were 48,742 deaths, not counting stillbirths.

Of TB 4,570, 6,443 of cancer, 5,656 of heart disease, 4,818 of vascular diseases, 5,140 of strokes, 2,419 of pneumonia, 961 of whooping cough, 562 children died of diphtheria, 123 of scarlet fever, 93 of measles, 3,640 died in infancy. There were 42,696 births.

The dead are lying in their graves, the attendant walks around with a pointed stick, picking up bits of rubbish.

It's half past six, still light, and a young woman in a fur coat, no hat, is sitting on her grave under a beech tree, lowers her head and doesn't speak. She is wearing black kid gloves, a piece of paper in her hand is a small envelope, Franz reads: 'I can no longer be among you. Greet my parents for me, and my baby. Life has become a torment for me. Bieriger is to blame. I hope he's enjoying himself. He used me as a toy and emptied the life out of me. A big cruel bastard. He's the only reason I went to Berlin, and he alone made me unhappy. I have been ruined.'

Franz passes the envelope back to her: 'O woe, o woe, is Mitzi here?' Don't be sad, don't be sad. 'O woe, o woe, where is my little Mitzi?'

There is another grave like a big soft ottoman, a learned professor is reclining on it, smiling down to him: 'What afflicts you, my son?' 'I wanted to see Mitzi. I'm just visiting here.' 'Whereas I'm already dead, it doesn't do to take life too seriously, or death either. Make everything easy on yourself. When I'd had enough and became ill, what did I do? Am I supposed to waste away? What for? I had them leave a bottle of morphia at my bedside, then I asked for music, piano, jazz, the latest hits. I asked to be read to from Plato, the great Symposium, those beautiful dialogues, and secretly the while I administered injection after injection to myself under the sheets, I counted them, three times the lethal dose. And all the while I listened to the tinkle and parp, and my friend reading to me about old Socrates. Yes, there are some clever people, and some not so clever.'

'Never mind reading aloud and morphine. Just tell me where to find Mitzi?'

Terrible, a man hanging from a tree, his wife stands by him wailing just as Franz approaches: 'Come and help me, cut him down, please. He doesn't want to stay in his grave, he keeps climbing up in his tree, and hangs there crookedly.' 'O my God, why?' 'My Ernst was sick for such a long time, no one could help him, and they didn't want to transfer him either, they kept calling him a malingerer. Then he went down into the cellar and got himself a hammer and nail. I can still hear him hammering away down there, I'm thinking what's he doing, I'm glad he's working at something and not just sitting around, maybe he's building a new hutch for the rabbit. Then he didn't come up in the evening, and I began to worry and think, what's keeping him, are the cellar keys where they're supposed to be, no, they weren't. Then the neighbours went down and they sent for the police. He hammered a strong nail into the ceiling, even though he was no great weight himself, I suppose he wanted to make sure. What are you looking for, young man? Why are you whimpering? Do you want to kill yourself?'

'No, but my sweetheart was murdered, I'm not sure if she's here or not.'

'Oh, you'd best look round at the back, where the new ones go.'

Then Franz is lying on the path beside an empty grave, incapable of howling, so he bites in the earth: Mitzi, what did we do, how could they do that to you, you never hurt a fly, Mitzi. What can I do, why don't they throw me in a grave too, how long can I go on for?

And then he gets up, he can hardly walk, pulls himself together, totters out between the rows of gravestones.

Then Franz Biberkopf, the gent with the stiff arm, piles into a cab that takes him to Bayrischer Platz. Eva has an awful lot to do, an awful, awful lot. Eva has days' and nights' work cut out for her. He doesn't live and he doesn't die. Herbert doesn't show up much.

There are a couple of days when Franz and Herbert take off after

Reinhold. Herbert is packing, and he keeps his ear to the ground, he wants Reinhold. To begin with Franz doesn't care much either way, then he gets into it, it's his last medicine on this earth.

The fortress is completely surrounded, the last sallies are undertaken, but they are nothing but diversionary tactics

We are into November. Summer is long past. With the autumn has come the rain. The weeks of pleasurable heat in the streets are a distant memory, when people went around in light clothes and the women wore little more than their petticoats: a white dress and a cloche hat was what Franz's girl, Mitzi, wore when she went out to Freienwalde that time, never to come back, that was summer. Before the court is the case of one Bergmann, who was an economic parasite and common danger and without scruple. The *Graf Zeppelin* arrives in Berlin in poor visibility, the sky was starry when it left Friedrichshafen at 2.17. In order to avoid the bad weather reported over central Germany, the airship takes its course via Stuttgart, Darmstadt, Frankfurt am Main, Giessen, Kassel and Rathenow. At 8.35 it is over Nauen, 8.45 over Staaken. Shortly before 9 a.m. the Zeppelin appears over the city, in spite of the rain the rooftops were occupied by curious onlookers who hailed the airship's arrival with jubilation as it meandered on over the north and east of the city. At 9.45 the first mooring rope came down in Staaken.

Franz and Herbert are prowling through Berlin, they are out most of the time. Franz stays in Salvation Army shelters and men's homes, wanders through the August refuge on Auguststrasse. He sits in the Dresdener Strasse, in the Salvation Army, where he went with Reinhold. They sing # 66 from the songbook: 'Say, why wait, my brother? Arise and join our merry throng. Your Saviour has been calling you, to give you peace and quiet. Refrain: Why? Why? Why not join the merry throng? Why? Why do you not want peace and quiet? Don't you feel it in your heart, brother, the living tug of the spirit? Don't you want relief from your sins? O fly to Jesus, brother, do! Say, why wait longer, my brother. Quickly death and judgment approach. O come, while the gates are still open. And Jesus's blood will speak for you!'

Franz goes to the homeless shelter on Fröbelstrasse, to the Palme, to look for Reinhold there. He lies down on the charpoy, today on one, next day on another, 10 pfennigs for a haircut, 5 for a shave, there they all are, sorting out their papers, trading shoes and shirts, Christ, is this your first time here or something, keep em on, not unless you want to go looking for them in the morning, see, this is what you do, you put the foot of your bed in each boot, they steal everything here, even false teeth. Do you want a tattoo? And peace, nights. Black peace, snoring like a lumberyard, I never clapped eyes on him. Quiet. Bim bim bim, what's this, prison, I thought I was back in Tegel. Wake up. Fight going on. Back on the street, 6 a.m., the women standing there, waiting for their man, accompany him to the alehouse, gamble away what they've managed to get from begging.

Reinhold's not here, stupid idea to go looking for him, he'll be chasing skirts, Elfriede, Emilie, Karoline, Lili; brunettes, blondes.

And at night Eva sees Franz's rigid face, he doesn't react to caresses, doesn't react to kind words, barely eats, barely speaks, knocks back coffee and spirits. He lies on her sofa, sobbing. 'We won't find him.' 'Let him go, then, Christ's sakes.' 'We can't find him. What can we do, Eva?' 'Leave him be, there's no sense in it, you're running yourself into the ground.' 'You don't know what we're doing. You – you haven't experienced it, Eva, you don't understand, Herbert does, a little bit. What we gonna do. I want to get him all right, I'll go to church and pray on my knees if it means I get him.'

But all that's not really true. Everything's not really true; the whole chase for Reinhold isn't real, it's groaning and indescribable fear. Just now the dice are being thrown for him. He knows the score. Everything will acquire a meaning, a terrible, unexpected meaning. Your hide-and-seek won't go on much longer, boy.

*

He stakes out Reinhold's pad, his eyes are no good, he looks and sees nothing. Plenty of people walk past the building, a few of them go inside. He went in there himself, was taken in, oh just on account of the chingderada bumderada bum.

The building starts to laugh at him when it sees him standing there. It would like to move, to summon its neighbours at the back and either side, just to look at him. There's a man standing there with a wig and an artificial arm, a fellow burning, full of spirits, standing there babbling.

'Morning, Biberkopfchen. 22 November today. Persistent rain. You'll catch your death of cold. Why not pop into your local and get something warming, if you take my meaning.'

'Give him here!'

'Give it up!'

'You give Reinhold up!'

'Go to Wuhlgarten, your nerves are shot.'

'Give him here!'

Then one evening Franz Biberkopf is working in the building, concealing petrol canister and bottle.

'Come out, wherever you are, you poison git, you smutty dog. You haven't got the balls to show yourself.'

The building: 'Whoever you're talking to, he's not here. Come in and see for yourself.'

'I can't look all over.'

'He's not here, who would be crazy enough to be here.'

'Hand him over! You've got it coming otherwise.'

'All I hear is otherwise. Go home, fellow, get some sleep, you're drunk, no wonder, you never eat anything.'

The next morning he's there minutes after the newspaper woman.

The street lamps see him running, they sway: 'Eia weia, there'll be fire.'

Smoke, little jabbing flames out of the attic windows. By seven the fire brigade are on the spot, Franz is with Herbert, clenching his fists: 'I don't know nothing and you don't know nothing, no need to tell me, but now he's got nowhere to stay any more. That's right. I torched his place.'

'Christ, you didn't think he was living there, did you.' 'It was his building, he'll know when there's a fire that it was me. We've smoked him out, mark my words, he'll come now.' 'I'm not so sure, Franz.'

Reinhold doesn't come forward, Berlin continues to clatter and trundle and din on its way, the papers don't say they've nabbed him, he's given them the slip, he's abroad, they'll never get him.

And there's Franz in front of Eva, doubled over, howling. 'I can't do nothing, and I have to stick it out, he's breaking me and he's killed my girl, and I'm standing there like a weakling. It's so unfair. So unfair.'

'Franz, nothing's changed.' 'I can't do nothing. I'm finished.' 'Why do you think you're finished, Franz?' 'Because I done what I could. So unfair, so unfair.'

There are the two angels flanking him, Sarug and Terah are their names, talking together. Franz is in the throng, walking in the throng, he is silent, but they can hear his wild crying. Policemen walk down the street, they don't recognize Franz. Two angels are flanking him.

Why is Franz being flanked by two angels, and what sort of game is this, where angels flank a human being, two angels on Berlin's Alexanderplatz in 1928 alongside a former manslaughterer, then burglar and pimp. Yes, this story of Franz Biberkopf, of his difficult, true and illuminating existence, has now gone so far. The more Franz Biberkopf doubles up and froths at the mouth, the clearer everything will become. The point is approaching at which everything will become clear.

The angels speak next to him, Sarug and Terah are their names, and their conversation – while Franz is studying the window displays at Tietz's – runs as follows:

'What do you say, Sarug, what would happen if we left this person to his own devices, abandoned him to be arrested?' Sarug: 'It wouldn't make that much difference, I think, he would be picked up one way or another, that's inevitable. He's been to look at the red building, and rightly so, in a few weeks he'll be in it.' Terah: 'In that case we're basically superfluous?' Sarug: 'To some extent – given that we're not permitted to whisk him away.' Terah: 'I think you're a child, Sarug, you've only been studying these scenes for a couple of thousand years. If we take him away from here and move him somewhere else, into a different existence, has he done what he could have done here? For every thousand existences, as you must know, there are at least seven hundred, no, more like nine hundred that are stymied.' 'What reason is that then, Terah, for sheltering this one particular individual, he is an ordinary human being, I don't see why we should step in.' 'Ordinary, extraordinary, those are words. Is a beggar ordinary and a millionaire extraordinary? The millionaire may be a beggar tomorrow, and the beggar a millionaire. This man here is close to regaining his sight. Many have made it that far. But he is also close to feeling, do you hear me. You see, Sarug, someone who has experienced much and learnt much has a tendency merely to know, and then to slip away, to die. He is used up. He has been through the span of experience, and he has grown tired, and his body and spirit are exhausted. Do you understand?' 'Yes.'

'But after one has experienced and understood many things, to cling on, not to go down into death, not to slip away, but to stretch, to feel, to present oneself with one's soul and stand there, that amounts to something. Sarug, you don't know how you came to be what you are or what you were, or how it came about that you were put here to go with me and protect other creatures.' 'That's true, Terah, I don't know that, my memory has left me.' 'It will come back to you. One is never strong on one's own, from one's own doing, there is always something at one's back. Strength is not innate but acquired, you don't know how you acquired it, but somehow you one day stand there and things that are lethal to others are harmless to you.' 'But he doesn't want us, your Biberkopf, you said so yourself, he's trying to shake us off.' 'He wants to die, Sarug, no one has yet taken such awful strides without wishing to die. And you're right, most are vanquished.' 'But you have hopes of this one?' 'Yes, because he's strong and not used up, and because he has twice already stood firm. Let's stay with him, Terah.' 'Yes.'

*

A young doctor, a bit of a knock-out, sits in front of Franz: 'Good morning, Herr Klemens. Go away somewhere, this is often the way of things after a fatality. You need a change of scene, in your present condition Berlin will get you down, you need a change. Wouldn't you like some distraction? You are his sister-in-law, does he have anyone to accompany him?' 'I could go, if required.' 'It is; I'm telling you, Herr Klemens, it's the only thing for it: peace and quiet, recuperation, a little gentle distraction; not too much. That can be counter-productive. Moderation in all things, eh. It's prime season, now; where would you like to go?' Eva: 'Would a tonic be good, lecithin, for better sleep?' 'I'll write it all down for you, here, adalin.' 'I've given him adalin already.' (That junk does him no good at all.) 'Then try phanodorm, one last thing at night, with some mint tea; tea is good too, it's an excellent solvent, and makes for quicker absorption. Take him to the zoo.' 'Nah, I don't like animals.' 'Well, then the botanical gardens, a bit of distraction, not too much.' 'Can you give him something to strengthen his nerves?' 'Maybe he could take a little opium to improve his mood.' 'I drink, doctor.' 'No, on second thoughts, opium's a different box of tricks, but I will give you some lecithin, a new compound, instructions on the packaging. And baths, baths are soothing. I take it you have a tub, madam?' 'Everything's there, of course, doctor.' 'Aha, that's the advantage of these new flats. You may say "of course", but there's no "of course" about it for me. I had to get all that installed, it cost an arm and a leg, the room, the decoration, you'd rub your eyes if you saw it, you don't have that to deal with. So: lecithin and baths, say, every other morning, and a masseur, thorough kneading of all the muscles gets the organism going.' Eva: 'Yes, that's right.' 'Thorough kneading coming your way, that'll loosen you up a bit, Herr Klemens. You'll be in the pink in no time. And then a trip somewhere.' 'It's not easy with him, doctor.' 'Never mind, just a matter of time. Well then, Herr Klemens, how're you feeling?' 'What?' 'Chin up, don't forget to take the medication, plus sleeping draughts and massage.' 'I've got it all under control, doctor. Goodbye, and thanks for now.'

'Well, Eva, you had it your way.' 'I'll arrange the baths and the medicine.' 'Yes, you go.' 'And you wait here for me.' 'Yes. You bet, Eva.'

Eva puts her coat on and heads out. And so, a quarter of an hour later, does Franz.

Battle is joined. We ride into hell with a great fanfare

The battlefield beckons, the battlefield!

We're riding into hell with a great fanfare, we're fed up with this world, we don't care what happens to it, with everything in and on and under it. All its humans, its men and women, the whole infernal kit and caboodle, there's no one we can depend on. If I was a little birdie I'd take a great big pile of shit and throw it behind me with both feet and clear out. If I was a horse, a dog, a cat, there's nothing you can do better than drop your dirt on the earth and move on.

There's nothing going on in the world, I don't feel like getting shitfaced again, though I know I can do it, drink, drink, drink, and then the infernal shit begins all over again. I know God made the world, but I wish a priest would tell me why. Though he made it better than the priests know, he gave us leave to piss on the whole thing, and gave us two hands and a length of rope, and away with it, that's in our remit, and then the hellish shit is over, enjoy, blessings, we're going to hell in a handcart.

If I could lay my hand on Reinhold, my rage would be over, I could grab him by the throat and break his neck and not let him live, and then I would feel better, I would feel satisfied, and everything would be in order, and I could have peace. But the bastard who has done me so much harm, who made me into a criminal again and broke my arm, he's somewhere in Switzerland laughing at me. I'm running around like a dog, he can do what he likes with me, no one is on my side, not even the police, who are chasing me, as if I was the one who done Mitzi, when it was that motherfucker, he's managed to pin that on me too. Every day the jug goes to the well, until one day it breaks. I've taken enough and done enough, I'm at the limit. No one can claim I haven't fought back. But too much is too much. So because I can't kill Reinhold, I'm going to kill myself. I'm going to hell with a great fanfare.

Who's this on Alexanderstrasse, very slowly pushing one foot after the other? His name is Franz Biberkopf, and you know his story. A ponce, a grave criminal, a poor man, a beaten man, his time has come. Damn the fists that beat him! The terrible fist that grabbed hold of him! The other fists hit him and let him go, there was a wound, an opening, it healed, Franz stayed the way he was, and hurried on his way. But this fist won't let him go, this fist is incredibly big, it shakes him body and soul, Franz is walking along with little tiny steps, and he knows: my life is no longer mine. I don't know what I have to do now, but Franz Biberkopf is finished.

It's November, late evening, nine-ish, the boys are hanging round Münzstrasse, and the electric tram and the bus and the newspaper vendors are all making a lot of noise, the police march out of their barracks with their nightsticks.

On Landsberger Strasse there's a protest with red flags: wake up, you damned of this earth.

'Mokka-fix' on Alexanderstrasse, nonpareil cigars, cultured beers in mugs and glasses, card games forbidden, guests are responsible for their own coats, I'm not taking the rap. Signed, the Landlord. Breakfast from 6 a.m. to 1 p.m., 75 pfennigs, one cup of coffee, two eggs any style, bread and butter.

Franz sits himself down in the Kaffeeklappe on Prenzlauer Strasse, and they jeer at him: 'Your Grace!' They pull the wig off his head, he unstraps his artificial arm, orders a beer, folds his coat across his lap.

There's three fellows in attendance, grey faces, and sure enough they're cons, probably just released, can't stop talking, all of them talking crosswise.

So I'm thirsty and I says why walk so far, there's a basement with

Polacks living in it, I show em my sausage and cigarettes, and they don't ask me where I got them from, and they buy, give me a schnapps, I leave everything there. And in the morning I watch them go, and I scoot into the basement, I've got hooks with me, it's all there, my sausage, my cigarettes, and I pick up the lot and scarper. Not bad, eh?

Police dogs, they're smart. Five men got out through the walls. I can tell you how and all. Both sides lined with metal, tin sheets a quarter of an inch thick. What they do is they go through the floor, what's that you're thinking, cement floor, dig a hole, every night under the wall. Then the police comes along and they say how come we didn't hear that. Well, we was asleep, weren't we. Stands to reason. Why should we be the ones to hear it.

Laughter, merriment, o du fröhliche, o du selige, they strike up a song round the table, widdeboom.

And then of course someone turns up, police constable, senior constable, Schwab if you please, throws his weight around and says: he's heard all this day before yesterday, only he was away on a business trip. Beezknees treep. Whenever there was anything going down, he was always on beezknees. Another half, me too, and three ciggies.

A girl is combing the hair of a tall blond gentleman at table, he's singing: 'O Sonnenburg, o Sunny Burg.' And as soon as there's a break, he starts singing again, always something involving the sun:

'O Sonnenburg, o Sonnenburg, how green are all your branches! This summer I was twenty-nine, but not in Berlin or Danzig did I serve my time, nor in Königsberg, either, where was it anyway? Don't you know, you mug, why, in Sonnenburg, in Sonnenburg.

'O Sonnenburg, how green are all your branches! You're a model jail all right, where humanity rules from morn till night. There they don't beat you, don't razz you, don't maltreat you, they don't make life hell for you; there a fellow gets his fill, grub and smokes and beer to swill.

'Fevvers in the beds, brandy, beer and cigarettes. Yes, it's certainly very grand, our guards are devoted heart and hand, we'd like to make a present of military boots to the officers, if they'd only give us cigarettes, heart and hand, isn't it grand. Just let us booze, with heart and hand, we'll let you sell your army boots and uniforms left over from the war, it's grand, we won't have them altered, and you can sell them on the spot, we need the cash, for we are just poor prisoners in jail.

'There are a few proud comrades who'd like to give us away, but we'll break their bonces for em, so they'd better think well before they start to bray, or we'll properly dust em up, and sorry will be the day when we bust em up.

'But the governor is a mug, why, he never notices anything. The other day a fellow came and wanted to inspect the free penitentiary of Sonnenburg, it disagreed with him. Why did it disagree with him? I'll tell you all about it. We're in the canteen together. Two officers are sitting near, and while we enjoy our booze and beer, who should turn up – yes, who should turn up, I ask you?

'It is, boom-boom, it is boom-boom, it's the Inspector, what do you say to that? We say cheers, we say bottoms up, Inspector, cheers, stick to the ceiling, have a jar, sit by my side.

'What does the Inspector say? It's me, the Inspector, boom-boom, make way for the Inspector, I am the Inspector, boom-boom there he is, I'll have the lot of you behind bars, cons and screws, you've nothing you to amuse, you've got it coming, boom he stands there, boom-boom he stands there, boom-boom.

'O Sonnenburg, o Sonnenburg, how green are all your branches! We made his life a hell, till he had to run to his wife, and take his revenge on her; boom-boom, united they stand, boom-boom, isn't he grand, boom-boom, the Inspector. Now don't you look like a fool! Ah, don't be angry, just keep cool!'[10]

Brown trousers and black serge jacket. One pulls a brown prison jacket out of a parcel. To the highest bidder, rock-bottom prices, the new black, one jacket, going cheap, just one shot of spirits. Who needs a jacket? Merriment, o friends, o du fröhliche, o du selige, brother, your sweetheart decrees, have one more on me. Next up: a pair of canvas shoes, detailed acquaintance with the layout of chokey, straw soles, ideal for doing a bunk, and then one blanket. Christ, you should have left that with the governor.

The landlady sidles along, shuts the door: keep it down, you lot, I've got customers. One sees to the window. His neighbour laughs: window, no chance. If there's a hue and cry, look here. – And he reaches under the table and pulls up a trapdoor: the cellar, and from there straight to the next courtyard, no need to climb any walls, all nice level paths. Just keep your hat on, else you'll catch someone's attention.

An old fellow growls: 'That was a nice song you sung. But there's others too. They're not too shabby either. Do you happen to know this one?' He pulls out a piece of tatty paper with wobbly handwriting on it. 'The Dead Convict'. 'No sad songs, please!' 'What do you mean sad. It's just as true as yours.' 'Now don't cry in your beer, I do believe you've got a lump in your throat, don't blub.'

'The dead convict. Poor, yet full of youth's enchantment, once he walked the righteous highway, sacred were to him things noble, mean things he left on the by-way. But misfortune's evil spirit lay in ambush, him a-spying, held suspect of evil actions in the law's nets he is lying. (The chase, the chase, the accursed chase, the accursed dogs were after me, how they chased me, they almost killed me. On and on, you don't know what to do, on and on, you never knew you could run that fast, you run as fast as you can, and in the end they nab you anyway. Now they've caught Franz, now I throw myself to the ground, now it's time, well cheers.)

'All his crying, all his protests, all his rage was idle prating, evidence was dead against him, and the cell for him was waiting. The judges were mistaken (the chase, the chase, the accursed chase), when his sentence they had spoken (how those damned dogs did chase me), but what availed his guiltless innocence, since his honour's shield was broken. Man, oh fellow-man, he whimpered, why oppress, why ruin me, did I do you injury? (It happens, there is no answer. And further and further he runs, it's not possible to run so fast, and he does what he can.)

'When from prison gates returning, he came back with outraged feeling, things were now the same no longer, in the dust they found him kneeling. To the river's bank he stumbled, but he found the bridge broken, back into the night he wandered, sick at heart, and full of loathing. All refused to still his hunger (the chase, the chase, the accursed chase), bitterness oppressed him starkly, then he yielded to his fury – "guilty this time," said Life darkly.

'(Guilty, guilty, guilty, he, that's the thing you have to be, the thing to be, to be a thousand times over!) Such a deed is punished harshly, custom, morals have this meaning, to a cell within the prison back he wandered, void of feeling. (Franz, hallelujah, hear that, a thousand times over, a thousand times over.) Yet once more a leap to freedom, murder, robbery and plunder, and without the smallest pity, tear that Beast, Mankind, asunder. He was gone, but soon in fetters he came back again. How fleeting was his first revel! A life sentence was his greeting. (The chase, the chase, the accursed chase, he was right, he did it right.)

'Now he wailed no more for pity. Let them curse! It doesn't matter. Mute, he bore the yoke upon him, and he learnt to feign and flatter. Dully he went at his labours, always doing the same thing daily, long his spirit had been broken, like the dead he wandered palely. (The chase, the chase, the accursed chase, they were always on my trail, I always did my best, now I am stuck fast in the dirt and I am not at fault, what was I to do. My name is Franz Biberkopf, and that's what I still am, watch out.)

'And today his course is ended, with the springtime's golden gleaming, in the sod he's being lowered, that's the cell the convicts dream of. Now the prison bell is ringing, it's farewell with eerie sadness to the man who lost his bearings and found death in prison madness. (Watch out, gentlemen, you don't know Franz Biberkopf yet, but he sells himself dearly, when he is compelled to go to the grave, he will take someone with him on every finger to announce him to the Almighty and say: first it's us, and Franz is on his way. No surprise, God, that he comes riding along with such a team, you were hunting him yourself, now he's joining the great team in the sky, he was no account here on earth, let him show his worth in heaven.)'[11]

They are still singing and talking round the table, so far Franz Biberkopf has been dozing, now he feels fresh and alert. He kits himself up again, buckles on his arm, we lost it in the war, we're forever going to war. The war doesn't end as long as you live, the main thing is standing on your own two feet. Then Franz is standing on the street, in front of the iron stairs to the Kaffeeklappe. Outside it's piddling and sheeting, it's dark, and there's a crowd on Prenzlauer Strasse. And there's some commotion opposite, on Alexanderstrasse, the cops are on the scene. And Franz turns and slowly directs his feet to see what's what.

The Police HQ is on Alexanderplatz

It's twenty past nine. In the well of the headquarters building, two fellows are standing around talking. They are telling jokes and stretching their legs. A young detective comes along and says hello. 'It's ten past nine, Herr Pilz, did you specify that we needed the car at nine sharp.' 'There's someone upstairs right now calling the Alexander barracks; we ordered the car yesterday.' Someone else chips in: 'Yes, they say the car's been sent, it went out at five to nine and lost its way. They're sending another one.' 'Great. Lost its way, and meanwhile we're waiting.' 'Well, so I ask about the car, and he says: who am I speaking to, I say Secretary Pilz, he says, this is Lieutenant Such-and-Such. So I say: well, Lieutenant, I'm asking on behalf of the commissioner, we booked cars yesterday for a raid at nine o'clock, the order was put through in writing to the Vehicular Department, I just want confirmation that you've received the order. You should have heard him, the lieutenant, butter not melting in his mouth, of course everything's in train, a mishap, and so on and so forth.'

The vehicles roll in. A few ladies and gentlemen pile into one of them, detectives, commissioners and some lady officers. This is the wagon in which Franz Biberkopf will shortly draw up, in the presence of fifty assorted men and women, his good angels will have quit him, his expression will be different from what it was when he left the Kaffeeklappe, but the angels will dance, ladies and gentlemen, whether you believe it or not, it will happen.

The car with the male and female occupants is on its way, not a military vehicle, but a vehicle of law and public order, a truck, people sit on long benches, it drives across Alexanderplatz with innocent commercial vehicles and taxis, the people in the truck all look cosy, this is an undeclared war, they are going out in furtherance of their work, some are quietly smoking pipes, some have cigars, the ladies ask: that one gentleman at the front, he's from the press, isn't he, so this will all be in the papers tomorrow. They drive contentedly up the right of Landsberger Strasse, they take roundabout routes to their destinations, otherwise the places will know too early what's coming. Passers by have a good view of the truck: they don't look at it long, it's a grim, frightening, thing but it's soon past, they're rounding up criminals, terrible that such a thing should be, let's go to the movies.

They get off at Rückerstrasse, the police truck waits, they walk back up the street. The little street is deserted, the troop walk up the pavement, there's the Rückerdiele.

Cover the entrance, sentries posted outside, more people opposite, everyone else inside. Evenin all. The waiter grins, he knows what's coming. Can I get the gentlemen a drink? No thanks, no time; cash up, raid, everyone's coming back to the station with us. Laughter, protests, well, really, don't take on, scolding, laughter; easy does it, I've got papers, well, lucky you, then you'll be back here in half an hour, what do we care, I'm busy, calm down, Otto, free tour of police HQ with atmospheric nocturnal lighting. Step this way. The truck is full to bursting, one man sings: 'Who rolled the cheese to the station, rolled along the cheese, how dare he do such a thing, nobody's paid the custom taxes for the cheese, for the cheese, so the cops looked down on it and began to frown on it, because they rolled along the cheese for which they hadn't paid the fees.'[12]

The truck moves off, everyone waves: who rolled the cheese to the station.

Well, that was easy enough. We'll go back on foot. A natty gent across the street tips his hat, evening, Commissioner, Captain. They walk into a house entrance, the others scatter, meeting point is the corner of Münz and Prenzlauer.

The Alexander-Quelle is heaving, it's Friday night, whoever's earned a wage drops in there for a drink, music, radio, the police barge past the bar, the young commissioner speaks to a gentleman, the band stop: this is a police raid, everyone back to the station. They are sitting round tables, laughing, unbothered, they go on talking, the waiter goes on taking orders. One girl is in tears with two of her friends in the passage: I've just moved, and I'm not re-registered yet, well, then you'll spend the night with us, it's no big deal, I'm not coming, I'm not letting any of you lay a finger on me, don't get worked up, it's not good for your health. Let me go, what do you mean let me go, you can go when your turn comes, the car's just left, then why don't you have more cars, you leave that up to us. Waiter, a bottle of champagne to wash my legs. You, I need to go to work, who's going to pay for my lost hour, I have to go to my building site, this is distraint of trade, everyone's coming with us, you too mate, calm down, they just need to do a raid, otherwise they won't know what they're here for.

People leave in dribs and drabs, the cars keep shuttling back and forth between the bar and the police headquarters, the police go back and forth, there's a certain amount of hysterics in the ladies' loo, one damsel is lying on the floor, her swain is standing by, what's he doing in the ladies'. She's got her cramps, can't you tell; the police smile, have you got papers, right, well, why don't you keep her company. She'll go on screaming her head off, you mark my words, then when everyone's gone she'll get up, and the two of them will dance a tango. I tell you, the first one to touch me gets a haymaker, and one more of those would be vivisection. The bar is almost empty. By the door stands a man who's been grabbed by a couple of officers. He's yelling: I've been to Manchester and London and New York, and these kinds of things don't happen in

Manchester or London. They move him along. All right, let's be having you, how're you, thanks, by the way, commiserations on your dog.

At a quarter to eleven, by which time the raid is pretty far advanced, and only a few of the tables at the side and at the back, going up the stairs, are still occupied, someone walks in, even though the joint is supposed to be sealed off. The police are energetic and won't let anyone through, but now and again a girl peeks in at the window: I'm sposed to meet my boyfriend here, no miss, come back at twelve, we'll be keeping your Romeo at the station till then. But the old gentleman watched the last consignment leave, finally the police were weighing in with their nightsticks at the entrance, because more people were coming out than would fit in the car, now it's gone, and the crowds have thinned out a bit. The man walks calmly past the two cops on the door, each of them looking the other way because more people are trying to get into the bar, and are shouting at them. From the barracks a column of police is just advancing, to ribald commentary, up the other side of the road, the men tightening their belts as they march. The grey man makes his way through the bar, orders a beer and takes it up the steps, where the woman is still screeching away in the ladies' and the other customers, the few still left, are talking and laughing and generally carrying on as though they hadn't a worry in the world.

The man sits down at a table by himself, makes a hole in his beer, and looks round the bar. His foot nudges something against the wall; well, fancy, he reaches down, a revolver, someone must have got rid of it, well that's nice, now I've got two of em. One on each finger, and if God asks me why, I say: I'm coming with a big team, something I never had down below is OK up here. They're doing a raid, and quite right too. Somebody's had an extra cup of coffee at HQ, he says, we have to have a raid, summing needs to happen that I can read about in the paper. It's time they realized upstairs that we work too, and maybe someone wants his promotion, and his wife wants a fur coat, that's why they go out and on a Friday of all days when people have just had their pay packets.

The man has kept his hat on, his right hand is stuck in his pocket, his left is too, when it's not picking up his glass. A policeman with a badger brush on his little Bavarian hat walks through the bar, empty tables everywhere, cigarette packets on the floor, newspapers, chocolate wrappers: all right, get ready, the last ride'll be along in a minute. He asks the old gentleman: 'Have you paid up already?' The old gentleman mutters something and stares into space: 'I just got here.' 'Well, you shouldn't have done, but we'll have to take you in as well.' 'Let that be my worry.' The policeman, a solid, broad-shouldered fellow, looks down at him, the expression on that man's face, he wants trouble. He doesn't say anything, just walks down the steps to the bar, then he notices the old man's glittering eyes, Christ, what's the matter with him, those eyes. He goes over to the door where the others are, a whispered consultation, and they go out together. A couple of minutes later the door swings open again. The police are back: last lot now, come on, let's be having you. The waiter laughs: 'Take me with you next time, I wouldn't mind seeing this shower from above.' 'Oh, you'll have em all back in an hour, mark my words, there are people waiting outside that we picked up in the first lot.'

'You too, sir, if you please.' He's talking to me. If you have a bride you trusted, with a body for which you lusted, you don't ask what sort of miss, just so long as she can kiss.

The gentleman doesn't stir. 'You, I'm talking to you. Are you deaf or something. Get up.' You were sent me by the new year, because before I never had you near. I want to wait for a few more, this one guy won't do me, I want more.

There are three police by the steps, the first of them comes up, the others after. The lanky young commissioner leads them, they're in a hurry. They've chased me enough, I've done what I could, I am a human being or am I not.

And he pulls his left hand out of his pocket and, not getting up, shoots the first policeman who is heading angrily in his direction. Bang. So we've done everything we had to do on earth, and we can go to hell with a fanfare, with a great fanfare.

The man staggers and drops, Franz gets up, he wants to back

against the wall, bag more where they came from. Let's be having you then, the more the merrier. He raises his arm, there's someone behind him, Franz barges him aside, then he feels a blow on the hand, a blow in the face, a blow on the hat, a blow on the arm. My arm, my arm, I've only got the one, they're breaking my only arm, what shall I do, they're killing me, first Mitzi, then me. It's all no use. All no use, it's all no use.

He collapses by the balustrade.

Before he can go on shooting, Franz Biberkopf has collapsed by the balustrade. He's given up, curses existence, has handed in his weapons. Lies there.

The police push the table and chairs aside, kneel down at his side, turn him onto his back, the man has an artificial arm, two revolvers, where are his documents, hang on, this is a wig. And Franz Biberkopf opens his eyes to find them pulling his hair. Then they shake him, pull him up by the shoulders, set him on his feet, he can stand, he has to stand, they jam the hat on his head. Everyone is already outside in the car when they lead Franz Biberkopf through the door by a chain round his left wrist. There's hubbub on Münzstrasse, a crowd had gathered, wasn't that shooting in there, watch yourself, here he comes, he's the one that done it. The wounded policeman has already been taken away by ambulance.

So this is the car that the commissioners and detectives and lady officers left HQ in at half past nine, they drive off, Franz Biberkopf aboard, the angels, as already indicated, have abandoned him. In the station yard the human freight is unloaded, marched up a flight of stairs to a long wide corridor, the women are put in a room by themselves, and whoever is released with his papers in order needs to exit through the barrier between the police, they pat everyone down, chest, trousers down to their boots, the men laugh, there is a continual scolding and pushing in the corridor, the young commissioner and the officers walk back and forth calming people down, asking for patience. The police watch the doors, no one gets to go to the toilet unaccompanied.

At the tables inside are officials in civvies, quizzing suspects, sifting through documents, where they can be produced, writing on large sheets: place, local jurisdiction, place of arrest, police station, IV K. So what's your name, remanded to, last arrested at, believe me, I gotta go to work, Secretary of Police, section 4, delivered morning, afternoon, night, first name, second name, marital state or profession, date of birth, month, year, place of birth, vagrant or of no fixed address, supplied address turned out to be bogus after follow-up inquiries. You have to wait here till your local station gets back to us, bide your time, they've got other things to take care of, and they've had people who gave an address, which was the right address and there was someone living there of that name – only, we show up and find someone else living there, and he just had his papers, so they were stolen, or borrowed, or some other business. Check the list of open warrants, data on grey card, grey card is missing. Evidence on file and items associated with the present or previously committed crimes, items with which the detainee might hurt himself or others, personal items, stick, umbrella, knife, revolver, knuckle-duster.

They produce Franz Biberkopf. Franz Biberkopf is over. They've got him. They bring him in on a chain. His head is hanging. They want to question him downstairs, on the ground floor, in the room of the duty sergeant. But the man won't speak, he is obstinate, he keeps touching his face, where the right eye is closed by a blow from a nightstick. He is quick to drop his arm, which also took a couple of blows.

Meanwhile, others who've been let go cross the dark courtyard to the street, gander arm in arm across the yard. Once you've got yourself a squeeze, and she does her best to please, and so we go with song, with song, with song, into one or other restaurant. I confirm that the information collected here accords with the truth. Signature of the detainee, name and number of the official making the booking. Court Berlin Mitte, section 151, to magistrate Herr—.

At the very end of all, Franz Biberkopf is presented and remanded in custody. This man fired a shot during the raid on the Alexander-Quelle, and has committed other infractions. He was found stretched out in the Alexander-Quelle, and half an hour later it was established that, in addition to eight other wanted individuals and the usual cluster of runaway juveniles, the police had pulled off a major coup. For the man who collapsed after the shooting had an artificial right arm and was wearing a grey wig. From that, and from a file photograph, it was established that the man was being sought as a person of interest in connection with the murder of the prostitute Emilie Parsunke in Freienwalde, being the previously punished Franz Biberkopf, guilty of manslaughter and prostitution offences.

He had been living unregistered for a long time, here's one, it won't be long before we nab the other.

Chapter Nine

And now Franz Biberkopf's race is run. It is time for him to be broken. He has fallen into the hands of the dark power called Death, which seems fitting enough. But he learns what it thinks of him in a way he wasn't expecting, and that exceeds everything he has so far experienced.

It talks turkey with him. It reveals to him the nature of his errors, his arrogance and his ignorance. And with that the old Franz Biberkopf collapses, his life is over.

The man is broken. A new Biberkopf appears on the scene, whose boots the old one is not worthy to lick, and of whom it is to be expected that he will fare better.

Reinhold's Black Wednesday – but this section can be skipped

And, as the police assumed: 'We've got the one, it won't be long till we've got the other', so indeed it comes to pass. But not in the way you might have expected. Because – it turns out they've got him already, he's passed through the same red-brick HQ, and other hands and rooms, and is already doing a stint in Moabit.

Everything with Reinhold happens quickly, and this was no exception. The boy don't like to hang around. We know what happened with him and Franz the last time; it took him a day or two to work out what Franz's game is, and then blam.

One night Reinhold headed off to Motzstrasse, and then he says, those wanted murder posters on the advertising pillar, I need to do a little job and get myself caught with false papers, a handbag or something. Prison is the safest place when there's trouble brewing. And everything works out as planned, except maybe he hit the lady a little bit too hard. But never mind, thinks Reinhold, time to disappear for a while. In the police station they eye his false papers, a Polack pickpocket, name of Moroskiewicz, off to Moabit with the fellow, they haven't got a clue who he is, and he's never done time before neither, but then who can be expected to know the lists of every wanted man by heart anyway. And his case proceeds discreetly and unobtrusively, just the way he crept through the station. But because he's a pickpocket wanted in Poland, and the rotter has gone out on the street in a nice part of town, and given a lady a whack over the head and ripped the handbag off her, that's a scandal, this isn't Russia, what were you playing at, we're going to make an example of you, and they throw the book at him, he gets four years' hard, and loss of civil rights for another five, placed under police supervision, and whatever else they can come up with, and his knuckle-duster is even taken away. The accused is to pay costs, ten minutes' break, it's stifling in here, please open a few windows, accused, have you anything to say?

Reinhold of course has nothing to say, he's thinking of an appeal some time down the road, he's glad to be talked to in that way, nothing will happen to him inside. So after two days everything's put behind him, everything, and we're over the worst. Bloody nuisance that business with Mitzi and that idiot Biberkopf, but for now we've done it, and things are on course, hallelujah, hallelujah, hallelujah.

This is the point things have got to therefore. By the time they nab Franz and take him back to the station, the real murderer Reinhold is already in Brandenburg, no one's thinking about him, he's lost and forgotten, and the world could end before it occurred to anyone to investigate him. He's not racked by any guilt pangs, and if things pan out the way he imagines, then he'd either still be sitting there, or else he'll have done one on a transport.

However, the world is arranged in such a way that the daftest sayings have their truth, and if a man thinks that's enough, it's by no means enough. Man supposes, God disposes, and the jug goes to the well every day till it breaks. The way they eventually found out about Reinhold and his grim implacable course thereafter is something I am coming to. But if the reader is not interested in pursuing that, he can simply skip the following few pages. This *Berlin Alexanderplatz* book of mine is about the fate of Franz Biberkopf and everything in it is correct, you will want to read and inwardly digest it, it has its palpable truth. But Reinhold has fulfilled his function in this narrative. Only because he represents cold violence, which is always the same, I will show him in his last hard struggle. You will see that he is hard and stony to the very end, his life moves on unmoved – whereas Franz Biberkopf bends, and finally is like an element that is subjected to radiation and turns into a different element. It's an easy thing to say, but we're all human. If there is a God, then we differ from him not only in point of good and evil, but we all have a different nature and a different life, we are different in kind and whither and whence. And now listen to the end of Reinhold.

So Reinhold is in the penitentiary in Brandenburg, weaving, of all things, mats, with someone who is also a Pole, but a genuine one, and a real pickpocket, and a tricky customer, and he also knows the real Moroskiewicz. When he hears 'Moroskiewicz' and thinks I know that name, so where is he, and then claps eyes on Reinhold, he says to himself: he's changed, and how can such a thing be possible. And then he pretends he doesn't know the guy at all and has never heard of him, and in the toilet one day he sidles up to Reinhold where they go to smoke, and gives him half a cigarette and talks to him and it turns out the guy don't even speak Polish. Reinhold doesn't like being addressed in Polish, and he tries to weasel out of the mat-weaving shop, the supervisor takes him, because he sometimes has these fainting fits, and uses him as a trusty in the cell wing, where the others can't get at him so easily. But Dluga the Polack doesn't give up. Reinhold goes from cell to cell calling out: put out your finished work! And they've got to Dluga's cell with the master, and the master is just counting up the finished mats, when Dluga whispers to Reinhold that he knows Moroskiewicz from Warsaw, a pickpocket, is he related to you? Reinhold gets a shock, and he slips the Pole a package of tobacco, and he goes on his way: put out your finished work.

The Pole's happy with his tobacco, but thinks there must be more mileage in this thing, so he starts blackmailing Reinhold, who always seems to have funds from somewhere.

The business could have turned nasty for Reinhold, but luck's still on his side, and he manages to parry the blow. He puts it about that his countryman Dluga is in the mood to make a general confession, a little birdie told him. So one day in the middle of recess there's an enormous free for all, and Reinhold manages to give the Pole a bit of a skelping. That earns him a week in solitary, with bedding and warm food from day three. And when he comes out everything's nice and peaceful.

But then our Reinhold gets above himself. All his life it was women this, women that, and now it's love once more that does for him. The episode with Dluga brought him irritation and rage at having to sit here all this time, and be bossed around, and there's no joy in his life, and he's so all alone, and the feeling deepens with each passing week. While he's sitting around, wishing he could murder Dluga, he gets involved with a young fellow, a burglar, also in Brandenburg for the first time, but due for release in March. It's the tobacco trade, and badmouthing Dluga that first gets them associated, but eventually they get to be really close friends of a kind Reinhold never had before, too bad he's a boy and not a woman, but it's still nice, and Reinhold in the fortress of Brandenburg is happy again: at least the damned business with Dluga has been good for something. Too bad the boy's time is almost up.

'I gotta wear the black cap and brown jacket such a long time yet, and when I'm sitting here, where will you be, my little Konrad?' Konrad is the boy's name, or at least it's what he goes by, he's from Mecklenburg, and he gives every indication of becoming a major player. Of his two mates he did break-ins with in Pomerania, one is still here, doing ten. And when the two friends on a black Wednesday, on the eve of Konrad's release, find themselves together in the cell once more, and Reinhold is doing his nut about being on his tod again, and not having anyone – oh, something'll turn up, just you wait, you'll get a cushy place in Werder or some other facility – then Reinhold can't keep it down, he can't get his head around the fact that his life has gone so badly off the rails, with that bitch Mitzi and that fuckwit Biberkopf, what have I got to do with pathetic specimens like that, I could be the big man on the outside, it's just poor wretches who are stewing in here. Then it really gets to Reinhold, and he's whimpering and wailing and begging Konrad, o please take me with you, take me when you go. The boy comforts him to the best of his ability, but there's nothing doing, you can't seriously urge someone to bust out of here.

They've got this little bottle of alcohol from one of the French polishers in the carpentry shop, and Konrad gives Reinhold the bottle, he takes a drink from it, and so does Konrad. He can't escape, there's a couple of guys who escaped or tried to escape, and one of them made it as far as Neuendorfer Strasse where he tried to hitch a ride when he was picked up, the man was bleeding all over him from the damned broken glass they left all over the tops of the walls, they had to lay him down in hospital, who knows if his hands will ever be the same again. And his mate, well, he was the wiser, he got as far as the broken bottles, and he said sod this, and dropped back into the yard.

'Don't even think about it, Reinhold.' And then Reinhold was all crushed and soft, he's got another four years of this to look forward to here and all on account of some stupid break-in on Motzstrasse and the bitch Mitzi, and the idiot Franz. And he knocks back more of the white spirits, and he feels a wee bit better, they've put their things out already, the knife is on top of the bundle, the key's been turned in the lock, twice, the doors are bolted, the beds are fixed up. Then they're whispering together on Konrad's bed, Reinhold is in his hour of gloom: 'Here, when you get to Berlin. Once you're out, go look up my bint, who knows who she's going with now, I'll give you the address, and you tell me what's what, know what I mean. And then listen out, see what you can pick up regarding my story, you know, Dluga got wise to something. I knew this guy in Berlin, a real fool, Biberkopf, Franz Biberkopf—'

And he whispers and he tells him and he clutches hold of Konrad, who opens his ears and keeps saying yes, and before long he knows the whole story. He has to help get Reinhold into bed because he's so beside himself with desolation and rage at his condition that he's incapable of doing it himself, and sits there caught in the trap. Nothing Konrad says makes any difference; Reinhold refuses and refuses, he can't stand it, he can't live like that, he has a regular case of stir-crazy prison blues.

So that's black Wednesday. By Friday Konrad is with Reinhold's bird in Berlin, and gets a warm welcome from her, and gets to talk for days, and she gives him money and all. That's Friday, and by

Monday it's all over for Reinhold. Because that's when Konrad meets a friend on Seestrasse, a bloke he was in borstal with, currently out of work. And Konrad starts prating to him about how well he's doing, and he pays for their drinks, and they pick up a couple of birds and go to the cinema. Konrad tells wild stories about his time in Brandenburg. Once the girls have gone home, they spend half the night till Tuesday up at the friend's place, and Konrad talks about Reinhold, only he goes by Moroskiewicz, and he's a top man, it's not easy to meet blokes like that on the outside, he's wanted for big crimes, who knows what reward is offered for information leading to, etc. And no sooner has he said that than he realizes it was stupid of him, but his friend swears by all that's holy not to say a dicky bird, honest, and he puts the bite on Konrad for another tenner.

Then it's Tuesday, and the friend is in police HQ, squinnying at the wanted posters to see if it's true that Reinhold, that was his name, is really wanted, and if there's a reward going, or if Konrad was just showing off.

And he's floored when he sees the name, Jesus Christ, murder of the prostitute Parsunke in Freienwalde, and there he is, it's gorra be him, 1,000 marks' reward, 1,000 bleeding marks. He's so impressed, 1,000 marks, that he scoots off, and comes back in the afternoon with his girlfriend, who says she's just seen Konrad, who asked about him, yes, he has some inkling of what might be coming, what should he do, should he do it, Christ, how can you doubt it, he's a murderer, what's that to do with you, and Konrad, what do I do about Konrad, just don't see him for a while, and anyway so what, how will he know it was you, and think about the cash, 1,000 marks, you're on the dole, and you're wondering yay or nay. 'Do you think it's him?' 'Come on, let's go in.'

Inside he tells the duty detective what he knows in so many words, Moroskiewicz, Reinhold, Brandenburg – only, he doesn't say how he came to know it. Since he's got no papers, he and his girlfriend are required to stick around. And then – everything pans out.

When Konrad goes out to Brandenburg on Saturday to visit

Reinhold, and he's got lots of things to take him, from Reinhold's bird, and from Pums, there's a newspaper in the train compartment, an old paper from Thursday, and it says on the front page: 'Freienwalde Murderer Arrested: in Prison under False Identity.' The train rattles under Konrad, the points clash, the train rattles on. When is the paper from, what paper is it, *Lokal Anzeiger*, Thursday, late edition.

They've got him. He's been taken back to Berlin. And it's all my fault.

The love of women brought fortune and misfortune to Reinhold all his life, and so at the last it led him to calamity. They transported him to Berlin, where he behaved like a madman. He wasn't far short of being taken to the same institution that housed his onetime friend Franz Biberkopf. So he waits, once he's calmed down in Moabit, to see how his trial will go and what might come from over there, from Franz Biberkopf who was his accomplice or his mastermind, but there's actually no knowing at this stage how things will pan out with him.

Buch insane asylum, closed ward

In remand, in the police headquarters called the panopticon, their first feeling is that Franz Biberkopf is putting it on, because he knows he's facing a capital charge, but then the doctor takes a look at the prisoner, he's taken to the infirmary in Moabit, and there's not a word to be got out of him, the man seems really to be mad, he lies there perfectly rigid, just blinking his eyes a little. After he's refused nourishment for two days, he's driven out to the asylum at Buch, where they put him in the closed ward. Whichever way you look at it, it's a prudent decision, because the man has to be kept under observation.

First they stick Franz in the day room, because of his habit of lying around buck-naked. He refused to cover himself, he even pulled off his shirt, for a few weeks that was just about the only sign of life coming from Franz Biberkopf. He kept his eyes squeezed shut, lay there stiffly and refused all nourishment, so that they had to have recourse to the feeding tube, and for weeks all he got was milk, egg and a little cognac. On such a diet the strongly built man dwindled rapidly, a single warder could carry him easily to the bath, which Franz seemed to enjoy, he even said a few words in the bath, and opened his eyes, and sighed and moaned, but there was no sense to be got from him.

The institution at Buch is just beyond the village of that name, the closed ward is just past the asylum where the others go, who are only sick and have committed no crimes. The closed ward lies on open terrain, in the middle of the flat land; the wind, the rain, the snow, the cold, the day and night can beset the building with all their force and vim. No streets block off the elements, a few trees and bushes and a handful of telegraph masts, but other than that it's all rain, snow, wind, cold, day and night.

Voom, voom, the wind puffs out its chest, it sucks in its breath, then it exhales like a barrel, each breath heavy as a mountain, the mountain is approaching, it crashes against the building; the bass growls. Voom, voom, the trees sway, they can't keep time, they have to go right, they're still facing left, and they go over. Plunging weights, hammering air, cracking, creaking, crashing, voom voom, I'm yours, come to me, we're almost there, voom, night, night.

Franz hears the calls. Voom, voom, without stop, why should it. The warder sits at his table reading, I can see him, he's not put off by the gale. I've been lying here a long time. The chase, the accursed chase, they've been chasing me up hill and down dale, I've broken my arms and legs, my neck is broken. Voom, voom, listen to the wailing, I've been lying here a long time, I'm not getting up, Franz Biberkopf will never get up. Even at the sound of the Last Trump, Franz Biberkopf won't get up. They can make all the noise they want, they can pierce me with their tube, now they're feeding me through the nose because I won't open my mouth, but eventually I will starve, what can they do with all their medicine. Filth, damned filth, that's all behind me now. Now the warder's drinking his beer, that's all behind me now as well.

*

Voom crash, voom crash, voom blow toss, voom gate bang. With heave and rush and crash and sway the forces of the storm come together and debate, it's night, how to get Franz to wake up, not that they want to break his bones, but the building is sturdy and he can't hear what they're calling to him, and if he was closer to them on the outside, then he would feel them and hear Mitzi's screams. Then his heart would be opened, his conscience would rouse and he would get up, and it would be good, but for the moment they don't know what to do. If you have an axe, and strike hard wood, then even the oldest tree starts to scream. But this lying there rigidly, flinching and insisting on misery, that's the worst thing in the world. We mustn't let up, either we break into the sealed house with a battering ram, or we smash the windows, or prise open the roof; when he feels us, when he hears the screams, Mitzi's screams which we carry with us, then he will come to understanding. We need to terrorize him, he's not to have any rest, I will pluck up his blankets, I will spill the warder's beer and blow his book away, voom voom, I will upset his lamp, smash the bulb, maybe there'll be a short circuit in the house and fire will break out, voom voom, fire in the insane asylum, fire in the sealed institution.

Franz jams his ears shut and lies there rigid. Round the sturdy building, alternation of day and night, clear skies and rain.

By the wall stands a girl from the village, chatting to one of the warders: 'Can you tell I've been crying?' 'No, just your cheek is a bit swollen.' 'It all is, my whole head, the back of my skull, everything.' She cries, produces a handkerchief from her little handbag, pulls a face. 'Even though I never done anything. I was supposed to go to the baker to get something, I know the girl there and ask her what she's doing, and she says she's going to the bakers' party. Can't always sit around at home in bad weather. And she's got a spare ticket, and offers to take me. Won't cost a penny. It's nice of her, isn't it?' 'Very nice.' 'But then you should hear my parents, my mother. I'm not allowed. Why not, it's a respectable ball, and you want to have a little fun from time to time in your life. No, we're not letting you go, the weather's so bad, and your father's not well.

And then I say, I'm going anyway, and I got such a beating, what do you think of that?' She cries and wails to herself. 'The whole of the back of my head hurts. Now you've learned your lesson, and you'll stay here, says my mother. Isn't that awful? Why shouldn't I go out, I'm twenty years old, I'm gone for the weekend, says my mother, well, but this is a Thursday and the ticket was going begging.' 'If you want, I can give you the loan of a handkerchief.' 'Ach, I've got through six of them already, and I've caught a cold from crying all day, what will I say to the girl, I can't go in the shop, not with my cheek looking like this. I wanted to go out, I wanted to think of something else, not just your friend Sepp the whole time. Now I've written to him to tell him we're through, he hasn't written back, so we really are through.' 'Leave him be. You can see him in town with a different girl every Wednesday.' 'I'm very fond of him. That's why I was desperate to go.'

An old man with an alcoholic's blue nose is sitting on Franz's bed. 'Hey, open your eyes, I know you can hear me. I'm in the same boat as you. Home sweet home, you know, well, for me that's in the ground. If I can't be home, I want to be in the ground. The peabrains want to make a troglodyte out of me, they're trying to make a cave-dweller out of me. You know what I mean by troglodyte, don't you, that's us, wake up, damned of the earth, starved all your lives, you've been sacrificed in war, in love of country, you gave everything for your people and love and happiness and freedom. That's what we are, man. The despot feasts in gaudy chambers, drowning his turmoil in wine, but the hand has already started to inscribe the menacing letters on the board. I'm an autodidact, I've had to learn everything by myself, in prison, and now they've locked me in here, they slapped a care order on the people, I'm too dangerous. Yes, that's me. I'm a free-thinker. You see me sitting in front of you, I'm the calmest man in the world, but if I'm riled. There's a time coming when the people will rise up, the mighty, powerful and free people, so rest, my brothers, you've sacrificed yourselves nobly and magnanimously for the cause.

'What about this, comrade, open your eyes so I can tell you're listening to me – that's good, that's all I need, I won't betray you – what was your crime, did you kill one of the tyrants then, death to you, hangmen and despots, sing it. You know, you're lying there all the time, and I can't sleep, it keeps going voom voom outside, you hear it, it'll knock the whole place for six anytime soon. Quite right too. I was doing sums in the night, how many times does the earth go round the sun in a second, I'm working it out all night, and I make the answer to be twenty-eight, and then I get the feeling my old lady's lying by my side, so I wakes her and she says: don't be cross, old man, but it was just a dream.

"They locked me away because I drink, but when I drink it makes me angry, but angry with myself, and I smash everything in my path, because I'm not my own master. Sometimes I go to the office to pick up my pension, and there's the officials sitting up there nice and snug, suckling on their pens and imagining they're gentry. I tear the door open and say my piece, and they say: what do you want here, who are you anyway? Then I bang on the table: who asked you, I've got no business with you, Schögel's the name, I'd like a copy of the phone directory, I want to talk to the governor. And next thing I know I've smashed the office to matchwood and two of the officials with it.'

Voom crash, voom crash, voom ram, voom gate bang. With heave and slam and crash and sway. Who is this deceitful fellow Franz Biberkopf, fever drop, lindyhop, let him wait till it starts snowing, then he'll think we'll be gone and won't be back. Think, the fellow can't think, he's got no brains to think with, he wants to lie around and be uncooperative. We'll settle his hash for him, we've got bones of iron, crash gate, look out, crash gate, hole in the gate, break in the gate, watch out, no gate, empty hole, cavern, voom voom, watch out, voom voom.

A rattling, there's a rattling in the storm, in the midst of the howling gale there's a rattling sound, a woman turning her head on a scarlet beast. She has seven heads and ten horns. She's yacking away and has a glass in her hand, she's mocking, she's lying in wait for Franz, she toasts the storm powers: grr, grr, calm down gentlemen, one man's not worth that much, there's not much going on in him, he's only got one arm, there's not much flesh and fat on him, he'll be cold ere long, they're already putting hot-water bottles in his bed, and I've got most of his blood, he's not got much left, he can't throw his weight around much. Pish, I say, calm down, gentlemen.

It's all happening before Franz's eyes. The whore moves her seven heads, yammers and nods. The beast settles its feet under her, its head swings back and forth.

Dextrose and camphor injections, but in the end a different consultant is involved

Franz Biberkopf fights the doctors. He can't tear the tube out of their hands, can't pull it out of his nose, they pour oil on the rubber and the probe slides down his throat, and the milk and egg mixture flows into his stomach. But when the feeding is over, Franz begins to retch and vomit. It's laborious and painful, but he can do it, even if they keep his hand tied so he can't stick a finger down his throat. You can train yourself to vomit up everything, and we'll see who gets their way, them or me, I won't let anyone bully me again in this goddamned world. I'm not here for medical experiments, and they have no idea what's wrong with me anyway.

Franz is winning. He is getting weaker and weaker. They try all kinds of things, talk to him, feel his pulse, lay him with head raised, lay him with head lowered, make up caffeine and camphor injections, squirt dextrose and cooking salt into his veins, enemas are discussed round his bedside, perhaps they should administer extra oxygen, he won't be able to tear the mask off. He's thinking what are these medical gentlemen bothering their heads about me for. A hundred people die in Berlin every day, and if someone's ill you can't get a doctor along to see them unless they can pay. Now here are all these clowns, but they're not here because they want to help me. They don't give a shit about me today just as they didn't give a shit about me yesterday, but I'm a challenge to them and they're annoyed with me because they can't crack this case. And they're not going to let that happen, not for all the tea in China, dying is against the rules here, it's bad for morale. If I die they might get a carpeting, and anyway they want to haul me up in front of the judge over Mitzi and what all else, hangmen's assistants is what these guys are, not even hangmen themselves, assistants, under-assistants, touts, and these people swan around in white coats and feel no shame.

There is a sardonic whispering among the inmates when the doctors have done their rounds and Franz is lying there same as before, and they've tried everything with him, injections up the keister, soon they'll stand him on his head, just now they're think-ing of blood transfusions, but where are they going to get it from, no one here is so stupid as to volunteer his blood for that purpose, they should leave the poor guy alone, a man's will is his own, if he's set his heart on it that's the way it is. The whole establishment won-ders what Franz is going to get injected with today, and they snigger about the doctors, because whatever they try it's no use on him, he's a knothead, one of the hardest, he'll show them, he knows what he wants.

The doctors change into their white coats in the consultation room, present are the senior registrar, assistant registrar, a couple of junior doctors and a medical assistant, and what they all say is: persistent vegetative stupor. The younger gentlemen take a par-ticular interest in him, they are inclined to take Franz Biberkopf's condition for psychogenic, his stiffness takes its start from his soul, it is a morbid state of inhibition and torpor that psychoanalysis would clear up, perhaps primal regression, if only – the great if only, shame, but there you are – if only Franz Biberkopf would speak to them, and sit around the table with them and work at setting aside his conflict with them. The younger gentlemen have in mind a sort of Locarno Agreement with Franz Biberkopf. Of the younger gen-tlemen, the two junior doctors and the assistant come back to Franz in the little barred ward after each of the morning and afternoon rounds, and try as hard as they can to get some sort of conversation started with him. They try for instance to ignore him: talking to him as though he could hear everything they said, which happens to be the case, as if you could tempt him out of his isolation so that he would break through his barrier himself.

When that fails to work, one of the doctors brings along an electric shock machine from the main house, and Franz Biberkopf is faradized on the upper body, and finally the Faraday stream is applied to the jaw, the throat and the under-jaw. These are the parts that stand in need of stimulation.

The older doctors are hard-boiled men of the world who don't mind walking out to the closed ward, and they permit all sorts of things. The senior registrar studies the case files in the consultation room, the nurse passes him the files from the left, the two younger gentlemen, the young guard, assistant and medical trainee stand by the barred window and chat. They have been through the list of sedatives, the new nurse has introduced himself and has stepped outside with the senior nurse, the gentlemen are closeted together, they browse through the protocols of the latest congress at Baden-Baden. The senior registrar: 'Next thing you'll be trying to tell me paralysis is psychically caused, and the spirochetes are lice on the brain. The soul, the soul, this modern myth! Medicine on wings of song.'

The two other gentlemen exchange a look and smile to themselves. The older generation talks a lot, but after a certain age calcium is deposited in the brain, and a man stops learning. The senior registrar smokes, signs another piece of paper, continues:

'Electricity's not a bad idea, better than your endless chit-chat anyway. But a low current won't achieve anything. And if you apply a strong one, then hang onto your hats. We had that in the war, electricity treatment, by golly. Not allowed any more, reckoned to be torture.' The young men pluck up courage and ask him what he would recommend, say, in the Biberkopf case? 'Well, first of all, you make a diagnosis, and ideally the correct one. Apart from the immortal soul – and of course we've all read our Goethe and our Chamisso, even if it's been a while now – there's still things like nosebleeds, corns and broken legs. They need to be treated as a proper fracture or corn needs to be treated. Someone has a broken leg, and it won't get better if you talk to it, it won't even respond if you play the piano to it. What it wants is for you to apply a splint, and set the bones correctly, and then it'll start to knit right away. Same with a corn. It wants you to apply ointment, or buy a pair of better-fitting shoes. The latter is the more expensive course, but in the long run it's more effective.' The wisdom of pensionable minds, intellectual pay grade zero. 'So what should we do in the Biberkopf case, do you have a view?' 'Arrive at the correct diagnosis. In this case – according to my haha, superannuated skills – catatonic stupor. Unless there's an underlying organic condition, a growth, something in the midbrain, you know, the kind of thing we ancients used to call a head cold. Perhaps we'll see something mind-boggling in the post-mortem, wouldn't be the first time.' 'Catatonic stupor?' Needs to buy himself some new shoes, methinks. 'Yes, anything lying there that rigidly, those sweating fits and occasional eye movements, he's capable of observing everything we do, and doesn't say a word, won't eat, that all looks to me like catatonia. The faker or psychogenic eventually relents. Doesn't take things as far as starvation.' 'And how do you work with such a diagnosis, sir, I mean, it doesn't help him any.' We'll squeeze him here. The senior registrar laughs, gets up, walks over to the window, pats the junior doctor on the back: 'Well, firstly, he gets some relief from you two, my dear colleague. He'll be able to sleep in peace. That's to the good. Don't you think he gets a bit bored by the stuff you and that colleague of yours say to him? Do you know what I'd base my diagnosis on now, rock-solid? There, I've got it now. He would have gone for it ages ago, by Christ, if it had been his so-called soul. When one of those hard-boiled jailbirds but thinks, here come these young gentlemen who know bugger all about me – forgive me, but we're amongst ourselves here – they want to give me the talking cure, well, you're what a fellow like that dreams about. He can cope with that. And what does he then do, would have done long ago? You see, colleague, if the man had had sense and rationality—' Now the blind chicken thinks it's found something: hear him kikeriki. 'He's inhibited, registrar, in our view it's a kind of blockage, but triggered by emotion. Loss of contact with reality, following various disappointments and failures, and then infantile emotional demands, futile efforts to restore contact.' 'Spiritual moments, my eye. Then he would just go on to have different spiritual moments. Then he would give up his blockages and inhibitions in a hurry. He'll make a present of them to you for Christmas. In a week with your help he'll be up and about, God, some therapist you are, all praise to the new beliefs, send a wire to Freud in Vienna, a week later your man will be trotting down the corridors with your help, wonder of wonders, hallelujah; another week and he'll know his way around the yard, and one more and with your help he'll have scarpered while your backs were turned.' 'I don't follow, registrar, but maybe it's worth a shot.' (I know everything, you know nothing, kikeriki, we know everything.) 'But I do. You'll pick it up in time. Called experience. So, I would stop tormenting him, take my word for it, it doesn't do him any good.' (I'm going over to building 9, these greenhorns, just let God do his thing, it must be dinnertime soon.)

Franz Biberkopf is unconscious and absent, very pale, yellowish, with swellings at the joints, hunger oedema, he smells of hunger, of sweetish acetone, anyone setting foot in his room realizes straight away something unusual's going on in here.

Franz's soul has reached a very low ebb, his consciousness is intermittent, but the grey mice who live in the attic understand him, and so do the squirrels and hares that go leaping about outside. The mice sit in their holes between the closed ward and the big central building at Buch. Then something blind flits from Franz's soul, wandering and seeking and hissing and asking, and goes back to the breathing husk that is still lying in the bed the other side of the wall.

The mice invite Franz to eat with them, and tell him not to be sad. What's upsetting him so. Turns out he doesn't find it easy to speak. They insist, want him to call a halt. Man is an ugly animal, the arch-enemy, the most perverse creature on the planet, worse even than cats.

He says: it's no good living in a human form, I would rather hide under the ground, scamper across the fields and eat whatever I can find, and the wind blows and the rain falls and the cold comes and goes, all that's better than living in a human form.

The mice run off, and Franz is a field mouse and burrows with them.

In the closed ward he is lying in bed, the doctors come and hold his body there by main force, he is fading fast. They admit they won't be able to hold onto him much longer. The animal part of him is running across the fields.

Now something slinks out of him and feels its way and seeks and frees itself, something he has only rarely and dimly felt in himself. It swims past the mouseholes, snuffles round the grasses, feels in the ground where plants conceal their roots and their seeds. Then something speaks to them, they can follow it, it is a blowing this way and that, a knocking, it's like when seeds fall to the ground, Franz's soul is giving back its plant seeds. But it's a bad time, cold and frozen, who can say how many will take, but there's room enough in the fields, and Franz has many seeds in him, every day he blows out of the house and scatters fresh seeds.

Death sings his slow, slow song

The powers of the storm are still now, another song has begun, a song as familiar as the one singing it. When he lifts up his voice to sing they all fall silent, even these who are most turbulent on earth.

Death has begun his slow, slow song. He sings like a stammerer, repeating every word over; when he has sung a chorus, he repeats the verse and begins again. He sings like a saw being drawn. Very slowly, carefully it commences, then drives deep into the flesh, screaks louder, higher and brighter, then with one tone it's at the end and rests. Then, slowly, slowly, it goes backward, and scrapes, and higher and firmer is its screaking tone, driving into the flesh.

Slowly Death sings.

'It is time for me to appear to you, because the seeds are flying out of the window and you are shaking out your bedding as though you weren't going to lie in it any more. I am not a simple mower, I am not a simple sower, I have to be here because it is my duty to preserve. O yes! O yes! O yes!'

O yes! is what Death sings at the end of each verse. And if he happens to make a strong movement, then he sings o yea! too, because he likes to. But those that hear it, they shut their eyes, because they cannot bear it.

Slowly, slowly Death sings, wicked Babylon listens to him, the powers of storm listen to him.

'I stand here and must record: the one who lies here and desires to give up his body and his life is one Franz Biberkopf. Wherever he is now, he knows where he is going and what he wants.'

A pretty song, certainly, but is Franz listening, and what does it mean anyway, to have Death sing? Printed in a book or read aloud, it is a little like poetry, Schubert's songs are a bit like this, Death and the Maiden, but what is it doing here?

I want only to tell the pure truth, and this truth is: Franz Biberkopf hears Death, he hears this Death, and he hears him singing slowly, like a stammerer, with many repetitions, and also in the manner of a saw, cutting into wood.

'I must record, Franz Biberkopf, your lying here and desire to come to me. Yes, you were right in wanting to come to me, Franz. How can a man prosper if he doesn't seek Death? Actual, true Death. You saved yourself up your whole life. Saving, saving, that's such a timid demand of humans, it means they stay in one place, and never get anywhere.

'When Lüders cheated you, I talked to you for the first time, you were drunk and you – you saved yourself. Your arm broke, your life was in danger, Franz, admit it, you didn't for one moment think of Death, I sent you all I had, but you didn't want to know me, and when you sensed me you grew wild and appalled and – you ran away from me. It never crossed your mind to reject yourself, and what you had begun. You gritted yourself and wanted strength, and the cramp still hasn't cleared, it's no use, you felt it yourself, it's no use, the moment comes and it's no good, and Death doesn't sing you a gentle song, lays no choking band around your throat. I am the life and the true strength, at last, at long last, you are no longer trying to preserve yourself from me.'

'What? What do you think of me, what are you hoping to do with me?'

'I am the life and the truest strength, my strength is stronger than the biggest cannon, you will not live in peace from me anywhere. You want to feel yourself, you want to test yourself, life is worth nothing without me. Come, Franz, come closer to me so that you see me, see how you're lying in an abyss, I will show you a ladder, and you will find a new way of seeing. You will climb across to me, I'll hold it steady for you, you have just one arm, but seize hold, your feet will tread firmly, seize hold, step up, come to me.'

'I can't see any ladder in the dark, where have you got it, nor can I climb with one arm.'

'You don't climb with your arm, you climb with your legs.'

'I can't hold on. What you're saying doesn't make sense.'

'You're unwilling to move closer to me. Let me make light for you, then you'll find your way.'

Then Death takes his right arm from behind his back, and it becomes apparent why he had kept it behind his back.

'If you lack courage to come in darkness, I'll make light for you, creep closer.'

An axe flashes through the air, there's a flash, it goes out.

'Creep closer, creep closer!'

And as he brings the axe down from behind his head in an arc described by his arm, the axe seems to slip from his grasp. But already, his hand is up behind his head again, swinging. There's a flash, a descent, a guillotining in a semi-circle through the air, striking, striking, another whoosh, whoosh, whoosh.

Take it back, bring it down, chop, take it back, bring it down, chop, take, bring, chop, take bring chop, take chop, take chop.

And in the flashing of the light and during the taking back and bringing down and chopping, Franz crawls along, feels the ladder, screams, screams, screams. And doesn't creep back. Franz screams. Death is at hand.

Franz screams.

Franz screams, crawls forward and screams.
He screams all night long. Franz has got going.
He screams into the day.
He screams into the morning.
Take bring chop.
Screams into noon.
Screams into afternoon.
Take bring chop.
Take, chop, chop, take, take chop, chop, chop.
Take chop.
Screams into the evening, into the evening. Here comes night.
Screams Franz into night, into night.

His body inches forward. On the block his body is being chopped into pieces. His body inches forward, has to, can't do anything else. The axe cleaves the air. It flashes and drops. He is being chopped up, an inch at a time. And beyond, beyond that inch, the body is not dead, it pushes itself forward, slowly forward, nothing falls, everything lives on.

Those walking past in the corridor, stopping at his bedside, thumbing up his eyelids to check the reflexes, taking his pulse, which is like a thread, they don't hear any of his screaming. They just see: Franz's mouth is hanging open, and conclude he must be thirsty, they carefully give him a few drops to drink, hope he doesn't vomit them up, it's as well he's stopped gritting his teeth. How is it possible that a man can remain alive so long.

'I'm in pain, I'm in pain.'
'It's good to be in pain. Nothing is better than that you should be in pain.'
'Oh, don't leave me in pain. Make an end.'
'There's no point in ending. It's ending now.'
'Make an end. It's in your power.'
'I've just got an axe. Everything else is in your power.'
'What have I got in my power? Make an end.'
Now the voice is roaring, it sounds completely different.

The endless rage, uncontrollable rage, wild uncontrollable rage, the whole endless rolling rage.

'It's come to this, to me standing here talking to you. Standing like a hangman and torturer, having to choke you like a poisonous snapping animal. I kept on calling to you, you think I'm a gramophone, you take me for a gramophone record to put on when it suits you, then I have to shout, and when you've had enough of it, you turn me off. That's what you take me for, isn't it. Well, go on, take me for it, but now you can see the situation's different.'

'What did I do. Did I not suffer enough. I don't know of anyone who's been through what I have, so pathetic, so wretched.'

'You were never there, you bastard. I haven't seen Franz Biberkopf in all my life. When I sent you Lüders, you wouldn't open your eyes, you folded like a camp stool, and then you drank, schnapps and schnapps and drinking all the time.'

'I wanted to be honest, and he cheated me.'

'And I say you never opened your eyes, you crooked hound. You wax indignant about thieves and rascals but you never look at people, and never ask how come and what. What sort of judge of people are you if you never open your eyes. You were blind, and you were cheeky on top of it, stuck up, Herr Biberkopf from a fancy part of town. The world has to be the way he says. It's different, mate, all right, remember that. It doesn't care about you. When Reinhold grabbed hold of you and threw you under the car, you lost your arm, and even then Franz Biberkopf never batted an eyelid. He's lying under the wheels, and he's vowing to himself: I'm going to be strong. Doesn't say: I need to think about this – no, he says: I'm going to be strong. And not notice that I'm talking to you. But you're listening now all right.'

'Not notice, why? What's the point?'

'And then there's Mitzi. Franz, shame, shame. Say: shame. Yell: shame.'

'I can't. I don't know why.'

'Yell shame. She came to you, she was lovely, she protected you, she liked you, and you? There was a woman, a woman like a flower, and what do you do: you go prating about her to your mate Reinhold. That's as good as it gets with you. After all, you just want to be strong, don't you. You're happy you can josh around with

Reinhold, and you've got one over on him, and you go and flaunt her at him. Why don't you think about who's to blame for her not being alive any more. And you never shed a single tear for her, who gave her life for you, no one else.

'It was all talk, all "I" this and "I" that and the "wrong that's been done to me", and how noble I am and how fine and no one lets me show what kind of fellow I am. Say shame! Yell shame!'

'I don't know!'

'You lost the war, sunshine. It's all up with you. You can pack up. Put yourself in mothballs. I've had it with you. You can squawk and wail all you want. What a wretch. Got given a standard-issue heart and head and eyes and ears, and thinks it's enough if he's decent, or what he calls decent, and sees nothing and hears nothing and lives into the day and doesn't notice a thing, try as I may.'

'Well what, what should I do?'

Death roars: 'I'm not telling you, don't talk to me. You've got no head, no ears. You weren't born, man, you were never alive. You're an abortion with delusions. With cheeky ideas, Pope Biberkopf, he had to be born so that we notice how everything works. The world needs different people than you, more alert, less impudent, capable of understanding how things work, not pure sugar, but sugar and shit mixed together. Man, I want your heart so it's over with you. So I can toss it in the dirt where it belongs. You can keep your chatter to yourself.'

'Let me be a while. Let me think. A little bit longer. Just a little bit.'

'I want your heart, mate.'

'A little bit.'

'I'm coming for it.'

'A little bit.'

And now Franz hears the slow song of Death

Lightning, lightning, lightning, the lightning lightning stops. Chop fall chop, the chop fall chop stops. It is the second night of Franz's yelling. Falling chopping stops. He no longer yells. Lightning stops. His eyes are blinking. He lies there stiffly. A room, a ward, people walking. You mustn't pinch your mouth shut. They pour warm stuff into his mouth. No lightning. No chopping. Walls. A bit, just a little bit, what else. He shuts his eyes.

And as Franz shuts his eyes, he starts to do something. You don't see what you're doing, you just think he's lying there and maybe he'll be done for soon, he's not moving a finger. He calls out and moves and walks. He calls everything together that is his. He walks through the windows onto the fields, he shakes the grasses, he creeps into the mouseholes: get out, get out, who are you, what's your business here? And he stirs the grass: get out of it, what's the point, it's no good, I need you, I can't let anyone go, I've got work to do, cheer up, I need all of you.

They tip broth into him, he swallows, he doesn't retch. He doesn't want to.

Franz has Death's word in his mouth, and no one will tear it away from him, he turns it in his mouth and it is a stone, a stony kind of stone, no nourishment spills from it. In this situation innumerable people have died. There was no Beyond for them. They didn't know that they were only required to put themselves through one more pain to get along, that just one small step was needed to move on, but they couldn't take that step. They didn't know it, it didn't happen quickly enough, it was a weakness, a cramping of minutes and seconds and already they were over, where their names were no longer Karl, Wilhelm, Minna or Franziska – replete, sinisterly replete, purple with rage and rigid desperation, they slept across the divide. They didn't know that all they had to do was to continue to glow white-hot, and then they would have become soft, and everything would have been as new.

Suffer it to approach – night as black as you like, a void. Suffer it to approach, black night, the fields with the hard frost on them, the frozen roads. Suffer them to approach, the lonely brick houses giving out a reddish light, suffer them to approach, the freezing travellers, the drivers of the carts bringing vegetables into the city, with the little horses pulling. The great, flat, mute plains that the suburban trains and the expresses rumble across, spilling white light in the darkness to either side. Suffer them to approach, the people at the station, the little girl saying goodbye to her parents, she is leaving with two older friends, she is crossing the water, we have tickets already, my God, a little girl like that, well, she'll make her way over there, be a good girl, then everything will be all right. Suffer them to approach, and take them in, the towns all in a line, Breslau, Liegnitz, Sommerfeld, Guben, Frankfurt an der Oder, Berlin, the train goes from station to station, the towns appear in their stations, the towns with their great and small streets. Breslau with Schweidnitzer Strasse, the great loop of Kaiser-Wilhelm-Strasse, Kurfürstenstrasse, and everywhere flats where people try to stay warm, look fondly at each other, sit coldly side by side, dirt holes and bars with a piano playing, baby, an old song, as if there weren't nothing new in 1928, for example: 'Madonna, you're bonnier', or 'Ramona'.

Suffer them to approach, the cars, the cabs, you know how many of them you sat in, rattling along, you were on your own, or else there were one or two in there with you, No. 20147.

A loaf of bread is pushed into the oven.

The oven is free-standing, a stack of bricks by a farmhouse, at the back is a ploughed field. The women have sawed a lot of wood, collected kindling, all that's next to the oven now, and they cram it in. Now someone crosses the yard with the big trays laden with dough. A boy pulls open the door, it's glowing within, a fierce heat, they push the trays in with poles, the bread will rise in there, the water will evaporate, the dough will brown.

Franz half sits up. He's swallowed, he waits, almost everything is present to him that was once running around out there. He's trembling. What was it Death said? He needs to know what Death said. The door opens. Here it comes. The scene is about to begin. I know him. Lüders, I've been waiting for him.

And they walk in, trembling, knowing they're expected. What's up with Lüders. Franz gives signals, they thought he's short-winded from lying flat, but he just wants to pull himself upright. Because here they are now. Now he's upright. Let's go.

And singly, here they come. Lüders, poor chap, little manikin. Wanna see how yer doing. He walks up the steps with his shoelaces. Yes, that's what we done. Mouldering in his ancient togs, reconditioned military uniform, Makko laces, madam, I just wanted to ask, could you spare a cup of coffee, where's your husband, probly fell in the war; slips his hat on: all right, let's see how much money you got then. That's Lüders, he was with me. The woman has a glowing face, one cheek is white as snow, she rootles around in her purse, she cackles, she tumbles to the ground. He rifles through her drawers: load of old trash, I'd better run before she starts screaming. Down the corridor, squeeze shut the door, down the stairs. Yes, he's done it. Steals. Steals a lot. They give me the letter she wrote, what's the matter with me now, all at once me legs have been taken off, me legs have been taken off, what for, I can't stand up. Do you want a brandy, Biberkopf, probably a death in the family, yes, wherefore therefore, why have me legs been taken off, I don't know. Must ask him sometime, must put it to him directly. Listen, Lüders, morning, Lüders, how you doing, not so hot, me neither, come over here, sit down on the chair, don't go yet, what have I done to you, don't go.

Suffer them to approach. The dark night, the cars, the frozen roads, the little girl saying goodbye to her parents, she's leaving with an older couple, she'll settle down over there, I've no doubt, behave yourself, and you'll be all right. Suffer them.

Reinhold! Ah, Reinhold. The divil, the wretch. There you are, what are you doing here, putting on airs again, no rain will wash you clean, crook, murderer, criminal, take the pipe out of your mouf when yer talking to me. I'm glad you came, I missed you, come here, you filth, you piece of shit, haven't they caught up with you yet, you got a blue coat? Just you wait, you'll end up in it. 'Who do you take yourself for, Franz?' Me, you wretch? Least I'm no murderer. Do you know who you murdered? 'And who showed me the girl, who didn't care about her, bigmouth had me crawl under the sheets, who was that?' Didn't mean you had to kill her, did it.

'So what, didn't you half knock her block off yourself? And then isn't there another one lying on Landsberger Allee, she didn't go to the churchyard by herself, did she? So what do you say now? Cat got yer tongue. What does Franz Biberkopf, Franz Bigmouf say now?' You threw me under the car, I lost my arm. 'Haha ha, well, you can always strap on your cardboard one instead. If you're such a fool as to get involved with me.' A fool? 'Well, has it escaped your attention that you're a fool. Now you're in Buch playing the wild man and I'm all right, Jack, so which of us is the fool?'

And there he goes, and hellfire flashes from his eyes and horns sprout out of his head, and he squawks: let's box, come on show me what you got, put em up, Frankie boy, let's see em, Frankie Biberkopf, little Biberköpfchen, ha! And Franz presses his eyelids. I shouldn't have tangled with him, I should never have got involved with him. Why did I ever take him on.

'Go on, Frankie, let's see em, you're a strong lad, aincha?'

I shouldn't have fought. He can still get a rise out of me, oh, he's a devil, I should never have done it. I'm no match for him, I shouldn't have done it.

'Strength, Frankie.'

I shouldn't have needed strength, not for him. I can see I was mistaken. The stuff I tried. Away with him, begone.

He won't go.

Begone, you—

Franz yells, he wrings his hands. I need to see someone else, is no one coming, why has he stopped?

'Oh, I know, you don't like me, doesn't taste good. Someone else'll be along.'

Suffer them to approach. Suffer them to approach. The great, flat plains, the lonely brick houses giving out a reddish light. The towns all in a line, Frankfurt an der Oder, Guben, Sommerfeld, Liegnitz, Breslau, the towns appear with their stations, the towns with their great and small streets. Suffer them to approach, the cabs, the sliding, shooting cars.

And Reinhold goes and then he's standing there again, winking at Franz: 'Well, who's done it, who's tops, Frankie boy?'

And Franz trembles: I haven't won, I know it.

Suffer to approach.

Next please.

And Franz, sitting up a little higher, has his fist clenched.

A loaf of bread is pushed into the oven, the enormous oven. The heat is unbelievable, the oven is creaking and snapping. Ida! Now he's gone. Thanks be to God you're here, Ida. That was the greatest villain there is in the world. Ida, it's good that you're here, he's been teasing and tormenting me, what do you say, I've had a bad time, now'm sitting here, do you know where that is, Buch, the loony bin, I'm here under observation or maybe I've gone mad already. Go on, Ida, don't turn your back on me. What's she playing at? She's standing in the kitchen. Yes, the girl's standing in the kitchen. She's pottering about, probly doing the dishes. But she keeps collapsing, one side of her has given way, like she's got roomatism or something. Or someone's biffing her, in the side. Stop hitting her, man, that's not human, don't, leave her be, leave her alone, leave that girl be, oh yes, oh go, who's hitting her, she can't stand up, stand up girl, turn round, look at me, who is it hitting you, it's terrible.

'It was you, Franz, you hit me and I died.'

No no, I never did that, that was established in court, I just did GBH, I weren't to blame. You mustn't say that, Ida.

'Yes, it were you that killed me. Watch yourself, Franz.'

He shouts no no, he clenches his fist, he throws his arm up over his eyes, he can't stop seeing it.

Suffer them, suffer them to approach, the travellers, they're carrying sacks of potatoes on their backs, a boy is pushing a handcart along after them, his ears are cold, it's 10 below, Breslau with Schweidnitzer Strasse, Kaiser-Wilhelm-Strasse, Kurfürstenstrasse.

And Franz moans: I'd be better off dead, who can stand this, I wish someone would come and strike me dead, I didn't do all that, I didn't know. He whimpers, he lisps, he can't talk. The warder understands that he wants something. He asks him. The warder gives him a sip of mulled wine; the other two patients on the ward insist on it, he has to heat him up some wine.

Ida lurches over. Ida, stop lurching, I was in Tegel, I done my time. Then she stops lurching, she sits down, she presses her head down, she gets smaller and smaller and darker. There she lies – in the coffin – not moving.

Groans, Franz groans. His eyes. The warder sits down next to him, holds his hand. Someone should try and take that away, push the coffin away from him, I can't get up, I can't.

And he moves his hand. But the coffin doesn't budge. He hasn't reached it. Then Franz weeps with frustration. And stares and stares in frustration. And in his tears and in his frustration the coffin disappears. But Franz is still weeping.

But what is Franz Biberkopf weeping about, gentle readers? He is weeping because he is suffering and because of what he is suffering, and also for himself. That he did these things and behaved like this, that's what Franz Biberkopf is weeping about. Franz Biberkopf is weeping about himself.

It's broad noon, in the institution lunch is being brought out, the food cart is just going back to the main building, the kitchen warder and a couple of the better-off patients are pushing it out of the building.

Here is Mitzi with Franz. She has a calm, sweet expression on her face. She is wearing a street dress, and has a tight cloche hat on that covers her brow and goes over her ears. She looks candidly at Franz, calmly, intimately, the way he remembers her, when he sometimes ran into her on the street or in the bar. When he asks her to come nearer, she does so. He wants her to give him her hands. She gives him her hands, her two in his one. She has kid gloves on. Take yer gloves off, won't you. She takes them off, gives him her hands. Come on over here, Mitzi, don't be a stranger, gimme a kiss. Calmly she steps closer, looks at him candidly and intimately, and kisses him. Stop a minute, he says to her, I need you, you gotta help me. 'I can't, Frankie. I'm dead, you know I'm dead.' Stop here. 'I'd love to, but I can't.' And she kisses him again. 'You remember, Franz, from Freienwalde. You're not cross with me, are you?'

She's gone. Franz writhes. He tears open his eyes. He can't see her. What have I done? Why've I not got her any more. If I hadn't have showed her off to Reinhold, then I wouldn't have got involved with him again. What have I done. And now.

His contorted face produces a stammer: he wants her back. The warder just hears 'again' and he pours more wine into his open, dry mouth. Franz has to drink, he has no choice.

In the heat lies the dough, the dough rises, yeast pushes it, bubbles form, the bread rises and browns.

The voice of Death, the voice of Death, the voice of Death:

What's the use of so much strength, what's the use of going straight, oh yes, oh yes, look at her, discern, rue.

Whatever Franz has he throws from him. He holds nothing back.

In which is described what pain is

Here we describe what pain and suffering are. How pain burns and tears. Because it is pain that has come. Many people have described pain in their poems. Churchyards see pain every day.

Here we describe the effect of pain on Franz Biberkopf. Franz can't stand up to it, he throws himself down before it, he is its prey. He lays himself in the burning flame, so that he may be killed, destroyed and incinerated. We celebrate the effect of pain on Franz Biberkopf. We speak of the devastation wrought by pain. Snapping off, topping, casting down, dissolving, all these things it does.

To every thing there is a season: to kill and to heal, to break and to build, to cry and to laugh, to complain and to dance, to seek and to lose, to rend and to sew. There is a time to kill, mourn, seek and tear.

Franz wrestles and waits for Death, for merciful Death.

He thinks Death, the merciful and conclusive, is now approaching. He trembles as he pulls himself upright to welcome him.

For the second time they come to him, those who threw him down at noon. Franz says: let it all happen, this is me, don't leave without Franz Biberkopf, take me with you.

With deep quaking he receives the image of the pathetic Lüders. Foul Reinhold trudges up to him. With deep quaking he receives Ida's words, Mitzi's face, it's her, now everything is fulfilled. Franz howls and howls, I am guilty, I am not a human being, I am a beast, a monster.

At that hour of the evening, Franz Biberkopf, former transport worker, housebreaker, pimp, manslaughterer, died. Another lay in his bed. This other has the same papers as Franz, looks like Franz, but in another world he bears a different name.

So this was the end of Franz Biberkopf, which I wanted to describe from the moment he left Tegel prison to his end in the mental asylum Buch in the winter of 1928–9.

Now I would like to append a short report on the first hours and days of a new man who has the same papers as him.

Departure of the evil harlot, triumph of the great sacrificer, drummer and axe-swinger

Dirty snow on the fields, in the bare landscape outside the red walls of the institution. There is drumming and drumming. The whore of Babylon has lost, Death has won, and drums her away.

The whore spits and carries on and drools and screams: 'What's so good about him, what do you see in him, Franz Biberkopf, cook him till he's sour, your Gottlieb Schulze.'

Death beats his drum roll: 'I can't see what you've got in your cup, you hyena. Franz Biberkopf is here, I chopped him into little pieces. But because he's good and strong, he is to put on a new life, get out of my way, we both have nothing more to say.'

And she humps her back and screeches, and Death moves off, gets going, his grey giant coat flaps up, then paintings and land-scapes become visible swimming around him, all of them, swirling around him from his feet to his chest. And cries, shots, noise, triumph and tumult around Death. Triumph and tumult. The beast under the woman shies away, lashes out.

The river, the Beresina, the marching legions.

Marching along the Beresina the legions, the icy cold, the icy wind. They have come all the way from France, led by the great Napoleon. The wind blows, the snow whirls, the bullets whistle. They fight their way across the ice, they charge, they fall. And always the cries: vive l'empereur, vive l'empereur! Sacrifice, sacrifice is death.

Trundling of locomotives, cannons bang, exploding of grenades, barrage fire, Chemin des dames and Langemarck, 'Lieb Vaterland magst ruhig sein, lieb Vaterland magst ruhig sein'. The shelters buried, the troops slumped. Death spins his coat, sings: oh yes, oh yes.

Marching, marching. We're moving into battle with firm stride, we have 100 companions on our side, dawn red, dusk red, light us until we're dead, 100 companions drum, widdeboom widdeboom, if things aren't straight, they're skew, widdeboom widdeboom.

Death spins his coat and sings: oh yes, oh yes.

An oven burns, an oven burns, before an oven stands a mother with seven sons, the groaning of the people is behind them, they are to forswear the god of their people. They beam and stand there peaceably. Will you forswear and join us. The first says no and suffers the torture, the second says no and suffers the torture, the third says no and suffers the torture, the fourth says no and suffers the torture, the fifth says no and suffers the torture, the sixth says no and suffers the torture, the seventh says no and suffers the torture. The mother stands there, encouraging her sons. In the end she says no and suffers the torture. Death spins his coat and sings: oh yes, oh yes.

The woman with the seven heads yanks at her mount, the beast refuses to get up.

Marching, marching, we're marching into battle, with us are 100 companions, they pipe and drum, widdeboom widdeboom, one's all right one's all wrong, one stops still the other falls down, one runs on, the other lies still, widdeboom widdeboom.

Cheering and shouting, marching by sixes and twos and threes, marches the French Revolution, marches the Russian Revolution, march the Peasant Wars, the Anabaptists, they all fall into line behind Death, there is cheering in their wake, they are headed for freedom, the old world must fall, wake up, the dawn air, widdeboom widdeboom, in sixes, in twos, in threes, brothers, to the sun, to freedom, brothers to the light, in stride and left, right, left, right, widdeboom widdeboom.

Death spins his coat and laughs and grins and sings: oh yes, oh yes.

The great Babylon at last pulls the animal to its feet, it starts to trot, it races across the fields, it sinks into the snow. She turns back and howls in the face of grinning Death. Under the roaring, the animal collapses, the woman sways over the neck of her mount. Death spins his coat. He sings and grins: oh yes, oh yes. And the field soughs: oh yes, oh yes.

Beginnings are difficult

When the deathly-pale bedridden man who once was Franz Biberkopf could once more speak and look in Buch, the detectives and doctors asked him lots of questions, the detectives to help them with their inquiries, the doctors to help them with their diagnosis. From the detectives the man learnt that they have arrested a certain Reinhold, who earlier in his life, or in his earlier life, played a certain role. They tell him about Brandenburg and ask whether he knew one Moroskiewicz, and where he might be found. He is told these things several times over, and remains quiet. He was left in peace for the whole of one day. There is a reaper, Death yclept. He sets his knife to the whetter, now it cuts better. Careful, wee blue flower.

The following day he made his statement to the detective superintendent that he had nothing to do with the business in Freienwalde. If this Reinhold party says different, then – he's mistaken. The shrivelled, pale figure is to put together his alibi for that time. Everything in the man jibs at going back that way. It feels blocked off to him. With groans, he brings up a few dates. He groans that they're to leave him alone. He flinches like a beaten dog. The old

Biberkopf is gone, the new one is sleeping and sleeping. He says not one incriminating word about Reinhold. We all lie under one axe. We all lie under one axe.

His information checks out, it tallies with statements from Mitzi's gentleman and his nephew. The doctors do a little better. Catatonia is forgotten. It was a psychic trauma and ensuing semi-trance state, the man has traumatic events in his past, it's clear that alcohol plays a part. In the end, the whole argy-bargy over the diagnosis is left behind, the fellow obviously wasn't malingering, he was suffering from severe shock, and that's the main thing. So, draw a line under it, and he's left accountable for the shooting in Alexander-Quelle under Paragraph 51. Wonder if he'll be back here ever.

The wobbly fellow, whom they call Biberkopf in memory of the departed, doesn't know as he traipses about the building, sometimes helping out at mealtimes, and no longer subject to questions – he doesn't know that there's still lots of things going on behind him. The detectives are exercised about what happened with his arm, where he left it, where he was treated. They ask around in the Magdeburg clinic, it may all be ancient history, but the police are interested in ancient history, even if it's twenty years old. But they don't come up with anything, we've got to the happy end now, Herbert is a pimp as well, the boys have all got these golden girls, they blame them for everything, they claim to have got all their money off them. None of the police thinks that's true, maybe they get a little bit from the girls every now and again, but in between they're up to something. The brothers keep mum about that.

The storm, that storm as well, passes the man by, he's to be forgiven for all this too. Looks like you got yourself a return ticket this time, my son.

Then there is the day he is released. The police leave him in no doubt they will continue to take an interest in him. The things that belonged to the old Franz are produced from the cupboard, everything is restored to him, he puts his togs back on, there's still a bloodstain on the jacket, that's where a cop whacked him over the head with a nightstick, I don't want the false arm, and you can keep the wig as well, if you ever get to play-acting here, oh, we do that all the time, but just about the only thing we don't wear is a wig, you've got your release form, goodbye, nurse, come and visit us one day when the weather's good, will do, and thank you, I'll let you out.

So that too is now behind us.

Dear Fatherland, don't worry, I shan't slip again in a hurry

For the second time Biberkopf leaves an institution in which he was confined, we are near the end of our long road, and will take just one more short step with Franz.

The first establishment he left was the prison in Tegel. Timidly he hugged the red wall, and when he peeled himself off it and the 41 tram came and took him into Berlin, then the buildings wouldn't keep still, the roofs were falling on top of Franz, he had to walk and then sit for a long time before everything quietened down, and he felt strong enough to stay there and start over.

Now he is exhausted. He can't stand the sight of the locked institution. But there, as he gets off the train at the Stettiner Bahnhof, the suburban station, with the Baltic Hotel in front of him, he feels – nothing. The buildings keep still, the roofs are firmly anchored, he can move around freely in their lee, he doesn't need to be creeping into some courtyards. Yes, this fellow – let's call him Franz Karl Biberkopf, to distinguish him from his predecessor, Franz was baptized with a middle name as well, for his maternal grandfather – this fellow is now walking slowly up Invalidenstrasse, past Ackerstrasse, towards Brunnenstrasse, past the yellow market building, and he's looking coolly at the shops and the buildings and the people all running around, and it's been a long time since I last saw this, and now I'm back. Biberkopf was gone a long time. Now Biberkopf is back. Your man Biberkopf is back.

Suffer them to approach, suffer them to approach, the wide plains, the red-brick buildings with lights on inside them. Suffer them to approach, the freezing travellers with sacks on their backs. This is a reunion, more than a reunion.

He goes into a bar on Brunnenstrasse and picks up a newspaper. Will he find his name anywhere, or Mitzi's, or Herbert's, or Reinhold's? Not a sausage. Where shall I go, where will I go? Eva, I'll visit Eva.

She's not living at Herbert's any more. The landlady opens the door: Herbert's gone, the police have been through all his stuff, he hasn't come back, his things are all up in the attic, should I put them up for sale, I don't know, I'll ask around. Franz Karl runs into Eva out west, in the flat of her put-put patron. She takes him in. She's happy to see Franz Karl Biberkopf.

'Yeah, Herbert's gone, he got put away for two years, I do what I can for him, they asked about you a lot too, first in Tegel, and what are you up to, Franz?' 'I'm fine, I'm out of Buch, they gave me my hunting licence.' 'Yes, I read it in the paper.' 'Wonder what they've got to write about. But I'm weak, Eva. Institution food is institution food.'

Eva sees the look in his eye, a still, dark, questing look that she's never seen before in him. She doesn't say anything about herself, she's been through stuff too, on his account, but he's very feeble, she looks for a place for him, she helps him, he's not to do anything. He says himself when he's sitting in his new place and she's about to go: no, I can't do anything any more.

So what does he do? He slowly starts going out on the street again, and walking around Berlin.

Berlin 52° 31' north, 13° 25' east, twenty mainline stations, 121 suburban stations, twenty-seven circular-railway stations, fourteen S-Bahn, seven shunting yards, tramway, overhead railway, autobus network, yes, but there's only one imperial city, there's only one Vienna. Desire of women, three words expressing all desires of women. Imagine a New York company bringing out a new cosmetic that gives yellowing irises the fresh blue of youth. The most beautiful eyes, from sapphire-blue to deep brown, all coming out of a tube. Why spend all that money getting your furs cleaned.

He walks around the city. There are many things that can make you healthy, if only the heart is healthy.

First off, the Alex. It's still there. It doesn't let on much, the winter was terribly cold so they stopped work and left everything the way it was, the big ram is now in Georgenkirchplatz, that's where they're digging out the rubble from Hahn's emporium, they've laid down a lot of tracks, maybe they're going to build a station here. And there's lots of other things going on in the Alex, but main thing: it's still there. And there's always people walking across it, it's dreadfully dirty, because the city fathers of Berlin are so hands-off and humane and they let all the snow just gradually melt away and turn to dirt, they don't want anyone to touch it. When there're cars driving past, you need to jump in the nearest entryway else you'll catch a hatful of slush and a summons for theft of public property into the bargain. The old 'Mokka-fix' is shut, on the corner is a new joint called 'Mexiko' which is supposed to be a world sensation: the chef at the grill in the window, an Indian blockhouse, and they've put up a security fence round the Alexander barracks, who knows what's going on there, they're knocking out windows. And the electric trams are stuffed with people, they're all of them busy, and the price of a ticket is still 20 pfennigs, a fifth of a mark in cash; but if you want you can pay 30 or buy yourself a Ford instead. The S-Bahn is still going, there's no first and second class, just third, everyone's sitting pretty on their cushioned behinds, if they're not standing, which has been known to happen. Getting off between station stops is forbidden and carries a fine of 150 marks; you'd have to be a mug to do that, given that you stand to pick up an almighty electric shock as well. Admiration for a shoe, kept clean and supple by new Ägü. Please enter and leave quickly, move back inside the carriage, plenty of room inside.

These are all fine and dandy, they help a man get back into the swing of things, even if he's feeling a bit weak, so long as the heart is healthy. Don't stand by the door. Well, and Franz Karl Biberkopf is healthy all right, would that everyone was keeping time like him.

Wouldn't be worth doing anyway, telling a long story about someone who wasn't good on his pins. And when a travelling bookseller one day stood on the street in mizzle and bellyached about his poor takings, Cäsar Flaischlen went up to his box of books. He listened to the bellyaching, then he patted the man on both shoulders, said: 'Quit bellyaching, keep the sun in your heart', and disappeared. That was the occasion for the celebrated sun poem. A sun like that, not that one but similar, is in the heart of Biberkopf too, and a tot of brandy and a lot of extract of malt stirred into the soup, that will do its bit to reinvigorate the man. We would like to offer you a share in an extraordinary vat of 1925 Trabener Würzgarten at a preferential price of 90 marks for fifty bottles, including emballage from here, or just 1.60 per bottle, sans glass and crate, which we will take back in the accounted price. Dijodyl for arteriosclerosis. Biberkopf doesn't have arteriosclerosis, he's just a little weak, he was fasting like a madman when he was in Buch, and it takes a while for a man to get replenished. Still doesn't mean he needs to see the magnetopath that Eva wants to send him to, because he helped her one time.

And when Eva accompanies him out to Mitzi's grave at the end of the week, she straight away has occasion to mark him and how much better he's feeling. No crying, just a handful of tulips he lays out, strokes the cross, and then he takes Eva by the arm and walks off with her.

He sits opposite her in the café, eating Bienenstich[13] in memory of Mitzi, because she could never get enough of it, and it tastes all right, though it's not really his thing. So we've been to see little Mitzi, and one shouldn't go to too many graveyards, you'll only catch cold, maybe next year, on her birthday. You see, Eva, I've no need to keep running to Mitzi, you can believe me and all, for me she's there even without the grave, and same with Reinhold, I'll not forget Reinhold, not even if my arm should grow back, I'll not forget him. There's some things where you're no more than the clothes you stand up in and not a human being at all if you forget them. So Biberkopf talks to Eva, and eats his Bienenstich.

Eva fancied being his girlfriend before, but she's gone a little cold on the idea now. The whole business with Mitzi and then the madhouse, that was all too much for her, no matter how fond she still is of the man. And the baby she's expecting from him, turns out that never happened either, she miscarried, it would have been lovely, but it weren't meant to be, so that's for the best as well, especially as Herbert's not around, and her patron prefers her without too, because it finally dawned on the man that it wouldn't necessarily be his anyway, and you can't really blame him.

So they sit quietly side by side, thinking backward and forward, eating Bienenstich and a Mohrenkopf with whipped cream.

And by the right quick march left right left right

We next see the man at the trial of Reinhold and the plumber Matter, aka Oskar Fischer, for conspiracy to murder and murder of Emilie Parsunke of Bernau on 1 September 1928 in Freienwalde outside Berlin. Biberkopf is not in the dock. The one-armed man is the subject of general interest, big excitement, the murder of his sweetheart, love life in the underworld, he went a little mad after her death, was suspected of complicity, tragic situation.

The one-armed man is called as a witness, who, as the expert reports say, is now restored to health and able to stand: the dead woman, whom he refers to as Mitzi, had no relationship with Reinhold, he and Reinhold were close, but Reinhold had a terrible unnatural sexual appetite, and that was how it all came about. He doesn't know whether Reinhold had sadistic inclinations from the start. He assumes Mitzi will have put up resistance to Reinhold in Freienwalde, and that he will have done it in a temper, or, as they call it, affect. Do you know anything about his youth? No, I didn't know him then. Did he not talk to you about it? What about drinking? Yes, that was this way: he used not to drink, but lately he started, how much he is unable to say, he used not to be able to take a sip of beer, just lemonade and coffee.

And that's all they can get out of Biberkopf on the subject of Reinhold. Nothing about his arm, nothing about their falling out, their fight, I shouldn't have done it, I should never have tangled with him. Eva sits in the public gallery, along with several of Pums's people. Reinhold and Biberkopf lock glances. The one-armed man has no sympathy at all for the accused between the two guards, who is looking at a long sentence, just a curious tenderness. I had a comrade once, I'll never have a better. I need to look at him and keep looking at him, nothing is as important as looking at you. The world is made of sugar and shit, I can look at you without batting an eyelid, I know who you are, I meet you here, my boy, in the dock, outside I'll meet you another thousand times, but that won't turn my heart to stone.

Reinhold is intending, if something should cross him in the hearing, to send the whole Pums group sky-high, he would shop the lot of them if they taunt him, he's kept that up his sleeve, especially in the event that Biberkopf should smarm up to the judge, the fuckwit, the whole thing is his fault anyway. But there they are in the public gallery, Pums's people, there's Eva, there's a few detectives, we know which ones they are. And then he calms down, hesitates, bethinks himself. He's relying on his friends, eventually a man does get out, and you need them on the inside too, and it's all better than doing the cops a good turn anyway. And then Biberkopf has been unexpectedly decent. They said something about him having been in Buch. Strange, how the sillybilly has changed, funny expression on his face, as if he can't move his eyes, maybe they rusted fast when he was in Buch, and the ponderous way he speaks. There's still something odd about him. Biberkopf knows, when Reinhold declines to give evidence, that he has nothing to be thankful to him for.

Ten years' labour for Reinhold, manslaughter in a state of aggravated passion, exacerbated by alcohol, compulsive character, and a difficult upbringing. Reinhold accepts the penalty.

In the public gallery someone screams when the sentence is announced, and then starts sobbing loudly. It is Eva, the thought of Mitzi has overpowered her. Biberkopf turns round on the bench when he hears her. Then he collapses into himself, and props his head in his hand. There is a reaper, Death yclept, I am yours, she came to you in love, she protected you, and you, scream shame, scream shame. Straight after the trial Biberkopf is offered a job as assistant porter in a medium-sized factory. He accepts. Beyond that there is nothing to report on his life.

We have reached the end of this story. It is long, but that is because it had to stretch and keep stretching till it reached its climax, that point of peripeteia where light strikes the whole thing.

We have been down a dark alley, first of all no lamp was burning, all we knew was that this is the way, gradually it grew brighter and then a little brighter still, and finally there is the lamp and below it we can read the name of the street. It's been a revelatory process of a particular sort. Franz Biberkopf did not walk down the same street with us. He ran pell-mell in the dark, he ran into trees, and the more he ran the more trees there were for him. It was dark already, and when he struck a tree, he pressed his eyes shut in horror. And the more trees he ran into the more he clamped his eyes shut in horror. His head full of holes, almost insensate, he finally reached the end. In falling, he opened his eyes. There was a lamp burning over his head, and he could read the street sign.

We leave him as an assistant porter in a medium-sized factory. He is no longer standing all alone on Alexanderplatz. There are some to the right and left of him, and in front of him are some, and others are behind him.

Much misfortune comes of walking alone. If there are several of you, that is already better. You have to get used to listening to other people, because what others say concerns me. Then I see who I am and what I can take on. My battle is being fought on all sides of me, I have to pay attention, before I notice anything it's my own turn.

He is an assistant porter in a factory. What is destiny? One thing is stronger than me. If there are two of us, it's difficult to be stronger than me. If we are ten, still harder. And if we are a thousand and a million, then it's very difficult.

Also, it's nicer and better to be with others. Then I feel and know everything better. A ship isn't secure without a sheet-anchor, and a man may not be without many other men. I know better now what is right and what is wrong. I have been taken in by words before now, and have had to pay bitterly for it, that won't happen to Biberkopf again. The words come rolling towards you, you need to watch yourself, see that they don't run you over, if you don't watch the school bus it'll make a mess of you. I won't swear on anything again in a hurry. Dear Fatherland, rest easy, I'm awake, I know what's at stake.

They often march past his window with flags and music and singing, Biberkopf coolly sticks his head out the door and remains calm. Shut your mouth and walk in step, march along with the rest of us gits. If I join their parade, I'll only have to pay for it later with my life. That's why I first calculate everything, and when the time comes and it's in my interests, then I'll go. Men have been given reason, oxen have herd instinct.

Biberkopf does his job as assistant porter, takes the numbers, checks the wagons, watches over the comings and goings.

Be alert, be a lert, things are happening in the world. The world's not made of sugar, you know. When they throw gas bombs I'll choke, you don't know why they threw them, but that's not the point, you had time to think about it.

When there's a war on, and they enlist me, and I don't know why, and the war is there even without me, then it's my fault, and it serves me right. Be alert, be a lert, the country needs lerts. The sky may rain and hail, you can't do anything about that, but there are plenty of other things that you can do something about. Then I won't shout like I used to: destiny, destiny. You don't need to respect something as destiny, you should look at it, turn it over in your hand and destroy it.

Be a lert, eyes wide, watch out, a thousand belong together, whoever doesn't wake is either a laughingstock or doomed.

The drums whirl behind him Marching, marching. We're going into battle with firm stride, with us are 100 companions, dawn red, dusk red, light us the way to early death.

Biberkopf is a little worker. We know what we know, we had to pay dearly enough for it.

The road is into freedom, into freedom, the old world is doomed, wake up, dawn air. And link arms and right and left and right and left, and marching, marching, we're marching into war, with us are 100 comrades, they drum and play, widdeboom widdeboom, one's all right, the other's all wrong, one stops still, the other falls down, one runs on, the other lies still, widdeboom, widdeboom.

THE END

Appendix

Alexanderplatz[14]

Omnibus halt number two. Alexanderplatz – Königstrasse – Schlossplatz – Unter den Linden – Brandenburger Tor – Friedrich-Ebert-Strasse – Lennéstrasse – Viktoriastrasse. Frequency every four (off-peak six) minutes, lines marked with a * offer service at night. Alexanderplatz, Alex, my poor smart Alec, worrave they done to yer? It hurts to see you this way. They stole yer sweetheart Berolina, and you used to be so nice and green, now you're nothing but hoardings and holes in the ground. Tietz has hoisted four white flags, what signifies Christmas sales, up on top the globe is lit, the police headquarters is a dirty red; I put my hand in my pocket, I must leave you, we can be friends no longer. All fares please, 20 pfennigs. Torn, crumpled or illegible tickets are invalid. All tickets are non-transferable. Valid on day of purchase only. Extract from see transport by-laws over.

We stagger off, beetle off, shuffle off. The thing has a Maybach engine, is the size of a house, and runs like an eel. How would you like to wind up under something like that? You couldn't pay me to. 'No standing room! No pedestrians!' But we're driving, according to the by-laws, valid only on day of purchase. They're already sitting at Aschinger's, I'd rather be sitting at Aschinger's myself than here, 'No standing room, no pedestrians', we know, here's the first stop, Alexanderplatz station. Look out, and you're amazed to see the human tide crossing the road. Where can they all be coming from? Well, the ones on the left, they've had business in the court or with the police, and on the right they're coming from the market, and then there are some that are heading for the train station, oh, do stay, it's quite nice in Berlin, I'm driving quietly down Königstrasse, enjoy life, it's not as though Werneuchen has that much more to offer. – Then the monster winds up again, they've been building this bridge for a hundred years, a blind man can see that, they're putting in new supports, and once they're in they take them out again and try different ones, that's progress for you in Berlin. Wertheim, *grüss Gott*, inexpensive Christmas goodies, New Year's gifts, cards, joke items. And now hold your breath, this you won't believe: they've tore off the top of Salamander shoes, but Salamander himself isn't going anywhere, nothing up top and a shop on the ground floor, the earth may be quaking, but he's still selling his boots. After all, you need boots, even in a hearthquake. And over the way there's Leiser's, who sells boots, oh God, and then there's Dorndorf, with his boots, and Stiller: what's going on here? It's amazing, all the barefoot people of the east are hotfooting it here, I think I'd better get off, but then the thing has moved off again. Gumpert's and Dobrin's are behind me, largest selection of domestic and international papers, and the best drinks and sweets, American iced drinks, ice cream sodas, milk shakes (heated up, for an extra 20 pfennigs). Rathaus stop. – This is the Berlin city hall, it stands here and watches over everything in the city, and behind it stands the town hall, which also watches over everything in the city, and then there are municipal offices, which also watch over everything in the city. They never sleep, except at night. Six passengers get off, three get on, this is the Berlin bus, *en passant*. The Rathaus is on the left, on the right people are crowding into the shops. The boots they didn't manage to sell earlier, you'll find them here at Mercedes; Spaeth sells lottery tickets at the top and the Reverend Fahsel's sexual problems further down, Brockhaus encyclopaedia in monthly instalments of 6.50, he claims: animals are watching you,[15] but I've yet to see that myself, leastwise not on the bus. Later on, I'm going to Spaeth's to buy myself the winning ticket in monthly instalments. On, across Spandauer, the corners are tenanted by Grumach and N. Israel. Oh, the mighty tribe of Israel! Its premises stretch all the way from Poststrasse to Simons

Pharmacy! Across the street is the post office, the one with the rootin-tootin horn. A No. 12 passes us, it spreads its blue sheen through Berleen: Hildebrandt Drinking Chocolate, that would be. The post, the post, to make a payment you need to go around the corner, telephone exchange east, section Berolina and Königs-graben. Report breakdowns to Room 274, send me a letter, write me a card. We're moving again, the Maybach motor is turning, extract from see transport by-laws over, Kurfürstenbrücke, Marstall, Schlossplatz. I will get off and someone else will get on in my place (because man is noble, well-intentioned and good).[16]

(trans. M. H.)

Notes

1. These words, 'The cry resounds like thunder's peal, / Like crashing waves and clang of steel: / The Rhine, the Rhine, our German Rhine, / Who will defend our stream divine?' are from the nineteenth-century patriotic song 'Die Wacht am Rhein'. For obvious reasons, it was highly popular during the First World War. See also pp. 9, 50, 81–3, 121, 213, 429, 439.

2. The 'Heckerlied' of 1848, here in its original revolutionary form, not in the obnoxious anti-Semitic adaptation sung by the Nazis. See also pp. 76, 85.

3. 'Onward, brothers, to light and freedom', a socialist rallying song.

4. Setting of Ludwig Uhland's nineteenth-century poem 'Der gute Kamerad', sung throughout the twentieth century at German military funerals. In the Weimar period and the Third Reich, it was instrumentalized by the Right as a celebration of sacrifice and heroic death in battle. 'I once had a comrade, / You will find no better. / The drum called to battle, / He walked at my side, / In the same pace and step. // A bullet came a-flying, / Is it my turn now or yours? / He was swept away, / He lies at my feet, / Like it were a part of me . . .' See also pp. 138, 278, 279, 437.

5. *Berlin Alexanderplatz: The Story of Franz Biberkopf*, trans. Eugene Jolas (London: Penguin Modern Classics, 1978), p. 96.

6. 'Hast du geliebt am schönen Rhein', a popular Weimar song, lyrics by Hans Willi Mertens (1865–1921).

7. Derisory spoonerist version of the opening of Schiller's 'Die Glocke', substituting *Mehl* (flour) for *Lehm* (clay).

8. Manoli was a German make of cigarette. In 1910, the earliest illuminated advertisement in Berlin showed the letters of the word 'Manoli' dispersing in a cloud of coloured lights; this led to 'Manoli' becoming a term for loopy or dippy.

9. *Berlin Alexanderplatz*, trans. Eugene Jolas, pp. 292–3.

10. *Berlin Alexanderplatz*, trans. Eugene Jolas, p. 419

11. *Berlin Alexanderplatz*, trans. Eugene Jolas, p. 421.

12. *Berlin Alexanderplatz*, trans. Eugene Jolas, p. 425.

13. 'Bee-sting' and 'Moor's head' are the macabre names of two types of German confectionery, both very sweet.

14. Döblin's contribution to 'Writers' Relay on the Omnibus', in *Berliner Tageblatt*, 1 January 1929.

15. *Tiere sehen dich an*, by the popular author Paul Eipper, published in 1928, and filmed in 1930. Georg Salter, who designed the cover, also designed the charming original cover for *Berlin Alexanderplatz*.

16. 'edel sei der Mensch, hilfreich und gut': Goethe.

Afterword

The literary name and fame of the city of Berlin, if not the idea of modern city literature altogether, are founded on the novel in your hands, first published in October 1929, two weeks before Black Friday and the Wall Street Crash. Others had written about their cities – New York and Boston and Paris and London and Rome for tens or even hundreds of years. Berlin – itself a new and brash and rather unappealing place, so new, in fact, that the joke was that no one was actually *born* there, its inhabitants all coming from elsewhere, like Döblin himself, who arrived there as a boy, from the Baltic city of Stettin, now Szczecin in Poland – is at once invented and immortalized and brilliantly and commensurately styled in *Berlin Alexanderplatz* Even then, it was thought, there's something wrong with this picture (as though Germans, the 'belated nation' in Helmuth Plessner's influential phrase, could not invent anything by themselves, or at least not anything new), and the author of the novel was and apparently still is, quite wrongly and needlessly, described as the German Dos Passos, or the German Joyce, whom Döblin had indeed read and admired, in Georg Goyert's translation of 1928, but to whom he thought he owed no debt, as he sought to prove by writing the name as 'Yoice', the spelling ironically following the soft German pronunciation (the Berlin dialect even softens hard 'g's).

A masterpiece is always a mixed blessing: other things being equal – they aren't – one would almost sooner not have one. *Berlin Alexanderplatz* is the one popular success in the large and extremely varied output, before and after, of its author; as Wilfried Schoeller, Döblin's biographer, writes, it is the tombstone overlaying, nay, burying, crushing, obliterating the possibility of any interest in his

447

other work[i]. When Döblin returned to Germany in 1945 from Californian exile (he was one of the more abject and less amphibian of the celebrated group that fetched up there, including the Mann brothers, Bertolt Brecht, Lion Feuchtwanger and Franz Werfel), hoping to interest readers and publishers in his new manuscripts, the only thing anyone wanted from him was a new printing of *Berlin Alexanderplatz*, in 20,000 copies. Before that, there was only the glare of unsuccess, without, evidently, the masterpiece's long but occasionally beneficent shadow. He wrote: 'Despite my unstinting literary endeavours and having my name more or less constantly in the papers, the authorship of eleven volumes earned me less than 400 marks a month in 1924, and that of twelve in 1925, less than 300.' What may look like black humour here – even more books, even less money – is probably a chance resemblance, and is nothing more than *Huh!* grievance and characteristic mordancy. It is a life full of breaks, rancour and invective. A literary magazine's horoscope published on New Year's Day 1926 – a comic, gossipy feature, but who knows, and Döblin, who went to palmists, certainly had time for such things – saw him with malign accuracy: 'Alfred Döblin, born on 10 August, 1878, came into the world at a moment of deep psychic disharmony, through poorly aspected Moon in Capricorn. Venus is opposed: to him the goddess is no friend. The conjunction of Mars and the Sun gives rise to combativeness and discord and is an impediment to production.'

In 1928, Döblin's monthly stipends were finally stopped by his publisher, Samuel Fischer, who had some time before been warned that his author's talent exceeded his ability to manage either it or himself, in other words that he was liable to prove difficult and unpopular. He had turned fifty, an atheistical Jew (later to convert to Catholicism), he was married with four children (all sons), and he was running a second penurious livelihood as a doctor and psychiatrist with a practice in the working-class Friedrichstrasse district in the east of Berlin.

Sometime in October 1927, Döblin embarked on *Berlin Alexanderplatz*. He didn't write about the process much, either at the time or afterwards (even before it appeared, he had, as was typical of him, 'moved on'); correspondence, if there was any, has disappeared; then the chance discovery of a suitcase full of materials (the so-called *Zürcher Fund* or 'Zurich trove', clippings and documents and postcards and the author's own photographs, many presented in the 1978 Marbach exhibition and catalogue) supplied hard evidence of the extensive work of pillage and improvisation and sampling involved in what was really for twelve or fifteen months almost a 'live' book. People talk airily about 'jazz' rhythms and forms, but this is the real thing: weather reports, articles on nutrition, local news items, personal interest stories, letters from patients, all incorporated into the novel. For a time Döblin must have been a sort of literary cistern, inflow, outflow, and mysteries of drift and whirlpool and obscure current in between. The work-in-progress of the book matched the work-in-progress of the city – one can imagine the former, too, with its own duckboards and drillings and tunnellings and detours and demolitions and temporary closures and promised improvements. In a Dantesque vignette, Wolfgang Koeppen remembers sighting Döblin at about this time, as a twenty-year-old (Koeppen, that is) in Berlin, in the Romanisches Café, frequented by writers and popularly known as 'Café Grössenwahn', the Megalomania Café:

Pale face, pointy nose. The features above the stiff collar could have belonged to a clergyman. Jesuitical, which I propose as a positive here. Learned, finical, ascetic, disciplined. But the eyes behind the spectacles, which were oval, and I seem to remember, wire-rimmed, they were tired, veiled, elsewhere, only half-intent on the board and the figures. Alert, like a huntsman, but somehow passively so. It was clear that he wanted to win the game, and in time he did win it. But straightaway it became a matter of indifference to him. Perhaps he was observing himself, seeing into himself, thinking, what am I doing here, I should be in Babylon.

Babylon was Berlin. Berlin was a Moloch. Berlin was the jungle, was Upton Sinclair's Chicago or Brecht's Mahagonny or Paul Bowles's Wen Kroy, was any big rapacious modern city, but it was also the provincial – both senses – capital of Brandenburg. Döblin wrote: 'And now Berlin. The chaos of cities. In the process of becoming a London of cosmopolitanism: first, a mix of people, now a mix of peoples.' It was both what was outside and what was mythically and compulsively inside, the reality and the dream, the statistical facts and the caricature. A much younger Döblin had referred scathingly once to 'the Brandenburg Nineveh' or maybe 'Nineveh-on-Spree'. There is a photograph of the time, a slightly elevated view of the Alexanderplatz, looking across at Hermann Tietz's pincushion-cum-*Pickelhaube* department store; the dirty white or grey space of the square in the bottom half of the picture might be the sandy soil of some edge-town like Marrakesh or Tashkent, but seems actually to be snow, chewed up by tyre tracks; the tiny scurrying human figures and vehicles look like a combustible confusion of infantry and artillery; there seems to be a rickety wooden police watchtower of preposterous elevation; while bizarrely, the building facing Tietz's has black smoke issuing from it, as though it had suffered a direct hit from a bomb or shell. It's a picture of peace and prosperity, but it might almost be a war photograph. To walk or ride anywhere here in this camel encampment is surely to risk life and limb.

Throughout the twenties, Döblin wrote pieces about Berlin for the papers, almost unfiltered impressions, breathless, canny, fast-forward. A relay of nine writers was commissioned to write accounts of travelling on one of Berlin's new omnibus lines. Döblin was given the section from Alexanderplatz to Schlossplatz. His 'hood. 'We stagger off, beetle off, shuffle off. The thing has a Maybach engine, is the size of a house, and runs like an eel. How would you like to wind up under something like that?' The soon-to-be-notorious transcriptions of routes and tickets and prices and transport by-laws are deployed, zany little rhymes appear, wares, voices, pedestrians. Consciousness is in constant flux; the style is osmotic, adaptive, gauzy. Shoe shops, police, American-style milkshakes. 'Six passengers get off, three get on, this is the Berlin bus, *en passant*.' He is not so much a camera as a non-specific recording device, the involuntary ear as much as the selective or beguiled eye, in equal parts bombarded and hungry. Perhaps from there it is not so far to the

idea of Franz Biberkopf, or as sometimes here (and why not?),
'Frankie BBK', a man playing catch-up, pinball to flipper, hero as
anti-hero as victim, mammal restored to herd after technical time-
out, because, as has been remarked, his antagonist in the novel is
not so much the coffee-and-lemonade Reinhold with his furrowed
face and strange strength and woollen sea-boot hose as reality itself,
as the everything-that-is-the-case-and-then-some of the city hoisting
itself onto the scales. On one of his earlier jaunts, in 1923 ('A sunny
morning; I set off on a circumambulation of the Alexanderplatz'),
Döblin encountered a busker:

From the entrance of one of the houses comes a sound of singing; people
are standing around; I walk in. There in the courtyard, accompanied by
all sorts of theatrical caperings, a rather down-at-heel fellow, no longer in
the first flush of youth, is padding around, singing – yes, and singing
what? *Heil dir im Siegerkranz.* Every verse; I last heard it in 1918, and am
thunderstruck. There is some giggling, others are aghast; he just carries
on belting it out.

Surely, as the critic Klaus Müller-Salget surmises, this scene, from
an article in the *Berliner Tageblatt* called 'Eastwise round the Alexanderplatz', is the earliest germ of the novel: the veteran singing
wartime songs in the courtyard for pennies.

Other things played into the book (as much as anything else, literature is about chance, or is not without chance, or getting chance
to work in your favour, and with the resolutely non-planning Döblin, rather more than most). A friend gave him a glossary of Berlin
words and expressions, *Der richtige Berliner.* Now, Döblin had partly
grown up with Berlin and its *Schnauze* or slang (among the principal elements or tendencies of which are criminality, the self-conceit
of the capital city, Yiddish, a humour both grinding and flippant,
and deliberately bad grammar, like the switching of accusative and
dative); as an author and wordsmith he was attuned to it, and interested in it; and as a doctor he would have come across it all the
time. But even so, seeing the 1925 edition, which Döblin worked
with (or I could say, from), brings many shocks of recognition.

Then he was asked to write the introduction to a collection of Berlin photographs by one Mario von Bucovich. Here, for the first time, he made an extensive use of statistics, claimed that brute scale rather than any particular characteristics defined the city, and argued that the essence of Berlin was invisible – an unusual argument to advance in a book of photographs, Schoeller notes, but it chimes with the auditory Döblin, in whom the visuals may be distorted, may be caricature, but the sounds are authentic. Perhaps one last bit of chance was Döblin's reconciliation with his publisher, Samuel Fischer. Fischer, as said, had washed his hands of his author, but one of his editors, aware of *Berlin Alexanderplatz* and no doubt its unusual potential, persuaded Fischer's wife Hede to invite Döblin to give a reading from the manuscript at the Fischers' villa in Grunewald. Fischer was won over, and opted in again. He did insist, though, on the subtitle, 'The story of Franz Biberkopf'; 'Berlin Alexanderplatz', for Fischer, was the name of a railway stop, not a title for a book.

Remains to describe the novel's success, which was extraordinary for anything so adventurously composed and with, on the face of it, such a resolutely ignoble focus on murder, prostitution, theft, betrayal, drunkenness, poverty and crippledom: following its serialization (in excerpted form) in the *Frankfurter Zeitung*, it was reviewed, overwhelmingly positively, some 120 times; negative reactions, like the fury and disdain of Communist reviewers, who either disliked the self-professed petit-bourgeois author Döblin, or couldn't see a proper proletarian role model in his criminal, and worse, apolitical hero, if anything helped further. The book quickly sold out its 10,000 first print run, and sales were quite soon pushing 50,000; an interesting radio adaptation followed the next year (with Döblin himself involved: like the single father in the tenement section of the novel, he loved the new medium); and in 1931 a more conventional film version starring the popular and imposing Heinrich George (not unlike Oliver Hardy on the poster) gave further currency to the title and the story (though ironically it did scant justice to the fluid, film-influenced techniques of the book – say, Walter Ruttmann's 1927 documentary film *Symphony of a City*). In

Afterword

short order, translations came out in Dutch, English, French, Spanish, Italian, Danish, Swedish, Hungarian, Czech and even – in 1935, and in the teeth of continuing opposition from the German Communists – Russian. Still, it wouldn't have been Döblin if it had all been roses and gravy ever after. The awarding of the 1929 Nobel Prize to Thomas Mann less than a month after publication (with a staggering 700,000 additional sales of a new popular edition of *Buddenbrooks* rushed out by Fischer, who also happened to be Mann's publisher) all but crushed *Berlin Alexanderplatz*. With the coming to power of Hitler in January 1933, prospects for the book, any further payments to the author, and the possibility of a continued life in Germany all suddenly and completely ceased for the next dozen years. Warned by friends, Döblin left Germany the day after the Reichstag Fire.

Berlin Alexanderplatz has had time on its side. Which is to say that fiction, inasmuch as it has developed at all in the last ninety years, has gone its way: the way of greater chaos, absorptiveness, allusiveness, speed, a kind of interiority that is indistinguishable from exteriority (and of course vice versa). We know as readers that what we see and hear we are; we know the world is a violent and intoxicating place; we know that a lot of our lives is sub-rational, and that a lot of what we know is trivial or doesn't matter. Hence, Beats, post-Moderns, a great deal especially of the American writing of the last fifty years, documentary fiction, experimental and difficult texts – but also simple and popular writing, crime fiction and so forth – all are in its debt or shadow. Döblin was long dismayed that writing addressed itself to such a tiny potential audience, or rather, that good books (heck, even bad books!) excluded, *a priori*, the overwhelming majority of people. He thought – in view of his reputation and the difficulty of reading him, ironically – that things should be made easier and more tempting for the reader. But simplicity, ease of access, folk-speech, they are in him as well.

I used to think of *Berlin Alexanderplatz* that it had good bones; I still do. The story of Franz as told in the little chapter summaries and episode titles – of how he comes out of prison; regains his bearings in Berlin; is cheated by Lüders; goes into a great alcoholic sulk; starts over; meets Reinhold; takes a turn to the bad; is run over and loses an arm; falls in with his old pals Herbert and Sonia; meets Mitzi and becomes her pimp; sees Reinhold again; forgives him; rejoins Pums's band of fruit sellers, this time with real commitment; loses Mitzi; is distraught; is violently arrested; seeks, by starving himself into a cataleptic state, to die; and is finally restored to Berlin, given a middle name and a menial job and a new beginning – is an almost ideal blend of surge and turn, or oomph and twist. What took me longer to understand or appreciate were the extrinsic features of the book: the things that didn't advance the story, or that were put there to amplify it, or provide a counterpoint to it. I was impatient with, or perplexed by, the biblical and mythological episodes, cosmic or cosmological connections, other narratives. So intent was I on Franz, and if not on Franz, then on his creator, that I was blinded to the fact that the novel was not primarily biographical, much less autobiographical (other than the conversation of the doctors in the 'closed institution' of Buch near the end, where Döblin worked from 1906 to 1908, it's not easy to think what that might be), but documentary: not a slice but the whole pie.

The book contains a great deal that is simply there for its own sake. Robert Musil talked about Döblin's 'pursuing the principle of interest: an interesting idea, one immerses oneself in it, keeps out other things, and all done with panache'. And then: 'Intellectually, it's not enough, but it's enough for the better kind of reader.' There does seem to be a prodigality, an unworked-out-ness, a roughness-at-the-edges if not an outright scruffiness about Döblin, as he offers the reader not a biographical, but a kind of intellectual collage, put together from some of the diverse things he knew about and thought about. And there we see the one and the many, the interest in systems, in mass-explanations, both a scientist's and a spiritual man's sense of le tout, sometimes an almost touching wish to explain how things hang together, how they work: the law; the slaughterhouse; bread-making; Newton's First and Second Laws of Mechanics; psychiatry; sugar and starch; trees; the avatars

Adam and Abraham and Job; mythology; solar energy; weather; the city and mass-transportation; trades unions and politics; ventilation; communications from beacon to telegraph; manned flight; sexuality; storms; sacrifice and healing; angels and birds. The systems exist, they are not codified, there is no über-system, except perhaps the book itself, which is one of those vying (with, among others, *Peter Rabbit*, according to Malcolm Lowry, who was an early admirer) for the title The Great Book of Everything. Perhaps Musil is right, and *Berlin Alexanderplatz* does run on interest, on capacity, on variety, on a jostle of ideas as much as language and characters. Truly, the competing and the reinforcing explanations crowd the ether. In an unused preface for the book, Döblin wrote: 'There are two paths in this world, one visible and one invisible.' Franz Biberkopf, as Klaus Schröter says, walks both of them[ii] He is there from gutter to stars, though he may not always know it, he is (in one of the few myths not used or alluded to in the book!) both the earth-hugging Antaeus and the Hercules who would pick him up and throw him away.

One of the ways in which things have moved Döblin's way is that language – including the language of books – has become so much more demotic. It is hard to imagine a contemporary novel being taken to task for this, the way Eugene Jolas's translation of *Berlin Alexanderplatz* was in certain quarters in 1931: 'There is not a word known to our profanity, vulgarity, obscenity, slang and gangster-dom that is not found in it . . . It has been, however, a bit overworked; there was really no need of perfect indecency'.[iii] Standard practice has, to some extent, caught up; we all talk more like thieves, and some of us write more that way too. Döblin got there early, and was waiting for us. Perfect indecency is more or less where we're at. In a sense, it's made him easier to translate now than when his book came out.

I admire the spirit of Jolas, who is remarkably wholehearted as a translator, and competes feistily with his author. In Anke Detken's survey of some of the early translations of *Berlin Alexanderplatz* he usually fares best, certainly compared to the first Spanish version, which translates street names (the title is *Plaza de Alejandro*, if you will!), or the first French translation, which more insidiously anti-quates, literarizes, cuts and domesticates – substitutes the inevitable City of Light for – the place Jolas is happy to leave as Berlin[iv]. I haven't seen him be really badly wrong anywhere, and I have been grateful to take over almost word for word his translations of a hymn, a couple of rhymes and a ballad, for which I confess I lacked the appli-cation. If he has a fault for the English reader, it is that everything gets a little monotonous and strenuous, is like an exotic muscle or a fog or a pudding in a museum. Over the many years I have been working and not working on *Berlin Alexanderplatz* – it may be the only book I've translated that seems to have demanded anything like an 'approach' from me – it has gradually become clear that more normality, a slightly speedier rhythm (English is much less patient than German, never mind the talky, self-relishing, almost baroque Berlin dialect), and more of what I call 'signalling' is what I want to do. The worst thing, to my mind, would have been to leave the English reader quite at sea in this bitty, yeasty collage, which seems to have been how many people experienced the Jolas, which got a mixed reception when it came out, and seems to be widely and unfairly disliked now. But then it's hard to think of translators other than Constance Garnett that are still well thought of a hundred years later.

It is one thing to be lost in an original, something else to be lost in a translation. A translation is unwilling, perhaps, to allow or stand up to the amount of interrogation from the reader that an original must expect: it has everything to fear, it is, after all, an imitation, a performance, a substitution. Every word of it is wrong – perhaps especially if it is called *Plaza de Alejandro*. It seems to be a difficult thing, in some ways even a dereliction of duty, for a transla-tion to be baffling, or to transmit in a passive way bafflement. There is a component in what I've done that is to clarify or interpret or guide. I've tried to stay light on my feet. 'What he means is this,' I've known to intimate, or couldn't help myself intimating, 'this section is from the coffee leaflet', 'here he is washing the glasses', 'they are on the tram', rather than some riddle or opacity. The opaque is my enemy. This is what I mean by 'signalling'. The occasional explanatory note seemed worthwhile – Jolas has none. Leaving the odd thing in the original as well. Perhaps the time of 'total translation', of which he was an example, is over. I've had some guides. As I say, the quicker rhythm of English. More economy, less creativity in the idiom, because, honestly, it isn't there in English, which is, certainly by now, a more normed, predictable, usage-driven language than federated and regional German, and certainly less flamboyant, less idiosyncratic than *Berlinerisch*. (As David Bellos has argued, translation will most likely tend to plane away the highs and lows of diction anyway.) So: underplay, gesture at something, rather than go any whole hog. *Der richtige Berliner* was a big help – it allowed me to think that some of what I was grappling with was itself researched and got up, not the work of a GP in a poor area with an infallible ear over decades. (Translation fears the deeply real.) A couple of slang dictionaries came in, one English, one American: how I wish there was a thesaurus of slang, or an English-Slanglish dictionary, for me to have looked up 'prison' or 'woman' or 'half-pint'! I was happy to try and go for what my colleague Anthea Bell cleverly dubbed the regional unspecific: contractions, dropped endings, a bit of colloquial, a bit of vulgar, the odd odd word: there is nothing else I am fitted to do in any case. My speakers say what they mean in a swift and low half-sentence, rather than speak two whole ones in what would probably be felt to be a pompous and attitudinizing and implausible way. (Some of what I call the book having 'good bones' is found in that.) I don't like dropping letters and misspelling words in speech the way Dickens does, until I found that the effect is entirely different if you just do it, without the rather self-congratulatory apostrophe, which is the perfect mark of bad faith. (I had forgotten, but there are recent Scots prose writers who proceed exactly in this way.) Also, when I found that Döblin often has it in him to speak like his characters, that seemed to improve things; there isn't the distribution of tones and levels, and the use of dialect isn't something done with excessive subtlety or purpose, at *some* moments, or for *some* characters. It seems to be a function of intensity, but generally within reach of all – and I was happy with that.

Berlin Alexanderplatz is a montage of passages, many of them remarkable, and some of them remarkably beautiful. It is the combination of so much, so many, and so varied that makes the book: the Job playlet; the refrains from Ecclesiastes and Matthias Claudius; the retelling of Agamemnon and Clytemnestra; a lot of the transitional and walking-around scenes; some of the quick stories (and the stories within stories); the anatomization of the tenement building; the undoing of Reinhold. Everyone will have their favourites; mine is probably the song to the outgrowths of Berlin: 'Suffer them to approach. Suffer them to approach. The great, flat plains, the lonely brick houses giving out a reddish light. The towns all in a line, Frankfurt an der Oder, Guben, Sommerfeld, Liegnitz, Breslau, the towns appear with their stations, the towns with their great and small streets. Suffer them to approach, the cabs, the sliding, shooting cars.'

Michael Hofmann
Hamburg, July 2017

i   Wilfried F. Schoeller, *Döblin: eine Biografie* (Munich: Carl Hanser, 2011)
ii Klaus Schröter, *Alfred Döblin in Selbstzeugnissen und Bilddokumenten* (Reinbek: Rowohlt, 1978)
iii Alfred Döblin, *Berlin Alexanderplatz: The Story of Franz Biberkopf*, trans. Eugene Jolas (London: Secker, 1931; Penguin Modern Classics, 1978)
iv Anke Detken, *Döblins 'Berlin Alexanderplatz' übersetzt* (Göttingen: Vandenhoeck & Ruprecht, 1997)

TITLES IN SERIES

For a complete list of titles, visit www.nyrb.com or write to:
Catalog Requests, NYRB, 435 Hudson Street, New York, NY 10014

J.R. ACKERLEY Hindoo Holiday*
J.R. ACKERLEY My Dog Tulip*
J.R. ACKERLEY My Father and Myself*
J.R. ACKERLEY We Think the World of You*
HENRY ADAMS The Jeffersonian Transformation
RENATA ADLER Pitch Dark*
RENATA ADLER Speedboat*
AESCHYLUS Prometheus Bound; translated by Joel Agee*
LEOPOLDO ALAS His Only Son *with* Doña Berta*
CÉLESTE ALBARET Monsieur Proust
DANTE ALIGHIERI The Inferno
KINGSLEY AMIS The Alteration*
KINGSLEY AMIS Dear Illusion: Collected Stories*
KINGSLEY AMIS Ending Up*
KINGSLEY AMIS Girl, 20*
KINGSLEY AMIS The Green Man*
KINGSLEY AMIS Lucky Jim*
KINGSLEY AMIS The Old Devils*
KINGSLEY AMIS One Fat Englishman*
KINGSLEY AMIS Take a Girl Like You*
ROBERTO ARLT The Seven Madmen*
U.R. ANANTHAMURTHY Samskara: A Rite for a Dead Man*
WILLIAM ATTAWAY Blood on the Forge
W.H. AUDEN (EDITOR) The Living Thoughts of Kierkegaard
W.H. AUDEN W. H. Auden's Book of Light Verse
ERICH AUERBACH Dante: Poet of the Secular World
EVE BABITZ Eve's Hollywood*
EVE BABITZ Slow Days, Fast Company: The World, the Flesh, and L.A.*
DOROTHY BAKER Cassandra at the Wedding*
DOROTHY BAKER Young Man with a Horn*
J.A. BAKER The Peregrine
S. JOSEPHINE BAKER Fighting for Life*
HONORÉ DE BALZAC The Human Comedy: Selected Stories*
HONORÉ DE BALZAC The Memoirs of Two Young Wives*
HONORÉ DE BALZAC The Unknown Masterpiece *and* Gambara*
VICKI BAUM Grand Hotel*
SYBILLE BEDFORD A Favorite of the Gods *and* A Compass Error*
SYBILLE BEDFORD A Legacy*
SYBILLE BEDFORD A Visit to Don Otavio: A Mexican Journey*
MAX BEERBOHM The Prince of Minor Writers: The Selected Essays of Max Beerbohm*
MAX BEERBOHM Seven Men
STEPHEN BENATAR Wish Her Safe at Home*
FRANS G. BENGTSSON The Long Ships*
ALEXANDER BERKMAN Prison Memoirs of an Anarchist
GEORGES BERNANOS Mouchette
MIRON BIAŁOSZEWSKI A Memoir of the Warsaw Uprising*
ADOLFO BIOY CASARES Asleep in the Sun

* *Also available as an electronic book.*

INTIZAR HUSAIN Basti*
MAUDE HUTCHINS Victorine
YASUSHI INOUE Tun-huang*
HENRY JAMES The Ivory Tower
HENRY JAMES The New York Stories of Henry James*
HENRY JAMES The Other House
HENRY JAMES The Outcry
TOVE JANSSON Fair Play *
TOVE JANSSON The Summer Book*
TOVE JANSSON The True Deceiver*
TOVE JANSSON The Woman Who Borrowed Memories: Selected Stories*
RANDALL JARRELL (EDITOR) Randall Jarrell's Book of Stories
DAVID JONES In Parenthesis
JOSEPH JOUBERT The Notebooks of Joseph Joubert; translated by Paul Auster
KABIR Songs of Kabir; translated by Arvind Krishna Mehrotra*
FRIGYES KARINTHY A Journey Round My Skull
ERICH KÄSTNER Going to the Dogs: The Story of a Moralist*
HELEN KELLER The World I Live In
YASHAR KEMAL Memed, My Hawk
YASHAR KEMAL They Burn the Thistles
WALTER KEMPOWSKI All for Nothing
MURRAY KEMPTON Part of Our Time: Some Ruins and Monuments of the Thirties*
RAYMOND KENNEDY Ride a Cockhorse*
DAVID KIDD Peking Story*
ROBERT KIRK The Secret Commonwealth of Elves, Fauns, and Fairies
ARUN KOLATKAR Jejuri
DEZSŐ KOSZTOLÁNYI Skylark*
TÉTÉ-MICHEL KPOMASSIE An African in Greenland
GYULA KRÚDY The Adventures of Sindbad*
GYULA KRÚDY Sunflower*
SIGIZMUND KRZHIZHANOVSKY Autobiography of a Corpse*
SIGIZMUND KRZHIZHANOVSKY The Letter Killers Club*
SIGIZMUND KRZHIZHANOVSKY Memories of the Future
SIGIZMUND KRZHIZHANOVSKY The Return of Munchausen
K'UNG SHANG-JEN The Peach Blossom Fan*
GIUSEPPE TOMASI DI LAMPEDUSA The Professor and the Siren
GERT LEDIG The Stalin Front*
MARGARET LEECH Reveille in Washington: 1860–1865*
PATRICK LEIGH FERMOR Between the Woods and the Water*
PATRICK LEIGH FERMOR The Broken Road*
PATRICK LEIGH FERMOR Mani: Travels in the Southern Peloponnese*
PATRICK LEIGH FERMOR Roumeli: Travels in Northern Greece*
PATRICK LEIGH FERMOR A Time of Gifts*
PATRICK LEIGH FERMOR A Time to Keep Silence*
PATRICK LEIGH FERMOR The Traveller's Tree*
PATRICK LEIGH FERMOR The Violins of Saint-Jacques*
D.B. WYNDHAM LEWIS AND CHARLES LEE (EDITORS) The Stuffed Owl
SIMON LEYS The Death of Napoleon*
SIMON LEYS The Hall of Uselessness: Collected Essays*
GEORG CHRISTOPH LICHTENBERG The Waste Books
JAKOV LIND Soul of Wood and Other Stories
H.P. LOVECRAFT AND OTHERS Shadows of Carcosa: Tales of Cosmic Horror*
DWIGHT MACDONALD Masscult and Midcult: Essays Against the American Grain*